Love Finds You™

in

CALICO

— CALIFORNIA —

Love Finds You

IN

CALICO

CALIFORNIA

BY ELIZABETH LUDWIG

summerside
PRESS™

Summerside Press™
Minneapolis 55438
www.summersidepress.com

Love Finds You in Calico, California
© 2010 by Elizabeth Ludwig

ISBN 978-1-60936-001-6

Scripture references are from The Holy Bible, King James Version (KJV).

The town depicted in this book is a real place, but all characters are fictional. Any resemblances to actual people or events are purely coincidental.

Cover design by Kirk DouPonce | www.DogEaredDesign.com.

Interior design by Müllerhaus Publishing Group | www.mullerhaus.net.

Cover and interior photos of Calico provided by Elizabeth Ludwig.

Published in association with Chip MacGregor of MacGregor Literary Agency.

Summerside Press™ is an inspirational publisher offering fresh, irresistible books to uplift the heart and engage the mind.

Printed in USA.

Dedication
....

To my sisters…and all my sisters-in-love.

Your encouragement has carried me through this journey.

I love you all.

Acknowledgments

....

I wish to acknowledge my wonderful critique partners, Janelle Mowery, Marcia Gruver, Sandra Robbins, Susan Sleeman, Jessica Ferguson, Ane Mulligan, Jessica Dotta, Michelle Griep, and Ginger Garrett. Without you, this story would not have been possible. To my agent, Chip MacGregor—you're the best! Thank you for your hard work and encouragement. To all of the folks at Summerside Press, I say thank you. Your dedication to quality Christian fiction does more than provide entertainment. You bring light to a world in desperate need of hope. I am honored to work with you.

And finally, a huge thank-you to Serena Steiner, historian at Calico Ghost Town. Your willingness to share your knowledge proved to be invaluable.

And why take ye thought for raiment? Consider the lilies of the field,
how they grow; they toil not, neither do they spin:
and yet I say unto you, that even Solomon in all his glory
was not arrayed like one of these.
Wherefore, if God so clothe the grass of the field,
which to day is, and to morrow is cast into the oven,
shall he not much more clothe you, O ye of little faith?

MATTHEW 6:28–30

Calico, California

TEN MILES FROM BARSTOW, DOWN INTERSTATE 15 IN SOUTHERN California, Calico Ghost Town rises like a specter from the sands of the Mojave Desert. Calico boomed from 1881–1896, when silver and borax mining swelled the population from a handful of souls to approximately twelve hundred. Along with an assortment of saloons and gambling halls, Calico supported a school, a church, and a local newspaper called the *Calico Print*. In the mid-1890s, a drop in the price of silver and the end of borax production in the region made mining in Calico economically unviable. By 1904, the town was completely abandoned.

In 1951 Walter Knott of Knott's Berry Farm purchased the town and began its restoration. He donated the town to San Bernardino County in 1966, and today, Calico is a regional park with attractions such as mine tours, Civil War reenactments, and an annual Heritage Fest. In 2005 Calico was designated the "official state silver rush ghost town" of California.

Elizabeth Ludwig

Chapter One

. . . .

Calico, 1883

"Fire! The mine is on fire!"

Abigail bolted upright in her bed, the blankets clutched to her chest. Pounding feet and strangled cries mingled with the wispy fingers of her dreams. Outside her window, an eerie orange glow illuminated the night sky.

"Papa?" Thrusting back the covers, she jumped from the bed, her legs chafed by the straw poking out from the ticking, and ran from her room. Next to the fireplace, her father's pallet lay empty, the blankets tossed aside as though he'd scrambled from them in a hurry. Her worried gaze traveled to the door, where the heavy oak beam used to secure it stood propped against the wall.

He's gone to the mine.

Her father's repeated warnings rang in her head, but she ignored them and darted across the cabin, flinging open the door. People carrying torches rushed by on the street, their voices lifted in panic.

"What's happening?" she shouted. It was no use. Snagged by the brisk wind whipping down from the mountains, her words carried to no one in particular.

Their tiny home lay on the edge of town, across from the livery. Perhaps Nathan Hawk, the livery's new owner, knew something. Sucking in a lungful of sharp air, Abigail yanked her shawl from its peg next to the door and threw it around her shoulders, struggling a bit as it tangled in her long, dark curls. The shawl was scant protection, but at least her nightgown was covered. Her red boots rested in the corner, but pausing to slip them on would waste precious seconds and Papa needed her *now*.

She whirled and hurried into the cool air, wincing as the stone-encrusted ground bit into her feet.

Raucous laughter spilled from one of Calico's many saloons and drifted down the street. The drunkards inside cared nothing for the smoke billowing from the mine. They were too wrapped up in their whiskey to notice the shouts and panicked neighing of the horses. Perhaps they'd be too preoccupied to notice one witless girl scurrying through the night, helpless as she was to run or defend herself if one of them attacked.

"Hold it right there."

The harsh demand sent a jolt through her heart. She skittered to a stop, peering through the gloom for a glimpse of the speaker's face.

"Didn't you hear the explosion? Don't you know it's not safe?"

A gun barrel glinted in the pale moonlight cascading from the mountains. Abigail clutched the shawl tighter to her shoulders. "M–Mr. Hawk?"

"Miss Watts?" He sounded as incredulous as Abigail felt. Lowering the rifle, he said, "Land sakes, woman, hasn't your father ever warned you—?"

"Papa's gone. I think he might be in the mine. It's on fire." Speaking the words birthed fresh panic. "I was hoping you could help...." She couldn't finish. Desperation boiled in her chest. "Oh, please!"

Nathan's strong hands grasped her shoulders. Without a word,

CALICO
1883
CA

he drew her into the livery and struck a match. The dim glow of the lantern drove away the shadows, but it did nothing for the darkness crowding her heart.

"You say your father is in the mine?"

Now that she could see his face, Abigail read genuine concern in Nathan's features. His brows were drawn, the muscles along his jaw bunched. She nodded. "I think so, but I didn't dare go there alone to check—"

"Absolutely not." His hazel gaze sharpened. When she flinched, his tone softened. "You'd only be endangering your own life. Anson wouldn't want that."

Her father's name rolled easily from Nathan's lips. The two had become good friends over the past couple of months, after her father took the newly arrived livery owner under his wing.

Nathan gestured toward one of the stalls. "Come. Sit with Lizzie while I see what I can find out."

Abigail looked in the direction he pointed. She needed Nathan's help and Lizzie couldn't be left alone, but the idea of waiting helplessly while he went to the mine filled her with frustration.

"Miss Watts?"

She shook the shackles of indecision from her limbs and picked her way across the dirt floor. A tangle of arms and legs, Nathan's five-year-old daughter slept soundly in the sweet-smelling hay. Abigail had taken an instant liking to the spunky little girl—and she to Abigail, often following her around town while she delivered mended clothing. Abigail sank to her knees alongside the sleeping child and peered up at Nathan.

"You will hurry?"

He nodded. By the light of the lantern, his grim face appeared even more somber than usual. "You should be safe in here, but—do not leave Lizzie's side for any reason. Is that clear?"

Warning sharpened his tone, but Abigail managed to bob her head. Nathan was a big man, rough-hewn and hard, but with a sadness in his eyes that said he was neither cruel nor unfeeling. Once she'd given her promise, he hooked the lantern on a nail above his head then strode out the door with his rifle gripped in his hands.

Outside, the shouts grew louder. Abigail kept her gaze fastened to the cracks in the splintered door, every moment hoping Nathan would return with her father in tow. At the same time, she feared that another figure with a more sinister intent might materialize.

She crouched closer to Lizzie. Would she ever feel safe in Calico? In the daylight, when the sun sparkled on the mountainside and wildflowers bloomed in abundance, Abigail talked easily with the prospectors. She laughed at their antics and enjoyed when they gathered with their families for a meal on the school grounds, which doubled as a church on Sundays. But at night...

Clutching her shawl to her chest, she breathed a silent prayer, wishing the confidence she felt singing hymns on Sunday was more tangible now.

Lizzie sighed, and Abigail thought she might awaken. Instead, the child rolled to her side, dislodging the thin blanket she'd been wrapped in. Grasping the edge of the covering, Abigail pulled it higher around the girl's slender shoulders. The blanket would do for now, while the last traces of summer sun heated the sands of the Mojave, but in the winter? Chilling storms and dropping temperatures were not far away. Perhaps by then Nathan would have sufficient funds to finish the house he was erecting beside the livery. If not—

Winters were harsh in this part of California, even more so for a child as young as Lizzie. Abigail reached down and stroked the girl's flushed cheek, tears gathering in her own eyes as she did so. She and Lizzie had both lost their mothers. What would Abigail do if she lost her father too?

A sharp gust of wind ripped through the entrance and thrust the door open with a crash. Abigail stared, her heart pounding. Then, with a muted cry, she threw herself between the entrance and Lizzie.

Her worst fears were realized. Outlined against the fiery night sky was the hulking figure of a man.

* * * * *

Nathan shoved easily through the crowd gathered at the opening of the Silver King Mine, using his height and size to added advantage. Many of the faces were Oriental. Torchlight created eerie valleys in the hollows of their cheekbones, but there was no disguising the fear in their eyes.

He jerked his head toward the gaping hole that formed the entrance to the mine as he spoke. "Does anyone know what's happening in there?"

His booming voice quieted the crowd.

A stubby woman dressed in black stepped forward. "Blasting powder. Caps, maybe." She shrugged. "We heard the explosion and come a-runnin'."

"Mrs. Bailey." Nathan eyed her compassionately. She was still mourning the loss of her husband who'd died in the mine less than eight months ago. Of all the people he'd met, he liked her best, apart from Anson Watts and his daughter. The stout little widow seemed to be cut from the same ore carved from the mountain. He glanced toward the mine. "Is Joseph—?"

"My Joseph is in there"—she jabbed her gnarled thumb toward the mine—"helping with the rescue. He and a handful of others were the only ones as would see to it."

At least her son hadn't been caught in the blaze. Nathan strode toward the entrance. The billowing smoke had lessened some, which meant that either the miners had wrestled it under control or it had burned itself out, choked by a lack of wood fuel and oxygen. He squinted against the ash stinging his eyes and poked his head inside. "Any idea who all might be down there?"

"Hui. Hui inside." A slender Chinese woman gestured frantically. "Many odders. You help, please? You go?"

"A couple of them Orientals volunteered to go with Joseph," Mrs. Bailey said, her brow lowered in a frown.

That explained Hui's presence. He wouldn't have been allowed inside otherwise. Another woman—Nathan vaguely remembered seeing her around town with Abigail—stepped forward to wrap the Chinese lady in a hug. "It'll be all right, Lin. They'll find the miners and get out. We just have to be patient."

"Everyone away from the mine. Move. All of you!"

Along with the rest, Nathan turned to see who issued the order. Gavin Nichols. Nathan grunted. The man thought too highly of himself, especially now that the Silver King had new ownership and Gavin had been elevated to the superintendent's position.

Gavin stomped through the crowd toward Nathan. "What's going on here? What happened?"

Thrusting out his chin, Nathan stared down at the smartly

dressed man. "I figured you'd know, Nichols. Those are your miners trapped inside, aren't they?"

Air popped from Gavin's mouth in a flustered rush. "Why, I came as soon as I heard."

Maybe. But after he'd taken the time to change his clothes. His embroidered vest probably cost more than Nathan made in a month, and his shoes were polished to a high gleam. The mine superintendent's position paid well, and Nichols wasn't ashamed to let everyone know. Nathan turned away, disgusted, just as a shout rose from the gloomy mine entrance and the cage that lowered the miners into the shaft rumbled.

"They're coming!" Mrs. Bailey cried.

Signaling the people around him, Nathan ushered those who waited into a line. The first rescuer came into view, supporting an injured miner around the shoulders.

Daniel McAdams. Nathan winced at the burned condition of his hands and face. Daniel would be lucky to avoid infection.

Nathan rushed forward to help draw the injured man out. After that a line of miners, their wounds varied, streamed from the hole in the mountain. Last to emerge was Joseph Bailey and Anson Watts. Between them, they carried a limp, charred body. The long, dark braid dangling from the man's topknot brushed the ground.

"Hui!" The Oriental woman, Lin, ran forward, crying and screaming in Chinese. "My Hui!"

Nathan caught her by the shoulders before she could throw herself on the body. She was too thin in his opinion; the ridges along her spine poked through her ramie tunic. He held her carefully as she sobbed her grief against his chest. "I'm sorry, ma'am," he murmured. "So very sorry."

A hush fell over the stunned crowd—except for the Chinese, who had separated themselves into a tight circle. They took Hui's body from Anson and Joseph and, with foreign prayers falling from their lips, carried him east toward their section of town.

The young woman who had comforted Lin before moved forward and grasped her forearms. "Come, Lin. Let me walk you home." To Nathan, she said, "I'll stay with her through the night. She's going to need someone close by to help with the baby."

She had a kind face, this woman, and compassion shone from her eyes. Nathan released Lin to her care. "Thank you, Miss—?"

"Martin. Caroline Martin."

The Martins were well-known in Calico. Lin would be in good hands, at least for tonight. Nathan could only hope she had kin who would see to her needs after that.

Miss Martin and Lin followed the mourners, raising a small cloud of dust with their shuffling feet. Nathan sighed then turned to look for Anson. His friend leaned wearily against an ore car, ragged grief etched into the lines of his brow. As the crowd dispersed to care for their family members, Nathan made his way toward him.

"It's business as usual tomorrow!" Gavin shouted, rocking on his tiptoes. "I'm as sorry as anyone to see men injured, but we have a mine to run."

Nathan froze and then turned slowly on his heel. "Injured? A man died, Nichols. His wife is a widow tonight."

The accusation in his tone froze the men and their wives. Their gaze bounced from him to Nichols while they waited for the superintendent to respond.

The insufferable dandy tugged on the tails of his string bow tie then gave a gruff shake of his head. "He wasn't a miner. He was Chinese."

"You think his wife cares about that?" Nathan looked around. Some in the crowd stared back at him, but no one broke the uneasy silence, even the handful he'd seen walking to church services on Sunday mornings.

Grimacing in disgust, he whirled from the pious display and continued toward Anson. Let them sort out for themselves the prejudice from their religion. He'd have none of either.

He clapped a hand to the older man's shoulder. "You all right?"

Anson shrugged, the muscles in his back rippling against his sweat-dampened shirt. Given his gentle nature, Nathan suspected Anson would rather heft a book than a shovel, but the mountain had chiseled him and cleft the softness from his body. Had the harsh conditions in Calico wrought the same effect on all people, or just the men? His thoughts winged to Lin.

"I'll be all right," Anson said. His gray eyes fastened on the retreating back of the mine's newest widow. "It's Mrs. Chen I'm worried about. Hui worked as a cook at the Calico Hotel. He was their only means of support, and they have a new baby at home." He heaved a sigh that must have rattled his bones.

So that was what Miss Martin had meant by her comment. Nathan shook his head. "Why do they come? Why even risk it?"

"Same reason as us, I suppose. Dreams of a better life." Anson rubbed his large palm across his face, smearing streaks of dirt and thick, red mine dust. His voice dropped and his gaze darted to the miners. "Some dream, eh? The silver trickling out of this hole isn't worth a man's life."

This was the second time in less than a week that Anson had mentioned the dwindling silver production. His concern rumbled from deep inside, like the explosions the miners set off to create new tunnels.

Nathan eased closer and lowered his voice. "Is it as bad as all that?"

Eyes somber, Anson studied him a moment before sighing. "I have my suspicions, nothing more."

"What does Nichols say?"

"What he always says—the silver will pick up once we dig deeper into the mountain." Anson grunted and crossed his arms. "I think he arranged to have that last wagonload of immigrants transported here just so he could prove to folks that Calico's still booming." Bitterness tinged his laughter. "High price to pay just so one man can keep up appearances. I hate the way the Chinese are treated here, like cattle with no right to seek after the very thing that brought all of us, but what can I do? Prejudice is ingrained pretty deep."

Concerned by the weariness in Anson's voice, Nathan straightened and gestured toward the livery. "We'd best get home. Abigail is waiting with Lizzie, and she's worried sick."

Anson looked startled for a moment, as though his daughter's concerns had not occurred to him, and then he shoved off the ore car and joined Nathan. "Of course. Poor Abigail. When she hears the cries of the Chinese, she'll probably think—" He shuddered.

Nathan knew exactly what she would think and how it would make her feel—dismay, despair, unbearable sorrow. He shook off a flood of memories. "Let's go." Urgency quickened Nathan's steps. He didn't know Abigail as well as he did Anson, but he still couldn't wait to put her fears to rest.

Chapter Two

Abigail crouched in front of Lizzie's sleeping form. Fear set her limbs to trembling, yet giving in to panic would mean their deaths—hers *and* Lizzie's.

She squared her shoulders and thrust out her chin. "Who are you? What do you want?"

Despite her show of bravado, she nearly shrieked when the stranger stumbled closer, into the full glow of the lantern. His dark hair poked out in every direction. Sweat and grime caked his face. Even without the layer of filth, she doubted she'd recognize him. The only miners she knew were the ones who attended the church services at the schoolhouse.

"Light—in the barn."

He motioned toward Lizzie. Creeping backward, Abigail placed a protective hand on the child's back.

"Little girl?" He took a step, tripped over his feet, and grabbed the wall to regain his balance.

Abigail searched the stable for a shovel—a pitchfork—anything to hold the man at bay. Why hadn't she armed herself when Nathan left? Her gaze swung back to the stranger. "There's no liquor here, mister. My father and—Nathan"—she forced the familiar use of his Christian name from her lips—"will return soon. You'd best leave now."

He wagged his shaggy head and bent toward Lizzie, a foul odor wafting from his body. In the dim glow of the lantern, she saw the glazed look in his eyes. Battling dismay, she breathed a silent prayer and then tensed to fight. He wanted Lizzie? He'd have to get through her first.

Suddenly, she heard it—the shouts and cries of people returning from the mine.

"They're coming." She jerked her eyes from the stranger's ragged face to the door. "They're on their way—"

Without warning, the stranger groaned and pitched forward. Abigail screamed and grabbed Lizzie to her chest, no longer caring if the girl awoke.

"Stay back! I mean it, mister. I'll claw out your eyes...."

The man lay still as a felled tree, his arms splayed from his sides like broken limbs. Her chest heaving, Abigail's voice faded into silence. He'd passed out? Was he so drunk he'd fallen to the floor in a stupor?

The stranger groaned and Abigail paused. Pain filled the sound, not liquored babbling.

"Is it morning?" Lizzie struggled in Abigail's arms then lifted a chubby palm and rubbed at her eyes. "Abigail? Where's Pa?"

Soothing the child softly, Abigail shifted her to sit in the straw. "Your daddy is on his way, sweetheart, but in the meantime, I have to check on that man." She held a warning finger in front of Lizzie's face. "You have to promise to stay here. All right, Lizzie? Wait for me here?"

Lizzie's blue eyes widened as she stared at the stranger. "Who is that?"

"I don't know, but I think he needs my help. Will you wait here?"

The child crawled onto her knees, tugged the blanket to her chin, and nodded.

CALICO
1883
CA

For a moment, Abigail hesitated. Urged by another groan from the stranger, she inched cautiously to his side on her hands and knees. The closer she got, the stronger the odors of dirt and sweat grew, which were mingled with the charred scent of something else.

"Abigail?" Lizzie's whisper floated softer than goose down. Her expression was one of fear—probably the same one that was reflected on Abigail's face.

She put her finger to her lips.

"Shh. It's all right, sweetheart." Rising, she lifted the lantern from its nail and lowered the light toward the figure.

The man's tattered leather vest had protected his back and shoulders, but one of his arms looked raw and a burn covered his hand. Blood from a wound to the back of his head trickled over his temple, and it was obvious by the singed hair that the flames had reached there, too.

Abigail gasped. He had to have been one of the miners trapped in the explosion. She gripped the lantern then rushed to the tack room for salve and clean towels. Nathan kept his supplies in neat order, but nowhere among the jars of oil and liniment did she see anything for burns.

"Abigail?"

Whirling, Abigail nearly fainted with relief. "Papa?"

Her father stood in the entrance to the livery, outlined by the glow of the rising moon. Nathan hovered at his heels, and they both stepped into the light cast by the lantern. Nathan's gaze flicked from Abigail to Lizzie to the figure lying on the floor. Grasping the barrel, he hefted the rifle to his shoulder. "Are you all right?"

Abigail nodded. "We're fine, but this man is injured. I think he's one of the miners."

"What?" Her father quickly knelt beside the stranger. Gently he rolled the man to his side and swept the shaggy hair from his face. "Tom Kennedy."

Nathan cocked his head. "Nobody noticed he was missing? Didn't they know he was working the mine?"

"Don't believe he was. Now that the weather is turning colder, he and his brother make their home in one of the tunnels." Her father glanced toward the door. "Nathan, help me get him up. He's going to need to see Doc."

Hustling closer, Nathan grasped one of Tom Kennedy's arms and her father the other.

"No," the stranger groaned, the first coherent sound he'd made since before he passed out. "Must—help—George."

Nathan peered at the man. "Who?"

A sharp breath whistled through her father's teeth. Abigail followed his gaze as it flitted back out to the darkness, fingers of apprehension wiggling up her spine.

"The other Kennedy brother," her father replied, rising. "He must be in the mine."

Chapter Three

Nathan straightened and went to stand next to Anson at the door. "We'll have to go back for him. But first, this one's going to need a doctor." His gaze flashed to Abigail. "Will you stay while I fetch him?"

"Pa?"

Cut short by his daughter's plaintive voice, Nathan hurried to Lizzie and caught her to his chest. Like two wiry bands, her arms snaked around his neck and held tight. "Don't be afraid, sugar," he said, chastising himself for not comforting her sooner. What must she be thinking, watching the events of this night unfold before her eyes? Charlotte would never have been so callous.

Just the thought of his wife struck knifelike pain to Nathan's chest. He squeezed Lizzie tighter before setting her down and tipping her tiny face up to his. "I'll be back soon. I promise. In the meantime, I need you to be very brave for your old pa, all right?"

Lizzie's blue eyes widened. She bobbed her head, the muscles in her cheeks and jaw twitching as she fought to look courageous, but the trembling of her chin gave her away. Thankfully, Abigail drew next to them and grasped Lizzie's small hand.

"Of course she'll be brave. She takes after her pa, don't you, dear?"

Lizzie peered up at Abigail and then back at him before nodding. Though a worried frown tugged at her slender brows, making her look all the more like her mother, she pressed close to Abigail and waved him a good-bye. Guilt roiled through his belly. He hadn't protected Charlotte, and now he was leaving Lizzie in the care of another.

Nathan exchanged a quick look with Abigail. She was a kind girl, more capable than many a man he'd met, and he was glad for her presence. Nodding his thanks, he whirled and walked into the night with Anson.

Despite the late hour, tinny music and shouts of laughter spilled from the saloon nearest the livery. Belle's place. Nathan had only met her once, but she'd seemed a nice enough sort. Her clientele, on the other hand...

He quickened his pace. Anson huffed to keep up.

"Where do you suppose George Kennedy is?" Anson said.

"Could be anywhere in that labyrinth, I suppose. Any idea what part of the mine they call home?"

Anson gave a curt nod. "I think so, but if my hunch about the fire is right, they were right in the thick of it when the blast roared through. I'm surprised either of them crawled out at all."

They left the dirt road that divided the town down the middle and swung onto the boardwalk, their boots clumping heavily on the wooden planks. By now, they'd left the livery far behind; Doc's office and residence lay near the heart of Calico. Nathan scratched his head. How the man managed to sleep through the worst of the ruckus from the saloons night after night was a mystery.

"Well, let's hope George is familiar enough with the nooks inside the mine to have found himself a hidey-hole," Nathan said as they drew to a stop outside the doctor's door. Pushed by the wind, a sign bearing Doc Goodenough's name swung from rusty hinges. Nathan tipped his head toward it. "That sign any indication of the man's skill?"

CALICO
1883
CA

Anson flashed a crooked grin. "Nah, he's the best doctor in all of Calico."

Right. He was the only doctor in Calico. Nathan grimaced and lifted his fist to pound on the door. After a moment, a sleepy-eyed man with disheveled hair badly in need of cutting answered. In his hand, a lantern illuminated features surprisingly devoid of wrinkles. Taken back by his youth, Nathan fell speechless.

The doctor looked him over from boots to brim and then glanced over Nathan's shoulder. "Anson? Who's this you've got with you?"

"He owns the livery next to my place."

Jerked from his silence, Nathan shoved out his hand. "Nathan Hawk, sir."

Doc Goodenough fumbled in the pocket of his nightshirt for a pair of wire-rimmed spectacles. He slid them on then accepted Nathan's outstretched hand. His grip was unexpectedly firm—though when he thought about it, Nathan supposed a doctor's hands would have to be strong.

"We're in sore need of ya, Doc," Anson said. "There's been a fire down at the mine."

Doc's gaze sharpened. "What? When? No one told me."

Anson dipped his head to study the ground. Nathan watched him with curiosity. Why *hadn't* anyone roused the doctor?

"Ah, well, I suppose that's because—"

"Save it, Anson, old friend. I know what they say about me 'round town. No sense adding to the list for which you'll have to give heavenly account." Doc sighed, expelling a breath that smelled suspiciously of whiskey, and reached for a tweed coat hanging from a peg next to the door. "How many were hurt?"

"Eight or nine, some more serious than others."

"I take it they went to Mattie?"

Anson nodded.

Nathan felt a swell of disbelief. "The old widow woman who lives next to the cemetery?"

"Look at it this way, son," Anson said, clapping him on the back. "At least they haven't got far to go when old Mattie Jenks finishes with 'em."

Pulling his suspenders over his shoulders, Doc Goodenough hitched up his trousers, grabbed his medical bag, and slipped on his coat before joining them on the porch. "They can't all have gone to see Mattie if you two fellas are in need of my services."

The men left the steps and started back through town. Nathan spoke up. "No, sir. One of the Kennedys ended up in my livery. He's bad off, but it's his brother we're worried about. We think he may still be in the mine."

Doc's brows rose. "Which one?"

"The youngest," Anson said. "George."

Doc shook his head sadly. "God be with him if he's trapped somewhere in those tunnels."

They passed a series of shops, small establishments where the owners carved out a living repairing jewelry, watches, and clocks; fashioning hats; or selling shoes. In the greasy light cast by the street lamps, Nathan saw Anson's eyes glisten.

"God *is* with him, Doc. His presence is obvious all over these painted hills." Anson's hand swept in front of him to encompass the slopes rising like shadows in the distance.

"Humph." Doc gave a low grunt before jumping from the boardwalk and following Nathan across the street. Behind them, Anson's soft chuckle wafted on the night air.

Nathan pointed toward the livery, where the rising moon cast the stable into relief. "There it is."

Not waiting for Nathan or Anson, the doctor hurried forward and disappeared into the barn. When Nathan followed, he saw that Abigail had resumed her place next to Tom Kennedy and gripped his hand tightly, though the man had once more drifted into unconsciousness.

"Will he be all right, Doc?" she said, her voice tight.

Nathan's gaze swung to the doctor, as anxious as Abigail for the answer.

He gestured for the lantern. "Bring that light closer and let me get a better look at his wounds."

Nathan grasped the lantern and held it so that the light fell fully on Tom's back and shoulders. Poor wretch was worse off than he'd thought. He shuddered and backed up a step.

Doc shook his head, mussing his tousled hair further. "No good. Can't see a bloomin'"—he paused to correct himself—"your pardon, ma'am. I can't see a thing with just this feeble light. We'll need to get him back to my office so I can clean up those burns and give him something for pain. He'll need it when he wakes." He snapped his bag closed and motioned for the men to draw near. "Anson, Nathan, help me get him up."

Anson hastened toward his daughter first. "Abigail, take Lizzie and go on back to the cabin. You'll be safer there. After Nathan and I finish here, we're going to head up to the mine to see if we can't find George. It could be a long night, and I don't want you or the child out here alone."

Abigail's eyes widened. "Should I fetch someone to help?"

His shoulders drooped. "No sense in it. More'n likely we're searching for a body."

As though he heard, Tom groaned.

Anson gave Abigail a gentle push. "Go on with you now, and be sure to bar the door. Nathan, you can come by to collect Lizzie after you've had a chance to rest up."

It was a good plan, and far safer than if the girls stayed in the barn. Nathan nodded gratefully then bent to wrap Lizzie in a hug. "Be a good girl for Miss Abigail, and don't try to wait up or you'll be sleepy tomorrow at school. I'll come get you first thing in the morning."

Lizzie's lips puckered for a kiss, which Nathan gave, and then without a word of protest, she reached for Abigail with one hand and rubbed sleepily at her eyes with the other.

Abigail swung Lizzie easily to her hip. Her soft eyes, so warm with compassion, sought Nathan's face. "We'll be fine. I'll make sure she's safe."

Stirred by a wealth of unwelcome emotions, Nathan could only nod. He watched as Abigail carried his daughter through the open door into the night. Though he knew he should feel nothing at all, an odd sense of relief flooded over him. At least for tonight, Lizzie would be safe and warm. She was with Abigail.

Chapter Four

....

Abigail tucked the covers tighter around Lizzie's body. The little girl lay snuggled against Abigail's side, but she'd begun stirring and would probably wake soon.

"Ish it mornin' yet?" Muffled by the blankets, Lizzie's sleep-drugged voice came out more sluggish than Papa's old mule.

"Not quite, sweetheart. It's still early. You can rest some more if you like."

Lizzie tugged her arms free and stretched them over her head. "Where's Pa and Mr. Anson?"

"Not back yet." Abigail tried to sound cheerful, but a curious dread weighed heavily on her chest. She'd spent the night in anxious prayer and, when she couldn't rest, had risen to dress and wash. Rather than direct yet another glance at the door, she tapped Lizzie on the nose before sliding out from under the covers. "Are you hungry?"

Lizzie's voice followed as Abigail bent before the hearth to stoke the fire. "No, but Pa will be. He's got a man's apple-tite." Sitting up in the bed, she patted her stomach.

Abigail laughed and reached for the kindling. "Who told you that?"

"My pa." Lizzie scrambled out of bed and squatted next to the hearth, her fingers already reaching for a piece of wood. "Can I help?"

Abigail gently pushed her a safe distance from the smoldering fire. "You can, but you mustn't get too close. Your nightdress could catch flame and you'd be burned. You must promise to be careful."

The somber look in Lizzie's eyes said she understood. Abigail patted the child's shoulder and pointed to a box next to the fireplace. "Hand me some of that wood."

Lizzie grunted as she grasped a sizable log with both hands. Once Abigail had the flames dancing, she dusted off her hands and led Lizzie to the kitchen. "That'll do it. Our cozy fire will soon chase off the chill."

Lizzie nodded and copied Abigail's motion of dusting off her hands. "Yep, that'll do it."

Grabbing a box of matches from a shelf high above the counter-top where she washed dishes, Abigail brought them to the table and showed Lizzie. "You saw where I got these?"

Curiosity shone in the child's eyes. "Uh-huh."

"Well, you mustn't play with them, all right? I use these matches to light the lamps, but you must promise to never handle them when I'm not around."

Again Lizzie nodded, only this time she slid her hands behind her back and watched while Abigail lit the lantern. Burning coal oil in the morning was an extravagance Abigail usually tried to avoid, but Papa would understand. She blew out the match and pushed the lamp to the center of the table where she and Papa ate their meals.

"All right, now. Why don't we get dressed and then start on breakfast? It's early, but Papa and Mr. Hawk will likely be hungry when they return."

At Lizzie's giggle, Abigail leaned down and braced her hands on her knees. "What's so funny?"

"His name is Pa, not Mr. Hawk."

Abigail laughed too. "That's fine for you, Little Miss, but to me, he's Mr. Hawk." She took hold of one of Lizzie's long blond braids. The twist was clumsily done, and sleeping on straw had left bits of chaff tangled in her hair. "Why don't I warm up a kettle for you and we'll give you a bath before your pa comes? Then you'll be all ready for school. Would you like that?"

Lizzie's nose wrinkled. "Do I have to?"

She shook her head. "No, but I'll let you use a bit of my rose water if you do."

"Rose water?" The disgust cleared from Lizzie's face. Her eyes widened, and she tipped her head. Her brow puckered. "What's that?"

The child had never heard of scented waters? Abigail tried not to look surprised. "Why, it's just the most heavenly smelling thing you've ever put your nose to." She tickled Lizzie under the chin, and as the child giggled, Abigail straightened and went to fetch the chamber set. "Come on, then. You won't want to miss this chance to smell pretty for your pa."

The promised rose water had the desired effect. Lizzie played happily in the tub Abigail dragged from the back of the cabin. A bit of lye soap and a dash of rose scent later, the child stood clothed and dry in front of the fire. Abigail smiled as she ran a brush through Lizzie's silky tresses. A ray of sunlight peeking above the horizon shone through the window and set the golden curls afire.

"There now," she said, laying the brush aside when she finished with Lizzie's braids. "Won't your pa be surprised when he sees you?"

Twin dimples appeared on Lizzie's cheeks. "Yes, he will." She seized the brush and held it aloft. "My turn?"

Abigail's thoughts flew to breakfast. The men would return any moment. She knew she should get started, yet how often did Lizzie get to enjoy female company? She smiled and swiveled on the stool.

"All right then, but we haven't long. Your pa—"

Heavy boots echoed on the porch, driving the words from her mouth. The dread returned, stronger than before and as tangible as a rattler coiled in the room with them.

"There they are!" Lizzie exclaimed. Dropping the brush with a clatter, she scrambled off the stool and darted toward the door.

Abigail rose as sunlight streamed into the room. Framed in the now-open doorway stood Nathan. He caught Lizzie in his arms, but his eyes sought Abigail. A wealth of sorrow brimmed in those hazel depths, and he gave a sad shake of the head.

Abigail's breath caught. Nathan had returned—but he was alone.

* * * * *

Nathan wrapped his arms around his daughter, knowing he should return some of the enthusiasm of his daughter's hug, but at this moment, with the dreadful news of Anson's accident burning in his chest, he couldn't muster the strength.

"Are you hungry, Pa? We're about to make breakfast. Do you like my hair? Don't I smell good?" Lizzie rattled off questions, not waiting for one answer before firing off another. "Is Mr. Anson with you? What took you so long?" She licked her thumb and ran it down his face. "Your cheek is all dirty. You need a bath. Maybe Miss Abigail will let you have some of her rose water. It smells like flowers, Pa." Grabbing a lock of her hair, she jammed it under Nathan's nose. "See?"

"Yes, I see." Setting her gently on the floor, Nathan crouched until they looked eye to eye. "Lizzie, I need a moment alone with Miss Watts. I have something very important to tell her."

"And then we'll make breakfast?"

Innocence shone in his daughter's eyes. Nathan wanted to stare into them forever rather than face the agony he already saw in Abigail's. He squeezed Lizzie's shoulder and led her onto the porch. "Special treat today. We're having breakfast at the Calico Hotel before I take you to school."

Lizzie's mouth formed a surprised O. "Really, Pa?"

"But you're going to have to change first. Put on one of your pretty dresses. Can you manage that all by yourself?"

Lizzie gave an excited nod.

"Good. Go on back to the livery, then, and wait for me there. I won't be long."

In seconds, her bare feet carried her quickly down the steps.

"Lizzie!"

At the sound of Nathan's voice she hurtled to a stop just shy of the wooden gate. "Yes, Pa?"

A knot so thick he could barely form the words rose in Nathan's throat. "I—I love you."

Lizzie giggled. "I know that, Pa." She whirled and, with her golden braids bouncing, she dashed toward the livery.

No more delay. Feet heavy, Nathan turned slowly and reentered the cabin. Abigail stood just where he'd left her, pinned, it seemed, to the same spot on the floor.

"Where's my father?"

Her stark question froze him at the door. There was no easy way to say it, no kind way of breaking the news. He grimaced and blew out a sigh. "Abigail, there's been a horrible accident." He tried to soften the words, to blunt the pain they would cause, but her piercing gaze cut him to the marrow.

"Where is he?"

He stepped forward and reached for her arm. She shrank away until her back pressed against the cabin wall. There was nothing for it, then. She wanted none of his comfort. He drew a deep breath. "I'm so sorry, Abigail. Your father—your father is dead."

The words fell like ice from his lips. On Abigail's face he read the same disbelief, the same stunned sorrow he'd felt just a short time ago, yet she didn't cry out as he'd expected. Instead, silent tears streamed down her cheeks.

He gestured to a bench at the sawback table. "Will you sit?"

Her wooden movements tore at his already frayed heart. It was better if she railed at him, pouring out her grief in agonized wails.

Her gaze clung to him as she pulled out the bench and sat, her lips and face white. No longer able to bear the pain in her eyes, Nathan focused on her clenched fingers.

"We were in the mine," he rasped. He cleared his throat and started again. "Anson thought we'd find George deeper in than where the other men were located, so we grabbed a couple of lamps and started searching. It wasn't long before we realized—" He paused, regretting the decision all over again. "We realized we'd cover more area if we split up."

She gasped, her eyes wide with shock. "You left him?"

He'd been berating himself with the same accusation since the moment he'd heard the faint rumble start, a warning sound that said the fire had made portions of the mine unstable. He lifted his gaze. "I am so sorry, Abigail."

She said nothing for a moment as she fought to compose herself. "Did—did he fall? Was he burned? How—?"

Nathan grabbed her hand, and she broke off and stared at him. He shook his head. "None of that. Part of the mine caved in, a section probably weakened by the fire." He squeezed her fingers tightly and softened his voice to a whisper. "He didn't suffer, Abigail."

She tore her hands away. "How do you know that?"

The jagged words sounded as though they had been ripped from her. What could he say? That her father had died instantly, crushed beneath the weight of dirt and stone? No. He didn't want that picture stamped forever in her head. He steeled himself and looked her in the eyes. "It didn't take me long to reach him. By the time I got to him, Anson was gone."

That much was true.

Her tortured look said she struggled to accept his story, and then a sob escaped and she dropped her face into her hands. Saying he was sorry again wouldn't help to ease her sorrow. Neither would saying he wished it had been him who'd taken the deeper shaft into the mountain rather than remaining in the drift that ran horizontal to the main vein. His muscles aching and spirit heavy, Nathan pushed up from the table.

"What about George?" Abigail whispered.

Nathan paused. "What?"

"The other Kennedy. Did you find him?"

That much, at least, he could offer as comfort. Nathan gave a curt nod. "We did. He's with Doc now, getting checked for a concussion. He's going to be all right in a day or two, once he gets over a few nasty bruises."

She grimaced as though the knowledge pained her. Nathan stepped closer to the table. "If there's anything I can do—"

She shook her head, cutting off the rest. "Thank you, but there's nothing. If you don't mind—I'd like to be alone now."

What more could he say? Nathan made his way to the door, pausing one last time to look over his shoulder at the somber, beautiful woman grieving silently at the table. She was alone in the world. Completely, utterly alone—and it was all his fault.

Chapter Five

....

A patch of wooden crosses sprouted in Calico's tiny cemetery like a forest of winter trees scrubbed free of leaves. Abigail had never dreamed she'd be standing among them, nursing a hurt so deep it almost crippled her. She lowered her gaze and forced herself to breathe—small, jerking puffs that tore at her raw throat. Beneath her dress, the tips of her worn, leather shoes peeked out, scuffed and covered in dust. She hadn't had the heart to put on her red boots. They reminded her too much of Papa.

"Is there anything I can do for you, dear?"

Worn out from crying, Abigail found it difficult to answer her friend's question. She stared in mute silence.

Tears welled in Caroline's eyes as she stroked Abigail's arm. "Anything at all?"

Since hearing of Anson's death, Caroline had fixed herself to Abigail's side—yet the lonely hole caused by her father's absence remained. She shook her head.

"All right, then." Sorrow colored Caroline's voice. "I'll see you shortly? I can wait for you at the cabin, if you wish."

"No, I—that is—" The words faltered and died on her lips. She feared hurting Caroline's feelings, and yet her spirit craved time alone. She grasped her friend's hand. "I can't thank you enough for all you've done."

Caroline moved as though to dismiss her thanks, but Abigail continued swiftly.

"It's just—when I sort through Papa's things"—she swallowed and steeled her resolve—"I'd prefer to be alone."

Instead of the recrimination she'd feared, understanding dawned in Caroline's eyes. Her friend's fingers fluttered up to her face, and she nodded. "Of course, dear. How thoughtless of me. But I insist that you let me stop by tomorrow to check on you."

She waited until Abigail mumbled her agreement before giving her hand a pat and moving away.

Sighing, Abigail returned her gaze to the crude wooden cross marking her father's grave. Her soul was as scarred as the landscape where it stood. Memories she'd thought buried in the grave of her childhood clawed to the surface—suffocating and painful. Whispers that Anson would never amount to anything and the sly looks at her and Momma's modest, meager clothing echoed through her brain and rattled her heart. Like Papa, she'd hoped to leave those things behind when they left Virginia for a fresh start in Calico. With effort, she shook free of the painful thoughts and focused on her father's name.

ANSON JEROME WATTS. Nathan had carved the letters deep and with care, and for that she was grateful. This plot would remain forever memorialized, not windblown and sanded into obscurity like the other markers scattered about the small cemetery.

"It's a beautiful cross." Gavin Nichols picked his way toward her, his boots making crunching sounds on the rocky soil.

Abigail pinched her lips shut and cut short a sigh. Well-wishers were to be expected. It was foolish of her to think that she could mourn her loss alone. "Thank you." The words rasped from her dry throat.

A few feet from the grave site, Gavin swiped his hat from his head and held it clenched in his gloved hands. "Your father was a good man. Hardworking. I'm going to miss him."

CALICO
1883
CA

Peeking through her lashes at him, Abigail saw only genuine compassion on his face. So why did she dislike him so? It was unfair of her, when he was making such an obvious effort at kindness. She swallowed her distrust and forced a small smile. "Thank you. I appreciate your saying so."

His fingers played along the rim of his hat—round and round. Finally he said, "Do you have everything you need? Is there anything I can do? Are you"—he cleared his throat—"all right by yourself in that cabin?"

Curious, the way his gaze kept darting away from her face, like he had a question weighing on his mind that couldn't find its way to his mouth. Abigail gripped her shawl tighter. "I'm fine, Mr. Nichols. Thank you for asking." She half turned, hoping he'd realize she wanted to be alone.

"It's just…" Instead of moving away, he stepped closer. "Calico is such a rough town, Miss Watts. I hate the idea of you all alone…." He trailed off, the tips of his mustache quivering.

Abigail laid her hand briefly on the rough fabric of his sleeve. He was just being polite, after all. "I'll be fine, Mr. Nichols. Thank you for your concern."

He shook his head. "Even so, a young lady such as yourself should have someone to care for her. Someone who can provide for her needs. Someone like…"

Him. The unspoken word hung in the air between them. Anger uncurled like tendrils of smoke in Abigail's belly. The frontier was a rough place, where harsh conditions demanded split-second decisions, but surely the man didn't mean to propose right here, while she stood next to her father's grave? She put up her hand to stop whatever he meant to say next. "I'm sorry, Mr. Nichols. I've barely had time to think about anything these last few days. I'm sure I'll have a lot to face in the days ahead, but now is not the time."

His head bobbed, faster and faster until she thought his neck would snap. "Of course. My apologies, Miss Watts. It's only your welfare I was concerned about. There will be plenty of time to talk. Next week, perhaps? When you're feeling better?"

With every word he uttered, Abigail's anger burned hotter. Could he actually believe a week was all it would take for her to recuperate from the loss of her father? Fortunately, she was spared an answer she would have regretted later.

"Miss Watts?"

The preacher stepped forward, the compassion in his eyes settling upon her and offering comfort she could not accept. At his side stood a slender Chinese woman. Her face was damp, as though she, too, had been crying.

Gavin clapped his hat onto his head, obviously displeased by the interruption but not inclined to say so. "We'll talk another time." He tipped his head to her and the preacher but ignored the Chinese woman completely. A moment later, he skittered down the hilly slope and disappeared out the gate.

Abigail cut her gaze to the preacher. Suddenly her mouth felt as dry as the desert landscape. "Hello, Pastor Burch." He dipped his head and looked at her expectantly. She fumbled for appropriate words of gratitude. "Um, thank you for the message you shared today. I appreciate your kindness."

A sad smile crept across his face. "It was more than simple kindness. I meant what I said. Your father loved the Lord and showed it by supporting His church."

It was true. Papa often prayed for Calico's fledging congregation. Bitter tears pricked Abigail's eyes at the memory of her father's many supplications in front of their fire. His prayers went unanswered despite the countless hours spent on his knees—and so had hers. Though the words rose like gall, she forced them out through tight lips. "Papa did believe in seeking God's favor for His people."

Pastor Burch's eyes widened slightly with surprise. A quick glance passed between him and the Chinese woman before he returned his attention to Abigail. "Oh, it was more than that. He gave to the offering every Sunday. Quite generously, I might add."

Abigail frowned. How many times had she fretted over the evening meal and scrimped and saved to stretch Papa's meager earnings to cover the few extravagances they could afford—things like wheat flour and sugar. She shook her head. "I'm sorry, Pastor, but you must be mistaken. Papa couldn't give in the way you are implying."

Puzzled, he pushed back his flat-brimmed hat and scratched his brow. "I'm quite certain, Abigail. He brought it himself, oftentimes after Sunday service, because he said he didn't want anyone to know—not that I think he'd mind now. He asked me to use it to see to the needs of the Chinese immigrants and their families. In fact, that's one reason Soo has asked to speak to you." He gestured to the woman at his side. "She wanted to express her thanks to the daughter of 'Mistah Anson,' as they called him."

Silent until now, the Chinese woman dipped her head at the mention of her name and grasped Abigail's hand. "Your fada, very good man." She pumped Abigail's palm and repeated the phrase, fresh tears streaming from her eyes.

"Soo owes her baby's life to your father," the preacher continued, slipping his arm around Soo's shoulders. "Anson paid to have the child sent to Los Angeles for treatment against scoliosis a few weeks back. Soo could never have afforded it otherwise, and little Jiao would most likely never have learned to walk."

Soo's gaze left the preacher and returned to Abigail. "Very good man," she whispered.

Emotions deep and varied washed over Abigail. The news should have made her glad. Instead, she felt betrayed. Why hadn't her father told her? Did he think she would begrudge the sacrifice? Had he not trusted her? She swallowed the resentment rising in her throat and forced a smile. "Thank you, Soo. I appreciate your sharing this with me."

She paused while Pastor Burch translated. Soo bowed so deep, her head dropped lower than her waist. A moment later, she said good-bye then scurried toward a handful of Chinese who ushered her back toward town. Still, Soo kept her eyes trained on Abigail until they disappeared from sight.

Abigail rubbed her temple. "I don't understand. Why didn't Papa ever tell me this?"

"It wasn't his way," Pastor Burch said as he placed a light touch on her shoulder. "Anson didn't need men to praise his generosity. He knew that his reward was in heaven with his Father. He's there now, surrounded by angels and claiming his crown."

Pain twisted inside Abigail's chest. What would Papa do with a crown? He'd never owned anything more than a beat-up cowboy hat. She shook her head. It made no sense that God would take her father now, especially if what the Chinese woman said was true—and when Abigail herself needed him so much.

The silence stretched uncomfortably thin. Finally Pastor Burch said, "Well, I guess I'd best take my leave. If there's anything I can do, you need but ask."

Though she struggled to process a proper thank-you, the words refused to come. He gave one last compassionate smile and then descended the gentle slope with the other mourners—a few sympathetic miners and their families, people whom her father had befriended.

When all had gone, Abigail turned back to view her father's sandy grave. To think, his final resting place was a barren, hostile desert, not alongside his wife in a fertile, green oasis back home in Virginia—the way he and his daughter had imagined.

The chilly day held a sharpness that warned of cooling temperatures, but overhead a cheerful sun burned her scalp, even through her bonnet. A rush of anger heated the blood in her veins. Why couldn't it be dark and rainy? Why couldn't the sky grieve with her over her father's loss rather than cast the sun's cheerful rays across the hillside?

Her heart felt pulverized—like the dust that came from the ore the miners pulled from the Silver King, stamped and mulled until only powder remained. Hands trembling, she studied the cross marking her father's grave then reached out to trace the letters of his name.

"Papa."

Though she whispered, his name blistered her lips with regret. Where was God in all this? Had He deserted her along with her father? Unbridled agony swept up from the depths of her spirit and sapped the strength from her limbs. She'd never hear her papa's voice again, or bask in the warmth of his smile. Never again would she rest in the safety of his loving arms....

Just as quickly as the painful thought came, two strong arms *did* encircle her, saving her from falling into a heap on the ground. She looked up into a pair of dark eyes shadowed with sorrow.

"Nathan?"

"I've got you," he said, sweeping her up into his arms. He carried her down the hill toward the cemetery gate, where his daughter waited, her blue eyes wide and filled with fear.

Lizzie pushed open the gate to let them pass then tugged at one of her braids with both hands. "Pa?"

"It'll be all right, sweetheart. Miss Abigail just needs to rest. Help me, now. We need to get her home."

Abigail wanted to protest, to demand that Nathan put her down and allow her to linger at the grave site, but the words wouldn't come and weariness made her head heavy. Last night had come and gone without sleep. If only she could let his concern ease the weight of her burdens, perhaps she could face the troubles ahead. But was that fair?

She struggled to lift her chin. "I can walk—"

His hold tightened as he looked down at her, but his steps did not slow. "Bosh. I'll have you home in no time."

Home? Abigail swallowed the bitter lump that rose in her throat. Papa was gone. She had no home now. Only an empty cabin.

As if conjured by her thoughts, the weathered planks of the cabin came into view. Abigail resisted the urge to bury her face in Nathan's shoulder, but she couldn't stop her eyes from closing, shutting out the once-comforting sight.

"Here we are, Pa," Lizzie said, her childish voice subdued. She scurried ahead and threw open the door.

Nathan carried Abigail to her room and gently laid her on the bed, but not before she glimpsed her father's pallet lying catty-corner on the living room floor. She choked back a sob and hid her face in the covers.

Nathan gave her shoulder an awkward pat. "There now. You'll be all right once you've slept."

When she didn't answer, he straightened and moved away.

His voice carried from the doorway. "How long has it been since you've eaten?"

She couldn't remember. Her stomach rumbled, but she didn't have the strength to worry about filling it. Whether he could see it or not, she shrugged and burrowed deeper into the bed. After a moment, the door closed with a soft click.

Finally.

It was what she'd wanted all day—to be left alone. Bit by trembling bit, she let go of the stranglehold she'd kept on her emotions and let the tears fall. With them came the anger and disappointment she'd been struggling to contain.

"Why, God?" she cried, anguish ripping the question from her heart. "Why did You let my father die? Why!"

She turned her face to the pillow, fearing in the depths of her spirit that she might never have the answers—and that her life, her faith, would never be the same.

* * * * *

Nathan stared at the bedroom door, his heart shredded and bleeding inside his chest. Though muffled, Abigail's sobs were painful to hear.

"Pa?"

He glanced down at his daughter, grateful for the distraction. "Yes, Lizzie?"

Her gaze skittered hesitantly to the door. "Maybe she needs a pretty."

Nathan lowered to his haunches until he and his daughter were at the same level. "What makes you think that, sweetheart?"

She shrugged her thin shoulders. Against her sun-kissed face, the light freckles scattered across her nose made her appear even more earnest. "You always give me a pretty when I feel bad. Should I look, Pa? Maybe it'll make her feel better."

Nathan felt a swell of pride at her compassion and drew Lizzie into a hug. "I think that's a wonderful idea, sweetheart." He breathed deep in her hair, using the moment to gather his emotions. Wiping the sheen of tears from his eyes, he cleared his throat. "I'm sure Abigail likes flowers. How 'bout you look for some, or maybe a shiny stone, while I make her something to eat?"

The sparkle returned to Lizzie's eyes with her smile. "All right." She pulled from his arms and skipped to the door.

Nathan stopped her before she slipped outside. "Not too far from the cabin, you hear?"

She nodded and tucked the tip of a neatly twisted braid into her mouth. Abigail had taken the time to fix Lizzie's hair before the funeral, right after she'd fashioned her own dark hair into a tight knot. Once again, Nathan felt a rush of admiration for Abigail's selflessness.

"Don't worry, Pa. I won't be gone long." Lizzie waved good-bye, and then her light footsteps skipped over the porch.

Sighing, Nathan wandered into the kitchen to scour the contents of Abigail's sparse pantry. He found a tin filled with cornmeal, and hanging from a hook near the stove was a side of salted pork.

Good.

Grabbing a brush and a small scoop from a nail, he bent to scrape the ashes out of the stove. Soon he'd have a cook fire going and he'd be able to feed Abigail's body, though not her spirit. Only time would do that, and only after many months.

"Time," he repeated firmly to himself. That was what she needed. He wouldn't fool himself into thinking help would come from anything—or anyone—else.

As he reached for the kindling and arranged it into a heap, fresh sorrow tugged at his heart. A part of him wished it wasn't so. A part of him wished he'd never learned firsthand *not* to depend upon God.

Chapter Six

....

She'd told herself she wouldn't look, but hunger and curiosity finally drove Abigail from the bedroom. The wonderful smells of savory pork and warm cornbread were tugging at her senses. She cracked open the door and peered out. Though the cabin was dimly lit, she saw no one, and renewed sorrow bubbled up from her midsection. Nothing her father ever attempted to cook smelled like that, and it served as a fresh reminder of his absence.

"Hello."

Startled by the deep voice, Abigail paused with her hand on the jamb. Nathan watched her from a chair near the fireplace. He rose, his tall frame out of place in the cramped space of the cabin, and gestured toward the flames. "I hope you don't mind. I thought it would take the chill off."

Of the room, perhaps. Nothing would ever warm her heart again. She clasped her hands tightly in front of her. "It's fine. Thank you."

A soft sigh rose from the corner, and Abigail turned to see Lizzie's tiny body forming a gentle mound on her father's pallet. At the edge of the covers, her small toes poked out.

"She was tired," Nathan said, almost apologetically. He approached, his warm gaze saying that he regretted hurting her even more than his tone did.

Abigail glanced toward the window, where the setting sun cast long shadows across the floor. Of course Lizzie would be tired. It had been a long day for all of them.

"I would've taken her home, to the livery, but I wasn't sure—that is—" He paused and slid his hands into his pockets. "I didn't think you'd want to be alone."

Though she knew he hadn't intended such, his words drove a dagger into her heart. The people she did have—a scattering of aunts and cousins back East, relatives who'd never loved or accepted either her father or her—didn't make her any less alone. She attempted a smile and failed. "I appreciate your thoughtfulness."

He nodded. It appeared as if he struggled a moment, for his jaw worked but produced no words. Finally he motioned toward the heavy iron stove, where the burner glowed red hot above a crackling fire. "Are you hungry? I figured you'd need to keep up your strength."

Abigail studied the soft-spoken livery owner with new interest. She would never have guessed him to be such a considerate man, although—she spared a quick glance at Lizzie—he obviously cared deeply for his daughter.

"I can move her." Nathan left the fire and approached the pallet. "I didn't mean to offend—"

Abigail raised her hand in protest. "No, it's all right. Leave her."

He drew to a stop, his broad shoulders still turned as though he meant to continue forward. "Are you sure?"

"I'm sure." This time she did manage a half smile. She motioned toward the table. "Will you join me?"

He nodded but took none of the pork from the platter. Instead, he poured himself a cup of black coffee and sat across from her at the table. Strangely, his presence did not trouble her, as she might have thought. There was something comforting in the sound of his quiet breathing, and he refrained from conversation as though he sensed her need for silence. Not wanting to appear ungrateful, she forced a few tasteless bites into her mouth. When she'd finished and pushed the plate away, Nathan lowered his cup and fixed her with his steady gaze.

"Miss Watts, I know it's not my place to ask—" He broke off and looked away as his fingers worked the rim of his cup.

She knew the words before he spoke them. They'd haunted her dreams, filling her with dread. She bent her head to study the dark whorls in the pine sawback. "What will I do now that my father is gone?"

His chair scraped back, and then his heavy steps paced the length of the small cabin. "I assume your father rented this place from the mining company?"

She swallowed. It was true—very few of the miners owned their own homes, her father included. They came, earned their fortunes, and moved away—or stayed and lived out their days working for the mining company. Awash with misery, she dipped her head.

"And now that your father no longer works for the mine?"

Her face twisted and she shrugged. "I haven't considered all my options yet, but I intend to speak to the company superintendent soon about continuing the rent."

His boots scraped to a stop. "Is that wise? Haven't you got family back East? Someone to whom you could appeal for help?"

He didn't know about her cruel, angry relatives, and she wouldn't tell him. She lifted her chin. "No."

He raised one brow and peered at her. "What will you do for money?"

In fact, she *had* thought about how she would support herself. Patching clothes for the miners had put food on the table, and she'd even managed to save a small pittance in a tin container beneath the floorboards. It wouldn't last long—a week or two if she was frugal. Still, her father had one last paycheck coming. Tomorrow she'd go see Mr. Nichols and determine her direction from there.

"I have enough to get by, at least for a while. Plus, the mining company still owes Papa for the days he worked last week. It won't be much, but it ought to carry me through until I decide what I should do next." She laced her fingers and tried to appear calmer than she felt.

"That's good," he said, though the concern remained etched on his brow. "There is still, however, another matter you need to consider." He dipped his head toward the porch, where, just beyond, the sound of revelers emerging from their beds had begun. "Once those men get wind of the fact that you're alone—and single—well, it won't be long before they're sniffing at your door."

A blush heated Abigail's cheeks, and she ducked her head to hide her embarrassment.

Nathan cleared his throat. "I beg your pardon, Miss Watts. It's just that, uh…" He hooked his thumbs in the top of his trousers, as if it was the only way to keep from wringing his hands. "If I might speak plainly?"

She encouraged him with a wave.

"A pretty gal like you, all alone—certainly you realize that it just wouldn't be safe?"

Rather than answer, Abigail rose and went to the pistol and holster mounted on a hook next to the fireplace. Grasping the butt, she pulled the weapon free with one hand, held it against her hip, then

CALICO
1883
CA

stared across the cabin at Nathan. "I assure you, Mr. Hawk, I am quite capable of protecting myself. Anyone who tries to break in here is going to meet with the business end of this gun."

To her surprise, the corners of his mouth lifted in a smile. "I'm sure you mean what you say, Miss Watts."

"I do." Her jaw hardened. "Trust me. I'm a very good shot."

He gave a brisk nod before crossing the room to Lizzie. "That's good. I'll worry less knowing you can take care of yourself."

There was an edge of laughter in his voice that made her think perhaps he mocked her, yet when he looked up, his eyes were warm—the color of fresh honey.

"I'll take Lizzie now and let you rest."

At the thought of spending another sleepless night in an empty cabin, Abigail's bravado fled. "Do you have to?"

She spoke too quickly, and he studied her intently. Despising the way her voice trembled, she took her time replacing the gun and then smoothed her hands down the length of her skirt until she felt her nerves steady. Finally she turned on her heel and faced him. "Lizzie is welcome to stay the night. After all, she is asleep, and the air promises to be cool. Why don't you let her lie where she is and collect her before school in the morning?"

She held her breath, waiting. When at last he nodded, she released it with a whoosh. The moment was inevitable, but for now, at least, she'd managed to postpone it—that horrible, empty hour when she'd be completely, utterly on her own.

Chapter Seven

·····················

Nathan rushed to wash and dress the next morning, splashing icy water from the trough over his head and face to speed his ministrations. He'd sensed a deep need for companionship in Abigail the night before. While he had no qualms about leaving Lizzie in her care, he couldn't wait to see his daughter. At least, he told himself it was his daughter he was anxious to see. He couldn't—wouldn't—think of anyone else.

Tending to the animals in the livery came first, however.

After feeding and watering them, he loosed them into the corral and then hurried to muck the stalls and spread fresh straw. Charlotte had always hated this work. Despite her claims that she could be happy anywhere as long as they were together, her nose had wrinkled at the pungent odors of the barn, and her displeasure at the smell that clung to his clothing as she laundered them was evident in her pinched fingers.

She never complained, he reminded himself as he completed his morning chores and covered the distance to Abigail's cabin in a few long strides. No matter how much Charlotte had missed her gentle friends back East, she never let it show, even after she took ill.

Shaking free of the memories, he raised his fist and knocked on the door. Abigail answered at once, giving rise to the suspicion that she'd not slept at all.

Pallor bleached Abigail's countenance, but she offered a weak smile. "Good morning."

"Pa!" Lizzie dashed around Abigail's skirt and up into Nathan's arms. "Abigail made me biscuits." She patted his cheek gently. "They're much better than the ones you make, but I still like yours. And she gave me real cactus jelly! It's not spiky at all."

"Spiky?" He lifted his gaze to Abigail for explanation.

"She thought the jelly would still have the spines." A hint of humor colored her voice, a welcome sound to Nathan after the heartrending sobs that had echoed through the cabin last night.

He pressed a kiss to the tip of Lizzie's nose and then deposited her onto the floor. "All right, sweetheart. Run on back to the livery. I'll join you in a moment."

"Did you feed Charlie?"

One of the more ornery mules that hauled ore from the mine to the stamp mill in Daggett, Charlie was by far Lizzie's favorite. Nathan suspected it was because of his shaggy coat and abnormally long ears. He smiled and nodded. "All done."

Lizzie's brows bunched into a frown.

Nathan bent and propped both hands on his knees so he could look into his daughter's face. "I'm sorry, sweetheart, but I couldn't wait for you this morning. Miss Watts has errands to run today, and I thought she might need my help. You wouldn't want Charlie to go without his breakfast while she and I tend to her business, would you?"

After pondering a moment, Lizzie shook her head. "No, Charlie needs his breakfast too. You think he might like some cactus jelly, Pa?"

Nathan chuckled. "I don't know, sweetheart. I reckon he might. Go on now. I'll join you in a minute."

Hollering her good-byes, Lizzie waved and then set off at a run for the livery. Nathan turned to Abigail and was surprised to find her watching him with tears in her eyes.

"Thank you," she whispered.

Suddenly uncomfortable, he shuffled his feet. "No need, Miss Watts."

She gave a determined shake of her head. "No, I mean it. You don't have to accompany me today, but I appreciate the offer. I can't tell you how much."

For the first time in as long a span as he could remember, Nathan felt a blush rise. It crept up from his neck until his entire face felt as if it were on fire. "It's no problem. Lizzie will be in school, so I'll be free until this afternoon. Besides, it's the least I can do," he managed with some difficulty. Criticism over his decision to split from Anson struck him anew.

"Well, I am grateful, nonetheless."

They were interrupted by a voice from the street. "Morning!"

Nathan stepped aside to give Abigail a view. The same young woman who'd volunteered to assist Mrs. Chen now bustled up the stone walk. She carried a basket in her arms, and on her face was a compassionate smile that reinforced his opinion of her kindness.

"I hope you don't mind—I thought you could use a few things." She climbed the steps and came to a stop next to them on the porch.

Abigail motioned toward the woman. "Mr. Hawk, have you met my friend? This is Caroline Martin."

Nathan extended his hand. "We've met."

Caroline hesitated and then smiled. "The mine."

"That's right."

She took his hand and gave it a shake before turning to Abigail. "I thought about you all night. How are you doing, dear?"

Abigail lifted her shoulders in a shrug. "I'll be fine—eventually." Her smile, though thin, hinted to her strength. She gestured toward the cabin. "Please, won't you both come inside?"

Admiration for her courage flared in Nathan's chest. He'd not given her enough credit. Perhaps she would be fine on her own. He cleared his throat. "Ladies, if you would excuse me, I have chores that need attending." They nodded, and he directed his gaze to Abigail. "If you need anything, please don't hesitate to ask."

Was it his imagination, or did her eyes warm as she looked at him? Stifling the rush of exhilaration the thought stirred, he swung off the porch and headed back toward the livery. The feeling was unwanted and unwarranted, and he would not allow himself to be caught up in boyish fancy.

Still, as he dodged rumbling wagons loaded with ore, he couldn't help but notice the quickness of his breathing and the racing of his heart. Whatever fables he might tell himself, he couldn't deny— neither one had anything to do with his brisk walk to the livery.

* * * * *

Despite what she'd thought earlier, Nathan's words did create a feeling in the general region of Abigail's heart that felt suspiciously like warmth. She lingered at the cabin entrance, watching him withdraw, until the stable door closed him from view. Finally, she drew a breath and let it go in a sigh.

Caroline's hand cupped Abigail's shoulder and she bent to whisper in her ear. "He's a nice man, that Nathan Hawk."

CALICO
1883
CA

That he was, and more. The way he put action to his compassion filled Abigail with hope. She managed a small nod before walking over to the table, where Caroline had set her basket down and was carefully unloading the contents. Along with a loaf of fresh-baked bread, she'd packed a small tin of flour, a few eggs, a pint of milk, and various other sundry items that Abigail knew would extend the money she'd stored under the floorboards a great deal.

She fingered the patch of checkered cloth and twine that secured the top of a jar of honey. "This is so sweet of you, Caroline."

Caroline's lips turned up in a pleased smile, and her eyes glinted with friendship. She grabbed the flour tin and pressed it into Abigail's hands then scooped up a small bag of sugar and followed her into the kitchen. "So, John tells me Mr. Hawk is fairly new to Calico. We've been so busy making wedding plans, I haven't had the chance to meet him."

Her hand on the cupboard's wooden knob, Abigail glanced over her shoulder at her friend. Just the mention of her fiancé's name brought a glow of happiness to Caroline's face and made her eyes sparkle. Though Abigail loved both John Gardner and Caroline, she felt a twinge of envy. What must it be like to be so free of care, so full of hope for the future? She tamped the unwelcome emotion and forced a smile. "Yes. Mr. Hawk and his daughter arrived just shy of six months ago."

"He doesn't work the mine, does he? What brought him to Calico?" Caroline went to the table and returned with another handful of items for the cupboard.

Abigail slid aside a jar of preserves to make room for the new supplies. "Like Papa, I think he heard there was work to be found. Papa was one of the first people Mr. Hawk met, and they formed a fast friendship. In fact, they'd even talked about staking their own claim together. Papa respected Mr. Hawk so much…."

She found she could not finish. Dipping her head to fight a sudden swell of tears, she was surprised to feel a gentle touch upon her shoulder.

"Never be afraid to let the tears fall, Abigail. It's God's way of rinsing away the grief and healing your spirit."

The sentiment brought no comfort. Abigail sniffed but accepted the lace hankie Caroline pressed into her hand. "Th–thank you," she said, the words broken by a hiccup.

Caroline gestured toward Abigail's bedroom and the washbasin. "I'll finish up here. Why don't you go splash some water on your face? You'll feel better."

Abigail's limbs felt as heavy as her heart. She dragged herself to the washbowl.

"What are your plans for today?" Caroline called from the kitchen.

A knot of dread formed in Abigail's stomach. She'd told Nathan she didn't need his help while running her errands, but facing Mr. Nichols alone raked slivers of fear inside her timid chest.

She braced both hands on the edge of the dry sink. "Ah, actually, I need to pay a visit to the mine superintendent."

"Mr. Nichols?" Caroline poked her head around the cupboard.

Pouring water from the pitcher into the basin, Abigail nodded. "I need to inquire about Papa's pay—the rest of the money they owe him."

Caroline closed the cupboard door and tapped her finger against her chin. "Yes, I'd forgotten that. I promised John I would join him for lunch, but that can certainly wait for another day."

"Oh, no," Abigail said, shaking her head. "You two have wedding plans to finalize. I'm fine by myself, truly."

In fact, her knees were shaking beneath the folds of her gingham dress, but she put on a brave face and tried to smile.

Caroline's eyes clouded with uncertainty. "Are you sure? John will understand if you need me to go."

Touched by her concern, Abigail wavered for a moment and then shook her head. "I appreciate the offer, but now that Papa's g–gone, I need to get used to doing things for myself." She plunged her hands into the washbasin to avoid meeting Caroline's gaze. Fear stirred in her stronger than she liked to admit, but if she allowed herself to dwell on the fact, she'd never leave the cabin. Scooping up a handful of water, she splashed her face and willed the bracing cold to harden her resolve.

Caroline entered the bedroom, carrying a towel she'd plucked from a hook next to the door. "Here."

Abigail took her time drying her face, and by the time she looked up, she felt more in control of her spiraling emotions.

"Better?" Caroline asked.

"Much. At least I won't face Mr. Nichols with puffy cheeks—though I can do nothing about these red eyes."

"I'm sure he'll understand." Caroline gave Abigail's shoulder a gentle pat. Grabbing hold of a comb that lay alongside the washbasin, she ran it through Abigail's long hair until the dark tresses gleamed. "There now, that's better. I've always admired the way your hair coils just so."

Abigail studied her brown curls in the mirror. "Papa always said I took after my mother that way."

Over her shoulder, Caroline's eyes met hers in the reflection. "I'm sure she was beautiful, then."

The feel of fancy silks and the scent of sweet perfumes niggled at her memory. Of course, that was before Mama had sold her nice things to help provide for the family. Still, even in a plain cotton dress, Olivia Watts was beautiful. Abigail lowered her gaze to the towel clasped in her cold fingers. "Yes."

Caroline set down the comb and turned toward the kitchen. "So, will you go now to inquire of Mr. Nichols, or do you have time for a cup of tea? I brought one of my favorites in the basket. I was hoping you'd have time."

Thankful for a friend as sweet as Caroline, Abigail felt a smile replace the urge to cry. She trailed after her, the hem of her skirt rustling softly against her scuffed brown shoes. "I wish I did, but there's no sense in putting off what must be done. Maybe this afternoon, after you've been to see John and I've finished up at the mine office?"

"Agreed." Caroline wrapped Abigail in a hug that warmed her to the core. "We'll be at the Calico Hotel until this afternoon, but I'll stop by the cabin afterward." She leaned back to peer into Abigail's face. "You'll call on me if you need me?"

"Of course."

"Very well, then. I'll come around three." After snatching her bonnet from the table, Caroline placed a quick kiss on Abigail's cheek and then made her way out the door and down the street.

Abigail hesitated on the porch, her mind riddled with reasons for postponing her meeting with the mine superintendent. The hour was early; he might not be at the office. And something in her empty stomach might make her feel better—she hadn't bothered eating any of the biscuits she'd prepared earlier for Lizzie. Abigail sighed. The excuses weren't convincing enough to make her wait. She grabbed her shawl and closed the cabin door, her leaden feet carrying her to

Gavin Nichols's office far too quickly. And the painted plank door swung open before she had a chance to knock—or answer the nudge inside her heart that said she should pray.

Gavin Nichols stared down at her, his eyes wide with surprise. "Miss Watts?" The surprise mellowed into something baser. Eyes sparkling, he leaned toward her—too close. Abigail sucked in a breath. He appeared not to notice, for his lips curled into a smile. "This is an unexpected pleasure. I intended to seek you out later, after you'd had a few days to, you know, sort things out."

Whatever "things" he thought she might need to sort, Abigail figured it best to ignore. She swallowed her apprehension and forced her chin higher. "Good morning, Mr. Nichols. I wonder if I might have a moment of your time."

His brows lifted at the businesslike tone she adopted. After a moment, he drew back and fumbled to pull a watch from a pocket of his vest. He flipped open the cover, peered at the face, then replaced it with a sigh. "It's getting on near midmorning. I'm afraid I've several errands to attend to after this week's unfortunate accidents."

"But, you see, Mr. Nichols, it's the accident"—she nearly choked on the word—"that I need to speak to you about."

Unease quickened her heart as Mr. Nichols's gaze roved over her from head to toe. Finally he stepped back and pushed the door wide. "I suppose I have a moment."

Clutching the shawl around her shoulders, she squeezed past him into an office larger than her cabin. Two small wooden benches hunkered in front of a massive desk, behind which sat a chair that looked suspiciously like a throne.

Mr. Nichols motioned for Abigail to be seated before circling the desk and sinking into his throne-chair. She sat across from him on one of the hard benches, her nerves twitching like so many ants creeping across her skin.

"If I haven't said it already," he began, "I'd like to express my sincere condolences for your loss."

Her head bobbed in what had already become a familiar gesture. "Thank you."

"Is there anything I can do for you? Anything you need?"

Abigail fidgeted with the fringes of the shawl, her eyes taking in the fancy, scrolled inkwell on his desk, the embossed leather ledger with the gently curling pages—anything but his face. Even though the money was due, asking for her father's last paycheck was difficult. She had hoped he would offer it without her having to voice the words.

Her gaze fell to the pine planks beneath her feet. "It's about my father's wages, Mr. Nichols."

His chair whispered softly as he shifted. "Go on."

Abigail lifted her head in amazement. He meant to force her into asking for the money outright? Very well. Squaring her shoulders, she looked him in the eye. "I believe my father had final wages coming. I'm here to collect whatever is due."

A sad frown turned the corners of Mr. Nichols's lips downward. Leaning forward, he crossed his arms upon the desktop before he spoke. "Miss Watts, I'm afraid there is no money due."

Uncertain she'd heard him correctly, she stilled. "What?"

He lowered his gaze and quickly followed that with a shake of his head. Abigail waited, while anxiety turned her stomach sour. Whatever he had to say, it wasn't good. She tensed as he rose, circled the desk, and stood beside her.

"Mr. Nichols—"

"Gavin."

She ignored his interruption and went on. "I'm not sure I understand. My father worked a full week for you before he died. He should have several days' pay coming."

The mine superintendent's face softened with compassion. When he sat beside Abigail on the bench, too close for comfort, she slid over to increase the distance between them. As if he understood the reason for her actions, he smiled, crossed his legs, and let loose a long sigh.

"Normally that would be true but, you see, Abigail—may I call you Abigail?"

She nodded curtly so he would continue.

"You see, Abigail, I'm afraid that there were some unfortunate circumstances surrounding the accident—facts that make it impossible for me to release the last bit of money your father had coming, insignificant as the amount might have been."

"What facts?"

"No one has told you?" His fingers worried the tip of his mustache. "I suppose I shouldn't be surprised. No one enjoys being the bearer of unsavory details such as these."

Though using his name felt wrong to her sensibilities, she forced herself to say it. "Gavin, what is it you need to tell me?"

He made a small clucking noise with his tongue before folding his hands over his knee. "There's just no easy way to say this except to come right out with it. Abigail, the accident at the mine wasn't as cut-and-dried as it first seemed. I'm afraid—"

He started to fidget and suddenly refused to look her in the eye.

"Go on," she said, her stomach tightening.

"Well, it was your father's carelessness that caused the explosion."

Outrage gripped her, which was quickly replaced by relief. Nichols hadn't been informed of the details of that fateful night, then—didn't realize that Papa hadn't been working the mine, only assisting in the rescue effort.

She gave a high, nervous laugh, cut short by a burst of despair so sharp that it sheared the words from her mouth. "No, you don't understand. Papa and Mr. Hawk were searching for another miner. When they couldn't find him, they split up, thinking they'd cover more area."

"Abigail—"

Her head wagged. "They were trying to save a man's life. Surely you didn't expect Papa to follow safety procedures when a man's life was at stake?"

The condescension in his gaze made her regret the decision to sit. He pushed to his feet at the same moment as she, and though he still towered over her, at least she didn't feel so helpless. She willed her sudden anger into her curled fingers, rending the knit of her shawl. She took a breath and forced her words to come more slowly.

"Tom Kennedy came to us for help. He said his brother was trapped, and Father and Nathan volunteered to look for him. What else were they to do?" Pleading crept into her tone, but with increasing desperation clawing at her stomach, she no longer cared if she begged.

At Mr. Nichols's smile, Abigail felt awash with relief. It really was a mistake, after all. He had no intention of robbing her of the last of her father's earnings. He simply didn't have all of the facts—

"You misunderstand, Miss Watts."

Suddenly Abigail realized it wasn't kindness she read in his smile, but pity. Reaching behind him, he pulled a sheet of paper off his desk and held it toward her.

A shudder took her, and she found she could no more have accepted the paper than if he had been offering a rattler. "What is it?"

"My report on the accident." He lifted one eyebrow. "Shall I read it to you?"

She remained still, as though she'd been carved from the same tree as the bench upon which she'd sat, dread cutting into her like slivers at what she would hear.

The paper rustled as he turned it and began to read. The words were unfamiliar at first, filled with a meaning she knew she should grasp but couldn't. It wasn't until he paused that the message sharpened into focus.

"C–could you read that again?" she stammered. Her face felt frozen, her hands ice-cold.

He glanced at her and then lowered his eyes to the sheet and cleared his throat. "'It is my conclusion, therefore, that the initial explosion, which injured no less than six miners and killed one other, was the direct result of blasting powder combined with a lantern flame that was left unattended.'"

Abigail shuddered again. Explosions and the cave-ins that could follow were constant fears. No man dared endanger his life or the lives of others by leaving burning candles or a lantern in the mine. How had this happened?

Mr. Nichols paused, his gaze searching Abigail's. Finally he blew out a long breath, laid down the report, and went to retrieve something from under his desk.

Abigail's chest tightened. She wanted to close her eyes, to block out whatever sight Mr. Nichols intended to reveal. Instead, her hand rose to cover her mouth, as if by doing so she could stifle the cry she felt rising. When he moved aside, it was too soon, too abrupt for her to do anything more than stare.

A charred lantern sat on the desk. Painted on the side of it in scorched, blackened letters, was the name ANSON WATTS.

Chapter Eight

....

"Is that...?"

The words trailed from Abigail's lips—emotionless, disbelieving. Papa cared about the mine. The people who worked in it were his friends. He would never have put their lives in jeopardy.

"This is your father's lantern, is it not?"

Abigail tore her gaze from the horrible lettered truth and stared into Gavin Nichols's compassionate eyes.

Swallowing hard, she plucked the words like cotton bolls from a dry field. "There must—be some—explanation."

"I had hoped so myself." Gavin grasped the lantern's handle and replaced the lamp under the desk. Once it was out of sight, he folded his hands in his lap and sighed. "Believe me, Abigail, I looked for another explanation. I questioned the miners who were working that night—even went to a few who weren't there, hoping I might be able to glean something that would hint to another possible cause. I found nothing."

"Then you didn't look hard enough."

Despite her strong words, fear had begun to mingle with the desperation Abigail felt—fear that all the horrible things that had ever been said regarding her father's future, and hers, were true. That neither of them would ever amount to anything, and her mother, whose family was wealthy beyond Abigail's imagining, had made a terrible mistake in marrying him.

Abigail whirled away from Gavin, wishing she could just as easily turn from the lies slamming her in the face. At the door she paused, knowing that there was still one thing they had yet to discuss.

Reluctantly she turned. "About the cabin…"

An even deeper look of pity darkened his face, and somehow she knew she didn't want to hear the answer.

"I'm sorry, Abigail," Gavin said, shoving his hands deep into the pockets of his trousers. "I'm afraid I have more bad news."

* * * * *

The early morning sun crested the mountains, its warm rays driving the chill from the livery. Nathan hustled to scrub the last bit of food scraps from the skillet he'd used to cook his breakfast before dunking the lot in a barrel of icy-cold water.

A passel of men from the mining company had arrived yesterday, all dressed in suits and sporting derbies. While the unexpected business meant his stable was full, it also delayed any extra work he'd hoped to accomplish on the lean-to he was building for himself and Lizzie. Plus, he couldn't help wondering what the men were doing in Calico—or if their presence had anything to do with Abigail.

Nathan eyed the door to her cabin, worry knotting his gut. It had been two days—and she'd only ducked out a couple of times to fill the water bucket. Even her friend Caroline had been unable to coax her outside for more than a few minutes. Something was wrong, and more than likely it had to do with the men who'd ridden in on the row of quarter horses munching his straw.

In the corral Charlie brayed, bringing Nathan's thoughts skittering back to the hungry mules.

He hitched up his pants and headed for the feed bin. "I'm comin'. Keep your harness on."

"Pa?"

Lizzie scrambled from her blanket, bits of hay clinging to her tangled braids. It was Saturday, and Nathan had decided to let her sleep late. He plucked a piece of hay loose and then dropped to his haunches and wrapped her in a hug. "Morning, sweetheart."

"Mornin', Pa."

"You hungry?"

She nodded.

"Good. Your breakfast is on the tack bench."

She grabbed a stray lock of tousled hair and twisted it around her finger. "You goin' to feed Charlie?"

"I'm on my way right now."

"Can I help?" Her eyes wide in her round little face, Lizzie's look turned pleading.

Though tempted to chuckle, Nathan resisted the urge and swiped his thumb down his daughter's smudged cheek. Mud even dotted the hem of her dress. "Tell you what. You go get washed up and put on a clean dress, and then I'll let you help me polish the bridles."

Lizzie's pink lips drooped into a frown. "I can't put on a clean dress. I don't have any, Pa." She lifted both hands, palms up, and shrugged. "They're all dirty."

Nathan's gaze bounced from her smudged toes to her grubby fingers. Charlotte would've been horrified to see her daughter in such a state. "Just wash up, then," he said, swallowing his guilt. Patting Lizzie's back, he added, "I'll see about the laundering tonight."

Her pout still in place, Lizzie shuffled off to do his bidding. At least he could be grateful for one thing—Charlotte could not have given him a more obedient child.

At the thought of his dead wife, a familiar ache throbbed inside

Nathan's chest. He turned from it and continued toward the feed bin. He'd really have to get a move on now, if he hoped to have enough daylight left after he finished his chores to be able to wash the few garments he and Lizzie owned.

By the time he'd finished oiling the leather harnesses for the mule teams, replenished the troughs with fresh water, and turned the horses into the corral for exercise, Nathan felt he'd gotten a decent jump on his workday. Now he'd find Lizzie and make good on his promise to let her help him polish the bridles.

Rags in hand, he headed toward the tack bench for a piece of lye soap and some beeswax. The soap and warm water would clean the bridles; the beeswax would polish and soften the cheekpiece and throatlatch. Lizzie, however, was nowhere in sight when Nathan reached the tack bench. Worse yet, her breakfast of bread crust and beans sat uneaten on her plate.

"Lizzie?"

Nathan shot a quick glance around the stable, nervousness setting his stomach to fluttering. Where could she be, and how long had she been gone?

Tossing the rags onto the bench, he hurried to the corral where he kept Charlie. The old mule lifted his shaggy head and blinked sleepily at him, as if surprised to see Nathan back so soon.

"Lizzie?" Nathan called again, this time cupping his hands to his mouth. The sides of the horse trough were damp where water had splashed, so he knew she'd washed up as he'd asked. In fact, the soap still lay in a frothy puddle where she'd left it when she finished.

"Lizzie!" Fear edged out every other emotion. In a town like Calico, it wasn't only the wild critters and harsh conditions that could kill a person. Rushing around the side of the stable, Nathan stared across the street at the weathered sides of Belle's Saloon. She wouldn't have gone over there, not when he'd warned her time and again to stay away. Surely—

"Pa!"

Nathan's heart jerked at the childish voice. Lizzie stood on Abigail's porch with her hand extended above her head.

"Over here, Pa," she yelled, adding a cheerful wave.

The nausea rolling in Nathan's stomach fled, swallowed by a mixture of relief and irritation. He reminded himself, as he strode across the yard, that Lizzie was only a child. Still, anger over the fear she'd caused made his limbs shake.

Upon reaching the cabin, he dropped onto one knee and grasped her by the shoulders. "Do you know how worried I was? How many times have I asked you to never leave the stable without telling me where you're going?"

Lizzie flinched at the sharpness of his tone, and tears filled her eyes. Tucking in her bottom lip, her chin trembled as she fought not to cry. "S–sorry, Pa."

"It's not safe, Lizzie. You shouldn't wander off." Fear flickered in her eyes. Feeling like a heel at having been the cause of her change in temperament, Nathan forced himself to calm down and wrapped his daughter in a gentle hug. Still, the father in him needed to remind her of the dangers outside their safe little world in the livery. He tucked his thumb under her chin. "Lizzie—"

The cabin door swung open. "Here you go. Milk to go with your pan—" Abigail broke off in midsentence. "Nathan. Hello." One hand held a tin cup filled with milk while the other fluttered upward to smooth her hair.

Nathan rose and stood before her in awkward silence, unsure of what to say but suddenly glad that Lizzie's little prank had brought him face-to-face with Abigail. The woman's eyes were red-rimmed, and she had an air of weariness about her that tugged at hidden places deep inside his chest, but at least she looked strong—beautiful even—if a little pale against the stark black of her mourning dress.

"Abigail."

Her name left his lips in a soft whisper. He hadn't meant to make it sound so tender. It surprised her, too, judging by the way her eyes widened. He cleared his throat and dropped his gaze to Lizzie's upturned face. "Sorry about the little one, here." He patted the top of Lizzie's head then smiled at Abigail. "Hope she hasn't been a bother."

"No bother. Lizzie and I were just having some breakfast together." This time it was Abigail who cut her gaze away. She held the cup toward Lizzie. "Here's your milk."

"Lizzie." Nathan directed a gentle scowl toward his daughter. "We've got plenty of food and milk over at the stable. You shouldn't be asking Miss Abigail for any of hers."

Lizzie grimaced. "Our milk is icky, Pa. Tastes like goats."

"It's from goats; it doesn't taste like goats," he corrected. "And it's perfectly fine."

Abigail smiled at Nathan. "It's all right. I have plenty."

Without further hesitation, Lizzie grabbed the cup and took a hasty swallow. Abigail gave an indulgent smile as Lizzie drew her sleeve across her mouth and then burped with satisfaction.

Abigail turned her gaze to Nathan. "Please don't worry. The pancakes were nothing, and I have milk aplenty. Caroline and her family bring me whatever they don't need from their cows. It's almost more than I can use, and after everything you've done"—her voice dropped to a whisper—"well, I don't mind."

Nathan missed the warmth from her fingers the moment she pulled her hand away—and immediately felt awash with guilt. Charlotte had only been gone a little more than a year. He shouldn't be missing any woman's touch but hers. Besides, he hadn't done a thing for Abigail except help to put her in the predicament she now faced. Troubled by what Anson would think, he shot a glance toward the wood box next to the cabin.

"Your firewood's low. I'll take care of it this evening."

Abigail didn't offer her thanks. Instead, she looked frozen. Had he said something wrong? Finally she gave a weak smile and waved her hand.

"Oh, don't bother. It's just me, after all, and the weather hasn't turned cold enough to warrant a fire every night."

Prodded by Anson's memory, Nathan shook his head. "It'll turn soon enough. Best if you're prepared before winter hits. When I have time, I'll see about fixing the holes in your chinking, too."

He nodded toward the cabin walls, where small patches of light filtered through the gaps between the logs. Nathan had noticed them before, but with cold wind and rain threatening, something would have to be done to keep drafts from chilling the house. Anson would have seen to it, had he lived. In his absence, Nathan would shoulder the responsibility.

Lizzie had finished with her milk. Nathan passed the cup back to Abigail and then took Lizzie's hand. "I'll be by this evening. Thanks for seeing to Lizzie." He'd cleared the steps and started toward the livery with Lizzie in tow when Abigail's voice stopped him.

"I can't pay you."

Glancing over his shoulder, he shrugged. "No pay necessary."

"You don't understand." A light breeze ruffled the cotton fabric of her dress. She caught the apron tied around her waist and gripped it tightly in both hands. "I don't have money to buy firewood—at least not right now. I intend to inquire around town this afternoon—to see if anyone has need of a seamstress."

Shock plucked the words plumb out of Nathan's head. Seeing the tension straining Abigail's features, he barely noticed the tug Lizzie gave to his fingers.

"We goin', Pa?"

Calico had begun to rouse. In the distance, a faint rumble spoke of charges being set off in the mine. Wagons and horses clopped noisily through town, and vendors began sweeping the boardwalks in front of their stores. No doubt Abigail didn't need or want to discuss her business near the street where anyone could hear.

Nathan bent to Lizzie's height. "Charlie is in the corral. Think you can fetch him some fresh straw? I'll be along in a little bit."

The freckles on her nose danced with her smile. "Yes, Pa."

She scurried straight for the livery. Though she'd be away a piece, Nathan had a clear line of sight to the corral, and he'd be able to see if she got into trouble. Satisfied, he rejoined Abigail on the porch. "Mind if we sit a spell?"

Her face was red and she refused to look him in the eyes, but she sank onto the old stump Anson had used as a stool. Nathan took that as an invitation and sat on a second stump next to her.

"What happened? I thought you said you were going to speak to Nichols about Anson's pay. I know it wouldn't have been much, but it seemed as if you thought it would be enough to carry you for a while."

Her shaking hands went to her temples, hiding her face from view. For a moment he thought she was debating whether to answer, until her throat worked to swallow several times. Nathan's gut plummeted. She was fighting not to cry.

Nothing made him feel more helpless than a woman's tears. Charlotte cried on occasion, sometimes for no reason at all, and Nathan never understood what drove it. This was different. In the short time he'd known Abigail, he'd come to learn that no small thing reduced her to tears.

Tugging a handkerchief from his pocket, he leaned forward and dropped it onto her knee. It was a pathetic effort, perhaps, but he was still far too conscious of his reaction from the last time they'd touched to risk further contact again. "What haven't you told me, Abigail? Maybe I can help."

She shuddered as she retrieved the handkerchief and pressed it to her nose. "At this point I doubt there is anything anyone can do, but I thank you for offering."

"How do you know?"

"What?" She lifted tear-filled eyes.

Nathan gentled his tone. "How do you know I can't help if you won't tell me what's wrong?"

"Nathan—"

"Your father helped me plenty when I first came to Calico. I owe him."

The stark words hung in the air between them, but he refused to draw them back. Abigail might not want or need his help, but he was determined to at least try.

"It's terrible," she whispered at last, and then her voice fell so low that he strained to hear. Even the cicadas humming in the distance threatened to drown out her words. "Papa—it's rumored it was his lantern that caused the explosion."

The wind whistled through Nathan's teeth as he sucked in a sharp breath. "I've heard no such rumor."

"Me either."

"Then why would you think such a thing?"

She dropped her hands to her lap, her fingers wringing the handkerchief. "I *did* speak to Gavin Nichols the other day. He told me about the gossip that's been circulating. Said he thought I should know."

Stunned, Nathan brought both hands to his head to help him think. Surely he'd misunderstood. He didn't work the mines, but he knew the repercussions if what she said was true.

"Did he say how he knew?" Nathan lowered his hands and formed the words carefully.

Shame flooded her face. "He showed me Papa's lantern."

Nathan quickly thought through the events of that night and realized the truth immediately. His jaw tightened. "What else?"

"Isn't that enough?"

"Not to destroy a man's reputation. It's true; we couldn't find Anson's lantern when we went back to the mine, looking for George Kennedy. We grabbed a couple of spare lights instead. Anson was human and he made mistakes, but there's no way he would have been so careless as to cause the mine explosion. There has to be another answer."

Gratitude softened Abigail's brown eyes. Her fingers shook as she reached out to grasp his hand. "Thank you."

The simple words, spoken so sincerely, filled Nathan with more pleasure than he'd felt in months.

"But until I can prove Papa's innocence," she continued, pulling her hand away, "I have to accept Mr. Nichols's explanation whether I agree with it or not."

Though he knew the answer, he still had to ask. "You don't, do you? Agree, I mean?"

She shook her head. "Of course not. Papa was many things, but he was never careless—especially when it came to endangering another's life." She bit her lip, worry drawing a thin line between her brows. "Still, according to Mr. Nichols… Somehow, I've got to prove that Papa wasn't at fault. Mr. Nichols offered to help, thank goodness, but I've been struggling for days just trying to figure out where to start."

Nathan choked back an angry retort. He didn't trust Gavin Nichols and wouldn't put it past him to throw the blame on someone else to cover his own mistakes. Right now, however, his suspicions did Abigail no good. Tamping a rising sense of frustration, he inhaled deeply and let it go. "So how does all of this affect the money the mining company owes you?"

Abigail looked down at the porch floor. "Mr. Nichols said he had no choice but to keep Papa's wages to help the families pay their doctor's expenses."

"They didn't have doctor's expenses. They all went to Mattie for treatment."

"Except for Tom Kennedy."

"His brother is alive because of Anson. I doubt that Tom would turn around and punish his daughter."

Pain flashed across her features before she closed her eyes. In the moment it took for her to regain her composure, he studied the smooth planes of her face. Anson had always said she reminded him of his wife, Olivia, but Nathan recognized the curve of her chin and tilt of her nose. They were Anson's.

Abigail walked across the porch and gripped the railing with both hands. Finally she sniffed and turned to face him. "There were also burial expenses."

Hui. Shamed to admit he'd not thought of him, Nathan swallowed hard. "All right. Still, if you subtract—"

"I told Mr. Nichols to give whatever was left to the Chens."

Of course. What was left to say? He let go a long sigh and rubbed his hands down his thighs. "You did the right thing."

She searched his face earnestly. "You think so?"

It put her in a difficult financial position, but Anson would have been proud. He nodded. "I do."

Her shoulders sagged, as though all of the tension seeped out of her body through her fingertips. "Thank you."

While she sat again on the stump next to him, he fished for the words to ask his next question. "Where does this leave you with the cabin?"

She stiffened, tightening the knot in Nathan's gut. "Rent was due on the first," he said, frowning. "Surely Anson paid it?"

"Normally he would have," she said, with a crack in her voice. Eyes pained, she leaned toward him. "But a few weeks back, Papa took one of the Oriental children to Los Angeles to see a doctor. He went to Mr. Nichols to ask for an extension on the rent, claiming he would catch up when he got paid. Mr. Nichols approved it."

"You mean—"

"I *will* be fine for a little while. Mr. Nichols gave me until the end of the month to decide whether to stay or go. Said it was the least he could do. I have the money I saved before Papa…" Her face twisted into a mask of grief and worry, and she rubbed the weariness from her eyes with her palms. "Anyway, I'll use the money I saved to pay this month's rent. After that—well—I'll worry about it when it gets here."

Three weeks. That gave her no time to recover from the loss of her father and barely enough time to search for a way to support herself. He clenched his jaw, fighting a whirlwind of helplessness and anger. "I'm sorry, Abigail."

She gave an almost imperceptible nod of her head, which was followed by a single tear that rolled down the smooth, rounded curve of her cheek and dripped off her chin. "It's not your fault."

Nathan disagreed. Cupping his fist in the palm of his other hand, he braced his elbows on his knees and brought his knuckles to his clenched lips. It *was* his fault, all of it, and once Abigail realized that, she'd probably never speak to him again.

Chapter Nine

....

Abigail risked a peek from the corner of her eyes.

Nathan sat with his head bowed and his broad shoulders hunched, as though he felt as miserable as she. It wasn't right, but somehow, it made her feel better to free the horrible words that had kept her cowering inside her cabin for days—unable to eat, unable to sleep, unable to pray. Plus, now someone else shared her fear and grief.

She placed a light touch on the sun-bronzed skin of his arm. At the flash of excitement that followed, she knew she should draw her hand back, but there was comfort in the muscled strength she felt there, peace in the sinewy tendons that said he was well capable of caring for the people he loved—and she found she didn't want to pull away. "I want to thank you for being such a good friend to Papa."

He let out a shuddering breath and lurched to his feet, his hand raking his hair. "Please don't thank me."

Hurt by his response, Abigail buried her tingling fingers in the folds of her cotton dress. "Why wouldn't I? Your friendship meant a lot to him—and to me now, knowing you cared so much."

"Of course I care. I just wish there was more—" He broke off and spun toward the far end of the porch.

More? With winter creeping toward them and him still desperate to finish building a home for his daughter? How much more could he do? Even so, she yearned for someone to share her troubles.

But not just anyone. Someone strong and dependable. Nathan. Her throat tightened at the knowledge.

He turned and watched her, his brow furrowed. Abigail squirmed under his steady gaze. Desperate for something to which she could credit her flushed cheeks, she rose and sought out a sunny patch on the porch next to the rail. A brisk breeze swept down from the hills. She let it whisk the heat from her face before she waved toward the livery. "You've enough worries of your own to see to without adding mine. I'm more grateful than I can say for everything you've already done."

Firm steps brought him closer to where she stood. Determination glinted in his eyes, along with something else she couldn't name. It was that thing that made her want to lean toward him—to rest in the strength she'd felt in his arms when he carried her from the cemetery to the cabin.

His finger gently caressed her cheek. "You have to promise you'll come to me if there's anything you need. Don't let pride keep you from asking for help—or money, if it comes to that."

She dropped her gaze. She could never bring herself to ask him for money, no matter how her spirits lifted at the offer. He laid hold of her arms before she could shake her head. This close, she could see the greenish-gold flecks in his hazel eyes and smell the fragrances of oil and leather clinging to his clothes. Her heart thumped against her ribs.

"I want to help you, Abigail, but not because I owe it to Anson. I want to help *you*."

All noise from the streets faded, even the shouts and whistles from the miners as they started their day, until only Nathan remained. Abigail stared at him, her breath trapped in her chest.

Suddenly she didn't feel so alone anymore, her troubles not so great. This was a man—a friend—she could rely on, as solid and sturdy as the rocks and soil rising behind him.

She managed a brief nod. When he stepped away, she resumed breathing.

"Good. I'll hold you to that." He smiled and jerked his thumb toward the woodpile then shoved his hands into his pockets. "Guess I'll see you this afternoon."

"Wait." Abigail searched for the words to say. Her gaze transferred to the livery and the small girl perched on the top rail of the corral. Lizzie's thin legs were wrapped tightly around the fence, and her braids swung crazily as she leaned over to rub her favorite mule's ears. Not only was her dress ragged and dirty, but it was beginning to look a mite small in the sleeves.

Perfect. She turned to him and knew just what to offer. "I can help you too."

He frowned. "What do you mean?"

Her excitement bubbled into a smile. "I'd like to sew a few things for Lizzie."

He stiffened and drew his hands from his pockets. "There's no need. Lizzie's clothes are fine—once I wash them, I mean. I intended to see to it this evening."

"I don't mean to imply—" She broke off. It hadn't occurred to her how her offer could be construed. Without meaning to, she'd probably insulted him. She spread her hands palms up. "It can't be easy having a child underfoot, with all the work you have to do. Adding laundry and other tasks when you're especially busy"—she gestured toward the full corrals—"like now, well, having a few extra things would lighten your load."

He crossed his arms, his face stern. "Didn't you just tell me you gave your papa's money to the Chens? How can I ask you to spend even a little bit of what you have left on clothes for Lizzie?"

"I wouldn't have to. I'll use one of my old dresses. As small as she is, I'll have plenty of cloth left over for a matching bonnet." Her tone turned teasing. "You might even get a break from looking after Lizzie. I'd need her for measurements and the occasional fitting."

Nathan squinted as he turned his gaze toward the livery. She could almost hear his thoughts whirring as he mulled over her proposition. Finally he scratched the side of his head, ruffling the sandy brown hair until it stuck out past his ears.

"She's a handful, you know. Asks a lot of questions and talks nonstop."

Abigail smiled. "She's a female, isn't she?"

He still looked uncertain. "You sure you won't mind having her around?"

She dismissed his concerns with a wave and then smoothed the folds of her blue-and-white striped skirt. "Of course not. She'll give me someone to talk to. Plus—" She hesitated, her heart thumping. "I won't feel so beholden to you for"—she motioned toward the cabin—"the work you do around here."

Truth be told, there were worse things than feeling beholden to a man like Nathan Hawk. Abigail smothered a rising tide of unwanted emotion and held her chin high. "Well? Is it a deal?"

His eyes narrowed thoughtfully, but after a moment he stuck out his hand. "Deal."

The skin of Nathan's palm was calloused and rough, yet he held her fingers gently as he shook her hand.

"You're a smart businesswoman, Abigail Watts. With a mind as sharp as yours, you'll be able to find work soon. Just be careful around town." He shot a glance toward the nearest saloon.

Abigail's gaze followed. Though it was early in the day, men were already stumbling down the steps. She shuddered. "Of course. I'll take good care of Lizzie."

"I have no doubt about that."

The certainty in his voice warmed her through. It felt good to be trusted by a man like Nathan—and even better that he was so confident in her abilities. She dipped her head. Honestly, the way the man made her blush was downright embarrassing. "Thank you," she murmured.

"You're welcome. I mean it, though. It's you I'm worried about. Don't take any chances."

She fought a smile. "I won't."

"And come to me if you need help."

"You'll be the first person I talk to—well, after Caroline."

He considered that a moment then nodded and moved off the porch. "See you this afternoon."

Yes, this afternoon. Her spirits now light, Abigail lifted her hand in farewell and held it there while he strode toward the livery.

Maybe she would be all right without Papa. Maybe all it would take would be a little encouragement and a lot of determination.

* * * * *

Encouragement and determination.

Abigail mentally repeated the words as she stared at the sign swinging from rusty hinges above her head. She hardly felt encouraged—or determined.

"Are we going in?"

Curiosity filled Lizzie's blue eyes—and why not? They'd been standing on the same spot, staring at the same sign, for a full minute.

Clutching her reticule tighter, Abigail sucked in a breath. "Yes. We're going inside."

"Are they gonna want some of your dresses?"

The question was prompted by an unsuccessful day. Though Abigail keenly felt the desire to clear her father's name, finding work to support herself and put food on the table had to come first. But after stopping by the schoolhouse, the tinsmith, and the shoemaker, she had yet to secure even one order. The women brave enough to make a home in Calico either sewed their own dresses or made do with what they owned. So after a few inquiries, she'd abandoned the idea of fashioning clothing for individuals and landed here, in front of the general store—her last hope.

She squeezed Lizzie's small hand. "I pray so, sugar."

Please, she breathed, as she reached for the curved brass handle to the general store door.

God hears our prayers, no matter how small or weak, her father had told her as a child. As Abigail stepped through the door onto the store's plank floor, she tried hard to believe he was right. God had taken the one thing that made sense in her world—her father. Surely He owed her this. It wasn't as though she was asking for charity, after all. She was willing to work, if she could just find someone to pay for her services.

The redolence inside the store was a strange mixture of spices, tea, tobacco, and dried goods. Abigail usually loved to spend time snooping through the different products Mr. Wiley had shipped in from the coast, things one would never expect to find in a town the size of Calico.

Lizzie stopped to look at the bell that had rattled above the door as they entered. "It's pretty," she said, pointing. "It makes a nice sound."

"Yes." She patted Lizzie's hand distractedly. Her thoughts were already scrambling for the best way to approach the store owner. She knelt and looked the little girl in the eyes. "Will you wait here for me while I talk to Mr. Wiley?"

Another patron walked into the store and skirted around them, setting the bell in motion once more. Barely sparing Abigail a glance, Lizzie nodded with her gaze riveted to the door.

Bereft of the comfort of Lizzie's small hand, Abigail wiped her damp palms on her skirt, licked her lips, and moved toward the counter. "Good afternoon, Mr. Wiley."

Theodore Wiley was an aging man whose tufts of white hair refused to be tamed even by the heaviest wax. Widowed by influenza a few years back, he often talked about packing his few belongings and moving west to the booming city of Los Angeles. Yet here he remained, beaming at Abigail over the wire rims of his spectacles.

The space around the counter was piled almost to the ceiling with barrels of dry goods, overflowing crates, and hastily stashed cutlery, but he squeezed his skinny frame through the mess and popped out on the other side next to Abigail.

"Morning, Miss Watts. You here to check on that new shipment of cloth I told you about?"

"Actually, no, sir. I'm not. I have plenty of material to keep my needles busy." She struggled to steady her nerves with a smile. "What I need are customers."

His ragged eyebrows lifted. "Oh?"

"Yes, sir."

"I figured you had plenty to keep you busy, what with all them single miners buzzing around, hoping to charm you by bringing you their mending. I've been tempted to bring you a couple of shirts myself." A merry wink of his blue eyes followed his chuckle.

Abigail tried to echo his laughter, but even to her ears it sounded pitifully thin. She shot a glance toward Lizzie, who had lost interest in the bell and was now perusing the rows of multicolored stick candy.

"Um"—she returned her gaze to the proprietor—"you see, Mr. Wiley, darning socks and mending shirts was fine when Papa was alive. But now that I'm on my own, I'm going to need something more along the line of full-time work." Hoping he wouldn't make her say more, Abigail held her breath.

His eyes darkened with compassion, and Mr. Wiley patted her arm. "Sorry to hear that, Miss Watts. I wondered how you would get along after your father—well, after he passed." The Adam's apple in his thin neck bobbed, and he shook his head. "Unfortunately, I haven't got a need for store help."

"Oh, no, sir. That's not what I meant." Abigail clasped her hands to hide their shaking. She hadn't figured this would be so hard—or that she would feel so frightened. "It's just—I've noticed that you do, on occasion, sell dresses already made."

"Yep, that's right," he said, scratching his chin. "But not too often. There isn't much call for store-bought dresses out here. What the womenfolk in these parts need, they make, and you probably know better than me, we ain't got no use for anything really fancy."

Abigail's spirits dipped lower. "Yes, sir. Still, I thought maybe one or two, just to keep on display..."

The words withered and died in her throat. What had she been thinking, coming here? She was practically begging. Papa would be ashamed. Her cheeks flamed as she took a step back.

"Forgive me, Mr. Wiley. I won't take up any more of your time."

"Uh…" He wagged his finger in the air. "Actually, I might could use a feminine touch here and there. Maybe it would draw the womenfolk into my place more often, for more than just pantry staples." He braced his hands on his bony hips. "Tell you what. You bring in a couple of those nice dresses of yours, and if they sell, well, I'll commission a couple more."

Abigail searched his face. No pity shaded his kind features, just a look of genuine interest. The fear pressing on her chest lifted ever so slightly, making room for her lungs. "Thank you, Mr. Wiley."

"No thanks necessary. I can't guarantee anything, you understand." His shaggy brows drew into a frown.

"No, sir."

"But I'll be glad to give it a try."

"I appreciate it very much."

"All right then." He stuck out his hand and gave a shake that jolted her bones. "It's a deal." Mr. Wiley then scratched one side of his head with a bony claw. "Say, before you go, did your papa ever speak to Gavin Nichols about those survey sheets?"

"Survey sheets?"

He shrugged. "Something about an appraisal he was doing on the various veins."

"Papa never told me anything about a survey." Her lips turned into a frown. "Did he say who ordered it?"

Mr. Wiley poked his spectacles higher on his nose with his thumb. "Don't believe anyone ordered it. Your papa was working on his own, far as I know. Seemed a little concerned, is all. I was just wondering if anything ever came of all that."

She shook her head slowly. "Not that I'm aware of."

Sadness clouded Mr. Wiley's eyes. "'Course, it wasn't all that long ago that he asked me about purchasing a tablet he could use to report his figures. Must not have even had a chance to use it."

"Must not. Anyway, thanks, Mr. Wiley. I'll get back to you about the dresses."

Abigail's thoughts whirled as she collected Lizzie and stepped from the general store into the brisk afternoon air. So much had happened in the span of one short day that her brain felt foggy. She'd committed to sewing one dress for Lizzie and at least one more for display in Mr. Wiley's store. While it wasn't much, the promised deal filled her with renewed hope.

A deal.

She'd never considered herself a businesswoman before, but as she passed through town toward home, she had to admit, she liked the idea. For the first time since losing Papa, the future didn't appear so bleak.

Lizzie sensed her mood and skipped alongside her, their feet making light, hollow thumps on the wooden boardwalk as they veered toward the post office for Abigail's weekly mail.

Yes, Abigail thought, lifting her chin, she might enjoy going into business for herself. Very much, indeed.

CALICO
1883
CA

Chapter Ten

....

Nathan's hammer rang against the horseshoe he was fashioning, splitting the air with a rhythmic *ping, ping, ping.* Most of Calico's blacksmithing responsibilities fell to him. Luckily, he didn't mind. He liked the feel of the hammer in his hand, relished the challenge of molding the metal to his will. Now that the weather had cooled, he enjoyed the chore even more.

Pausing to wipe the sweat from his brow, he stretched his back and shoulder muscles while he scanned the dusty street for a sign of Abigail and Lizzie. Abigail, especially, had been in his thoughts all day. She had gone in search of work, hoping to find a female or two willing to pay for the services of her needle. The money she'd managed to save wouldn't go far if she didn't find a job soon.

He threw a glance at the blue sky, which was dotted here and there with fluffy clouds. "I'm not asking anything for myself, You know." Bitterness rose in his throat. He knew better than to lay his own requests before God, but maybe Abigail's... How could God not love someone as kind and generous as her? "She's alone. She needs this. Help her—please."

The clouds continued to drift lazily across the heavens, as silent as ever. What had he expected? Thunder? Lightning? He was no Moses, and God no longer guided men from pillars of smoke and fire.

Fighting a rush of anger, Nathan tightened his grip on the hammer and delivered one final blow to the horseshoe. The jolt of metal on metal traveled up his arm to his shoulder.

It was good. Something tangible he could focus on. Not the wrestling match he'd been waging with an unseen God ever since Charlotte died.

He tossed the horseshoe onto a growing pile. It landed on top with a clang and then rolled off and settled in the dirt.

"Pa! Pa!"

He turned in time to see Lizzie break away from Abigail and hurtle across the street toward him at a full run. He held up his hand and brought her to a skittering halt.

"Mind the fire, Lizzie, and the hot water."

She stopped, her eyes wide, and waited while Nathan wiped his hands on a towel. When most of the grime was gone, he bent and scooped her up. "Well?" he asked as Abigail caught up to them. He searched the woman's face for a lessening of the anxiety he'd read there earlier. "Did you girls have a good day?"

Lizzie erupted into chatter, but his gaze remained locked onto Abigail. For the first time in many days, he glimpsed the hint of a real smile. Relief sagged his shoulders, but not wanting her to see it, he turned his face and pressed a kiss to Lizzie's cheek. "You did good work today, little one."

She grinned and then her blue eyes widened. "Pa, did you know Mr. Stacy has a mail dog? He has his own pouch and everything."

"A what?" Nathan laughed and looked at Abigail.

"The postmaster," she replied, her smile growing. "I stopped by today to see if there was any news from—any correspondence for me." She went on before he could remark on her choice of words. "It seems he has a new friend—a black-and-white shepherd he found laying on his porch."

"His name's Dorsey," Lizzie interrupted. She wiggled until Nathan put her down. Holding her hand up to her chin, she said, "He's this big, Pa, but he's not mean. He's nice. He likes to lick."

Probably the same cheek Nathan had just kissed. Abigail caught his grimace and laughed. "Don't worry," she whispered, bowing close. "All clean."

Nathan's heart jerked. Charlotte used to read his thoughts like that. It both startled and pleased him that Abigail could too. He turned his attention to Lizzie's insistent tugging on his hand.

"Mr. Stacy said I could visit Dorsey sometime, but Abigail said I need to ask you first. Can I, Pa? I want to see Dorsey delib"—she stumbled on the word, her small brow bunched—"libering—"

"Delivering," Abigail supplied.

"De–libering the mail. Please?"

As if he could deny that face anything. Nathan chuckled and pinched the end of Lizzie's nose. "He actually delivers mail?"

"Uh-huh." She rubbed the spot he'd tweaked, her gaze earnest. "Mr. Stacy puts the letters in his pouch and Dorsey carries them away."

Abigail smoothed a blond tendril from Lizzie's forehead. "Mr. Stacy has a partner in a mine near Bismarck, just outside Barstow. Apparently when the two need to correspond, they do it via Dorsey."

Unable to help himself, Nathan watched Abigail's hand tuck Lizzie's hair back into place. She did it almost without thought, as though it were second nature.

"Nathan?"

"Uh…" Caught staring, he blinked and dropped his gaze to his daughter's oval face. "That would be a sight."

"So you'll take me?" Eyes hopeful, Lizzie clasped her hands under her chin.

"Yes, sugar. I'll take you."

She squealed and sent her ruffled skirts flying as she ran off to play with Charlie. Her childish voice rose and fell as she told the old mule all about Dorsey.

Alone with Abigail, the need to fill the silence became pressing.

The smile remained on Nathan's lips as he crossed his arms and looked at Abigail. "A mail-carrying dog, eh?"

Her slender shoulders lifted in a shrug. "Mr. Stacy insists he's more dependable than the stage."

Nathan laughed and rested his hip against the anvil where he'd been working. "Which really isn't saying much."

She laughed too, her fingers absently twisting the string that bound her reticule. "No, I guess not."

In the distance, the normal sounds of the town floated sluggishly on the afternoon air, breaking what otherwise might have been an awkward silence. After a moment, Abigail looked away and plucked at the fabric of her dress. "Well, I guess I'd best see to that gown Mr. Wiley asked for."

Nathan lifted an eyebrow. So, God did still answer prayer—now and then. "He placed an order?"

She shook her head. "Not really—just agreed to let me display a couple of things in his store. If they sell, he promised to commission more."

He was stalling, Nathan realized, because he wasn't ready for his conversation with Abigail to end. It was good to see this side of her

CALICO
1883
CA

again—this less-troubled, more hopeful side—and he couldn't help but want it to continue. He shoved off the anvil and stood before her, squaring his shoulders. "I'm glad. I hope it all works out."

"Me too. If the dress sells, I may be able to look into the mining accident and try to figure out what really happened."

Her lashes swept up, revealing her sparkling brown eyes, and Nathan felt himself drawn to them—dangerously so. A man could lose himself in those depths. He swallowed, hard, and jammed his hands into the pockets of his trousers. "Well, I suppose I should let you get to work."

She swept a stray lock of hair behind her ear with one hand and pulled at the lace around her collar with the other. "Yes, you too."

"I appreciate your keeping an eye on Lizzie today."

"She was no trouble," she said quickly. "I enjoy spending time with her."

Abigail didn't appear in any hurry to leave either. Instead of backing away as he should have, Nathan found himself stepping closer. "I–I'm happy for you, Abigail. About Mr. Wiley, I mean."

Was it his imagination, or did her breathing quicken?

She licked her lips. "Th–thank you."

The air around them felt charged, like the split second before a bolt of lightning ripped the sky. A second longer and Nathan would have found himself irresistibly drawn to taste that same mouth he'd just been studying. Ashamed at where his thoughts had taken him, he whirled and fumbled to pick up the file he used to smooth the horses' hooves. He held the tool high. "Back to work."

"Back to work," she repeated, her voice a whisper.

The folds of her navy-striped skirt billowed as she spun away. She grasped its sides to keep it from brushing the dirt and almost ran the short distance to her cabin—in a hurry to get away from him, it seemed, and well she should. At that moment, he was no better than those mongrels from the saloon he'd warned her about.

Still, with each stride, Nathan willed her to turn, to send one last glance in his direction. In fact, she did turn just before her foot crossed the threshold, but not to look at him. Instead of wistfulness for his company, it was a scream that made her hesitate—a cry so filled with pain and fear that it sent rivers of dread coursing through Nathan's veins. The file slipped from his fingers and landed with a thump at his feet. That panicked voice belonged to—

Lizzie.

Chapter Eleven

....

Abigail could see the shock rippling across Nathan's face. Before she could blink, he dashed for the street.

Lizzie.

Dread darkened Abigail's senses, making her feel faint and momentarily immobile. But Lizzie needed her. She couldn't succumb to the horror and fear swirling within her. Hitching her skirts, she ran after Nathan, past the corral, across the dry, dusty grass, faster and faster. She skittered to a halt just shy of the street.

Two frightened horses snorted and stamped, their muscles bulging against the leads binding them to a flatbed wagon. High aboard the seat, a man struggled to control them. His face was pale, like the whitewashed sides of Wiley's General Store.

"Ho, there, Bill. Be still now, Bess."

A growing crowd practically drowned his harried words. Abigail pushed forward, afraid to see what drew them yet compelled to continue.

"I'm sorry, mister!" the man on the wagon shouted, straining against the reins. "She came out of nowhere. I didn't have time to stop."

The words birthed fresh horror in Abigail's chest. "Please, let me pass." She repeated it over and over until at last she broke through the jostling of elbows and shins.

The sight that met her forced her to gasp. Nathan huddled next to Lizzie's still form, his face twisted by fear and pain. Lizzie was unconscious in his arms, her face drained of blood and appearing as white as milk. In stark contrast, a purplish bruise had formed on the little girl's brow.

"Is she...?" The words faded from Abigail's mouth. She sank onto her knees next to Nathan.

His fingers trembled as he lifted a strand of hair from Lizzie's cheek. "Sweetheart?" Tears soaked his eyes as he scanned the crowd. "Someone fetch Doc Goodenough."

"I'll go."

Abigail's head rose at the familiar voice. Caroline stepped from the throng. Where she'd come from or how she'd heard, Abigail had no idea. Nonetheless, her friend's presence bolstered her courage. "Thank you," she mouthed—but Caroline was running down the street toward Doc's before Abigail could finish.

Nathan surged to his feet, startling the horses and bystanders even more. "Get back!" he roared, hovering protectively over his daughter's body. "Get those animals out of here!" He jerked his chin toward the wagon then bent and gently lifted Lizzie into his arms.

Though the seething fury in Nathan's voice set her insides to quaking, Abigail reached out and clutched his elbow. His head snapped toward her, his eyes burning coals that seared through to her heart.

"Not the doctor's office." Abigail lowered her voice to a whisper. "It's too far. Not the livery, either. It's not sanitary. Bring her to my cabin."

The anger in his gaze melted away, but what remained was far more devastating.

He clung to her with his eyes, pleading for reassurance she could not give. Instead, she grasped his arm and refused to blink, as though she might with that small gesture convey the strength he needed.

CALICO
1883
CA.

"Put her in my bed, Nathan," Abigail urged. "Doctor Good-enough can examine her there."

He nodded, his throat working, fighting a swell of emotion Abigail knew could erupt at any moment. The crowd parted as he passed, their silence lingering like a bad omen—except that Abigail didn't believe in omens. She lifted her eyes heavenward—only for a moment, but long enough to pour every ounce of energy she possessed into one simple word.

Please.

Her legs numb, she scrambled up the cabin steps ahead of Nathan. Murmuring quietly to Lizzie, he brushed past Abigail toward the bedroom and laid his daughter gently on the bed. Abigail wished it could be softer, more forgiving than the straw and ticking she'd slept on since moving to Calico. She rushed to a cedar chest next to the nightstand and pulled out a spare blanket.

Lizzie let out a sigh as Nathan settled her against the pillows. It was the first sound she'd made since being struck by the horses.

Abigail's gaze collided with Nathan's. "Did you hear that?"

He nodded, the hope lighting his eyes matching what she felt. She held her breath as he bent and whispered into his daughter's ear. "Sweetheart, if you can hear me, it's time to wake up. I'm worried about you. Can you open your eyes for me?"

Lizzie's mouth curled into a pucker, but she did not speak. The disappointment on his face bit sharply into Abigail's heart. She patted his arm and forced a small smile.

"It'll be all right. The doctor will be here soon."

In fact, footsteps sounded on the porch moments later. The door burst open and Dr. Goodenough rushed in, followed closely by Caroline.

"How is she?" Caroline's question hung unanswered in the small cabin. Her friend was red-faced and breathless, and Abigail figured she'd run the entire way to Dr. Goodenough's office.

Dr. Goodenough dropped his bag to the floor with a thump and leaned over Lizzie's tiny body. He grunted and laid his ear to the child's chest. "What happened?"

"Chasing a bird or a butterfly—who knows?" Nathan raked a hand through his hair. "The driver of the wagon said he didn't see her until it was too late."

Dr. Goodenough straightened and moved to Lizzie's feet. Beginning with her toes, he felt along her limbs, checking the bones for breaks. "Did she go under the wheels?"

Nathan paled, his knuckles white as he clutched one of the bedposts.

Abigail took his hand, waited until he shook his head, and then spoke for him. "We don't think so."

A sigh rumbled from Dr. Goodenough's chest. Moving to his side, Abigail's gaze remained locked on him. Redness rimmed his eyes and a shudder shook his hands, but the doctor was young and had shown some skill when he tended to Tom Kennedy after the fire. Surely he could care for one small child. He had to! She pinched her lips together and willed strength into his trembling fingers.

"Well?" she breathed when she could bear his silence no longer.

Dr. Goodenough moved to Lizzie's head and lifted first one eyelid and then the other. Something obviously satisfied him, for he drew back his shoulders and gave a nod, turning to peer at Nathan.

"She took a bad knock to the noggin"—he pointed at his own tousled hair—"but it looks as though nothing is broken. She should be fine in a week or so, but until then, no running or overheating herself."

"Fine?" Nathan appeared to be puzzled for a moment, uncertain whether to actually trust the doctor's words. His fingers ruffled his hair. "Then why is she still unconscious?"

Lizzie stirred as though in answer to his question. "Pa?"

Relief knotted in Abigail's throat. Dropping onto his knees next to the bed, Nathan grasped Lizzie's hand and briefly pressed it to his mouth. "Yeah, sweetheart?"

"My head hurts."

By the smile stretching Dr. Goodenough's lips, Abigail knew he was just as relieved by the words as she and Nathan.

"Like I said"—he bent to retrieve his black bag from the floor—"she oughta be fine in a week or two." He withdrew a small bottle from the bag and then pushed the handles closed with a *snap*. "A teaspoon of this mixed in a cup of water to cut the bitter taste. No more." His brows rose in stern warning. "And only if she requires it for pain. It should help her sleep."

Sensing Nathan was loath to leave his daughter's side, Abigail accepted the bottle and wrapped it firmly in both hands. A teaspoon. No more. She would remember.

"As for you, little girl," he said as he bent to peer kindly at Lizzie, "no playing near the streets. Doctor's orders. I'm sure you won't mind missing out on school while you get better, either."

Lizzie smiled, and Nathan sighed with relief. After a moment, he staggered to his feet. Dr. Goodenough tapped him on the chest with a bony finger and motioned him closer to the door. Abigail took his place next to the bed, a smile for Lizzie already fixed into place.

Dr. Goodenough's voice dropped, but there was no mistaking the note of concern. "Watch for dizzy spells. Fetch me if she shows signs of being disoriented, or if she becomes nauseous. I know I don't have to tell you how lucky she is."

A shudder shook Nathan's body and his head bobbed in glum agreement.

From the corner, Caroline spoke. "God was certainly watching over that child today."

All three started, as though none of them even remembered she was in the room.

Her hands lifted, and she shrugged. "It could have been much worse."

Though at first Nathan stiffened at Caroline's mention of God, his body gradually relaxed and he nodded. Strangely, his grudging acceptance of the remark eased the weight squeezing Abigail's chest. She turned her attention to Lizzie. The child was going to be all right. They were all going to be all right.

The weak hope sputtering in her chest since she'd left the general store flared into life. God hadn't abandoned them after all— He'd been right there alongside them the entire time.

* * * * *

Weariness settled across Nathan's shoulders like a yoke. After returning to the livery and spending a grueling day tending to the mule teams, he wanted nothing more than to take Lizzie home and settle in for the night—but he couldn't do that yet. Not without thanking Abigail for tending to his daughter first. So he dunked his head in the horse trough, ran a rag across his back and neck, then put on a clean shirt and headed for her cabin.

A firm knot of guilt formed in his belly—a feeling he'd been

CALICO
1883
CA

fighting all day. The last thing he'd wanted to do was leave Lizzie after her accident, but the work at the livery wouldn't wait. Nothing in this wilderness waited—not even long enough to grieve.

He knocked then spoke the moment the door opened. "How is she?"

Abigail pressed her finger to her lips. "She's fine. Sleeping." She pulled the door wider and motioned him inside.

Nathan shot a worried glance toward the bottle of laudanum Dr. Goodenough had left on the nightstand. Many a man had found himself addicted to the stuff, and he didn't like the idea of giving it to his daughter even in small doses.

Following his gaze, Abigail shook her head and then trailed after him to the bed. "No, she didn't need it. After I gave her something to eat, she drifted right off." She gestured toward a kettle dangling from the hook fastened to the wall next to the fireplace. "Are you hungry? I made chicken soup."

Which explained the savory aroma drifting through the cabin. Nathan hesitated, warring with the rumbling in his belly and the desire not to inflict undue strain on Abigail's already-taxed finances.

"I have plenty," she insisted, her face an irresistible mixture of expectation and encouragement.

Lizzie slept peacefully with her small fist pressed against her cheek. What harm could it do to allow her to rest while he and Abigail talked? At his nod, pleasure lit Abigail's eyes. She turned and went to the cupboard to retrieve a cup and a bowl from the shelf.

"There's fresh water in the pitcher." She indicated the counter with a tip of her head and held out the cup.

"Thanks." Careful to avoid her fingers, Nathan poured himself a drink while she spooned a hearty helping of soup from the kettle and placed it on the table.

"Sit," she said, laying a spoon alongside the bowl. "I'll cut you a slice of bread."

Bread, too? Nathan's mouth watered. He tried not to let the chair scrape and wake Lizzie while he took a seat. Already, the aroma from the soup tantalized his senses. His stomach rumbled, but he waited until Abigail returned with the bread and sat across from him before lifting his spoon.

"Mind if I say grace?" Her cheeks colored softly. "We have a lot to be thankful for, despite—everything."

Nathan's gaze dropped to the chicken and carrots bobbing in his soup. He hadn't prayed before a meal since before Charlotte died. Still, it felt right. He set down his spoon and laced his fingers.

"Father, we thank You for this food. Please bless it. Use it to nourish our bodies. Especially Lizzie's. In Jesus' name, amen."

That was it? He lifted his head in surprise, but Abigail was already rising and returning to the counter to fetch a jar from the shelf.

"Honey for the bread." She placed the jar beside his bowl and flitted back to the sink.

She's nervous, Nathan thought, watching her. Was it his presence alone, or the fact that she'd sensed his reluctance at facing God? He reached for the jar and used the tip of his knife to scoop out a portion of the thick, amber liquid.

"I have coffee, if you like," Abigail said, swishing a bit of water around in the pot to cleanse it. "I was just getting ready to brew some fresh."

"I reckon I could use a cup after the workload today."

"Busy?"

CALICO
1883
CA

Nathan nodded as he dug his spoon into the hearty soup. "Those fellas from the mining company sure rode in hard. I had to rub down every one of their horses before I put 'em out to pasture. When I finished with that, I put in a little extra time working on the lean-to. Figure it's best I get a handle on that before the real bad weather sets in."

She smiled, and the conversation settled into a comfortable flow as Nathan told her about his day and Abigail shared the details of her afternoon with Lizzie. Before long, his belly was full, some of the ache had eased from his tired back, and it was time to go. He rose and reached for his empty bowl.

"I'll get that." Abigail quickly claimed the dishes and carried them to the sink. "I hope it was to your liking."

"The meal was wonderful, Abigail. Better than I've had in months. Thank you."

"You're welcome." Hesitation flickered in her eyes. "Will you—will the two of you—I mean…"

He understood her concern. She'd seen the livery and knew the conditions there weren't ideal for nursing an injured child back to health, which was why Nathan had spent several hours converting the lean-to into a bedroom for Lizzie. He'd even rigged a canvas roof to keep her warm and make her feel as though she were in a tent instead of a shack attached to the barn.

"We'll be fine," he said, offering a smile of thanks.

She smiled back, setting off a curious wobble in Nathan's midsection. Suddenly he knew he'd best get Lizzie home—and soon. "Sorry to leave you with a mess," he said, striding toward the bed where his daughter lay, "especially after everything you did today."

Abigail's light tread was a gentle patter behind him. "I don't mind at all. In fact, I was sort of hoping you'd bring her by tomorrow."

Nathan bent, scooping Lizzie into his arms, and then paused. "You sure about that? She's bound to be underfoot, knot on the head or no."

Once again, a smile curved Abigail's lips. "She keeps me company. Makes this place not so quiet." Tears dampened her eyes, which she quickly tried to hide with a turn toward the nightstand. When she swung back, calm had returned to her face. She held out a bottle. "The laudanum Dr. Goodenough left."

"Think she'll need it?"

"She might. Best if you keep it on hand just in case."

Nathan nodded, but before he could shift Lizzie's weight and reach for the bottle, Abigail slipped it into his shirt pocket and gave it a pat.

"There you go."

Nathan held his breath. The motion had brought her closer. Even with his daughter between them, he could smell the clean scent of her hair, see the rosy complexion of her skin. She was a beautiful woman, alone in a town full of scoundrels and thieves. Nathan hated leaving her, but his first priority was to his daughter.

"Thanks," he whispered, drawing back a step.

Abigail spun toward the bed and returned with the cover she'd put over Lizzie. "Take this. I have another," she said, draping the blanket over Lizzie's small form.

Nathan adjusted his arms to let the blanket fall between his body and Lizzie's so he wouldn't lose it on the way to the livery. He didn't want to accept any more from Abigail; she'd already done so much. But she obviously cared for his daughter, and he wouldn't hurt her feelings by rejecting this last gesture of concern.

"Thanks," he repeated.

She held the door open while he and Lizzie slipped through. Not once did the child stir. In fact, her head lolled sleepily against his chest and she let out a murmured sigh that let him know she dreamed. He paused on the porch, certain there was more he should say before he left, but he was unable to find the words.

Grabbing a corner of the blanket, Abigail tucked it under Lizzie's arm then pushed a strand of yellow hair from her flushed cheek. "See you tomorrow, sweetheart," she said, surprising Nathan when she pressed a kiss on the spot where Lizzie's hair had been. Her gaze lifted to meet his, the gloom of evening making her eyes mysterious. "You too."

Mouth dry, Nathan could only nod. He eased toward the steps, hesitating when he reached the first one. "Abigail?"

Her hand on the door, she looked back at him. "Yes?"

"Make sure you bolt the door tonight. And if you need me..."

She smiled. "Thank you, Nathan."

Devoid of his hat, he tipped his head instead and hurried across the dry grass toward the livery. It had to be the extra work and worry that were making his thoughts such a scramble. Still, after he tucked Lizzie into her new bed, he couldn't keep his gaze from drifting to Abigail's window, where the glow from a single candle lit the night. She was alone in that house, but judging from her demeanor today, she was coping with it fine. Better, really, than Nathan had expected.

He smiled as he turned and pulled the suspenders from his shoulders. Anson had done a fine job, raising his daughter alone. Nathan could only hope he himself would do as well with Lizzie.

Chapter Twelve

Abigail awoke with her heart pounding.

From the window, moonlight spilled across the floor and came to rest on the pine armoire that hunkered against one wall. She listened, searching the shadows for clues. What had jarred her from sleep? Her gaze sought the window, where she half expected an orange glow to light the night sky. It was dark and cloudless.

Annoyed at her jitters, she relaxed against the bed pillows. She was being silly. Nothing stirred. It must have been a dream.

A whisper of cold air raised the hair on her arms and chilled her bare legs. She reached toward the bottom of the bed, where the blankets lay in a jumbled pile. Her fingers closed around the corner of one, but instead of drawing it over her body, she paused—sensing more than seeing that she was not alone.

"Hel—" Her voice cracked. She swallowed and tried again. "Hello?"

Dropping the blanket, her fingers crept for the candle and matches sitting on the nightstand next to her bed. She shook so much that she dropped the first match. The scuffle it made as it fell to the floor seemed abnormally loud, but it wasn't nearly as loud as the sound of something being scraped—wood on wood—coming from the window.

Panic rose in her throat. She jammed her fist to her mouth to keep a scream from spilling out. A split second later, she scrambled from the bed and hurtled toward the fireplace where Papa kept his pistol. Why hadn't she thought to keep it near the bed? Lizzie—that was why. She hadn't wanted to risk keeping it in a place where the child could get her hands on it.

The scraping at the window grew louder, and then the glass shattered with a *bang*. Abigail's heart stalled, and she let out a scream that fractured what remained of the peaceful night.

Frantic now, she stumbled across the room toward the weapon, jamming her toe on one of the chairs at the table. It fell over with a clatter. Abigail jumped over it, screaming again as footsteps thumped on the floor behind her.

"Hobble your lip, gal."

"Get out!"

"Where you at?"

Abigail cringed as the moonlight spilling from the broken window gave her a glimpse of the intruder. He had an almost puzzled look on his face, as though he found the surroundings strange.

His eyes haven't adjusted to the dark, Abigail realized with a start. The knowledge jarred her from her terrified stupor. If she didn't act now, she might not have another chance. She lunged toward the fireplace.

"There you are." The man's growl rasped across her skin. His arm shot out, and he snagged a piece of her nightdress. She tore from his grasp and clawed at the rough-hewn mantel, using it to leverage herself closer to the barrel of Papa's gun.

"Help! Someone help me!" she screamed, before turning on the intruder. "Who are you? What do you want?" Her questions bounced back to her unanswered. As the man regained his balance he jerked closer, his cruel fingers finding and pinching the flesh on her wrist.

"Got ya."

Satisfaction colored the man's whiskey-stained breath. He dragged her to his chest and clamped his hand over her mouth. In his eyes was a look she recognized, a glint she'd often witnessed around town from men who frequented the saloon. No one had to tell her what he wanted. She knew. Weakness flooded her knees.

Please, God, no. Help me, please.

Even as she thought the words, her fists balled. The intruder might be fuller than a tick, but he wouldn't take her without a fight.

He tilted his head just so, and the light of the moon illuminated a jagged scar that zigzagged across his chin.

Frozen in horror, Abigail stared. She knew him—Justice Fisher. He and Papa had argued once over the living conditions of the Chinese immigrants. His cruelty had seeped through his words and settled in his eyes, and Abigail still remembered the fear she felt when Papa refused to be cowed and instead stood toe to toe with him. Perhaps that was what she needed to do.

She stopped struggling and stood up straight, hoping her night-dress concealed the trembling of her body. "What do you want, Justice?"

His jaw went slack. In the same moment, his hold on her wrist loosened. She jerked away and snatched the iron poker from the fireplace. Wielding it like a sword, she thrust it at his face to keep the inebriated miner at arm's length.

"How dare you break in here! What exactly are you after?" she demanded. Justice was a big man, muscled from years of working the mine. If he lunged, she wouldn't be able to fend him off with just the poker, but hopefully her questions would distract him long enough to give her time to grab her father's pistol.

It didn't take long for the surprise of hearing his name to wear off. The grin crept back to Justice's face, and his dark eyes narrowed. "Aw, gal, I think you know what I'm after."

Abigail raised the poker as he inched closer.

"What do you suppose you're going to do with that?" he sneered. He wiped the back of his hand across his lips. "You think you're going to keep me from getting to you with that little stick?"

Though her knees shook, Abigail took a vicious swipe with the poker. "Maybe not, but I'll sure enough clean your plow until you do."

For a split second, hesitation warred with desire on Justice's face. Maybe the alcohol fogging his brain had lifted long enough for him to see reason. Abigail inched sideways toward the hook that held her father's pistol.

Justice's jaw hardened. "Hold on there, gal. What do you think you're doing?"

Abigail froze. He wasn't as drunk as she'd thought, which only made him more dangerous. Her grip on the poker tightened. "G–get out, Justice. I know who you are. I'll tell everyone what you've done. You willing to hang for a few minutes in my bed?"

Disgust at the thought made her stomach roil. A woman in the West barely stood a chance, but a soiled woman? How many men wouldn't hesitate to force themselves upon her if her innocence were lost? She shivered in fear at the bleak future she'd face.

Feet planted, Justice reeled in the center of Abigail's small cabin as the silence stretched. Finally he gave a grunt and lumbered back a step. "You got a point. There ain't nothing in this town worth dying for, even in the mine."

She didn't have time to ponder his answer. His shaggy head

swung toward the line of tins filling the shelf above the cookstove. Obscured by shadow, his dark gaze looked even more menacing.

"You got cash in them tins?"

Inside her chest, Abigail's heart melted like wax. "N–no."

His wicked grin was proof that she had taken too long to answer. "Where is it?" he said.

She had to act now, before he had a chance to discover her stash. Even if she failed to hold him off, she might be able to fire a warning shot to get someone's attention. She threw the poker at Justice's head then lunged for the pistol.

His meaty fist caught her on the temple before she reached it. The force of the blow knocked her into the mantel. Blood oozed into her mouth as her chin connected with the solid wood, and she sprawled onto the floor, her head throbbing, his large form looming over her.

"Don't give me cause to kill you," he warned, his voice low. He bent and picked up the discarded poker then used it to gesture toward the wall. "You git over there and stay until I find what I'm looking for."

Despite the spinning of the room, Abigail managed to edge toward the window as he had instructed. Like a wild hog he rooted through the tins, tearing off and discarding the lids one by one, tossing the containers onto the floor when they failed to yield the treasure he sought. When he reached the last one, he moved to the pantry.

"Please," Abigail begged, tears clogging her throat as a precious bag of flour exploded on the floor. "That food is all I have."

Justice growled in frustration and wheeled to stare at her. "You're lying, gal, and I know it. Now where is that cash?"

He stepped toward her, rage burning fiercely in his eyes. Abigail willed her shaking limbs to support her as she pushed off against the wall and stood. The mantel jabbed her shoulder, tangible evidence that the situation she faced was very real. She swallowed a burgeoning knot of fear. Was the pittance she'd saved worth her life? But without it, what would her life be worth? She might survive a week, possibly two, on what she could salvage from the floor. That money was her only hope.

Justice took another step. In the moonlight, his mouth formed a dark, angry gash against the pallor of his skin. "Last chance, gal. I ain't gonna ask you agin. Where is that cash?"

Abigail took a deep breath. She wouldn't tell him, no matter what he threatened to do—

The thought was still half formed when the floor beneath his feet creaked. She gasped, the horror she felt binding her lungs like a steely band. He was standing on the loose floorboard—the one she'd taken such pains to replace. Dismay washed over her as his gaze swept down and then back, knowledge gleaming in his eyes.

He knew. Justice had discovered her stash.

Chapter Thirteen

....

"Mr. Hawk, are you in there?"

Nathan poked his head above the stall door. A figure stood outlined in the entrance of the livery. It took him a moment to recognize Caroline Martin. He propped the pitchfork he'd been using against the wall and headed out of the stall. The moment he stepped into view, Caroline hurried forward.

"There you are. I'm sorry to disturb you."

In fact, she didn't look sorry. More agitated than anything else. Her face was flushed, and her bonnet had gone slightly askew. Nathan tipped his head in acknowledgment then grabbed a rag to wipe his hands. "Morning, Miss Martin."

"Mr. Hawk, have you seen Abigail this morning?"

Nathan looked across the livery yard at Abigail's cabin. No smoke rose from the chimney, even though she normally had her cook fire going by the time the sun crested the hills. Caution nudged his insides. The place did look unusually still. He dropped the rag on the tack bench and propped his hands on his hips. "I haven't seen her. Did you try her cabin?"

"Yes. I knocked, but she didn't answer."

A second nudge followed the first. *Maybe she doesn't feel well,* he mentally argued, *or decided to sleep in.* Not that she didn't need or deserve the extra rest. The last few days had been pretty traumatic.

Caroline's gaze remained fixed on him, earnest and searching beneath the wide brim of her bonnet. He gave a curt nod. It wouldn't hurt to check.

"Mind sitting with Lizzie for a bit?" he said, tipping his head in the direction of the lean-to where his daughter slept. "I'll go see what Abigail's up to."

Relief wiped the lines of worry from Caroline's face. "I don't mind at all. Be glad to. Thank you, Mr. Hawk. It may be nothing...."

Suddenly the nudge felt more like a push, mobilizing him into action.

"I won't be long," he said, striding through the livery and to the street. When he glanced back, Caroline was already standing outside the door of the lean-to, her hand resting on the jamb as she watched him go.

Nathan's stride quickened. A woman's instincts were rarely wrong. He'd learned that a long time ago, when Charlotte had warned against traveling west. She'd said she had a "bad feeling." Nathan had attributed it to a mother's natural caution. She didn't like the idea of them packing up all their belongings and leaving home, especially when they had a small child to care for. If he'd listened to her then, she might still be alive.

All of that has nothing to do with Abigail, he told himself as he climbed the steps to the cabin. She was fine. Probably tucked inside sleeping, wondering why half of Calico was bent on turning her out of her warm bed.

"Abigail?" He knocked and then paused to listen. "You in there?"

Slight scuffling drifted through the cracks in the door. The noise didn't make him feel better, as it should have. It wasn't like Abigail to leave a person standing on her doorstep, wondering if she was all right. He knocked again, louder.

"It's me, Nathan. I just came by to see if you needed anything." At the silence that followed, his hand fell to the latch. "Abigail?"

And then he heard it—more scuffling, followed by a soft moan.

"Abigail!" He pushed against the door. It gave a little, but something kept it from fully opening. Jamming his shoulder against the wood, he gave a hard shove. Finally it parted enough for him to squeeze through.

The dim sunlight filtering through a broken window revealed the shambles inside the cabin. The sawback table was overturned, the chairs strewn across the room. One of those chairs had kept the door from opening. In the middle of the floor, a large hole yawned. The plank that had covered it lay haphazardly across the hearth, and next to it—

Nathan's heart jerked.

Abigail was crumpled in a corner, her hands and feet bound and a gag in her mouth. Tears streamed down her face, what wasn't covered by the hair clinging to her damp cheeks, and her nightdress...

Before he could stop it, a groan ripped from Nathan's throat. Blood speckled her nightdress from her neckline to her waist. Thrusting the chairs out of the way, he ran to her and dropped to his knees at her side. He forced himself to be gentle as he worked the knot on the rag that gagged her mouth, but his fingers shook so that it took him several attempts to tug it free.

"What happened?" He had to force the words out, so thick was his voice with outrage and concern.

She only cried harder. He couldn't stand it. Nathan pulled her onto his lap and held her to his chest, his fingers smoothing the ragged tendrils of hair from her forehead. "Oh, Abigail, I'm so sorry," he whispered, closing his eyes against the sight of the bruise on her temple and the ugly, purple cut on her chin. Her whimpered sobs, however, sliced straight to his heart. He'd kill whoever had hurt her—hog-tie them and string them up from the nearest tree.

Abigail turned her face into Nathan's shoulder, where the collar of his jacket served to muffle her sobs. Though he could do nothing to erase the memories from her mind, he well understood that the power of her tears would wash away some of the fear. He held her close, murmuring to her until he felt her shaking subside. When she stopped crying, he shifted her weight until he could slip his knife from its sheath on his belt. With a quick flick of his wrist, he severed the ropes that bound her hands and then leaned forward to do the same for her feet. She was barefooted, her flesh clammy and raw beneath his fingers.

The muscles in his midsection clenched as he rubbed the angry, red skin around her ankles.

"What happened?" he managed after a moment. He lifted his head to look into her wide, tear-soaked eyes.

"A m–man—" Her throat jerked as the words caught.

"Someone broke in?"

She nodded.

He smoothed a strand of damp hair that clung to her forehead. And though it galled him to ask, he had to know. "Did he—hurt you?" His teeth clenched, he waited for her answer.

She shook her head. "He h–h–hit me, but he didn't—didn't—"

The relief was more powerful than Nathan could stand. He grabbed her and pulled her again into his arms, squeezing so tightly that she gasped.

"Sorry," he said, loosening his hold.

"It's all right. I'm all right," she stammered. "It's just—"

A second wave of tears rolled down her face, smudging the streaks of dirt and dried blood. Nathan pulled a handkerchief from his pocket and gently dabbed the tears away. "What is it?"

"He took the money. All of it." She pointed to the hole in the floor. "Everything I'd saved. There's nothing left."

Nathan peered at the hole. "I don't understand. There wasn't but a week's worth of wages in there. What could he have been after?"

Abigail shuddered. "I don't think he meant to rob me. I think he wanted—he was going to—"

With each word, her voice rose. Worse, Nathan knew nothing he could say would make any of it better. Pulling her with him, he stood and led her to the door. "Come with me."

She resisted before they stepped onto the porch, looking down at her soiled nightdress. "Wait, I don't think—I don't want anyone to see me and think—"

He shrugged out of his jacket. How foolish of him not to consider her modesty! Wrapping the jacket around her shoulders, he waited until her approval registered on her face before ducking back inside to retrieve her shoes. Only a pair of red boots sat near the door, but they had to be hers, so he grabbed them and slipped back outside. "Will these do?"

A strange look crossed her face as she gazed at the boots.

"Abigail?"

She blinked and then nodded slowly. "They're fine."

He followed the direction of her stare. Except for the color, they were ordinary boots—scuffed a little at the heel, but otherwise in good shape. He'd seen her wear them before, even caught himself smiling as she sauntered through town with the toes peeking out from the hem of her calico dress.

Her body shook as she stretched out her hand. A moment later she sat on one of the stumps, jammed her feet into the boots, and stood.

He didn't have to be a genius to figure out that the boots meant something to her, something he'd missed before, but she looked him in the eyes with her chin lifted and her shoulders squared. Rather than question her, he stepped forward and took her hand. She was doing her best to be brave, and if he could help by offering silent support, so be it.

For a moment, she did nothing but stare at their clasped hands. Finally she took a deep breath, ran her finger underneath her lashes one last time, and then bobbed her head. "I'm ready."

Nathan walked slowly with her toward the livery, moved beyond words that she would trust him enough to put herself in his hands and sensing as they went that he needed to let her set the pace.

Caroline waited for them at the entrance to the barn. One hand rested on her hip; the other shielded her eyes. When they drew close enough for her to see the bruise on Abigail's temple and the blood on her nightdress, she blanched, and her mouth dropped open.

"What happened?"

Aware of Lizzie's questioning frown behind Caroline, Nathan forced a smile. "We'll talk inside," he said, tipping his head toward his daughter.

Following his gaze, Caroline nodded then rushed forward to clasp Abigail's hands. "Come on, dear. Let's get you cleaned up."

In spite of himself, Nathan found he hated relinquishing care of Abigail to Caroline. Her small hand, which fit so perfectly in his, slipped from his grasp. Battling an unreasonable amount of disappointment, he turned and scooped his daughter into his arms.

"Come on, sugar. Let's get you some breakfast."

His noisy kiss on Lizzie's cheek served to dispel her concern. She giggled and threw her arms around his neck, but even as he started for the cook fire, his thoughts remained elsewhere and his gaze—his gaze stayed fixed on Abigail.

* * * * *

Her face, what she could see in Nathan's tiny shaving mirror, was puffy and red. The bruise on her temple felt as if it grew larger by the second, and the cut on her chin would require a stitch or two and likely leave a scar. Still, things could have been much worse.

Abigail shuddered, remembering how close she'd come to having more than just her home violated.

"Are you sure you don't want me to fetch the marshal?" Behind her, Caroline's dark eyes narrowed. "Surely there is something he can do? Maybe it's not too late."

A heavy sigh rose in Abigail's chest. She ran her fingers over the rope burns on her wrist. It would be nice to think that Marshal Harris might be able to catch Justice—maybe even recover some of her money—but he'd disappeared hours ago, and chances were slim.

"He's long gone," she said, digging her fingernails into the palms of her hands. "That's why he tied me up in the first place—to give himself a head start. Reckon he's halfway to the border by now."

Caroline placed both hands on Abigail's shoulders and bent to press her warm cheek against Abigail's cold one. Abigail breathed deeply, comforted by the familiar fragrance of Caroline's delicate perfume. At least that was still the same.

"I'm so sorry, sweetheart. I wish there were something I could do."

"I know," Abigail whispered.

"Try to believe that God has a purpose in all this, something we cannot see. He hasn't forgotten you. I just know He's going to take care of it all, in time."

Tears burned Abigail's eyes, but she refused to let them fall. She hadn't told Caroline so, but what hurt worse than anything was the fact that when she needed Him most, God abandoned her. Despite her wavering faith, a part of her had clung to the hope that after her father died, God would somehow step in and be a Father to her, seeing as how He'd seen fit to claim her earthly one. Instead, He'd left her to fend for herself.

Anger deeper than anything she'd ever felt flared inside her chest. She dipped her head to keep Caroline from seeing her emotion.

"Don't worry, dear," she cooed, obviously mistaking the movement for distress. "Everything will work out. We just need—"

"How?" Borne by rage, the word burst from Abigail's lips as her head came up. "How will it work out when I have no money, no job, not even a place to live?"

Confusion clouded Caroline's face. "What?"

"I have nothing, Caroline. Not even the cabin is mine, and in a couple of days…" What? Where would she go? The mountainous weight of it settled on her shoulders, pressing down, suffocating her.

"I—see." Caroline cleared her throat and then fidgeted with the frothy lace surrounding her collar. "Surely you have family to whom you can turn—"

Abigail whirled away, her arms clutched tightly around her

middle. Caroline didn't know about the suspicions regarding her father or how those suspicions had led to her decision to remain in Calico. She hadn't told her because she thought she'd have more time, a few weeks at least. Now...

Caroline's light footsteps glided to a stop behind her. She squeezed Abigail's shoulder. Compassion flowed from her, comforting but useless. "What will you do?"

Abigail shook her head and found she couldn't stop. "I don't—I don't—"

It felt as if the air had been drawn from the room. Her head began to throb. She put out her hand but found nothing upon which to steady herself. "Oh, Caroline, I just don't—"

"Marry me."

Both Abigail and Caroline spun in the same moment. Nathan stood at the entrance to the livery, his hat in his hands, his face solemn.

Caroline recovered first. She folded her hands at the wide blue sash around her waist, and when she spoke, she sounded surprisingly calm. "Did you say something, Mr. Hawk?"

He took a step toward them, and Abigail saw that he clutched his hat so tightly, his knuckles were white. "I said..." He paused, and his gaze swung from Caroline to Abigail. "You can marry me."

Chapter Fourteen

....

For several long seconds Abigail could only stare. In her wildest imaginings, she'd never pictured a proposal of marriage coming like this, in a barn, with her face as battered and bruised as her heart. She clutched at the buttons of her nightdress, refusing to blink, afraid to breathe.

"Um..." Caroline looked from one to the other then edged out from behind Abigail. "I think I'll go check on Lizzie while you two talk." With her hurried steps, her skirts rustled like a field of dry grass. At the door she hesitated, and her gaze locked with Abigail's. "*Believe*," she mouthed, before rushing away.

Abigail drew a quick breath. If only she *could* believe. Rather than face Nathan, she turned and sank onto the bench. After a moment, she felt, rather than heard, him sit beside her. Seized by trembling, she hid her hands in the folds of her nightdress. No doubt he thought her addled—she couldn't think of a single word to speak.

"I apologize if my offer offended you," he began, his voice hoarse. His face had gone a deep red except for his lips, which were clenched and white around the edges.

Abigail's heart sank a tad. So he intended to retract the offer. Despite the unexpectedness of the proposal, for a fraction of a second she had allowed herself to consider it. But no easy answer would come swooping down from the heavens. No, she was right back where she'd started before Nathan spoke—

"I probably could have phrased it more tactfully," he continued. "It's just—you were upset, and it seemed like a reasonable solution. Still, I should have waited until we were alone, instead of springing it on you in front of Caroline." He tipped his chin. "My apologies."

Abigail waited, her pulse rate spiraling. He'd never actually said he regretted making the offer. Could that mean—?

She shook her head. The idea was ridiculous. Clutching Nathan's jacket tightly around herself, she rose. "You're a kind man, and I appreciate your concern, but I could never ask…"

Words failed her. She gaped at him helplessly.

He sighed heavily and then stood to pace. "Before you answer, I think there are a few things you should consider."

Her shock growing, Abigail watched him stride the length of the floor and back. He was serious. He actually meant to convince her to marry him.

"First, I think you see now why I was so opposed to your staying in the cabin alone." A few feet away, he paused to look at her.

What could she say? Her nod dissolved into a shudder.

"So if we agree that you can't stay alone, your only other option would be to move into the hotel or—move in with me." He swallowed hard and ran his hands down his thighs. "And you can't afford the hotel."

True, she couldn't, but to ask him to commit to a loveless marriage…?

Nathan stepped closer. On his face was a mixture of compassion and shame. "Please understand, this is not purely a noble gesture."

About to reject his offer, she hesitated, curious as to what had him so ruffled.

CALICO
1883
CA

"It's Lizzie." Yanking a handkerchief from his back pocket, he ran it across his damp brow. "I thought I could raise her alone, but after her accident, I saw that it takes more than hard work to provide her with a home. She needs—a momma."

Abigail's heart lurched. She'd been without her own mother for so long, she couldn't even remember how to act like one. "Nathan—"

"This would be a business arrangement," he added quickly. "I wouldn't have any expectations of you other than caring for my daughter."

Here his face colored, his embarrassment so deep it was almost tangible. An answering blush rose on Abigail's cheeks. How had things deteriorated to the point where she now found herself having such an impossible conversation?

"I won't—touch you—in that way, or expect you to fulfill any wifely duties—"

She had to stop him. She stepped forward and held up her hand. "Nathan, please. I can't accept your offer."

He halted mid-sentence, his mouth slack. "What?"

Caroline's words came flooding back. *Trust. Believe.* If she were to do those things, she had to assume that God would provide her with the work she needed in order to save herself and the cabin. Maybe she just hadn't given Him enough time. Maybe the answer huddled around the bend, if she would only wait for it. The tiny drop of confidence in her heart warred with a flood of doubt. Finally Abigail lifted her chin.

"I have until the end of the month. It's only a couple of weeks, but who knows? Maybe I will have found work as a seamstress by then, or perhaps the dresses on display in Mr. Wiley's store will have garnered me some business."

Nathan jammed his hands into the pockets of his trousers. "That's not much time, Abigail. How will a sale help you if you can't fill it?"

His reasoning rang true, but still, Abigail shrugged. "Caroline thinks God will take care of me. I—think so too." At least, she wanted to. He frowned, but she rushed on before he could speak. "It's a fragile hope, I know, but it's all—" She faltered but forced herself to continue. "It's all I have."

Truly, believing in God was the only thing left to her, the only thing this rugged country hadn't ripped away. Like the dresses she would fashion for Lizzie, could she somehow manage to piece together the tattered remnants of her faith?

She shivered, afraid that the answer would not be the one she wanted. "Tomorrow I'll go by the mining camp. I made a little money mending shirts. Maybe I can gain enough business to carry me through the end of the month."

Nathan drew a deep breath and folded his arms across his chest. "All right, then. If your mind's made up?"

She nodded. "It is."

He retrieved his hat from the bench where he'd dropped it and slapped it onto his head. "I won't say that I think God is gonna take care of all of your problems, Abigail, but I respect your right to cling to hope, if it's what you want. Still, I'm here if you need me. Don't forget."

"I won't."

"As for the living arrangements—I suppose I can pitch a tent on the other side of the corral. That way I can keep an eye on your place and still listen out for Lizzie if she calls."

"Oh, I can't ask—"

It was his turn to hold up a hand. "It's the only thing I can think of for the moment. Maybe later we can figure out something more permanent. For now, it will have to do."

Dismay washed over her. She didn't mean to add to Nathan's cares, but every time something happened to her, he ended up shouldering the burden. She laid her hand on his forearm.

"I can't thank you enough for everything."

It was a feeble gesture of gratitude, but she hoped he knew how much she meant it. After a moment, something akin to disappointment flickered in his eyes. He stepped back, his smile as forced as his marriage proposal had been. "I meant what I said, Abigail. Still do. My offer stands—later—if you need it."

What could she say to that? Nothing. She nodded.

"All right, then." He fumbled a bit then managed a tip of his brim in parting. "I'll find Miss Martin for you."

Caroline. What would she think of the decision? Weariness descended like rain upon Abigail. Would life ever be simple again? Somehow she doubted it, and the thought filled her with fear.

Chapter Fifteen

....

Abigail rose and dressed the next morning, the scent of coffee tickling her senses as it simmered in a tin pot on the stove. While she wasn't particularly keen on the stuff, she'd gotten used to rising early and sharing a cup with her papa. She drained the dregs from her mug, rinsed it clean, and then turned and examined the empty cabin. It wasn't much, but while she and Papa lived there, it had been home.

She gave herself a shake before the thought could settle. No time for dwelling on the past. Her red boots sat next to the door, where she'd left them. She crossed the room and picked one up, her fingers lingering on the intricate stitching adorning the sides. In Virginia she'd laughed at their outlandish color, but Papa had claimed they would be right at home in the West and insisted they buy them. Now she needed the confidence they gave her whenever she put them on.

Drawing a deep breath, she slipped her feet inside the boots and headed out the door. The mining camp lay outside of town, and since she had no time to waste…

The first rays of sunlight peeked over the line of hills in the distance. It was early—the songbirds hadn't even finished their trilling—but no one in Calico slept much past the rising of the sun. Well, with the exception of a few. She shivered as she walked past Belle's Saloon.

They're lost, Abigail, not hopeless.

Her papa's words rang in her ears all the way to the mining camp.

As expected, several of the cabins showed signs of life. Smoke drifted lazily from the chimneys, and here and there, bare-chested men gathered around a campfire. They watched her approach, balancing their coffee cups between their fingers.

"Good morning." She tried to sound cheerful, though the men's hard stares made her nervous.

Two with familiar faces nodded in response. One man, his shirt patched and missing buttons, rose and met her on the rutted path.

"Morning, Miss Watts. Can I help you with something?"

Cotty Kay. Abigail remembered him from a prayer service last Christmas. He'd also been present at Papa's funeral. She greeted him with a smile and held out her hand. He took it and gave it a gentle shake, though his gaze bored into her chin. Suddenly Abigail realized what he must think of her battered appearance.

Heat suffused her face, and she had to force herself to speak. "H–hello, Mr. Kay. It's good to see you again."

Releasing her, he diverted his gaze and slipped his hands into his pockets. "You looking for someone?"

"Not exactly," Abigail said, aware that the attention of the miners was fixed firmly upon them.

She readjusted her shawl with trembling fingers but, not wanting to appear nervous, clasped her hands to still their fidgeting. As she did, an idea struck. She was in the mining camp and had been meaning to speak to the men about her father's accident. Mr. Kay looked friendly enough. Maybe she could accomplish both of her assigned tasks. She gestured toward his ragged shirt.

"Been doing your own darning, I see."

He grimaced as he looked down at the broken buttons and poorly applied patches. "Not well, I'm afraid."

Perfect. Abigail smiled. "I could help. I'm skilled with a needle, and my rates are reasonable."

He quirked a dark eyebrow. "You come here looking for work?"

Among other things, yes, but she knew better than to spook the miners by asking too many questions about the accident right away. She nodded. "With Papa gone, I'm going to need to do something to support myself."

Mr. Kay shifted his stare down to his toes. "Awful sorry about that, Miss Watts. A lot of us men really liked your pa."

"Why, thank you, Mr. Kay."

He dipped his head then ran his index finger along his stubbled jaw. "Come to think of it, I did hear you was as fine as cream gravy when it come to working with a needle. Didn't you do some work for old Dobbins?"

The owner of the hotel had enlisted her services on occasion and always paid well. Abigail nodded. "One of my regular customers."

Mr. Kay grabbed the edge of his tattered shirt and squinted at it. "I reckon I could use a hand with some of this. Never did care much for mending. You say your rates are reasonable?"

"Absolutely."

Abigail's heart thumped while the miner pondered the idea. Finally he bobbed his head once and smiled. "Yeah, I reckon I could use your services." He twisted to look at the other men. "Boys? Anybody else could use a woman's touch?"

A couple of the men guffawed. Mr. Kay flushed a deep red and then moved to cut her from the men's view. Clutching the open ends of his shirt, he muttered, "Sorry, ma'am."

She felt for him. It was obvious his comrades' bad behavior

made him uncomfortable, but since leaving Virginia, she had become accustomed to such remarks.

She waved her hand dismissively. "It's all right."

"I can speak to the men for you, if you'd like. See if any of them would be willing to spend part of their hard-earned money on their clothes rather than the saloon."

The offer would spare her from having to venture further into the mining camp.... Abigail quickly tossed aside the idea and shook her head. "No, thank you, Mr. Kay. I have other business I need to attend to while I'm here." She hesitated, and her gaze darted to the men gathered around the campfire. "I don't suppose..."

He peered at her, his brows bunched with concern. "Are you all right, Miss Watts?"

Forcing a cheery smile, she turned to him. "Would you mind if I asked you a few questions regarding the accident that killed my father, Mr. Kay?"

He frowned and crossed his arms. "Questions?"

She'd have to tread carefully. Abigail nodded. "Just simple things. I was wondering if you knew who was working the mine that night."

His face cleared and he shrugged. "Oh, that. Yeah."

Scratching his head, he appeared to think for a moment and then began reciting names, many of which were familiar. She would have plenty of people to ask regarding the explosion. Before she could form her next question, however, hoofbeats bade her turn. Gavin Nichols rode toward the camp, the tails of his tweed coat flapping in the wind. He pulled his mount to a stop, raising a cloud of dust that would have enveloped Abigail had she not stepped back.

"Miss Watts!" Unlike Mr. Kay, he stared openly at the bruise on her cheek and the cut on her chin. "Are you all right?"

Abigail thrust her shoulders back. "I'm fine, thank you."

He looked confused for a moment, before he threw one leg over his horse's back and swung from the saddle. "Pleasure to see you this morning. What brings you to the camp?"

"Errands, mostly," she said, trying her best to sound nonchalant.

"Errands." His head tilted as he studied her, and he fingered the ends of his mustache.

Resisting the urge to squirm, Abigail met his gaze squarely.

Finally he looked away and turned to Mr. Kay. "Cotty."

"Mr. Nichols."

Gavin clapped a hand to Mr. Kay's shoulder. "Everything all right this morning?"

He shrugged and dropped his eyes. "Same as always, I suppose."

"Good. Good to hear." Gavin swung so his gaze encompassed the men seated around the campfire. "Morning, boys."

They grunted in response, with only one or two actually mumbling a greeting.

"I see you're all tending to company business, eh?"

He barked a laugh that sent a shiver over Abigail's flesh. Tossing what remained of their coffee onto the fire, a couple of the men rose, dipped their heads toward Abigail, and then went inside their cabins. What was it about the mine superintendent that had the men so cowed?

"Never mind them," Gavin said, grasping Abigail's elbow and drawing her away from Mr. Kay and the others. "What are you doing here all by yourself? And what in blazes happened to your face?"

Abigail cast one last reluctant glance at Mr. Kay. There went her chance to ask questions. She couldn't very well do more with Gavin hovering at her side. Her shoulders slumped as she shook her head.

"I had a slight accident. Nothing serious."

Apparently not satisfied, he folded his arms across his chest. "I suggest you be more careful."

She fought the retort that rose to her lips and smiled instead.

"So, is there something I can help you with here?" He beamed down at her, looking quite pleased with himself above the collar of his white shirt and string tie.

The condescension in his tone worked like starch to stiffen her spine. While she knew he meant to be helpful, his attention only served to irritate her.

"I'm quite fine on my own, thank you. Good day, Mr. Nichols." She intended to walk away, but he caught her arm before she could turn.

"Abigail, wait. Please. I've been meaning to come by and see how you're doing."

His face softened with compassion. Acknowledging that her irritation was unwarranted, Abigail paused, drew a breath, and blew out her frustration on a sigh.

She touched his arm. "I'm fine, really. I appreciate your concern."

Gavin's gaze dropped to her hand, which she immediately withdrew. Too late, she realized as he looked back up, expectancy making his eyes bright.

"It must be difficult for you, all alone in that cabin. You don't have to be, you know. There are plenty of men"—he paused to straighten the lapels of his coat—"who would be happy to care for you, offer you shelter. A woman as pretty as you—"

Abigail held up her hand to stop him. "Gavin, please."

The miners and their families had begun streaming out of their cabins to begin their workday. Though many were too busy to spare them a glance, a few watched with curiosity lighting their faces. He looked at them and nodded. "Ah, of course. Not the time or place."

It wasn't what she meant, but at least it had stopped him. Abigail sighed with relief, a signal he mistook for regret.

He bent close, his hot breath fanning her ear and the nape of her neck. "Don't worry, Abigail. We'll talk soon."

Before she could stop it, she shuddered. He chuckled low in his throat and pulled away. No telling as to what he accounted her reaction. Dislike kindled like a smoky tendril in her belly. Shaking her head, she whirled and ran smack into the broad chest of one of the miners.

"What are you doing here?" the man demanded.

Abigail froze at the hostility in his voice. His face looked familiar, but though she searched her memory, she could not recall his name. Gavin came to her rescue.

"Joseph, you're up and about early this morning."

Joseph Bailey. That was it. The name snapped into Abigail's brain. But why did he look so angry with her? Aside from the time she'd delivered a basket of food to his family when his father died, she barely knew him.

Joseph jerked his chin toward Abigail. "The boys said she come around looking for work. Lotta nerve, considerin'." His eyes glittered like bits of ore.

Considering what? At a loss, she frowned.

Gavin eased between them and planted one hand firmly on Joseph's chest. "Now look here—"

"You look here," Joseph growled, thrusting Gavin's hand away. He jabbed his finger toward Abigail. "She ain't got no business coming around here, 'specially now."

Abigail looked at Gavin, who flushed under her stare.

He cleared his throat. "Now, Joseph—nothing's been proven. You know that."

Drawn by the raised voices, a crowd gathered, including Mrs. Bailey, who had followed her son outside. She glared at Abigail, her stance as rigid and accusing as those of the miners and their families hovered around her.

"Is it true?" she demanded, her bunched hands pale against her black dress. "Your father was responsible for the explosion?"

Abigail stood speechless. What could she say? How did they even know what Gavin had told her?

Gavin stepped forward, momentarily drawing the attention of the crowd. "Now, Mrs. Bailey, I've told you before, the facts of this case have not yet been resolved."

"But you ain't denying it. And neither is she." Mrs. Bailey gave a toss of her head. "How long before we know what really happened down there? If Anson wasn't the cause of the fire, what was?"

"We've got to know our men are safe," another woman said, her face a twisted mask of worry.

"Yeah," a man said. His face was red with anger. Shaggy hair and beard, dark eyes—his features looked vaguely familiar. One of the Kennedy brothers?

He spat a stream of tobacco juice to the ground, ignoring the disgusted snorts of the women present, and jutted out his chin. "What are you gonna do about that? We've got families to consider."

Gavin pulled his shoulders back and took his time straightening the folds of his silk vest. "Safety is always a priority at the Silver King. I can assure you folks of that. The mining company has sent a team here to investigate the cause of the fire and test the stability of the existing shafts."

He went on, but Abigail turned her attention to a slight rustling in the crowd near her. After a moment, Nathan appeared.

He bent to whisper in her ear. "I saw the commotion and headed over. What's going on?"

Already on the verge of tears, Abigail shook her head. He'd find out soon enough. Shame trickled over her. What if she couldn't prove her father's innocence? How would she ever look these miners and their families in the eyes again? Bit by bit she inched backward, until she hovered on the fringes of the crowd. At least the hostility had turned from her, but so had the possibility of seeking work. None of these people trusted her now, and the prospect of earning some sort of a living with them had dried up faster than the condolences they'd shared just a few days ago.

Just as she turned to go, another woman's gaze locked with hers. Belle, the saloon owner from across the street. Abigail's breath caught at the pity she read in her eyes. Or was it compassion? If anyone understood what it felt like to be an outcast, surely she did, even from a society as uncivilized as Calico's.

Her hands pressed against her midsection, Abigail whirled and headed away from the camp.

Nathan's quick strides brought him alongside quickly. "Where you headed?"

"Away from there."

"Surely you knew the word would get out. Didn't you stop to figure the consequences?"

Anger flaring, she skittered to a stop. "What I didn't figure was having to answer to you on top of everyone else." Shocked at herself, Abigail clapped her hand over her mouth. "Sorry. I didn't mean—"

He shook his head. "No, you're right."

Rather than try to dismiss the uncomfortable silence, Abigail resumed walking, and Nathan followed. Between them, she sensed the unspoken question looming. Would she reconsider his offer now that her options had become so limited?

"Abigail, wait." Behind them Gavin huffed to catch up. "Please, I need to speak to you."

Nathan eyed her critically. "He calls you Abigail?"

What could she say? She shrugged.

"I'll leave you two to your business." Nathan tipped his hat and strode away, the set of his shoulders echoing the disapproval she heard in his voice.

Wonderful. It seemed she did nothing right lately. She sighed and waited for Gavin.

"May I walk with you?" he asked, swabbing a silk handkerchief over the rivers of sweat running down his face.

Abigail nodded.

He gestured toward the mining camp. "I'm sorry about that. Are you all right?"

"Yes." Drawing a deep breath, she resumed walking.

Not wanting to add to his misconceptions regarding her feelings, she phrased her sentences carefully. "Thank you for stepping in, Gavin. I appreciate it very much."

Gavin's brows rose in genuine interest. Or was it pleasure? She couldn't tell which.

"You're welcome." He hesitated, and his lips drew into a frown. "What you witnessed back there was just a sampling. You realize that, right?"

Something about the way he asked stirred a sick feeling in her stomach. She managed a squeaky "Yes."

Gavin looked behind them at the miners, who were only now

beginning to disperse. "We can talk in my office. If you're free, of course."

It appeared she'd be quite free since she'd been unable to find much work. She nodded and followed in silence as Gavin detoured the livery and led her to the mine superintendent's office. Once again she found herself seated on the hard, wooden bench opposite his desk.

Already Abigail felt her control slipping. It happened more easily of late—the wobbly feeling that started in her stomach and settled in her chest. She clasped her fingers, hoping to disguise some of their shaking. "I know you said you'd give me until the end of the month to decide about the cabin, Mr. Nichols—"

"Gavin."

"Yes. Sorry. You see, Gavin, a couple of nights ago, someone broke into my cabin—"

"What?" He sat up and put both palms flat on the desk. "Is that what happened to your face? Did he hurt you?"

"No. I mean, yes, I cut my face while struggling to get away, but—" Suddenly the rope burns on her wrists began to throb. Tears filled her eyes. "I wasn't hurt. Not badly anyway. The point is—"

"Did you see who did it? Could you make out any features? It wasn't one of those Orientals, was it?"

What prompted him to think such a thing? Words froze in Abigail's mouth at the look of repulsion hardening his features.

"It'd be just like their kind to try to get back at you for Hui. Family honor and all that rubbish. Worse than savages when it comes to their pride." The longer he spoke, the more clipped his words became.

While Abigail hadn't considered possible retribution from the Chinese, she knew better than to think they'd had any part in the robbery. She'd seen Justice's face for herself. She shook her head. "No, Gavin. It wasn't the Chinese."

He drew up short, his brows lowered in a frown. "Who then?"

Once again, she rued the fact that Justice was long gone. She clenched her lips. "It doesn't matter. What is important is that he—they—took everything I'd saved over the last few months and left me with nothing—no money and barely any food."

The angry lines on his face softened, and he leaned forward across the desk. Under different circumstances, she might have thought him a handsome man, especially when compassion turned his brown eyes so kind and warm.

"I'm very sorry," he said. Clearing his throat, he fingered the edges of his collar and then slicked his hair with his palm. "Have you—given any consideration as to what the future holds?"

Abigail gritted her teeth. She wasn't interested in Gavin. Best if she was direct about that fact. She laid her hand on top of his, hoping the simple gesture would soften her words. "I'm not ready for marriage, Gavin. Especially now. It's important to me that I get back on my feet and figure out what really happened at the mine before I think about settling down."

Bewilderment sparked in Gavin's eyes, and then his gaze hardened. He pulled his hand from beneath her grasp. "Well then, there's nothing I can do."

Despite his tone, hope swirled inside her. "Actually, there is. I could use a little more time, raising the money for the rent on the cabin."

He eased back in his oversized chair, drawing the warmth and compassion he'd offered seconds ago with him.

"I'm n–not asking you to excuse the debt, you understand," Abigail stammered. "I fully intend to pay everything my father owed.

The problem is just getting the money together. I can do it of course, or I wouldn't ask. I should have work in a f–few days or so."

Now that she'd started, the words piled up on themselves and spilled out. Abigail continued rambling as Gavin hefted himself out of his chair and paced the length of his office.

"So you see," she finished lamely, "it's just as I said. A few days is all I need, I'm sure."

He eyed her steadily then retook his seat. His elbows propped on the desktop, he rested his chin on his laced fingers and sighed. "I'm afraid I can't help you, Abigail."

Despair rumbled through her. "What?"

"If you'd asked anything else—" He shook his head. "There's something I haven't told you. I'd hoped to break the news later—after you'd had a chance to recover some from the loss of your father, but I guess there's no help for it now."

She tensed. "Please, just tell me."

He lowered his hands to the desk. "Some of the miners aren't happy about you continuing on in the company's cabin. You saw for yourself"—he waved toward the window—"they think it was your father's fault that the accident happened in the first place—and that the mining company shouldn't be responsible for caring for his off-spring. They want me to evict you, Abigail. Some weren't even happy I gave you until the end of the month."

"Where do they expect me to stay?"

"At this point, I don't think they much care." He put up his hand. "Now, don't get me wrong, I don't think all the miners feel this way, just a few of the more—vocal ones. Joseph Bailey, for example. I've done my best to quiet the grumbling, but truth be told, I'm afraid there is some validity to their argument."

Her breath caught. "What?"

"Think about it—the mining company owns the mine and the cabins. Now that you are no longer affiliated with the mine, do I really have the right to continue with our lease agreement?" He stretched out his hand, and warm fingers curled around hers. "Not that I intend to toss you out into the street."

She hadn't even noticed when she'd laid her hands on the desk. Discomforted by his touch, she drew her hands away. "How long?"

"Excuse me?"

"How long can you give me?"

His mustache twitched. *Like the whiskers on a cat,* Abigail thought, *or maybe a rat.*

"Until the end of the week."

Her heart plummeted to the bottom of her boots. *Four days?* "But—that's not—"

His face somber, Gavin leaned toward her. "Perhaps you have family you could appeal to. A grandparent, maybe? Or an aunt? A nice girl like you has to have someone who will take her in."

His posture, his tone, his words—something in his demeanor suddenly made Abigail feel as though he were pushing her to leave Calico. Quite a change from a short while ago. She bristled as she stood.

"I appreciate your concern, Mr. Nichols, but I am quite capable of taking care of myself, without 'appealing' to any relatives."

He rose too. "Abigail, I didn't mean to offend you, but if you're not interested in settling down, what possible reason could you have for remaining—?"

She stiffened as he reached out to her. After a moment, he dropped his hand.

Her chin lifted. "I have your word, then, regarding the cabin? I have until Sunday?"

Folding his arms, Gavin nodded. "Until Sunday. I'll keep the miners at bay."

A brisk nod and a curt good-bye later, Abigail found herself outside and down the street. The painted letters above Mr. Wiley's general store swam before her eyes, taunting her, daring her to go inside. What would she do? Where would she go? She couldn't leave town, not until she found out what really happened in the mine. The Calico Hotel was a temporary option, but only if she could find work to pay for her stay.

Drawing a breath, she pushed open the door, the merry bell greeting her as she stepped inside.

"Well, I don't like it, is all," a stout woman dressed in gray muslin declared. "A young, unchaperoned woman in Calico can only mean trouble."

"She's long past marrying age, anyway," a second woman chimed. "Her father should have seen to it long ago."

Abigail recognized the pair from church. The stout woman had come to Calico as a mail-order bride several years ago and married one of the local ranchers. The other, the schoolteacher's wife and a pillar in Calico's society, rarely left her side. Between the two, they had Mr. Wiley so flustered that he didn't bother to look up when Abigail entered. Skirting a crate-laden table, she ducked behind a tall shelf to listen.

Mr. Wiley tugged at the collar of his shirt. "Mrs. Rusten, Mrs. Potter, please. Abigail Watts is only trying to earn a living. Now that her father is gone—"

Gertrude Rusten, the woman in gray, gave a very unladylike snort. Lips pursed, she reached out to clasp her friend's hand.

"Working for a living when there are so many eligible bachelors to be had—whoever heard of such a thing? Any respectable young woman would fetch herself a husband and settle down."

"Exactly." The shorter woman, Agatha Potter by name, narrowed her eyes and peered at Mr. Wiley. "And shame on you for encouraging this risk to the poor girl's reputation."

Mr. Wiley's eyes widened behind his spectacles. "Me? But I—"

Mrs. Potter pointed to the dresses on display. "Those are her handiwork, are they not?"

"Well, yes, but—"

"I thought so."

"Not that we have anything against honest labor," Mrs. Rusten said.

"It's not that at all," Mrs. Potter concurred.

"But a woman alone, working for a living? It's just not seemly."

"Exactly."

To Abigail's dismay, Mr. Wiley threw his hands into the air. "All right, all right, ladies. I see your point. I certainly never intended—"

Mrs. Potter's brows rose to form twin peaks. "Of course you didn't, Mr. Wiley. But we do hope that you intend to rectify the situation?"

Abigail's gaze dropped to the tips of her red boots. Despite her flashy footwear, she felt small inside—hopeless—totally unable to face down the two women hounding Mr. Wiley. Rather than speak and draw attention to herself, she inched out the door and down the street as fast as her leaden legs would carry her.

Chapter Sixteen
....

Abigail slowed her steps as the cabin's worn frame came into view. She wanted to run inside and hide, to bolt the door the way Papa had told her to a thousand times and never come out, but the days were slipping by faster and faster, weighing on her heavier and heavier.

Sick to her stomach, she stared down the long street toward the Calico Hotel. If she couldn't find a job as a seamstress, maybe she could work as a maid. She'd never done that sort of thing before, but she'd looked after Papa and kept the cabin clean. How hard could it be to tend to a handful of guests?

Her gut twisted into a knot. Hui Chen had worked at the Calico Hotel before he died. A few other Orientals who inhabited Calico worked there too. How would they feel about her robbing them of a job? Did she have a choice?

Balling her fists, she strode down the street, refusing to stop until she stood in the entrance of the hotel dining room. The lunch crowd had cleared out, and only a few stragglers remained to linger over their plates of roasted beef and buttery mashed potatoes. Suddenly taken shy, Abigail inched forward, avoiding the curious stares of the Orientals who scurried about with baskets full of dirty dishes and soiled linens.

A woman's voice rang from a door that opened into the kitchen. "I don't care if you need to spend more time scrubbing those stains out, Lu. These tablecloths need to be white, do you understand? White."

Abigail followed the sound, her heart pounding a rhythm faster than Nathan's hammer. Inside the kitchen, two women faced one another—one stout and fair, the other, an ancient Asian woman with a braid running down her back. The latter bowed over a basket of tablecloths.

"Yes, Missus Baker. Lu understand."

Mrs. Baker jammed her hands on her hips. "Good. Run along, then, and see that these cloths are laundered properly."

Lu backed out a side door, still mumbling her apologies and bowing over the basket each time another "Sorry, missus" fell from her lips.

Blowing out a sigh thick with frustration, Mrs. Baker keeled left and narrowed her beady eyes at Abigail. "Well? What do you want?"

Given Mrs. Baker's girth, Abigail couldn't help but be reminded of the great ships she'd seen out East. She tamped a rising swell of intimidation and looked her in the eyes.

"My name is Abigail Watts—"

"I know who you are."

Caught off guard by the interruption, Abigail faltered, her mouth agape. She knew who Mrs. Baker was too, having seen her in the general store from time to time. Still, the woman had yet to set foot inside the schoolhouse on Sunday for church, and they'd never been introduced.

Mrs. Baker crossed her arms. "The Orientals talk like everyone else in this town." Her eyes narrowed. "I ain't got no need of a seamstress."

"I didn't come looking for seamstress work."

"What'd ya come for, then?"

She was gruff, all right, with an exterior that matched her mood, but Abigail couldn't afford to be choosy. Her chin lifted. "I'll take any job you've got."

"Ain't got no jobs. Who told you I did?"

"I—"

"Well? Who told you?"

"No one; I just thought—"

"You thought wrong. What work I got I already give to them Orientals. They work hard and cheap, good qualities in the people I look to hire." She gave a raspy chuckle. "'Sides, their rent is part of their pay."

She jabbed her finger toward the side door where Lu had disappeared. It hung open on rusty hinges, and a line of lean-tos could be seen through the door, their roofs sagging like so many ancient mules. The walls, too, looked as if they might collapse at any moment. Tattered laundry fluttered from a rope strung between two of the makeshift cabins, and here and there a handful of children ducked under and around the clothing, their faces dirty but happy.

A wobble rose up from Abigail's middle and manifested in her voice. "Your workers—live there?"

Mrs. Baker's countenance hardened. "Ain't mine. Mr. Nichols is what hired 'em. 'Sides, what's wrong with those houses? Ain't no whites in this town what would want a bunch of Orientals living next door. They're lucky Mr. Nichols ain't that kind. There'd be plenty of folks who'd give their last tooth to stay in places as nice as what they got."

Those folks would include Abigail soon enough. She shuddered to think of the living conditions she might one day endure—a day that was fast approaching.

Swallowing the last dregs of her pride, she nodded. "Yes, ma'am. You're right. I'd be very grateful if you could find me a place here with your staff. Very grateful."

Mrs. Baker eyed her thoughtfully. After a moment, her chin jutted toward the table where a couple of Asian women worked, kneading bread. "Is it true what they say?"

A sinking feeling flooded Abigail's midsection. "Ma'am?"

"Your pa responsible for the explosion what killed a couple of their men?"

"One," Abigail said hastily. "One man died, but I'm not sure yet what caused the accident."

"Accident, huh?"

Her temper flaring, Abigail squared her jaw. "That's right. I don't know what others have to say"—she stole a quick glance at the two women, who now stared openly at her—"but I intend to prove that the explosion at the mine was purely accidental."

"How you gonna do that?"

"I—well—" Abigail slumped into silence. She had no idea how to go about proving her father's innocence. Until now, she'd been too concerned with finding work just so she could live. Several miserable moments later, Mrs. Baker straightened with a huff.

"'Swhat I thought." She shifted her bulky frame toward the dining room.

"Wait."

Abigail bit the inside of her cheek as Mrs. Baker peered over her shoulder at her.

"Yeah?"

"About the job."

Her persistence must have pleased the old proprietress. She nodded her approval then clucked her tongue. "Come back in a couple of weeks. Maybe I'll have something then."

"Two weeks!"

"Take it or leave it, gal. It's all I got."

Tears formed in Abigail's eyes, but she nodded and backed out of the kitchen the way she'd come.

Two weeks.

The wait seemed impossibly long.

* * * * *

Nathan bent over a horse's hoof, a handful of nails clenched in his teeth. Behind him, Lizzie's chatter rolled nonstop.

"That horse's shoes aren't like my shoes, are they, Pa? Why do horses have shoes? Do mules have shoes? What about Charlie? Are Charlie's shoes like mine?"

After each question Nathan gave a grunt, but his mind wasn't on Lizzie or the hoof he was filing to make ready for the new shoe he'd fashioned. It was on Abigail and her unexpected rejection.

Lizzie swung onto the second rail of the stall door and reached for the top.

"Careful," Nathan cautioned. "I don't want you falling off and hurting your head again." He set down the file and picked up a rag to wipe away the dust.

"I won't fall, Pa." Lizzie's voice turned singsong. "Humpetee Dump. Humpetee Dump. Off the wall."

Finally she managed to swing one foot over the top rail and wiggled herself so she sat astride. "How does the rest go, Pa?"

The horse nickered as Nathan let go of its hoof and set its leg back on the ground. Pulling the nails from between his teeth, he straightened and pushed on the horse's hindquarters so he could squeeze around it and stand next to Lizzie. Gripping the rail on either side of his daughter, he looked her in the eyes and tried not to smile as she winked.

"All right, Miss Chatty. Don't you have chores to finish?"

"I did them, Pa."

"Straw too?"

Lizzie's face fell at the reminder of the fresh straw that needed to be spread in each stall. "Well…"

"Excuse me."

Both Nathan and Lizzie turned toward the livery entrance, where the mine superintendent had entered unnoticed. Nathan grabbed Lizzie under her arms, lifted her off the stall door, and set her on the floor.

"Run along now and finish your work."

"All right, Pa."

She dashed away, and Nathan turned to the man. "What can I do for you, Nichols?"

"I, uh, I'm looking for Miss Watts. Have you seen her?"

Nathan took his time wiping his hands on a rag. What made the man think he would find Abigail here? He tossed the rag onto a workbench and braced both hands on his hips. "Did you try her cabin?"

Nichols had the grace to blush. Plucking his hat off the top of his head, he stepped out of the sunlight into the shaded interior of the livery. "All right, so it's not exactly Abigail I was looking for."

"Who were you looking for?"

"You."

Nathan narrowed his eyes. Instead of dropping his gaze, Nichols met his look squarely.

"All right, then."

Nathan pulled up a stool and motioned toward the bench for Nichols. Eyeing the bench critically, Nichols took his time brushing away the chaff and dust. Finally he settled himself and laid his hat beside him. "You have some ties to the Watts family."

It wasn't a question. Nathan nodded, intrigued. "I was a friend of Anson's, yes."

"I thought so."

As though his shirt had suddenly grown too tight, Nichols tugged at the collar. When that failed to ease his discomfort, he cleared his throat and then stroked his mustache between thumb and forefinger.

Nathan waited in silence. Whatever the man was going to say had to be important for him to risk muddying his spotless shoes. Finally Nichols leaned forward, his elbows braced on his knees.

"I'm worried about Abigail. I know she trusts you, but I don't think she's told you all there is to know about her situation."

"She's told me as much as she's inclined to," Nathan said carefully. As much as he wanted to know what had put the burr under Nichols's saddle, he didn't feel comfortable intruding where Abigail didn't want him.

Nichols grunted. "That was all well and good—before."

He clamped his lips and waited, extending the pause until Nathan felt downright irritated.

He rubbed his restless fingers against his scalp before motioning for Nichols to continue. "Go on."

"Well, someone has to step in and help that young lady see reason. I tried, but given my position with the mining company…" He shrugged, his smile much too smug. "I can only do so much."

Arms folded, Nathan frowned. "What is it you're asking me to do, Nichols?"

Except for the twitch, twitch, twitch of his moustache, Nichols stilled. Slowly his fingers began working the cuff of his jacket, and then he drew a deep breath and let it go. "Abigail is a beautiful woman, Hawk, as I'm sure you've noticed. She's young. Innocent. She has no idea of the kind of dangers a girl like her might face in a town as raw as this one."

Though Nathan had considered the same things, he still didn't like hearing Abigail's name roll off Nichols's lips—or that the man thought her beautiful. With his jaw clenched, he tipped his head in agreement.

"She needs someone to care for her, protect her. I'd be that man if I thought she'd have me." He fixed a measuring look to Nathan's face. "I've got a sneaking suspicion you would too." Chuckling, he leaned back and crossed one ankle over the other. "Unfortunately, I don't think that's the case for either of us. Am I right?"

"So?" Nathan ground between gritted teeth.

"Considering as how she's more than likely carrying around some romantic notion about marriage—most women her age do—I think the only recourse is to convince her she'd be better off seeking help from family." He lowered his gaze. "I understand she has people back East. Rich people. Folks who can see to her welfare." Nichols's expression, when he looked up, could only be called placid.

Just what had driven the man to dig into Abigail's past? Though he searched Nichols's face, from his wide, steady eyes to the tips of

CALICO
1883
CA

his waxed mustache, no answer revealed itself. Either the man was telling the truth about his concern or he was a consummate actor.

"All right," Nathan said slowly. "So what makes you think I can convince her if you can't?"

Nichols's smile widened. "No getting anything by you, eh, Hawk?" He flicked a piece of straw from the arm of his jacket. "Yes, I spoke to Abigail about going to her family for help. She flat-out refused."

"Well, then, there's your answer, eh, Nichols? After all, she has time to decide what's best for herself without help from me." Nathan stood and half turned to go.

"That's not exactly true."

Nathan paused. "What?"

Compassion dripped like honey down Nichols's face. He rose and paced the floor in front of the bench. "She only has until the end of the week. She probably won't tell you that, knowing the kind of woman she is—so proud and independent." Sighing, the mine superintendent swiped his hand across his brow. "I tried, but in spite of my best efforts, I had to recant my previous offer of extending her stay until the end of the month. Some of the miners aren't happy about her father's role in the accident, and they want her out."

Anger at the injustice boiled in Nathan's belly. "Abigail didn't have any part in that."

"Of course she didn't," Nichols said, the outrage in his voice matching Nathan's, "but at this point they don't care."

"So you're just going to give in to them? Toss her out onto the street?"

The tips of Nichols's ears flushed bright red. "What would you suggest I do? It's my job to keep the mine running smoothly, not to cater to the needs of one helpless female—no matter how I feel about her—or the situation."

He added the last bit quietly and, Nathan suspected, with difficulty. Maybe there was more to Nichols than he'd given him credit for. Finally he grunted his agreement, and Nichols bobbed his head.

"All right, then." Gripping the edges of his lapel, Nichols straightened his coat then bent and retrieved his hat from the bench. "Thanks, Hawk. I appreciate your help. My only concern is for Abigail and what's best for her."

"Mine too," Nathan said. No matter what his individual feeling toward Nichols, he couldn't help but admit that he read genuine concern in the man's gaze.

His hand on the livery door, Nichols eyed Nathan a moment before donning his hat and slipping outside.

With the man gone, Nathan finally felt free to expel the deep breath that had been building inside his chest from the second Nichols spoke Abigail's name. Somehow he'd managed to extract a promise from Nathan that he would help him convince her to leave. There was no doubt that Nichols was right—Calico was a dangerous place, especially now that she'd fallen out of favor with the townspeople. Nathan knew he should be thinking up excuses, reasons for her going that would curtail any arguments she might give, but how could he do that when everything inside of him wanted her to stay?

Chapter Seventeen

....

The noise spilling from the saloon hurt Abigail's ears. It was bad enough that the music and laughter warred to drown out the other, but mixed into the chaos was the occasional gunshot. She flinched every time another blast rang out.

Leave, a tiny voice inside her prompted—but how could she when every other establishment in town had turned down her services?

Once again, the look she'd seen in Belle McAllister's eyes burned into Abigail's memory. She wavered on the step outside the saloon, knowing her papa would have railed against her setting foot inside such a place—but knowing, too, that she had no other choice.

Beneath her hand, the swinging door pushed easily. Inside, a thick gloom covered the place, heavy with smoke and the scent of cigars. That wasn't the worst of it. The farther she penetrated, the more rancid the air became. Fighting the urge to cover her nose at the smell of sweat, whiskey, and urine, she pressed tightly to the wall and made her way toward the bartender.

Papa's pistol provided much-needed courage at her hip. She'd taken the time to retrieve it before coming to the saloon. Whether she could actually shoot a man was of no consequence. She merely hoped the weapon itself would provide a deterrent should any of the men who frequented the saloon think to approach her. Amazingly, not one of the drunkards perched at the gaming tables or on stools even spared her a glance.

She drew even with the bar and leaned forward to be heard above the ruckus of the piano and the men. "Excuse me."

One glance and the bartender's face twisted skeptically. "What can I get for ya?"

Abigail shook her head. "I'm looking for the owner, Belle McAllister."

His hearty laugh rang above the noise. "Belle ain't up yet."

It was after two. Abigail fought to cover her surprise. "I saw her myself this morning. She was at the mining camp."

Though he glared at her, Abigail braced both hands on her hips and refused to budge. Eventually he stopped wiping out the glasses and studied her with two beady eyes.

"That may be, sweetheart, but Belle always takes herself a nap before the evening rush, if you know what I mean." He angled his chin toward the men draped over their chairs at the bar.

Pulling her gaze back to the bartender, she said, "Do you know what time she will be up?"

"Not till dark, sweetheart," he replied with a chortle. "Unless..." He fixed her with a measuring look. "You ain't looking for work, are ya, gal?"

The way his eyes roamed over her figure left no doubt as to the kind of work he meant. The comment drew several stares from other men, and Abigail shivered despite her show of bravado.

Her hand inched lower on her hip, toward the holster. "Not the kind you're implying," she said, a surprising note of sternness in her voice. "I'm a seamstress. I thought maybe some of your—ladies—could use a skilled needle."

By now more than one man had drawn near, but mindful of the pistol she wore, they maintained a respectful distance.

Leave, the voice inside prompted again, more urgently this time. Still Abigail refused to listen, her heart speeding its rhythm faster and faster until she feared she might be sick.

Dropping the cloth he'd been using to wipe out the glasses, the bartender placed both hands palms down on the bar and leaned forward to peer into Abigail's face. "You sure that's the only kind of work you're after? Stitching up a few rags won't pay nearly as well as the job I'm talking about."

Shouts from the men followed his statement, drowning out the gasp of fear that squeezed from between her clenched lips.

She'd made a mistake coming here—a horrible, dreadful mistake.

Clutching the grip of the pistol tightly now, Abigail inched backward—straight into the solid form of a man.

* * * * *

Hur–ry, hur–ry, hur–ry.

The voice inside Nathan's head matched the whirring, back-and-forth whisper of his saw. At his side, the pile of planks he'd been working on grew higher. He tossed the latest addition on top then drew his sleeve across his brow. What had compelled him to spend the day finishing the lean-to was a mystery. All he knew was that he'd awoken with a pressing need to see it done.

Lizzie skipped around the pile, one hand patting each plank and the other waving a drooping wildflower. "Are all these for our cabin, Pa?"

"They are, sweetheart."

"Why do we need so many?"

"You want a nice big room of your own, don't you?"

"Yes."

"Well, that's why."

"I see."

Across the street and down a piece, another gunshot sounded from Belle's Saloon. Nathan gave a snort of disgust. It appeared the revelers were starting early today. It was barely past two in the afternoon. Thankfully, Lizzie seemed oblivious to the noise and went on with her game.

"Sixteen, seventeen, eighteen— Pa, what comes after eighteen?"

"Nineteen. Lizzie?"

Her skipping stopped. "Yes, Pa?"

"Charlie wasn't feeling so good this morning. I put him in the end stall next to Max. Will you do me a favor and check on him?"

"Sure, Pa." Hitching up her skirt, she hurtled into the livery, the lace on her bloomers the last to disappear as she rounded the corner.

A few yards off, two men in dapper gray suits approached— representatives from the mining company. Nathan recognized them from the day they'd brought their horses to the livery for keeping. Dropping the saw onto the stack of wood, he wiped his hands down his pant legs and went to meet them.

"Howdy, gentlemen."

"Mr. Hawk." The younger of the two men extended his hand and gave Nathan's a hearty shake. "My associate and I will be leaving in the morning. I wonder if you could have our mounts ready?"

"Of course." The man had a solid handshake, much firmer than Nathan had expected from an Eastern dandy. "I take it your job here is finished, then?"

"Quite," the second gentleman said. He was thinner than the younger man, with graying hair and a full beard. "Unfortunately, I wish we had better news to carry back."

Nathan frowned. "Was the mine not as stable as you had expected after the fire?"

"Fire?" the tall man said, his gray brows bunching into snowy peaks.

Nathan nodded. "I thought that's why you were here—to check on the stability of the tunnels impacted by the explosion."

A confused look passed between the two men, and then the younger spoke. "Um—yes. We had several things we needed to address while we were here."

Puzzled by their unsettled demeanor, Nathan said nothing.

"Well, we'll give our report to Mr. Nichols. Any information we have regarding the mine passes through him," the thin man said. "You'll have our horses ready?"

"Of course. I'll see to it."

"Thank you. Good day, Mr. Hawk."

"Good day, gentlemen."

Both men looked back at Nathan as they walked away, their heads tilted toward one another as they talked in low whispers.

What was that all about? Why had they seemed so befuddled when he mentioned the fire?

Company men, he thought with a grunt. He'd learned he couldn't trust Gavin Nichols. Now he wondered if any of them could be trusted.

He shook his head. Standing around and wondering about a couple of strangers' odd behavior wouldn't get the work finished on the lean-to.

He retrieved his saw and reached for a piece of wood that would make a fine rafter for the new roof. Before he could touch the blade to the wood, however, the crack of a pistol split the air. Worse, it was followed by a familiar scream.

Chapter Eighteen
....

Abigail stared at the pistol in her hands.

She couldn't remember drawing it, much less pulling the trigger, yet her ears rang with the report and a gray haze swirled above her head. The man she'd bumped into stared at her, openmouthed, his eyebrows inching toward his hairline with shock.

"All right, back away from the girl. All of you!"

Abigail's gaze darted to the slender woman glaring down at them from the top of the stairs. Her satin skirt swaying, she sashayed down the steps, one pale arm motioning toward the door. "Move—all of you—'fore that gal decides she's better off putting a hole through one of your thick skulls instead of my ceiling."

Amid the grumbling, more than one "Aw, Belle" met Abigail's ears. She stared in surprise at the woman, hardly recognizing the plain face, devoid of makeup, and brownish hair that hung unstyled down her back.

The pianist took up playing once more, having ceased at the gunfire, and gradually the saloon returned to normal. Belle came to a stop in front of Abigail.

"I assume you're the reason I was jerked from my nap?"

"I—I—" Abigail stammered.

Belle cut her short with a brisk wave. She turned to the bartender, whose wide smile for the owner spoke of his affection. "Get me some coffee, Matt. Quick. I'm gonna need it." She eyed Abigail, taking in her plain cotton dress and shaking gun in a glance. "One for my friend here too."

"Coming right up, Belle."

Her lips pursed, she tipped her head toward the gun. "You gonna put that thing away, honey, or stand there holding it all day?"

After several fumbled attempts, Abigail finally managed to holster the weapon and then looked up at Belle.

She nodded. "C'mon. Let's grab a seat." Rather than wait to see if she followed, Belle turned and headed for a table in the corner that was clearly off-limits to the other patrons. Except for a delicate glass ashtray, the table was vacant and clean. Before she could sit, though, Matt returned with the coffees for Belle and Abigail. He set them down and then pulled out Belle's chair.

"Here you go. Black, just like you like it."

Belle's slender hand looked even paler against Matt's cheek, as she gave him a pat. She sat down, lifted her cup, and took a sip. "Ah, that's good. Thank you, darlin'. Now go on back to your duties."

If he had a tail, it'd be wagging, Abigail thought sourly, taking a seat across from Belle.

Belle spoke first, pulling Abigail's attention away from the lovesick bartender. "So, Miss Watts, what can I do for you?" She peered at her with a gleam that said she saw much and knew more. Abigail instantly liked her.

"I need a job," she responded, somehow sensing that the saloon proprietress would appreciate her bluntness. "Needlework. I'm a seamstress."

"Are you skilled?"

"Yes."

"What do you sew?"

"Anything, if I have a pattern to follow."

Belle paused and leaned forward, her lips pursed. Once again Abigail was taken aback by the difference in her complexion. Belle was much older than she'd figured when their eyes had met at the mining camp this morning—and more shrewd than she liked to let on, Abigail realized with a start.

"You given any thought to what folks are gonna say once they learn you're sewing dresses for my girls? Those church women ain't gonna take kindly to it, you know. You ready to earn a living for yourself the rest of your days? Give up any notions of marrying a respectable fella?"

All because she needed work? The unfairness of it hit Abigail squarely in the chest. It wasn't like she hadn't exhausted other avenues—well, except for the one she absolutely refused to tread—the one that led to the state of Virginia and her aunts. All she wanted was time to prove her father innocent of any wrongdoing. After that...

"Uh-huh." Belle's head bobbed knowingly. "I thought so. You ain't given it a thought."

"Perhaps not," Abigail said, a streak of pure stubbornness giving rise to her temper. "Still, a girl's gotta earn a living, and right now I don't have many choices."

"But you have some."

Nathan's face flashed into Abigail's memory and drove the words from her mouth.

Her hips swaying, Belle stood, abandoning the remainder of her cooling coffee on the table. Her slender fingers tapped her shapely arms. "Girl, go home. Think about what you're doing and those 'choices' you've been so quick to say no to. Then, if you still think

I'm all you've got, come back. We'll see what kind of deal we can work out."

She walked away, and Abigail found she didn't have the gumption to call her back. The woman was right; she hadn't taken the time to properly think through her decision to appeal to Belle for help. In fact, she hadn't even spoken of her idea to Caroline because of what her friend would say.

Indecision swirled in her head. Did she stay and bear the brunt of the townspeople's reproach, or go and face the same with her aunts back East? Both were too awful to consider, especially if she added Papa's feelings to the mix.

Leaving her coffee untouched, she walked to the door. Her shoulders slumped beneath the weight of her despair. Tears burned her eyelids, but she refused to let them fall, at least not while she was still inside the saloon where anyone could see. She'd wait until she got back to the cabin to give in to her bout of self-pity.

With each step the waiting got harder, the hot tears closer to spilling over. She stumbled the last few feet out the door—straight into Nathan's arms.

* * * * *

Nathan's hold tightened instinctively around Abigail's shaking body. She looked like she was about to cry, but she was apparently unharmed. A surge of protectiveness welled up from his middle. He drew back and looked into her face. "I heard gunshots. Are you all right? What on earth were you doing in there?"

She tossed her head and stared as though she couldn't speak.

"C'mon. I'm taking you home."

Resisting the tug of his arms, she managed a soft "Lizzie?"

"She's with Caroline. I took her there the second I heard you scream."

And then I ran back to the saloon, my heart racing. He left that part unsaid, but the truth of his fear for her still made his blood pound through his veins. A shout rose from inside, and the look on her face tore at his gut.

"Please, Abigail. Let me take you home."

Not until the words rolled off his lips did Nathan realize how he meant them. It wasn't the cabin where he wanted to take Abigail. It was the lean-to. That was why he'd felt so pressed to finish. It was as much for her as it was Lizzie.

The knowledge left him weak-kneed. Who was he to think that he could care for Abigail? Was it purely selfishness that made him want to consider her a part of his family? A need for someone other than himself to act as caregiver to Lizzie?

These and a myriad of other thoughts whirled through Nathan's brain as Abigail surrendered her resistance and allowed him to lead her home—to her cabin. She hadn't given him permission to take her anywhere else.

Once inside, she unbuckled the gun and holster, dropped them onto a chair, and plopped heavily into a seat at the table. She put her face in her hands, and slowly tears seeped through her fingers—a sight Nathan wished he'd never again have to see.

Grabbing a chair, he scraped it across the floor and sat in front of her. "Want to tell me about it?"

She shook her head.

He took her hands and held them in his. "Would it matter if I told you I already know?"

She blinked, her red eyes mirroring her confusion. "What?"

"Nichols came by to see me." Though she tried to pull away, Nathan held fast. "He wants to help you, Abigail. So do I."

"You can't help. Neither of you can. I have to do this myself, only—only—" More tears washed her eyes. "Oh, Nathan, what am I going to do? I can no more prove Papa's innocence than I can provide for my own living. I've failed him. I've failed myself. Maybe the townspeople are right. Maybe it's ridiculous to think I can stay where I'm not wanted—"

Nathan leaned forward and, mindful of the cut on her face, tipped up her chin until she met his eyes. "You are wanted here, Abigail. You are."

She fell silent, a strange mixture of fear and hope reflected in her watery gaze.

Suddenly Nathan knew why she had refused his first offer of marriage. She wanted what every woman wanted—a home and family, a place where she knew she'd be safe. And love.

An aching resistance fanned to life in his soul. He'd sworn to never love another woman after Charlotte died. He'd vowed to make the best life he could for Lizzie—alone. Yet Abigail would accept no less than a man's full love and devotion. Could he convince her of his willingness to at least try?

She stared at him, waiting.

He dropped his hand, no longer touching her, but not moving away, preparing himself for an honesty that would likely saw them both in two. "We need each other. I need you," he amended, before the shuttered look returned to her eyes. "Abigail, I know I'm probably not the man you dreamed of marrying." Shame wormed its way up from his belly, but he pushed on. "I can hardly provide for my

CALICO
1883
CA

daughter, much less a wife, but I promise you, I'll try. You'll never lack for anything so long as I live. I can give you a warm bed, a roof over your head—and friendship, at least for now."

Her gaze remained steady, but she said nothing.

At least she's listening.

He drew a steadying breath, hoping it would somehow quell the pain thrumming inside his chest. "I loved my wife."

He watched her, gauging her reaction.

Sadness slipped over her face. "I know."

"There's a part of me that will always love her. You need to know that."

She nodded.

"But—I will try to love you too, Abigail, if that's what you want. I can't promise anything. You understand that, right?"

"Yes," she whispered, her lips trembling.

His heart hammering harder and faster, Nathan reached out to claim her hand. "I swear to you—I'll give you as much of myself as I can. I'll try to make you happy, and if I fail—" His throat felt thick, but he forced himself to continue. "I won't hold you to a loveless marriage, Abigail. I'll help you find whatever it is you decide you need, even if it means your leaving Calico forever."

She pulled her hands away and darted to her feet, but instead of following, Nathan slid off the chair and dropped to one knee. Her face pale and her mouth slightly open, she watched him.

Nathan knew he had to press on, to ask the question he felt rising, before his determination fled. Licking his lips, he then stretched out his hand and said, "Abigail, will you marry me?"

Chapter Nineteen

....

Abigail's heart fluttered as Nathan sank to one knee. Pain carved itself on his face and twisted the handsomeness of his features into something broken and sad. She almost said no. Would have said no, were it not for the tiny flicker of hope that accompanied the grief in his eyes. She clasped her hands and drew a deep breath.

"Yes, Nathan. I'll marry you."

The words were out before she had time to think. Nathan blinked in surprise then rose to his feet. He stood awkwardly, as though unsure what should come next. Finally, he drew close and wrapped her in a stiff hug.

Too quickly, he let her go. "I'll see to the arrangements."

"All right."

"I think the sooner we see to it, the better."

"I agree."

A muscle in his jaw ticked. "Will Sunday give you enough time to prepare?"

For the day she'd been dreaming about since she was a little girl? Sorrow tore at her heart, but she lifted her chin and steadied her voice. "Yes."

"All right, then. I'll go speak to the preacher now." At the door, he paused with his hand on the knob. "Is there—anything you need—for the ceremony, I mean?"

She had no dress, no father to give her away, no family to gather around and wish her well. What else was there? She started to shake her head but then stopped. "I'd like Caroline to stand with me, if you don't mind."

He gave a gentle smile that chased away a bit of the doubt crowding her heart. "Of course."

"And maybe Lizzie could serve as the flower girl?"

"She'd like that."

"Good." Her gaze skittered around her sparsely furnished cabin and finally settled on the toes of her red boots. "Well, then, I suppose that's all."

Instead of leaving as she expected, Nathan crossed to her, pressed a quick kiss to the top of her head, then whirled and went out the door before she could see what had compelled him.

Her knees shaking, she sank onto a chair at the table. So that was it, then. In less than three days she'd be a bride. She took no joy in the thought. The future loomed as forbidding and uncertain as before.

No, that wasn't true. As she lay with her head on her arms, listening to the minutes tick past on the clock above the fireplace mantel, she realized that one thing had changed. Her future now included someone other than herself. Though she still had no idea what that meant, a strange peace settled over her soul.

She wasn't alone any longer. She had Lizzie—and Nathan.

* * * * *

Abigail's face lingered in Nathan's thoughts early the next morning, as he prepared two horses for the departure of the mining company men.

She'd said yes, and in less than a week she'd be his wife.

His heart thrilled at the notion but quickly quelled when two long shadows darkened the livery door. With heads bowed, the men spoke to each other in low tones.

"You've wired San Francisco?"

"Yesterday when I went to Daggett. They'll have the paperwork ready when we get back."

"Good. The sooner this deal goes through, the better."

Nathan's thoughts whirred like locusts. Mining company men didn't ride out of San Francisco—and if they weren't with the Silver King, who were they and what were they doing in Calico?

Both men stopped talking when they spotted Nathan. He tipped his hat to them.

"Morning, gentlemen. Good day for a ride." He gestured to the sun just beginning to rise over the mountains.

The older man with the bushy eyebrows grimaced. "On another day, I'd be inclined to agree with you. Not today."

"You men have a long road ahead?"

The shorter of the two grunted. "You could say that."

Nathan did his best to look sympathetic. "But your trip was worthwhile, I hope?"

"That remains to be seen," the older man said, scratching his chin. "Indeed."

Acting on a hunch, Nathan rolled his shoulder and put on a contrite face. "Say, sorry about the mix-up yesterday. I assumed you were with the Silver King." Again, a flicker of interest and confusion lit their eyes. Nathan pressed his advantage. "Sure was a bit of bad luck, that fire."

The older gentleman cleared his throat. "About that—I don't suppose you could tell us what happened?"

As briefly as he could, Nathan recounted the event. To his surprise, the men looked relieved when he finished.

"It is unfortunate," the shorter of the two said. "But accidents like this are not uncommon."

"Just glad to hear the mine is back up and running—for the miners' sakes and that of their families," the older said, tugging at his mustache. He looked at his shorter companion. "Shall we?"

He couldn't hold them up any longer. Nathan held out the reins. "Good luck on your trip."

"Thank you, young man."

One hand on the horn, the older man swung easily into his saddle and then sat watching while the shorter man clumsily did the same. Before they wheeled to leave, however, the older man leaned down to Nathan.

"Anyone who rides into town would stop by here, isn't that so?"

Nathan shrugged. "Eventually, I suppose. If they intended to stay a bit and needed a place to stable their horses."

The old man nodded. "So that means if any other men, like us"—he gestured to his friend—"rode into town, you'd know it?"

Narrowing his eyes, Nathan nodded. "That's right. Can't say as I've seen anyone, though."

Giving a satisfied grunt, the older man straightened. "Good." He removed a card from his pocket and handed it to Nathan. "This is my address in San Francisco. I don't suppose you'd be willing to contact me if that changes?"

"That depends," Nathan said, examining the card briefly and then tipping his head toward the stranger. "What exactly is your business here?"

The older man chuckled and shot a glance at his friend. "You were right, Perry. Nichols is true to his word."

His hold on the reins tightened as he returned his gaze to Nathan. "A business transaction is what attracted us to Calico, friend. Purely business." Lifting his hat, he turned his horse and started out of town at a brisk pace. Much less gracefully, his short companion followed.

Still pondering the man's words, Nathan watched and thought. What kind of business drew interest from as far away as San Francisco?

The answer hit him like a punch to the jaw. The men seemed concerned that the production of silver hadn't slowed after the fire, yet they weren't with the mining company. That could only mean one thing...

They were interested in buying the mine.

Chapter Twenty

....

"You look beautiful."

Abigail studied her reflection in the mirror. With Caroline's help, she had managed to alter one of her mother's old dresses into a suitable wedding gown. A bit of lace, a strand of borrowed pearls— she certainly looked the part of a bride.

But beautiful?

She fingered the necklace. "I'll have these back to you tomorrow."

"No hurry. Enjoy the day." Caroline's hands lingered over Abigail's curls. Frowning in the mirror, she said, "Are you sure about this? You're certain this is what you want?"

Doubt stretched like a shadow over her soul. She wasn't sure, but she couldn't admit that to her friend. Caroline would only worry, and Abigail was worried enough for them both. "I believe I'm making the right decision."

"But have you prayed?" Caroline placed both hands on her shoulders and turned her from the mirror. "I've been so worried about you, dear. Ever since your father died, it's like your faith hasn't been the same. You know how much God loves you, don't you? You know He hasn't left you?"

"I..." Abigail's gaze fell to the handkerchief clutched in her hands. She wanted to believe, but doubt and fear filled her heart. She lifted pleading eyes to her friend. "I'm trying."

Caroline's face darkened with sorrow. "Oh, sweetheart, maybe you shouldn't be rushing into anything. Maybe you should wait a few days—"

"That's just it. I don't have a few days. My things are packed. I have to leave the cabin today."

"You could stay with me. At least for a little while, until you get your bearings."

"And after you and John marry? Then what? Your wedding is only a week away."

"John won't mind."

"But I will. I can't be a burden to you or anyone else." Turning back to the mirror, Abigail spoke to her reflection. "No, this is what I have to do. I'm grateful to Nathan for everything he's done. Now I'll do my best to be a good wife to him."

Caroline said nothing for a moment then leaned into Abigail and wrapped her in a hug. "I'll make sure everything is ready."

Grateful tears welled in Abigail's eyes. Caroline was a dear friend, and she was lucky to have her. In a wink she disappeared through the door, taking her brief moment of comfort with her.

Getting up from the vanity, Abigail walked to the bed and lifted her father's Bible from the coverlet. It was one of the few things that hadn't been destroyed when Justice Fisher ransacked the cabin. She'd found it when she and Caroline cleaned up the mess.

Her eyes fell on one familiar verse after another as the pages parted. To think, in just a few short days, she'd gone from listening to Papa's voice as he read from the Scriptures to being thankful she still had a small piece of him to cling to.

The mantel clock chimed the hour, and Abigail knew she needed to make the short walk to the schoolhouse. She didn't want to leave the preacher waiting.

Or Nathan.

Her heart fluttered at the thought. Soon she'd be married, but would she have a husband who loved her?

You'll have a home, she reminded herself, *and the time needed to prove your father's innocence.* Plus food, clothing, shelter—it had to be enough for now. It had to be.

Pressing the Bible to her body, she walked out the door, her feet steady on the gravel path that led to the schoolhouse and her new husband.

* * * * *

For the third time that morning, Nathan pulled his watch from his vest pocket and flipped open the lid. Five minutes past the hour. Abigail would be arriving soon. Even with the events of the past few days, she was foremost on his mind today.

Stuffing the watch back into his vest, he tossed one last glance around the schoolhouse. Silk flowers borrowed from the milliner were in place, candles burned from sconces on the walls, and in his hip pocket rested a slender gold band. Everything was ready. He could only hope she would approve.

Nervousness clutched at his belly. Strange, considering that the circumstances surrounding their marriage were less than ideal. Still, he found himself wanting to provide a memorable occasion for Abigail, not a hastily thrown together ceremony that meant little or nothing to either of them.

Caroline and Lizzie had fashioned bows to attach the flowers that now hung from the sides of the wooden benches. He straightened the nearest bouquet then stood back to survey his handiwork.

"How many times you plan on fixing those flowers?" Pastor Burch said, a smile on his face. "You sure you don't want to sit down until your bride arrives?"

Nathan shook his head. He couldn't sit. "Maybe I should go check on Lizzie."

Pastor Burch stayed him with a hand on his forearm. "Caroline is with her. Besides, you're needed here." He motioned toward a bit of lace that had worked its way loose from the trellis Nathan had built for the vows.

He quickly refastened it on the trellis then resumed his pacing. If he were honest, it wasn't just the wedding that had him so nervous. It was also being inside the schoolhouse with the pastor. He hadn't set foot in a church since Charlotte died, and he didn't like having to look at the preacher and be reminded of his neglect. Still, he knew Anson wouldn't have wanted his daughter wed by anyone else.

Pastor Burch cleared his throat. When Nathan turned to look, he quirked an eyebrow and gestured toward a bench.

Sighing, Nathan took a seat, and the aging pastor sat next to him. No telling what the man had to say. Would he criticize Nathan for not bringing his daughter to Sunday services? Would he question Nathan's motives for marrying Abigail—or wonder why Anson's daughter would settle for a surly, bitter man, such as he? He clasped his hands and waited.

"You're an answer to prayer."

Nathan's gaze flew to the pastor. "What?"

Crinkles formed around the pastor's blue eyes. In their depths, Nathan read great compassion.

"I've been so concerned for Abigail. I've been praying that God would send His provision. He sent you."

CALICO
1883
CA.

The conversation was rapidly making Nathan uncomfortable. He shook his head. "Look, Pastor—"

"What, you never saw yourself as being God's answer before?"

Hardly. Nathan squirmed under the man's steady gaze.

Pastor Burch smiled and crossed his arms. "Young man, let me tell you something about the God I serve. He rarely works in the way I expect or in a way I can understand, but He always, *always* answers prayer."

Anger flared inside Nathan's chest. "I prayed. When my wife took ill, I prayed she'd get better."

"And?"

"She died."

Pastor Burch shook his head sadly. "Not the answer you wanted."

Nathan's fists clenched. "Not an answer at all." He rose to his feet. "Sorry, Pastor. I wish I could believe—"

"Oh, it was an answer," Pastor Burch interrupted quietly, going on as though Nathan hadn't spoken. "See, that's the problem with most folks—always wanting God to answer their prayers in their time and in the ways they want. When He doesn't, they assume He ignored their request, but that just isn't so. He only took a different route. One that fit His plan."

"His plan?" Nathan snorted.

Pastor Burch lumbered upright and came to stand next to him. "It brought you here, didn't it?"

Grasping his shoulder, he turned Nathan toward the door, where Abigail stood outlined. The sun rested on her hair and gave her skin a healthy glow. Hope lit her eyes. Only the nervous twisting of her fingers around a bouquet of silk flowers gave away her nervousness.

At her side, Caroline offered silent support. Lizzie stood slightly in front, awestruck, as she stared up at Abigail. Yellow ribbon tucked with leaves had been fashioned into a wreath around Lizzie's head. It perfectly matched the flowery chain that draped her neck.

A queer feeling filled Nathan's stomach, a strange mixture of pleasure and pain. God's plan had brought him here? What kind of plan involved the death of a man's wife and a young woman's father, just to bring two people to a moment like this?

The questions rolled round in his head as Abigail left the entrance to the schoolhouse and made her way down the aisle. Nathan watched, mesmerized by the peace he read on her face.

She stopped next to him, her eyes questioning. Holding his breath, he stretched out his hand and felt a thrill of excitement when she placed her small palm in his.

Whatever had brought them to this place, Nathan realized as they turned to face the pastor, he was glad. He only hoped Abigail felt the same.

Chapter Twenty-one
....

Abigail stared in amazement at the finished lean-to. The place was much larger than she had expected—it could hardly be called a lean-to at all—and it smelled of sweet hay and fresh-cut lumber.

Lizzie tugged on her hand. "Do you like it, Abigail?"

Abigail's gaze fell on her new daughter, amazed and delighted that she already thought of her as such, and she smiled. "It's wonderful."

"It's not as big as the cabin," Nathan said, his face red.

Setting her reticule down on the dining table, Abigail walked into the lean-to. A new cookstove had been installed in the kitchen area—a pleasant surprise, considering she'd been expecting to have to prepare their meals over a campfire. Heavy curtains hung in the corner from the ceiling. Heat fanned her cheeks as she surmised what they hid. She walked past without stopping. There would be plenty of time later to consider the sleeping arrangements. Instead, she paused at a wooden rocker Nathan had placed next to the window.

"I thought the light would make it easier for you to see when you're sewing," he said, shuffling his feet. He placed his hands on Lizzie's shoulders and gathered the little girl close.

Suddenly Abigail was aware of how important it was to him that she approve of the lean-to. Warmth radiated from her heart, and she smiled. "It's perfect. Thank you, Nathan."

With those few words, the awkward moment passed.

Lizzie skipped over to lay claim to Abigail's hand. "Come see my bed. Pa says I have to be careful climbing the ladder, but I'm not scared. It's fun."

Laughing, Abigail gave in to the childish tug on her fingers and followed as Lizzie led the way to the loft. Just as she'd said, a ladder stretched upward toward the ceiling, but it was the two pallets situated beneath the rafters that captured Abigail's attention.

"That one's for me," Lizzie said, pointing at the smaller of the two, "and that one's for Pa."

Momentary relief mingled with disappointment, though why she should feel the latter, she couldn't fathom.

She lingered on the top rung of the ladder while Lizzie scrambled across the loft and hopped onto her pallet, releasing a fresh burst of hay scent into the air. "C'mon, Abigail. Try it." She gave the pallet a pat. "It's much softer than sleeping in the barn."

"I'm sure it is, sweetheart."

"Pa even put in a window so I can look out at the corral and see Charlie." She rose from the pallet and went to the small block cut-out. The peaked roof was just tall enough for Lizzie to stand without bumping her head. Thrusting open the shutter, she stuck her hand through and pointed. "See?"

"Lizzie, there's plenty of time to show Abigail the rest later. I'm sure she would like to get her things settled," Nathan called from below.

Regret clouded Lizzie's face. Abigail smiled. "It's all right, sweetheart. You can show me the rest tomorrow. Right now, why don't you come down and help me fix supper?"

Delighted, Lizzie scampered down the ladder after Abigail, her small hands and feet sure on the rungs. Nathan waited near the table.

"Your things are out back. I'll fetch them so you can unpack while I rustle up something to eat," he said.

CALICO
1883
CA

"I can do that," Abigail protested. She certainly didn't want her new husband doubting her skill as a cook on the first night in their new home.

Nathan placed a warm touch upon her shoulder. "Tonight it's my turn. Don't worry; I'll be only too glad to relinquish the cooking responsibilities once you're settled in. I'm sure Lizzie will be glad too. She's had to eat more than her share of burned pancakes."

His easy laugh set Abigail's worry to rest. She nodded, eager to know more about the man she'd married. While he carried in her things from the barn, she slipped behind the curtains draping the bed and changed out of her wedding clothes into something more practical—a blue-and-white-checked dress she'd owned for years. As she emerged, Lizzie met her with a frown.

"What is it, Lizzie?"

Her lips puckered, Lizzie pointed. "I like the other dress better. It was dreadful pretty."

The seriousness with which she said "dreadful" made Abigail smile. "Yes, it was," she agreed, bending to prop her hands on her knees, "which is why I don't want to get it dirty."

"But today is your wedding day. You're supposed to look pretty all day." The door creaked open and Nathan entered with an armload of Abigail's things. Lizzie scurried over to pull on his leg. "Isn't she supposed to look pretty, Pa?"

Amusement lit Nathan's eyes as Abigail straightened and peered at him. "Oh, I'd say she looks pretty enough."

Lizzie grunted but became distracted by a bug crawling through the door. She grasped the broom and swept the offending creature outside.

Abigail fought a rising tide of embarrassment as Nathan crossed the room to her and lowered his voice.

"Where would you like these?"

"The bed is fine for now. I'll take care of storing them later."

He bent to duck through the curtains but paused. "In case I didn't mention it earlier, you looked beautiful today. Anson would have been very proud."

His words echoed through Abigail's head long into the night. She stared up at the ceiling, recalling them over and over and liking the way they'd sounded, spoken in Nathan's deep, rumbling voice.

Flipping onto her side, she burrowed into the bed, comforted by the familiar scent of her own blankets.

Nathan thought her beautiful. She definitely thought him handsome. But was any of that a strong enough foundation upon which to build a marriage? Squeezing her eyes shut, she tried to wipe all thoughts from her head and finally slipped into a fitful sleep, her dreams plagued by the fear that the answer might prove a long time coming.

* * * * *

Abigail woke long before dawn's rays chased the shadows from the lean-to. She slid from the bed, dressed in a hurry to ward off the night's chill, and did her best to make breakfast without rousing the rest of the house.

Her efforts were only half successful. Nathan descended the ladder just as the coffee finished brewing. She poured him a cup and one for herself then sat across from him at the table.

"I'm sorry if I woke you."

He took a sip from the coffee cup before running his fingers through his tousled hair. "I had to get up anyway. Chores." Concern filled his hazel eyes as he looked at her. "You're up early. Did you sleep all right?"

CALICO
1883
CA

Her smile chased the frown from his brow. "I had to make up for neglecting the supper duties last night." She gestured toward the stove. While it had taken her some time to adjust to the newfangled thing, she had managed to get a pan of biscuits baking. "Breakfast will be ready in a moment."

Nathan took a long sniff. "Is that what I smell?" He set down his cup. "Where did you find the flour?"

"I had some left in the tins you brought from the cabin." She nodded toward a shelf he had secured to the wall above the stove. Her items formed a neat row.

Nathan's brows rose, and he swiped his palm across his face. "You did all that this morning? I must have been tired. I never heard a sound."

She flashed another smile and went to remove the biscuits from the pan. Strange how she only now realized how much she'd missed having quiet conversations with her father in the wee hours of the morning, before the rest of Calico roused from slumber.

Once she'd fried up some eggs to go with the biscuits and moved everything to the table, she and Nathan sat down to eat. He didn't pray with her, but neither did he protest when she stopped to bow her head.

"What are your plans for today?" he asked when she finished.

Abigail buttered a warm biscuit while she thought. "Gavin"—her eyes flashed to Nathan as she remembered his disapproval the last time she'd used the Christian name—"Mr. Nichols said he spoke to the men who worked the mine the day of the accident, but I still have questions. One of the men, Cotty Kay, told me who was working. I think I'll start by finding out whether they saw anything unusual."

About to take a bite of his eggs, Nathan paused and lowered

his fork. "You sure you want to do that? The miners weren't happy the last time you were at the camp. It might not be safe for you to go there alone."

She shook her head. "I don't have much of a choice. I have to clear Papa's name. The only way to do that is to find out what really happened in the mine."

Concern blazed from his eyes. She dropped her gaze to avoid being swept away by it. Nathan was being kind, but if she allowed his fears to influence her decisions, she'd lose her nerve and never know what really caused the explosion. Though he said no more about it, his displeasure swirled through the lean-to as they finished the quiet meal.

Afterward, Nathan picked up his plate, returned it to the sink, then went to the hooks along the wall and fetched his coat. "If you'll give me a couple of hours, I'll get started on my chores at the livery and then come back to collect Lizzie."

"There's no need," Abigail began. "I'll gladly watch her for you—"

The look in his eyes stopped her cold. His face somber, he crossed to the table near where she stood. "Abigail, I understand your need to prove your father's innocence. Were I in your place, I'd do exactly the same thing. I promised to help you, and I will. Anything I can do, you need but ask."

He waited and she nodded.

"But I cannot forget about Lizzie's safety." His eyes darkened as he peered at her. "I know you'd never intentionally do anything that would put her in harm's way—"

She clutched his arm. "Nathan, please say no more. I promise you, whatever I do, I'll do it alone." Her heart tightened painfully at the idea that he doubted her concern for Lizzie. He was just a father making certain his daughter was cared for, of course, but it hurt nonetheless.

He hesitated a moment longer, his long fingers working the brim of his hat, and then, satisfied by her assurance, he turned and strode out the door.

Abigail took her time in cleaning up the plates and cups they'd eaten on, pondering, as she dried and stored them all on a second plank attached to the wall, how she would know which of the men she could talk to. Caroline might know, since she'd spent the night with the Chens after Hui was killed, or possibly John Gardner, Caroline's fiancé, could tell her. But before she could think on it too deeply, scuffling sounded and Lizzie's bare legs poked out over the top rung of the ladder.

Tickled by the sight, Abigail smiled and slung her dish cloth over her shoulder. "Morning, sweetheart."

Grabbing a tin plate, she scooped out a healthy serving of eggs and added a still-warm biscuit. Her plans for the morning would wait. Right now, she had a new family to care for and, strange as it seemed, she was determined to show Nathan that she would do everything in her power to keep Lizzie safe.

* * * * *

Nathan's thoughts chased round and round as he moved from one stall to the next, adding oats to the feedbags and spreading fresh straw. Abigail was his wife now. He didn't like the idea of her digging into Anson's death alone. If he was right about the mine being for sale and the two strangers from San Francisco were only the first to come snooping around Calico, he didn't want her anywhere near the situation. Unscrupulous, money-driven men were dangerous.

He sighed. As much as he wanted to protect Abigail, their

marriage existed in name only. He had no right to voice his concerns or impose his will in the matter. Still, wouldn't Anson have wanted him to do all within his power to protect his only daughter? And was it only regard for Anson's wishes that had him sloughing through his thoughts like a wagon through mud? What about Lizzie? Didn't he have an obligation to consider her needs first? Back and forth the questions bounced until Nathan thought his head might burst.

Faint voices drifted from the back of the livery, pulling him from his musings. He left the tack bench and drew closer to the far wall to listen. A chair scraped the floor, followed by light footsteps, and then Lizzie laughed, the sound bringing a quick smile to Nathan's lips. His enjoyment of the moment was cut short, however, when Abigail's laughter echoed Lizzie's. His stomach tightened and his heart rate sped to an alarming pace as his scattered thoughts came sharply into focus.

Abigail's safety meant as much to him as Lizzie's.

He snatched a bundle of halters and carried them to the tack bench. The reason didn't matter, he assured himself, as he clipped the halters in place on a row of hooks. What mattered was that he didn't want a repeat of his failure with Charlotte, and if that meant going out of his way to protect both Lizzie *and* Abigail, so be it.

Finished with his morning chores, he wound his way out of the livery and turned with determined steps toward the lean-to. He and Abigail had much to discuss.

"Hawk! Hold up there. I need to speak to you. Just what do you think you're doing?"

Nathan's steps slowed. He knew that voice. Sure enough, Gavin Nichols bore down on him from the direction of Abigail's former cabin, his face red and rivers of sweat dampening his collar.

Chapter Twenty-two

· · · · · · · · · · · · · · · · · · · ·

Low voices drifted outside the door, one of them angry. Oblivious to the sound, Lizzie shoveled another bite of eggs into her mouth and munched happily, her stockinged feet swinging back and forth above the floor.

"What will we do today, Abigail? Can we go see Dorsey? Mr. Stacy said he'd have a message for him to carry soon. Maybe we can go watch him fill Dorsey's pouch."

Abigail pushed up from the table. "Um, maybe, sweetheart. We'll have to see what your father has planned first."

"All right, but maybe we could save Dorsey a biscuit. Do you think he likes biscuits, Abigail? I can put some cactus jelly…"

Her lively chatter continued, but Abigail stopped listening and moved to the door. Nathan was in conversation with someone, and whoever it was wasn't happy.

"I came to you out of concern, thinking you would help."

"I have helped."

"This is your solution? This is how you help her? What about the miners? I can't hold them off forever."

"Abigail will be safe as long as she's with me."

Gavin Nichols. Abigail cracked the door open far enough to see the mine superintendent standing toe to toe with Nathan. Though he was tall, he still looked up to Nathan. Sputtering, he flung the tails of his coat wide and propped both fists on his hips.

"Are you out of your mind? Didn't you see what happened to her face?"

"That had nothing to do with the miners," Nathan said. "The man who broke in was after her money."

"How do you know? Maybe he got spooked and took off before he got what he was really after, and maybe he's not the only one. These men are out for blood, Hawk. They want an explanation, and right now, the only one they're satisfied with is Anson's guilt."

A curious look flashed across Nathan's face, and then he shook his head. "That's because the accident is still so raw. Once your team from the mine company certifies that the mine is safe, this will all blow over—"

"They're not—! That is—" Gavin drew a deep breath then grabbed his hat in one hand and brushed a bead of sweat from his brow with the other. "All right." His limbs shaking, he shoved the brim of his hat into Nathan's face. "This is on you, Hawk. If anything happens to that woman—or your daughter, for that matter—it's on you."

A look of black rage dropped over Nathan like a blanket. Abigail sucked in a breath and curled her fingers tightly around the door's edge. She'd never seen him so angry. Gavin shrank back as Nathan took a step forward.

"You let me worry about taking care of my family, Nichols. They're no concern of yours, now or ever."

He'd called her "family"! Abigail's breathing quickened.

A cloud of dust settled over Gavin's polished boots and the cuffs of his trousers as he shuffled his feet. He jammed his hat on his head and nodded. "Fine. You see to it, then. In the meantime, I'll see to business on my end."

He strode away, but Nathan stood unmoving with his hands clenched at his sides.

Abigail looked over her shoulder at Lizzie. "Get a wiggle on and finish your breakfast, Lizzie. When you're done, climb up into the loft and see to the beds, yours and your pa's."

Her mouth stuffed with biscuit and jelly, Lizzie could only nod. Abigail offered a smile and then eased out the door. Lizzie would be fine, at least until she'd spoken to Nathan.

The morning sun had just crested the ridge of hills in the distance. Its pale rays provided little warmth, but they did illuminate the fire blazing in Nathan's eyes when he looked at her.

Abigail approached him carefully. "What was that about?"

The muscles in his jaw flexed. "You heard?"

"Some."

He glanced toward the lean-to. "Lizzie?"

"She's finishing her breakfast. What did Gavin want?"

Nathan blew out a breath and then motioned toward the shaded side of the lean-to. "Let's talk over there. Best if Lizzie didn't hear."

Abigail followed him around the house, though she had to hasten to match his long strides. For several moments he did nothing but pace, his fingers working themselves through his thick hair like a plow to a field. When he stopped, Abigail bit her lip and waited, her chest tight.

"Gavin thinks you might be in danger. Says the miners won't be satisfied with anything less than blood."

She shivered so hard her teeth shook. "Wh–whose blood?"

"In this case—ours."

Nathan crossed to her and planted both hands on her shoulders. The strength she felt in his grip made it hard not to feel safe, as though the miners and their accusations couldn't possibly touch her so long as he stood in their path, but the warmth of his fingers also reminded her of his humanity. She couldn't put him in harm's way, not when he had Lizzie to consider.

She shrugged from beneath his grasp. "Don't you mean mine? This doesn't involve you, Nathan."

His gaze hardened. "You're my wife now. What affects you affects me."

Abigail swallowed a surprising lump in her throat. "That wasn't the deal."

"I'm changing the deal," he said, his voice gruff. He took a deep breath and let it out slow. "Abigail, you have to promise me that you'll let me help you find out what really happened in the mine. Tell me you'll wait to ask your questions until I can be with you."

The sleeves of his cotton shirt were rolled to his elbows, revealing arms Abigail longed to fall into. It surprised her how much she wanted to say yes, to accept his help without question, but deep inside, she knew she couldn't wait. She'd go to the mining camp or seek out the Chinese, find anyone she thought might provide information, and keep doing it until she had the answers she sought.

And she would do it alone.

* * * * *

Nathan waited, his hands clenched at his sides, while a passel of emotions flitted across Abigail's face.

She had to listen to him. She just had to.

The vehemence of the thought shook him to the core. Though his arms ached to hold her, he resisted. He'd never let go if he gave in to the urge now.

A teasing wind plucked at her hair and tossed a strand of it into her eyes. She brushed it away with her left hand, where the gold band he'd placed on her finger just hours ago gleamed.

"Well?" he demanded, more gruffly than he intended.

The shuttered look he knew so well dropped over her face, and she lifted her chin. "You have my word. I won't go to the mining camp without telling you."

He searched her eyes. She stared back, guileless. Relief, deeper and wider than any canyon, opened up and swallowed the dread in Nathan's belly. He expelled a loud sigh and followed it with a smile.

"We'll figure this out, Abigail. I promise you, we won't stop digging until we know what really caused the mine explosion."

Once again, the faces of the two mining company strangers popped into his brain, followed by Gavin's obvious discomfort. Did he have any right keeping the information from Abigail? But wouldn't knowing the truth only push her to investigate further?

Before he could dwell on the answer, Abigail's features twisted into something earnest and sharp. "What if we don't?"

He blinked. "What?"

"What if we never prove my father's innocence?" Hugging herself, she peered up at him. "Will you share my father's shame? The livery could suffer and lose business. You and Lizzie—"

He did pull her into his arms then, and when she seemed as though she would continue with her protests, he gently laid his finger across her lips.

"I don't have the answer to that, Abigail, but I think—" Pastor Burch's words rang in Nathan's head, filling him with more hope than he'd felt in a year. He looked down into his new wife's eyes. She looked back, pleading for his assurance with her gaze. Everything in him wanted to give it, to be the pillar she could lean on when she was weary or frightened. He smiled. "I think that if we can find a way to pray, maybe—maybe God will hear."

Surprise sparked in the depths of her brown eyes for one brief moment and was quickly chased away by an even brighter flash of gratitude.

How strange, Nathan thought, tightening his hold on his wife as she slid her arms around his waist and squeezed. He'd always thought he knew what it meant to provide for a wife, but never in the years he'd been married to Charlotte had he ever considered that what she needed most was for him to rely on God.

Chapter Twenty-three

....

Abigail's promise haunted her the rest of the morning, as she familiarized herself with the new routine of being a wife and a mother. Heat that had nothing to do with the cook fire she tended fanned her cheeks.

She'd told Nathan a lie.

After adding a log to the fire, she adjusted the grate and then closed the stove door. Actually, telling Nathan she wouldn't go to the mining camp when she fully intended to seek out the miners in other places was more of an omission, but it still felt like a lie—ugly and embarrassing. Especially when she considered his last words.

She paused, remembering again the feeling that was stirred by hearing Nathan encourage her to remain prayerful. What a change from just a few short weeks ago!

Brushing the dust from her hands on an apron around her waist, she turned and went to the window, where she had two loaves of fresh bread cooling. Lizzie waved to her from outside. At her side, Dorsey the mail dog yipped and nipped at her clothes. The wool coat Lizzie wore dwarfed her small frame, but with the weather turning colder every day, Abigail didn't want her playing outside without one and had dug a spare from her chest of drawers. The first chance she got, she'd hem the garment and cut the sleeves so they didn't drag on the ground.

"Lunch will be ready soon. You'll need to come in and wash up," Abigail called.

Lizzie lifted her face from Dorsey's furry neck and laughed. The dog had obviously taken pains to lick the remains of her breakfast from her cheeks. His tongue had left wet streaks up and down her face.

"Yes, ma'am," Lizzie said, giggling. Curling her fingers deep into Dorsey's black-and-white coat, she buried her nose in his fur, inhaled deeply, then tipped her head back and blew out the breath. "Dorsey smells like rain."

More like dog.

Mirth bubbled in Abigail's chest. Lizzie would be returning to school soon, but in the meantime, she enjoyed caring for her. She sensed deep inside that she would enjoy caring for Lizzie's father just as much, but not when deceit had already crept between them, carving its way like shafts through the mountain.

Guilt burrowed its icy hooks deeper into her flesh. The one and only time she'd ever lied to Papa, he'd found out. Eyes misty, he'd told her that trust, once broken, was never the same, even if it was somehow forged together.

"Abigail, hello!"

Abigail lifted her head. From the dusty street, Caroline raised a gloved hand in greeting. Abigail smiled and motioned her to the door then left the window to meet her.

Opening the door wide, she said, "This is a surprise. I figured you and your mother would be finishing the wedding plans."

"I'm never too busy to check on a friend," Caroline protested, though her frown quickly dissolved into a giggle. "All right, so I was dying of curiosity." She embraced Abigail tightly then stood back to look at her. "Well?"

Disappointment pricked Abigail's flesh. "Well, what?" she said, trying to sound cheerful.

CALICO
1883
CA

Caroline's voice lowered to a whisper. "Your first night as a married woman. How was it?"

Abigail marched to the cookstove, where she had a kettle of water warming. "My marriage is in name only, Caroline. You know that."

Her friend's eyes darkened. "Yes, but—"

"But what? Nathan and I are content with the arrangement." She pointed to the loft. "He and Lizzie sleep up there, and I"—she motioned to the half-drawn curtains, where her neatly made bed peeked through—"sleep there."

A slender brow arched on Caroline's forehead. "Oh." After a moment she took off her gloves, removed a cup and saucer from the cupboard, and carried them to Abigail. "I'm sorry."

"Why? I had no misconceptions about what I was doing when I accepted Nathan's proposal. In fact, things are even better than I imagined." She swept her arm wide to encompass the room. "He's given me a place to live and food to eat. More importantly, he's given me the time I need to pursue the truth regarding my father. I couldn't ask for anything else."

"I guess not," Caroline said, though she sounded unsure and a puzzled frown marred her brow.

"Enough nonsense, now," Abigail said, ushering her to a place at the table. "Lizzie and I were about to eat lunch. Will you join us?"

"Can't." Rather than remove her bonnet and shawl, Caroline shook her head and waved toward the door, her gloves flopping like a pair of bagged birds in her hand. "I'm actually on my way to see John. I just wanted to check on you first—see how you're doing." The teasing left her gaze and she reached out to grasp Abigail's hand. "I'll be back this afternoon, though. I promised Nathan I would sit with Lizzie."

A pitcher of water in her hand, Abigail paused and looked at her friend. "Lizzie? Whatever for? Did he say?"

Caroline shook her head. "And I didn't ask. He asked me for a favor, and I was only too glad to help."

Strange. While Abigail pondered what he had mind, Caroline slid her fingers into her gloves.

"Tell him I'll come around three, would you?"

She placed a light peck on Abigail's cheek before showing herself to the door. Lizzie met her there, her childish voice raised in delight as she bade Dorsey good-bye.

"Lizzie, you remember my friend, Miss Martin, don't you?" Abigail said.

The little girl peered at Caroline. "Hello. Pa says you're going to stay with me later."

It appeared Abigail was the only one not aware of that fact. Planting her hands on her hips, she directed a pointed look toward Lizzie. "How did you know that, sweetheart?"

Lizzie swayed side to side, her freckled nose scrunched. "Pa told me. Said to tell you not to wait on him for lunch. He's finishing up his chores."

Chores? But surely he took time to eat. At least he had before he married her. Before she could stop herself, Abigail shot a glance at Caroline, who appeared to be as surprised as she by Lizzie's announcement.

The awkward silence stretched long, broken finally by Caroline.

"I guess I'd best get a move on. Otherwise, I won't be back in time to sit with Lizzie. See you this afternoon, sweetheart."

The little girl waved, and when Caroline left and closed the door behind her, she skipped over to the table. "What's for lunch?"

"Ham sandwiches," Abigail said, though her appetite had fled and the scent of fresh bread no longer held appeal.

Thoughts of Nathan kept her preoccupied as she slathered a slice of bread with butter and ham and set the plate alongside a cup of milk in front of Lizzie.

"There you go, sweetheart. Eat up."

"Ain't you gonna eat?"

"*Aren't*. No, I'm not hungry."

She patted Lizzie's head absently and then fetched the water bucket and filled the sink. At least she'd keep busy until Nathan returned at three.

Her eyes wandered to the clock she'd brought with her from the cabin. Because the lean-to lacked space, Nathan had placed it next to her bed. Walking over, she spread the curtains wider and secured them with the piece of rope she was using as a sash. Afraid she'd still be unable to track the time, she turned the clock an inch more. Satisfied, she went back to the sink to finish the dishes.

In fact, she'd dried and stored all of the dishes, swept the floor, and made several trips to the water barrel to fill the wash bucket for laundering before she heard Nathan's heavy steps outside the door. He entered, his face ruddy from the sun and wind.

Wiping her hands on her apron, Abigail straightened and went to greet him. "You're back." Her mouth dry, she swallowed and motioned toward a plate wrapped in a checkered cloth waiting for him on the table. "Are you hungry? I made you a sandwich."

He shook his head as he crossed to the washbasin, poured some water from the pitcher into it, and soaked a towel. "I'm fine. Took a biscuit with me from breakfast."

Abigail glanced at the clock. It was nigh unto three. Unsure of what to do, she waited awkwardly while he rubbed the towel over his face and neck.

"Where's Lizzie?" he said when he'd finished.

"Sound asleep." Abigail pointed to her bed. Lizzie lay with one leg draped over the edge and a tattered picture book propped open across her belly.

Nathan folded the towel then laid it next to the washbasin. "Just as well. Maybe now she won't ask so many questions or miss us while we're gone."

Abigail folded her hands over her middle, as if by doing so she could calm the nervousness fluttering in her stomach. "Are we going somewhere?"

To her surprise, he smiled and came to stand in front of her. "Into town to question the Chinese. I figured we'd best see to it before you were tempted to break your promise."

She widened her eyes. He'd known all along?

Somehow, he drew all the air from Abigail's lungs as he stepped closer and cupped her chin. "I know how important this is to you. It's important to me too. I hope you know that."

She did. It was reflected in his eyes and in the set of his jaw. She nodded.

Gradually the look on his face changed. His gaze dropped to her mouth, and his cheeks flamed red. Tingling from where he still touched her, Abigail swayed closer. His hand lingered on her jawline and then slid down her arm, slowly, like a caress. Only it couldn't have been, because Nathan still loved his wife—

A knock sounded on the door, jerking them both from the moment.

His gaze remained locked on hers as he dragged his fingers through his hair. "Caroline."

Shivering at the huskiness of his voice, Abigail rubbed her hands over her arms. "Yes."

"I asked her to sit with Lizzie."

"I know."

Still they stared at each other, unmoving, until a second knock propelled Nathan into motion. He strode to the door and yanked it open.

Surprise registered on Caroline's face. She stood with her fist half raised, her mouth slightly agape. "Am I late?"

"You're right on time." His lips stretched into a forced smile, and he motioned her inside. "I appreciate your help, Caroline. Abigail and I need to visit with a few of the Chinese who were present the night of the mine accident. It's best if Lizzie wasn't there."

"Of course." Her skirt swishing softly, Caroline whisked inside, took off her shawl and gloves, and laid them on the table.

Hooking his thumbs in his suspenders, Nathan rocked back on his heels. "Lizzie's asleep. She played outside all morning and came in plumb tuckered."

"Not a problem."

"We shouldn't be long," Abigail added, glancing at Nathan for confirmation.

"Bosh," Caroline said with a wave. "Don't worry about a thing. Lizzie and I will be just fine." She slid a book from her reticule and held it aloft. "In the meantime, look what John gave me."

Abigail traced the gold letters on the cover. Papa used to spend hours engrossed in such books. Back East, his shelves had been full. He'd sold most of them when they were preparing to move to Calico.

"It's *Oliver Twist*," Caroline continued, her voice quivering with excitement. "He knows how I love Dickens. I'm going to read while you're gone."

Abigail reluctantly returned the book. "That was sweet of him."

"Wasn't it?" She hugged the book to her chest, her sigh ringing with contentment. "He's always so thoughtful."

In spite of herself, Abigail felt the slightest pinch of envy—a feeling she quickly squelched. Caroline showed kindness to all, and her unfailing generosity had touched many folks in Calico, herself included. Caroline deserved love and happiness. She deserved John.

Startled by a light touch to her elbow, she looked up to see Nathan studying her through hooded eyes.

"Are you ready?"

She nodded quickly, gave Caroline a brief hug, and then followed Nathan to the door. He lifted her shawl from a hook and held it aloft.

"Temperature's dropping. You might need this."

She took it from him, their fingers grazing, but he turned toward the door before she could read anything in his gaze.

Once they left the livery, Nathan slowed his steps and gave her a sidelong glance. "I figured we'd start with a couple of Orientals who work over at Belle's Saloon."

"The saloon?" Abigail's feet faltered. "But I thought the Calico Hotel—"

Nathan shook his head. "No good. The people there work for Nichols. He owns the houses where they live. I doubt they'd go against his word."

A chill that had nothing to do with falling temperatures shook her. She pulled the shawl tighter around her shoulders. "You think he lied?"

"You don't?"

"I don't know." That much was true. She had doubts, nothing more.

Nathan snorted then took her elbow and guided her across the street. When they reached the saloon, he pulled her aside. "You know what you want to ask?"

Dismay took over. Not really. How did one go about uncovering a lie?

He lifted her chin with one finger until she looked him in the eye. "It'll be all right, Abigail. God—God will give you the words."

Her eyes widened and he chuckled. "Don't worry. I surprise myself lately." He motioned toward the saloon's darkened interior. "Belle is expecting us."

Once again, his actions threw her off-kilter. When had he spoken to Belle? And would she ever stop being surprised by her new husband? Shaking her head, she preceded him inside.

Like before, a handful of men occupied the saloon. The smell, too, remained unchanged. Abigail wrinkled her nose and pressed closer to Nathan. She didn't have Papa's gun, but at least this time she wasn't alone. Strangely, she felt safer shadowed by Nathan's tall presence than she had while cradling a firearm.

"Where is she?" Abigail whispered.

Nathan pointed, and her gaze followed. Belle sat at her table, the customary cup of coffee in her hands. No one spared them a glance as they wound through the round tables to her side.

Belle quirked an eyebrow. "You're back."

To which of them she spoke, Abigail was unsure. She looked to Nathan. He laid his hand on a chair.

"May we?"

Belle dipped her head. Unlike last time, when she'd been roused from her bed by a gunshot, her curls now twisted about her face in perfect little spirals, and she'd taken pains to apply powder to her cheeks. She pushed a half-full coffeepot across the table and motioned toward two empty cups. "Help yourselves."

With questions forming a knot in her throat, Abigail doubted she'd be able to squeeze down a sip of coffee, but Nathan poured her some anyway and more for himself.

Holding the dainty china handle between thumb and index finger, Belle took a sip from her cup. Eyes closed, she savored the brew and finally released a sigh. "That man sure knows how to make a cup of coffee."

She shot a flirtatious wink toward Matt, the bartender, and chased it with a smile. In return, he saluted her with two fingers and then went back to scrubbing the counter.

"So?" she said, returning her gaze to Nathan and Abigail. "What can I help you folks with today?"

Abigail rubbed her palms down her skirt. Where to start? She cleared her throat. "Um—you see—"

Belle quirked an eyebrow. "Sometimes, the best thing is to just say it, honey."

True, but plucking the questions from her dry throat was a lot like picking cotton with bare fingers—it stung. Abigail swallowed. "You see—I was wondering if maybe—" Desperate, she looked to Nathan for help.

She read only encouragement in his hazel eyes. He smiled,

reached over, and squeezed her hand. Gentle as it was, it gave her the confidence she needed. She turned to Belle.

"We'd like to question a few of your employees."

"My girls?" Belle's eyes widened in surprise. "Whatever for?"

"Not the girls." Abigail scanned the room. Just as Nathan had said, a couple of Oriental men—one old and bent, the other young but obviously related—lugged soiled linens down the stairs in large woven baskets. No doubt they were on their way to a washtub to launder them. With a tip of her head, Abigail motioned in their direction. "Them."

Suspicion darkened Belle's face, and her painted lips thinned in disapproval. "I'd rather you spoke to the girls. They, at least, can take care of themselves."

Surprised at the protectiveness in her tone, Abigail floundered for words.

Nathan came to her rescue. "We mean no harm, Miss Belle. It's just…" He paused and looked at Abigail. Sensing that he waited for her approval before he continued, she gave it with a slight nod. Whatever he meant to say, she trusted him. His eyes flashed with pleasure, and then he leaned forward and laid both arms on the tabletop.

"A few days ago, Abigail found out that Gavin Nichols suspects her father of causing the explosion that killed Hui Chen and injured several other miners. Abigail doesn't believe that and neither do I, but before we can prove different, we're going to need to find out exactly what happened that night."

Belle's slender fingers worked her bottom lip as she listened. She looked no less concerned when Nathan finished, and she shook her head. "What has that got to do with Tao and his son?"

"They were there." Nathan crossed his arms on the tabletop. "I saw them come out of the mine after the first rescue effort."

Abigail flinched. Nathan had gone looking for her father after she ran to the livery seeking his help. Of course he would know who'd been at the mine, but she hadn't thought to ask him. She turned pleading eyes to Belle. "We have to start somewhere. Maybe if these men can remember something about that night—"

Belle cut her off with a finger to her lips. Eyes narrowed, she scanned the occupants of the saloon then stood and motioned for them to follow. She didn't wait to see if they would, however. Her silk skirt swaying, she left the bar and mounted the stairs.

Abigail's voice dropped to a whisper. "Where is she going?"

Nathan gave a shrug that said he was as confused as she.

"Should we follow?"

"Do we have a choice?"

After rising, he slid out her chair and directed her toward the staircase. Abigail liked the sensation that came with his gentle touch to her back. It was a feeling of being protected and respected all at once.

At the top of the steps, several doors opened off a narrow hallway. Many overlooked the saloon, but the one farthest from the stairs nestled in a corner and could only be seen if a person stood directly across. That door hung slightly ajar. Nathan pointed. Abigail started that way—until a sugary voice sent pinpricks of irritation needling across her flesh.

"Hello, handsome. Ain't never seen you in here before."

Unseen until that moment, one of Belle's girls lounged on a velvet chaise, her pale skin made even more shocking by the scarlet dress that hugged her every curve. Her lashes fluttered suggestively as her gaze swept over Nathan from head to toe.

Suddenly Abigail understood why cats hissed. She linked her arm through Nathan's and thrust out her chin. "We're looking for Belle."

The girl appeared to be taken aback a moment, before pointing toward the half-open door at the end of the hall.

"Thank you," Abigail began, but Nathan already tugged on her arm. Strangely, she was quite pleased that he seemed as much in a hurry to get away as she.

The room Belle had disappeared into looked more like an office than the boudoir Abigail expected. Though a large bed swathed in a silk coverlet dominated one corner, the rest of the space housed a desk and several bookcases. Even more surprising was the number of books on the shelves. Abigail had nowhere near so extensive a collection.

Belle ushered them inside, closed the door, and then swept around the large desk and sat. "You should know," she said without preamble, "that there's no place in this town that's safe to talk—not openly anyway. I suggest you be a little more careful about where you direct your questions."

Abigail felt a flutter of fear. What did she know that they didn't? She licked her lips. "What about here?"

Belle leaned back in her chair, her fingers laced across her slender midriff. "This is safe enough, I suppose. It won't take long for people to get wind that you came, but at least they won't know what we talked about."

"People?" Nathan asked, gruffly.

Belle said nothing.

"You mean Gavin." It really wasn't a question, but Abigail asked it anyway.

One smooth shoulder rolled in a shrug.

Abigail shuddered. Just how far did the man's reach extend? And if he put a woman as confident as Belle on her guard, what chance did she and Nathan stand?

This time Nathan didn't bother pulling out a chair. He paced the room from one corner of the fancy Oriental rug to the other. Abigail herself couldn't sit. Her nerves were stretched tighter than a fiddle string.

Belle ignored him and prompted Abigail gently. "Time's short. Suppose you get to the point, honey."

Abigail nodded. "Papa's accident—"

"You sure it was an accident?"

It seemed she was determined to interrupt every time Abigail got started. "What?"

Belle's slender brows drew into a frown. "How do you know?"

"Nathan said…"

Belle's gaze swept to Nathan, and Abigail's followed.

His jaw squared, he looked back at Belle. "What exactly are you hinting at, Miss Belle?"

She gave a jaunty toss of her head that set her curls to bobbing. "It's rumors mostly. Whispers. But I pick up on things." Leaning forward, she propped both elbows on the desk and laced her fingers. "What do you know about the mine?"

What was there to know? Abigail shook her head and Nathan followed suit.

"Either of you aware of any rumbling that maybe the silver is petering out?"

A jolt shot through Abigail. What was it Mr. Wiley had said about Papa's suspicions?

Nathan gave a low grunt. "We've heard rumblings, but like you said, they're mostly rumors."

"Well, there are plenty of folk in this town who believe those rumors, except for one. Gavin Nichols keeps arranging to have Orientals brought here to work. Why do you suppose he does that?" She waited a moment and then went on. "He keeps insisting mine production is about to double. Says the increased income will have all of the businesses in Calico booming. The problem is, so far it hasn't happened."

Abigail asked the first question that popped into her head. "What about the Orientals?"

"What about them?"

"You said Gavin 'arranges' to have them brought here. What did you mean?"

As though intrigued by the answer, Nathan drew near and stopped next to Abigail. His hand warmed her shoulder.

Belle's lips thinned. "They pay him. Most times it's everything they own, but they're so desperate for a better life, they're willing to risk everything. Gavin puts them on a boat and ships them all over the country."

"The rent houses." Abigail peered up at Nathan. "Gavin owns all of the ones behind the Calico Hotel."

Belle nodded. "Exactly. So on top of charging them their life savings to come, he puts them up in rundown cabins they can barely afford. He practically owns them."

Nathan circled and plopped into a chair. "I don't understand. What does all of this have to do with Anson's accident?"

Belle's voice lowered, as though she feared being overhead even in the confines of her own bedroom. "Think about it, son. All of

Gavin's profits are tied up in that mine. If word got out that the rumors were true, that the silver was actually running out…"

Abigail felt as though a stone had settled in her stomach. "Papa thought the mine was about to go dry." Her legs shaking, she eased into the chair next to Nathan. "Mr. Wiley said he was working on some kind of report to prove that the mine was losing production. He bought a tablet to keep track of his findings."

Belle quirked an eyebrow.

"What happened to it?" Nathan said.

"I don't know. I never saw it." She grasped Nathan's hand. "Was it in Papa's things?"

He shook his head. "I packed everything that was left at the cabin. Never saw anything that looked like a notebook. Could he have hidden it?"

If he did, she would have no idea where to look. Dismay swirled over her as all three fell silent.

Finally Belle spoke. "Ask your questions. I'll let Tao know it's all right. Just make sure you do it in private."

Abigail's head lifted. "You'll help us?"

She surprised Abigail with her next words. Hesitating, she said, "I reckon I owe you." Her face darkened in a glower and she thrust her finger toward the Orientals' camp. "Besides, Gavin Nichols is a sorry scoundrel making a living on the backs of the poor people he fools into coming here. I'll help anybody who'll stop him."

She ended on a hiss that sent fear bleeding through Abigail's veins. Belle hated Gavin, but was it only the plight of the Orientals that caused it? She couldn't be sure.

Chapter Twenty-four
....

A fiery wave of protectiveness surged through Nathan as he and Abigail left the saloon. His face burned and his hands shook. What if Belle was right? The mine wouldn't be nearly as valuable if the silver was petering out. And if Anson knew about this but not about the prospective sale, it would explain the necessity of keeping him quiet. His notebook might be the key, but the added danger to Abigail left Nathan unable to think clearly.

Grasping her elbow, he pulled her around the side of the saloon into the shadows created by the overhanging roof.

"Nathan?" A tremor cracked her voice as she cast a quick glance around. "What is it?"

He took a deep breath. It didn't help. He paced. "This isn't good. We're going about this all wrong. We shouldn't be charging around town, asking questions."

"What?"

Her eyes rounded with disbelief, which only served to make her look more vulnerable. He steeled himself against the riot of emotions turning his insides to jelly and came to a halt in front of her. Crossing his arms, he said, "From now on, I'll go alone. It's not safe for you and—"

"It's not safe for you, either."

"That's different."

"Why?"

Her chin tilted stubbornly. Convincing her to stay home with Lizzie while he searched for information wasn't going to be easy, but he sure intended to try. He stepped closer.

"You're a woman, that's why, and you're my wife."

"But you said—"

"I know what I said. That was before."

"Before what?"

The tears filling her eyes were making it hard for him to focus. He stared at a crack in the water trough next to the street, where trickles cut tiny little rivers through the dry ground—only that reminded him too much of her tears. He jerked his gaze to the lamps that lined the street. No good. They were just a dim reflection of the light in her eyes.

"Nathan? Before what?"

She braced her hands on her hips and stared at him until he had no choice but to look at her. To his surprise, facing her was much easier than forcing himself to speak the words clogging his throat.

"Before I realized how hard it was going to be to assume responsibility for another person."

That wasn't what he'd meant to say, and yet the words were out before he could call them back.

"What?"

Angered at the way she was making him feel, Nathan stiffened and stuck out his chest. "The livery is my livelihood, Abigail. The work there doesn't stop just because we believe there's more going on at the mine than we thought."

"I know that—"

"I have to provide for my daughter. That means the livery comes first." He held up his hand to cut short her protest. "Now, I intend to do all I can to prove Anson's innocence, but seeing to your safety all day long is only going to slow me down."

With that, her shoulders slumped a bit and her hands slid lower on her hips. "I—I never asked you to do that."

Her lips trembled, and she looked ready to dissolve into tears any second, but he was too angry with himself and the emotions running amok inside to care. He gave a stubborn shake of his head. "You didn't have to. As your husband, that's my job, even if our marriage isn't real."

She flinched, but he forged on.

"Starting tomorrow, I expect you to honor my wishes and stay home. I'll do any digging that needs to be done to get to the truth, but I'll do it alone."

He felt like a brute. Worse, he sounded like one, but he couldn't make himself stop, even when the pain in her eyes made him want to kick himself.

"I—I—"

Something deeper than hurt shone in her gaze. She was angry too. He sucked in a breath and waited for her rant. Waited for her to accuse him of being all kinds of a fool and to say she'd made a mistake in marrying him. Instead, she lifted her chin, squared her shoulders, and looked him in the eyes.

"Fine."

He blinked, certain he hadn't heard right. "What?"

"I said fine."

Grabbing her skirt, she whirled and strode down the wooden boardwalk, her boots thumping her disapproval—but it was Nathan who felt the heel.

A growl of frustration ripped from his throat. Snatching the hat from his head, he jerked his fingers through his hair. Normally he prided himself on his ability to bridle his tongue. What was it about Abigail that made him lose control? Even when he tried to protect her, his words ended up a jumbled mess.

Heaving a sigh, he jammed the hat back on his head then swung off the boardwalk onto the dusty street after his wife.

* * * * *

He'd lied. He'd promised to help her, and now he was going back on everything he'd said and acting like an overbearing brute. Worse than that. A pig.

Abigail's fists tightened on the fabric of her skirt as she marched down the street. How she wished it were his neck instead! Maybe then she could—

"Abigail!"

She ignored Nathan's call and kept walking.

"Abigail, wait."

For what? Another broken promise? The thought wasn't fair, but she swiped angrily at the tears moistening her eyes anyway, glad when the lean-to came into view. Lizzie waved from the half-open door. At her side Dorsey barked a happy greeting, his tail wagging furiously.

Lizzie scrambled to her feet and brushed the dust from her dress, then grabbed Abigail's hand and gave it a tug. "You're back. We made cookies. Miss Caroline let me stir. Come on, I'll show you."

Perfect. Marching up the steps, Abigail grabbed hold of the door and closed it on Nathan's surprised face.

He wanted her to stay home? Fine. But that didn't mean she had to make it comfortable for either one of them.

Caroline stood at the table, a sheet of cookies she had pulled from the oven in one hand and a half-raised spoon in the other. "Hello, dear. How did it—oh."

Spying the look on Abigail's face, she broke off mid-sentence. The pan made a hollow *thump* as she set it on the table, dropped the spoon alongside, and hurried to Abigail's side.

"What happened?"

She could only shake her head for fear that if she tried to utter even one word, she'd erupt into tears.

"Lizzie, honey, would you see to that last pan of cookies for me? Careful now. Mind the pan. It's still warm."

As though she, too, had suddenly become aware of the tension flowing from Abigail, Lizzie gave a solemn nod and walked over to the table, her blue eyes round and fixed to Abigail's face.

"So?" Caroline's voice dropped to a whisper. She grasped Abigail's hands and led her to the rocking chair in front of the window. "Tell me what happened."

Abigail's nose threatened to drip, and her head throbbed from fighting tears. She heaved a sigh that rumbled from deep inside her chest.

"It's all right, honey. It can't be that bad," Caroline said, pulling a handkerchief from her sleeve and handing it to Abigail.

She took it and pressed it to her nose. After tossing a glance over her shoulder at Lizzie, who was patiently sliding cookies off the pan onto a plate, Abigail drew a deep breath and started.

"He lied, Caroline. He doesn't intend to help me at all."

"What? Who?"

"Nathan. He isn't going to help me find out what happened to my father."

Doubt and confusion warred on Caroline's face. She grasped a chair from the table nearby, spun it so it faced Abigail, and plopped down. "I don't understand. Did he say that?"

Abigail hesitated. She wasn't being fair. Shoulders slumping, she said, "Not exactly."

"Then…?"

"He said he wants me to stay home while he does the checking. He doesn't think it's safe for me to go with him when he questions the miners or the Chinese."

Caroline's face cleared and she smiled. "So he's concerned for your safety. Well, then, that makes sense."

Never did it occur to her that her friend would take Nathan's side. She stiffened and crumpled the handkerchief in her lap. "What!" Mindful of Lizzie's listening ears, she lowered her voice and said again, "What?"

Caroline grabbed her hand and gave it a squeeze, her smile a bit too condescending for Abigail's liking.

"Sweetheart, you're just not used to anyone worrying about you—"

"Of course I am. Don't be ridiculous. Papa used to worry about me all the time."

"I know he did, but this is different. It's been you and your father since the time you were ten. You've only been Nathan's wife for a few days. You have to give him time to adjust. It has to be hard on him, having lost his first wife."

The ire in Abigail's belly died a little. She fought to get it back. "I'm just as capable of taking care of myself as any man."

"I'm not saying you aren't. It's just—you have to understand how Nathan sees you."

Abigail paused. She knew how he saw her—as a helpless female who would only get in his way.

CALICO
1883
CA

As though sensing her thoughts, Caroline shook her head. "It's different with men, especially husbands," she said. "They see us as something vulnerable and fragile, something to be protected and cared for. I know your papa loved you, but he never looked at you as a woman. When he saw you, he only saw his tough, tomboy daughter. Nathan sees his wife, and in light of his failure with Charlotte—"

Abigail shot to his defense. "He didn't fail Charlotte. She took sick. Nothing he did could've prevented that."

Caroline patted her hand. "You and I know that, but he doesn't. He thinks he made a mistake, bringing her west. Her death left him with a hole in his heart that hasn't fully healed yet, and rather than risk adding to that hurt, he's bound and determined to do everything he can to keep you and Lizzie safe."

Lizzie, yes, but her?

"Talk to him. Let him know how you're feeling. It'll be all right. You're his family now, sweetheart," Caroline continued. "A man like Nathan takes that responsibility seriously."

Of course he did. Abigail knew exactly what kind of man Nathan was. She'd seen it for herself in the way he cared for Lizzie.

The last dregs of her anger melted from her in waves.

Caroline rose and pressed a kiss to the top of Abigail's head. "Everything will work itself out, I'm sure. I'll stop by tomorrow to see how you're doing."

At Abigail's glum nod, she turned and crossed the room to bid Lizzie good-bye. She then collected her things, slipped into her shawl, and, with a final wave, whisked herself out the door.

Determined not to let Lizzie see her mood, Abigail wiped the last tears from her eyes, forced a cheery smile, and went to the table. "So these are the cookies you and Caroline spent all afternoon baking."

"Uh-huh." She picked up a cookie and held it aloft. "Try one. They're oatmeal and raisins. Miss Caroline brought the raisins."

A rare treat. Abigail took a bite, letting the warm tastes of cinnamon and sugar slip over her tongue. Her enjoyment was short-lived, however, as she thought of Nathan. Somehow they had to find a way to fix the problems between them if they ever hoped to make their marriage work. And she wanted it to. To her surprise, she very much wanted it to.

Patting Lizzie's head, she offered a smile and bent to her level. "They're delicious, sweetie. You two did a wonderful job."

Lizzie's face brightened at the praise. "Thanks. I'll help you clean up now."

"Don't bother. I'll see to the dishes. Why don't you take one of these cookies to your pa while they're still warm?"

She held one up and gave it to Lizzie. Maybe the savory spices would work the same magic on Nathan that they had on her.

"All right." The cookie held flat on her palm, Lizzie skipped to the door. "Be back soon."

Yes, and in the meantime, Abigail intended to clean up the lean-to while she prepared what she needed to say. She'd have to hurry. Suppertime was closing in fast, and she wanted to have the argument with Nathan reconciled tonight.

This time a genuine smile curved her lips as she collected the scattered dishes and carried them to the sink for a soak. Caroline was right. Nathan wasn't arrogant or cruel, and he had no intention of going back on his word. They just needed to talk—work things out. She'd see to it they did that tonight, before any more misunderstandings piled up between them.

Her heart lighter, she set about her chores, listening all the while for the sound of her husband's boots upon the threshold.

Chapter Twenty-five

Frustration thrummed through Abigail's fingers as she bent over a washtub filled with laundry. Jerking her head, she tossed a damp tendril of hair from her eyes and scrubbed Nathan's work shirt even harder over the washboard.

A week.

It had been almost a full week since she'd determined to speak to Nathan, and still the problem between them lay unresolved. He rose earlier than ever, oftentimes before she stirred, and returned late at night, so exhausted he barely took time to eat before dragging himself up the ladder to the loft and flopping into bed.

Lizzie appeared to be oblivious to the situation, though it helped that she spent her mornings at school, far away from the tension filling the lean-to. After school, she chatted happily all afternoon long while Abigail fretted and wondered what Nathan had discovered— or if he was searching at all.

Slapping at the soapy water in the washtub, she gave a grunt. No. She wouldn't believe that he'd become so wrapped up in the livery that he'd ignored the mystery surrounding her father's accident. Surely…

Anxiety piled upon anxiety. She wanted to ask, and determined every day that she would; yet when he stumbled home each night with lines of weariness crisscrossing his haggard face, she couldn't bring herself to voice the words.

"Morning, Abigail."

Always a welcome sound, Abigail lifted her head to watch Caroline approach. Marriage agreed with her. She fairly glowed, and her eyes, though always bright, now sparkled with happiness.

The weight on Abigail's chest pressed harder than ever. Caroline and John shared a love she could only dream about. Banishing the thought from her mind, she dried her hands on the apron bound about her waist and then rose and enveloped her friend in a hug.

"Good morning to you. You're out early."

"I am. John and I are arranging for a cash shipment through Wells Fargo, but that's not till later. I wanted to stop by and see how you're getting along first."

"Wells Fargo, huh?" Abigail took her time in smoothing the apron over her plain brown skirt. "You're going ahead with your plans to buy Mr. Wiley's store, then?"

"We are."

Excitement flashed in Caroline's gaze. She and John had spoken to Mr. Wiley a few days ago, after he'd repeated his desire to pack up his belongings and move to Los Angeles. It seemed only right that Caroline and John take over his business, since apparently John had long dreamed of managing his own mercantile. Even with so many things unsettled in her own life, Abigail was happy for them.

She squeezed Caroline's hand. "Have you time for some tea?"

"I can't." Caroline's lips drooped in a frown. "Sorry. I just wanted to see how you and Nathan—"

Abigail's heart jerked in her chest. She cut her off with a wave. "The same, I'm afraid."

Her friend leaned forward and peered earnestly into her eyes. "Oh, Abigail, you just have to find the time to talk things out. This waiting isn't good for either of you."

"I know," she said, sighing miserably. "But what can I do? He works from sunup to sundown, so when he is home, I can't bring myself to add to his worries." She hesitated and caught her lip in her teeth.

Caroline tilted her head and blinked. "What is it?"

Abigail swallowed. "Oh, Caroline—what if he isn't trying to figure out what happened at the mine? Or hasn't had time to try," she corrected quickly, though not fast enough to halt the wave of guilt that washed over her. Hadn't she seen for herself how tired he was? Was it fair for her to expect so much?

Her mind set, she squared her shoulders and lifted her chin as she realized what she had to do. "What time do you think you'll finish at Wells Fargo?"

"It shouldn't take long. Why?"

"Do you think you could watch Lizzie for me after school? Maybe an hour or two this afternoon?"

"Of course, but—"

Abigail nodded, already feeling lighter now that she had a course of action. "Good. Thank you."

Caroline drew back. "Abigail, you don't plan to go against Nathan's wishes, do you? Not while the two of you still have things to work out."

She gave a stubborn shake of her head. "I don't have any choice, Caroline. Nathan is doing the best he can, but all of this, added to his chores at the livery, is just too much. I have to do something."

Though she still appeared worried, Caroline agreed to come by the lean-to once she and John had finished their business. Abigail happily counted the minutes while she attended her chores. It felt good to know that matters would once again be in her hands, not resting with a husband she barely knew. She'd pulled two loaves of fresh bread from the oven and had a hearty stew simmering by the time Caroline returned in the afternoon.

"You're sure about this, dear?" she asked Abigail, tugging the strings on her bonnet loose. "You're sure you want to go before you've had a chance to speak to Nathan?"

Abigail removed her apron and laid it on the table next to Caroline's bonnet. "Quite sure. Finding out what happened at the mine is my responsibility. I never should have asked Nathan to assume that burden."

"I thought you didn't ask," Caroline said, her eyes twinkling. "I thought he did that all on his own."

Abigail directed a stern look at her friend. While she knew Caroline meant no offense with her teasing, she also knew her friend would like nothing better than to see her marriage to Nathan become something deeper. She shook her finger at her then went to the hooks next to the door for her bonnet and shawl.

"All right, you, that's quite enough of that."

A sigh mingled with Caroline's light chuckle as she followed Abigail to the door. Her face reflected the worry she felt as she helped Abigail with her shawl and then handed her a small silk reticule.

"I'll be back soon," Abigail said softly, injecting a note of confidence into her voice that she hoped would lay Caroline's fears to rest. She slid her wrist through the loop on her reticule and then turned for the door. "Lizzie is out by the corral finishing up her schoolwork. She wanted to sit outside, and I told her it would be fine, since it won't be long before the weather gets too cold."

"I'll check on her."

"Thank you, Caroline. If she gets hungry, go ahead and let her eat. Nathan…" She paused with her hand on the knob. "Well, I guess I've already told you."

"I won't expect him until late."

"I'll be home before then," she promised. She gave Caroline a brief hug and then hurried outside, her feet carrying her in a beeline toward the mining camp.

Like before, a steady hum of activity buzzed through the huddle of makeshift cabins. Skirting a handful of women toiling over cook fires, Abigail wound her way toward a tiny little building near the heart of the camp. Her hands shook, but she swallowed her fear, raised her fist, and knocked. The door swung back a moment later and she stood face-to-face with a scowling woman dressed in black.

"Hello, Mrs. Bailey."

Lines of weariness crisscrossed the tiny widow's face, and despite herself, Abigail found she felt quite sorry for the old woman. Where was the spitfire who'd hurled accusations like stones the week before?

Mrs. Bailey crossed her arms and her lips formed a thin, pale line. "You're back."

"Yes, ma'am. I was hoping to ask you a few questions." Somehow, she'd managed to keep the quaver out of her voice. She peered at Mrs. Bailey for what felt like a full minute. Whatever the woman thought of her or her father, she was determined to show they had nothing for which to be ashamed.

Finally, Mrs. Bailey gave a nod and held the door open wider. "You'd best come inside. It wouldn't be good if Mr. Nichols got word that you and I been talking."

Abigail scooted past her and then stood, waiting, while Mrs. Bailey cast one last glance up and down the street before entering the cabin. Rattling the ill-fitting door until it closed, the widow then walked toward the only furniture in the tiny cabin—a sagging table with two chairs shoved in close. She took one and waved her visitor toward the other.

"Mrs. Bailey—" Abigail began, her fingers toiling over the fringes of her shawl.

"I reckon I owe you an apology."

Abigail's questions withered and died in her throat. "I beg your pardon?"

Mrs. Bailey sighed and clasped her gnarled hands on the table-top. "I know your papa didn't have nothin' to do with that fire. It was my anger that made me willing to lay hold of any explanation I could find, but I ain't had a moment's peace since. I figure that's the Lord's way of showing me what a fool I was, believing them rumors."

Abigail took a deep breath. If God was at work, it certainly wasn't because of her faithfulness in seeking Him out. She shot a silent apology heavenward.

She matched Mrs. Bailey's posture and leaned forward. "Tell me about the rumors. Do you have any idea how they got started?"

For the briefest second, fear flickered in Mrs. Bailey's tired gaze. The old woman fidgeted with the collar of her mourning dress, her fingers working, working, in an endless pattern around the edge. "Can't say as I know for certain"—her eyes flicked to Abigail's and then back to the table—"though I did hear Mr. Nichols's report about the accident hinted at your father's involvement."

Gavin started the rumor? Abigail's heart thumped painfully. Why? All along, he'd led her to believe he wanted to help.

Mrs. Bailey jerked from her chair, as though somehow she was too full of nerves to sit any longer. "Can I get you something to drink? I've got coffee on, or I can heat some water for tea."

Abigail shook her head. "No, thank you." Slipping her hands under the table, she wiped her damp palms on her skirt and then folded them in her lap. "If you don't mind..." The frown lifted from her brow as a sudden thought struck. "Mrs. Bailey, have you or others heard anything about dwindling silver production?"

Mrs. Bailey's face twisted in a decided look of concern. Her gaze darted to the window above the sink, which had been opened a tad to let the heat escape from the old potbellied stove dominating a corner of the kitchen. A kettle of beans simmered on the stove, and alongside it was the coffeepot. She jammed the window closed and then bustled back to the table and plunked herself down.

"Listen, gal, I like you. You got spunk just like your pa, but it ain't good to go round asking too many questions, especially when it comes to the mine."

"You *have* heard something." Abigail said it matter-of-factly, no longer needing Mrs. Bailey to confirm what had become a solid idea in her mind.

The woman's wrinkled hands spread in appeal. "I did, but only after I said those things about your pa the other day. I never would have made them accusations otherwise." She faltered a moment, her lips working silently. "I—hope you can believe that."

Though she regretted that the lines on Mrs. Bailey's face deepened with worry, Abigail couldn't help but press. "Will you tell me what you've heard?"

The severe knot in which Mrs. Bailey wore her hair tugged at the nape of her neck as she bowed her head. It said something about the woman herself—tight, rigid, pinned in place by things outside her control.

"The wives talk," she began hesitantly, "mostly when we're gathered round the washtubs. A couple of the women said their husbands have been worried, but they're keeping their mouths shut for fear of what happened to Anson."

Abigail's breath caught. "They think my father's death wasn't an accident?"

Mrs. Bailey gave a solemn nod. "They're starting to. Or the fire that killed that Oriental, neither. It's only whispers, mind, but the talk is that there's more going on than what first appeared."

"But nobody is saying anything."

"Ain't nobody brave enough. We've all got families to think of, and if the threat of another accident ain't enough, worrying about being put out of a job is."

"You think Gavin would do that?"

Mrs. Bailey's lips pinched shut. Finally she said, "All I know is, my Joseph still works in that mine and I"—she shuddered and then rose—"I've said more than I should. I'm afraid I'm going to have to ask you to move on now."

"But—"

"And don't you bother going to the other miners or their families. It's likely you'd do more harm than good if Mr. Nichols got wind of the fact that you come back to the camp to ask more questions. I only agreed to talk to you because…"

Suddenly she lost the proud set of her shoulders and her face crumpled with shame. "Well, I figured I owed it to ya after what I said about your pa."

Abigail rose too and joined Mrs. Bailey at the door. She hesitated a moment and then patted one of the woman's thin shoulders. "Thank you, Mrs. Bailey. I appreciate your courage."

The old woman gave a quick nod before pulling a handkerchief from her sleeve and pressing it to her nose. "I hope—I'm real sorry if I put you in more danger by talking to you. I'm going to tell you the same thing I told your man—be sure what you're looking for is worth the price you might have to pay later."

So Nathan *had* been by. Abigail shivered, knowing she'd been wrong and he'd somehow managed to keep his word all along. But how? When?

She thanked Mrs. Bailey again and then slipped out the door, thankful for the old widow's sake that the street remained empty. With any luck, no one would even be aware she'd been by.

Catching her skirt in both hands, her reticule swinging from her wrist, she hurried back into town toward the Calico Hotel. Despite Mrs. Bailey's warning, she still had one more person she needed to question, someone Nathan wouldn't know to seek.

Abigail rounded the rear of the restaurant this time, rather than entering through the front. Though she doubted she'd be able to keep her visit a secret, she didn't need the cranky proprietress hindering her from speaking to the Chinese.

Like the mining camp, tiny hovels with sagging roofs formed twin rows, but these were in much rougher condition. How they managed to remain upright, she couldn't imagine. Elderly women swept dust over dirt at the first two places she came to, but neither of them spoke English. She pressed on. At the third house, a young boy sat on the ground, playing with carved wooden animals, while an old man in a rocker picked at a bowl of rice.

Abigail approached cautiously, her fingers clutched around the edges of her shawl. "Hello."

The old man peered at her from beneath shaggy white brows. A grain of rice clung to his lips—startlingly white against the skin burned brown by the sun. He brushed it away with the back of his hand and kept on staring. The little boy, however, jumped up and ran to his side. A slight limp slowed his progress and one shoulder seemed to hitch higher than the other, but it didn't seem to bother him.

Abigail nodded politely to the man. "Good afternoon."

Neither the man nor the child replied. The boy wiggled from foot to foot, his black eyes wide in his round face.

She cleared her throat and tried again. "My name is Abigail Watts—er, Hawk. Do either of you speak English?"

The old man lowered his bowl and mumbled something to the child in Chinese, who whispered something back.

"Please, I'm looking for a woman named Soo. I believe she lives somewhere near here."

At the mention of the name *Soo*, the boy and the old man began conversing rapidly, both of their hands fluttering back and forth in some strange addition to their language. Finally the boy directed his gaze to Abigail.

"My grandfadder want to know, you Mistah Watts's daughter?"

Abigail had no problem deciphering the boy's broken English. She nodded eagerly. "Yes. I'm looking for a young lady about this tall"—she held her hand even with her shoulder—"and about my age. Her name is Soo. She has a little boy named Jiao. Do you know them?"

The little boy bent his head and repeated her words to the old man in Chinese. His eyes narrowing, the old man held out his hand and waggled his fingers. The boy promptly located a cane from behind his chair and placed it in the old man's hand. Bracing himself, he rocked to his feet and then hobbled toward Abigail. She waited while he examined her through milky gray eyes. Finally he nodded and motioned for the boy to go inside.

As though obeying an unspoken order, the boy scurried through the doorway and then returned a few moments later, with the woman Abigail had spoken to at the cemetery in tow. As before, she dipped into a deep bow the moment she caught sight of Abigail and then began chattering rapidly in Chinese with the boy and the old man. All three fell silent at the same time. Looking quite flustered, Soo stepped forward and bowed again.

"Miss Abigail." She said some words in Chinese and then motioned to the boy. Grasping his shoulders, she shoved him forward, indicating that he was to interpret.

"She says it is honor to see you," the boy explained, glancing up for approval. Soo nodded as though she understood.

Eyes wide, the boy waited earnestly for Abigail's reply. She returned Soo's nod and then looked at the boy. "Please tell her it is good to see her again, as well."

While she waited for the boy to translate, she glanced around the camp. As she'd feared, her presence had begun to attract attention, but there was no help for it. She had to question Soo.

She motioned to the rocker the old man had vacated and a wooden bench nearby. "May we sit?"

Soo recognized the motion and, without waiting for the boy's interpretation, eagerly took a seat and then patted the space next to her. Abigail took it and laid her reticule aside. The boy helped the old man resume his place in the rocker with a hand to his bent elbow and then circled around to stand at Soo's shoulder. Abigail offered him a smile.

"You must be Jiao."

The boy nodded.

"It's a pleasure to meet you, Jiao. I heard about you from the pastor." At his look of confusion, Abigail folded her hands as if to pray. "The church?"

"Ah." Jiao broke into a smile.

Soo patted his arm impatiently, and Jiao explained the exchange. She turned her dark eyes to Abigail. "Sumting we do"—she pointed at Abigail—"for you?"

Abigail gave a quick bob of her head. She looked at Jiao. "Would you please explain to your mother that I"—she laid her hand over her chest—"have questions I'd like to ask about my father's accident."

Jiao's brow furrowed at the word "accident," and Abigail made the motion of something exploding, followed by a sound she hoped resembled a bang.

"Ah." The frown cleared and Jiao began to speak rapidly to Soo, who nodded in understanding.

"I wonder," Abigail continued when he finished, "if she or any of her friends have heard anything unusual about the night my father was killed."

"On-you-sul." Jiao frowned as he pronounced each syllable, his dark eyes uncertain.

"Strange. Funny," Abigail added, sticking both thumbs to her temples and waggling her fingers.

Jiao laughed, but when he explained to Soo, her smile faded. She turned to the old man, said something, and then listened while he spoke.

By his tone, Abigail knew he discouraged Soo from sharing with her. She leaned forward to touch Soo's arm.

"Please. I wouldn't ask if it weren't important."

Jiao seemed to sense the urgency Abigail felt and pressed closer to his mother's shoulder while he explained. After what seemed like ages, Soo gave a hesitant nod.

Abigail breathed a sigh of relief and turned to Jiao. "Please ask your mother if there is anything she can tell me about the accident." Once again she made the motion of an object exploding and then realized with a start that she had begun to emulate the addition to her speech that the boy and the old man had used earlier. Jiao translated, rapidly.

Soo shook her head and spoke to Jiao.

"She say nothing on-you-sul," Jiao said, breaking into a wide smile. He sobered and then copied her blowing-up motion. "Black powda start big fire." His voice dropped to a whisper. "Hui Chen killed."

Abigail bit her lip. "Yes, I know. About the explosion—was there any warning? Did any of the men see or sense the danger?"

Jiao repeated her question in Chinese, waited while Soo replied, and then shook his head. "She say no Chinese in the mine when the fire start. Only after, when they look for miners."

"Yes, of course." Her brow furrowed in consternation. The Chinese were not permitted in the mine, so she would have to direct her questions to the things Soo might know. She scratched her head, thinking. "All right, let's talk about the rescue. Several of the Chinese went in to help. Do you think she might be able to tell me their names?"

As Soo began to recite them, Abigail withdrew a short pencil and a scrap of paper from her reticule and wrote them down. These, added to the men Nathan had already given her, made for a lengthy list. Abigail scanned the sheet from top to bottom then turned it over to Soo.

"Is this everyone?"

Soo looked uncertainly at Jiao, who translated and then read the list out loud to his mother. Soo shook her head and pointed to the paper. She said something and then looked at Abigail, her gaze expectant.

"I'm sorry; I don't understand," Abigail said, checking the list once more. "Did I forget someone?"

"She say someone not on list. She say one more man she think in the mine the night your fada killed."

Puzzled, Abigail mentally ticked off the names Soo had given her. "Who? Who did I forget?"

Leaning forward, Soo tapped the paper in Abigail's hands then motioned for Jiao.

He copied her gesture of tapping the paper. "Gavin Nichols. She say Gavin Nichols not on list."

CALICO
1883
CA

Chapter Twenty-six

. . . .

"Gavin Nichols." Abigail shook her head in confusion. *Gavin had been in the mine?* She turned to Soo. "Are you certain? Did you see him?"

Soo looked at Jiao, who quickly translated. She made an up and down motion with her hands and said something in Chinese.

Jiao shook his head. "She not see him in the mine. She say she wash his clothes. See the mine dust. Some of his stuff burned"—he pinched the edge of his sleeve and held it up—"on shirt. Here. She wonder why he not say more before now."

Of course. Like so many of the Chinese, Soo made her living doing laundry for the miners and working at the Calico Hotel.

Abigail leaned toward Soo and touched her hand. "Is it possible that Mr. Nichols's clothes were damaged some other way?"

Soo waited for Jiao and then shook her head and spoke.

Jiao listened a moment and then said, "No. Every day, she wash one shirt for Mr. Nichols. This day, she wash two shirts for him, but these have red dust on the pants and shirt. She say she know he in the mine." Eyes troubled, Jiao fell silent and looked at Abigail.

Abigail, too, felt a stirring of apprehension. Gavin had never said he *wasn't* in the mine the night her father was killed, but he hadn't volunteered the information, either. Was he hiding something?

Thanking Soo and Jiao for their time, she rose, bowed to the old man who had listened to their conversation from the rocker, and then turned and left the camp. If Gavin were somehow involved in the mine explosion, Nathan needed to know. She intended to tell him everything she'd discovered today and then do whatever it took to reconcile the rift between them. But first she needed to find him. Her stride lengthening, she made a beeline for the livery.

* * * * *

There was no helping it; Nathan needed to find Abigail and tell her everything he knew—about the men from San Francisco, his hunch about the sale of the mine—everything. Keeping the information from her wasn't right, regardless of whether the knowledge meant danger to her.

Angered by the thought, he jabbed his pitchfork deeper into a mound of hay and jerked out a forkful, spreading fresh bedding for the horses across the floor with one swift swing. Problem was, all he wanted to do was protect Abigail, and the more he talked with the miners, the more certain he became that she needed his protection—but from whom?

Pausing with his elbow propped on the pitchfork, he tugged a hankie from his back pocket and swiped the sweat from his brow. He'd managed to keep up with his chores the last few days by rising early and working late, but questioning the miners in between times had begun to wear on him. He felt the weariness in his bones. Not to mention he missed Lizzie.

He sighed, worried all over again that in trying to do his best, he'd failed both his wife and his daughter.

"There you are."

Nathan looked up, surprised when Abigail skittered into the

livery, her face flushed as though she'd been running. He reached out and caught her elbow as she stumbled to a stop next to him.

"What is it? Is everything all right? Where's Lizzie?"

"She's fine," Abigail panted. "She's with Caroline. I—I need to talk to you."

Nathan braced the pitchfork against the wall and led Abigail to the water bucket for a drink. Dipping the ladle for her, he held it steady while she took a sip.

"Better?" he said when she'd finished and wiped the back of her hand across her lips.

She nodded.

"All right, then. Why don't you sit down and tell me what this ruckus is about."

He motioned toward a bale of hay; she loosened her bonnet with a shake of her head. Ripping the thing from her head, she smoothed her hair before crushing the hat to her chest, her eyes wide and filled with remorse.

"Nathan, I went to see Mrs. Bailey today."

Taken aback, he crossed his arms and widened his stance. "You did what?"

"I know you asked me not to, but you've been working so late and you've looked so tired—I wanted to help."

He drew a steadying breath, surprised by the rush of anger he felt at the danger she'd put herself in. "Abigail—"

"I know you told me not to, but I just had to do something." Tears soaked her eyes as she stared at him, pleading. "You don't know how hard it's been to sit back, waiting and wondering."

Suddenly, she caught her lip between her teeth and lowered her gaze. "Still, I shouldn't have gone without telling you, and I'm sorry."

She was apologizing? Much as he would have liked to let her play the villain, he couldn't, not when he was as much to blame as she. Letting go a sigh, he crossed to her and gently lifted her chin until she looked into his eyes.

"It's my fault. I should have told you what was going on instead of making you guess at what I've been up to. Anson was your father. You have a right to know."

A shiver shook her, and when she blinked, the tears that had been balancing on the tips of her lashes spilled over.

Nathan pulled his hankie out once more and brushed at her damp cheeks. "I'm sorry, Abigail. Don't cry. Please. There's so much I need to tell you—"

She stilled beneath his touch. "I know you've been to the mining camp. Mrs. Bailey said she spoke to you."

He nodded.

"That's why you've been coming home so late—because you've been talking to the miners."

He shrugged. "For all the good it's done. They've all pretty much said the same thing—Anson caused the explosion."

"But I got the impression from Mrs. Bailey that the men are sticking to that story out of fear of Gavin Nichols."

Tucking the hankie back in his pocket, he recalled the unease with which the miners answered his questions, if they spoke to him at all. "I got the same feeling. Unfortunately, that's all it is—a hunch."

"Maybe not."

He quirked an eyebrow and tilted his head at her. "Meaning?"

Her face flushed redder than before, and she stammered as she spoke.

"A–after I left Mrs. Bailey's, I went to see one of the Chinese women."

Once again, Nathan's heart raced. He straightened, and his hand clutched the top rail of the stall beside him. "You what?"

"Before my father died, he helped this woman's child," she went on quickly. "I thought maybe she'd be inclined to help me or at least answer some of my questions."

He couldn't let her see his face, or she'd know how afraid he was for her. Turning, he rubbed his hand over his eyes until he was calm enough to speak. When he looked back, she stared up at him, the bonnet still crushed to her chest.

His speech carefully controlled, he said, "Well? Did she?"

"Help?" Her countenance brightened as she nodded. "Her name is Soo. She does some of the laundry for the Calico Hotel and for Gavin. She told me she washed two sets of clothes for him that day, one of which looked as though it was coated with red dust from the mine. The sleeve was burned too," she added, plucking at her dress. She crossed to him and grasped his arm. "Oh, Nathan, do you think this means he had something to do with the fire?"

He paused, thinking. "What reason could he have? It just doesn't make sense."

Abigail's shoulders slumped, and then she looked up, her grip on his arm tightening. "The silver production."

"What?"

"I asked Mrs. Bailey about it. She said there were rumors that the silver was petering out. Remember, Papa thought so too. He'd bought a notebook from Mr. Wiley so he could keep track of how much ore they dug out from the mine."

Nathan's mind whirled as he remembered his conversations with Anson regarding the mine. If Anson was right and Gavin had gotten wind of his findings—that certainly would have put a damper on the sale of the mine.

She shrugged as she continued. "I just wonder where he put it. I've searched..." She trailed off, and a look of horror crossed her face.

Nathan's chest tightened and he placed his hands on her arms. "What is it? What's the matter?"

"The night Justice broke in, he was looking for something. I thought it was just the money, but what if—"

He quickly saw her reasoning. "What if Gavin hired him to find that notebook?"

Eyes wide, she swallowed then shook her head. "It's too much speculation. Why would Gavin go to so much trouble and risk being caught, based on one man's suspicions?"

"I think I might know the answer to that." Nathan carefully explained what he'd learned about the men from San Francisco and his hunch regarding the reason behind their visit. "So you see," he said as he finished, "your father's suspicions may have been a lot more troublesome than we thought—and a lot more costly."

"Because the mine wouldn't be worth as much."

He nodded then clenched his jaw. "Abigail, did you see whether Justice took anything other than the money before he left?"

She covered her mouth with her hands, shivering as she relived the fear from that night. "I don't think so. It's possible, but I couldn't prove—I mean—I blacked out for a second when he hit me...."

With each word, she shook a little harder until Nathan felt compelled to pull her close and soothe away her fears. After a moment, he gave in to the desire to press his lips to her hair.

"All right. It's all right," he murmured, breathing deep of the rose scent that clung to her clothes and skin. She burrowed into his shoulder, stirring an ache in his heart that only intensified when she slipped both arms around his waist and clung tightly.

Closing his eyes, he bit back a groan. As hard as he'd tried to keep her at a distance, this woman had gotten under his skin, and now all he could think of was the danger she faced. It scared the fire out of him, left him feeling weak as a kitten. Yet somehow he had to find a way to shield her. Failing her the way he'd failed Charlotte would nigh kill him. He drew back and peered into her eyes. First he had to tell her the way he truly felt, or she wouldn't trust his reasons for keeping her out of harm's way.

"Abigail—"

A shrill voice cut the words from his mouth. "You there, livery-man. Can you help me?"

Drawing a quivering breath, he eased from her slightly and glanced toward the livery entrance. Two women stood there, one short, the other tall and slim, and both wearing the same disapproving frown. The taller one spoke.

"We're looking for a young lady by the name of Abigail Watts. Do you know her?"

Abigail straightened and pulled the rest of the way from him. "I'm Abigail Watts"—she glanced at Nathan and then back at the women—"Hawk. Can I help you?"

The two women exchanged looks and then folded their arms, a comical copy of each other with their piercing eyes and austere clothes.

"You can't possibly be the person we're searching for," the shorter woman said, shaking her head. "The girl we're looking for isn't married."

"Not at all," said the taller one, pushing her rigid shoulders back even farther. "You see, young lady, the person we're looking for is our sister's daughter. We've come to take our niece home."

Chapter Twenty-seven

....

The aunts.

Abigail's breath caught as she stared at the two women, who were each in their own way a life-sized copy of the photo she kept of her mother. Her legs shaking, she stepped toward the taller of the two women.

"Aunt Vivian?"

The woman's sharp eyes narrowed. Tugging a pair of gold-rimmed spectacles from her reticule, she held them up and peered at Abigail for what felt like a full minute. The shorter woman also stared, her mouth slightly agape.

"Well, I'll be," the tall woman said. "You certainly look like her." She tucked the spectacles back inside her bag then gestured once to herself, once to her companion. "I'm Hester Jane. That's Vivian."

The feathers on Vivian's hat quivered. "How do you do?"

Abigail's heart raced. She'd sent word to the family back East about her father's death, but she'd never expected a visit. A card perhaps, or a letter, but when neither had arrived, she'd begun to think they would ignore the news completely.

She tossed about in her mind for the words to say, but they refused to come, and with each passing moment, the aunts' glares became more critical.

Nathan stepped forward, his hand outstretched. "Ladies, it's a pleasure to make your acquaintance. I'm Nathan Hawk."

"M–my husband," Abigail stammered, somehow finding her voice.

The aunts gasped, staring first at her and then at Nathan. Slowly, Hester Jane accepted his hand, with the barest touch of her fingers. "You own this livery?"

He nodded. "If you have animals in need of care—"

"We came by the stage," Vivian interrupted, trilling the words like the proper little sparrow she resembled. "It was a frightful trip. I've never been jostled so." She pressed a jeweled hand to her chin. "My teeth even hurt."

"Don't be so dramatic," Hester Jane said, cutting her sister short with a scowl.

If Vivian was a sparrow, Hester Jane was a raven. Lifting her slender white fingers to the high collar of her black traveling dress, she preened a moment then narrowed her eyes and peered at Abigail.

"I suppose we have much to discuss. We'd best get on with it. Neither my sister nor I have any desire to remain in this dusty little town a moment longer than necessary."

Abigail's manners came tumbling back in an instant. She motioned in the direction of the lean-to. "Please, allow me to show you to our home. We can talk there. You have bags that need to be delivered?"

Her hand to her mouth, Vivian gawked at the door of the lean-to, her brown eyes wide in her scrawny face. "Oh, Hester, we've come just in time."

Hester Jane's lips pursed in disapproval. She jabbed her bony finger past Vivian toward the lean-to. "What—is—that?"

A rash of ire swelled from Abigail's midsection. How dare the old biddies be so critical after Nathan had worked so hard? Nathan opened his mouth to speak, but she stopped him and slid her arm through his.

"That, my dear aunts, is our home."

"Oh my," Vivian whispered, her hand sliding from her mouth to clasp her throat.

Hester Jane sniffed. "Yes, well, it's obvious the direction Anson's choices have led." She whirled before Abigail could reply and latched onto her sister's arm. "Come, Vivian." Turning sharp eyes to Abigail, she said, "We're staying at the Calico Hotel. You may come by for tea in an hour. Try not to be late. It's best we get things settled as quickly as possible."

Ignoring Nathan completely, she swept from the livery with her sister in tow.

For several seconds, neither she nor Nathan spoke, choosing instead to watch the swirl of dust motes left in the aunts' wake.

"Your mother's sisters?" Nathan said, still facing the door.

Abigail swallowed. "I'm sure she was nothing like them."

Nathan shrugged. "I don't know. The little one seemed nice."

The words hung in the air a moment, and then both of them burst out laughing. Only then did Abigail realize she still had hold of Nathan's arm. Her mirth fading, she lowered her gaze and dropped her hand.

Nathan cleared his throat as though he too became uncomfortable in the same instant as she. "What do you suppose they want?"

A shiver traveled her spine as Hester Jane's words came echoing back.

"We've come to take our niece home."

They'd come to take her back to Virginia? But that meant leaving...

Her heart thumped as she peered up at Nathan. He said nothing, his gaze measuring the expression on her face, the set of his jaw stern.

"I suppose I should go see them."

His face hardened and he crossed his arms. "I suppose so."

Her stomach sank. "Or we could go home and finish our discussion. The aunts can wait. Nathan—"

He shook his head, but it was the look in his eyes that halted the words in her mouth. Somehow she'd made him angry—or disappointed him. Both possibilities wounded her to the quick.

"Speak to them, Abigail. Find out what they want. We'll decide what to do after that."

He spun on his heel and was at the door almost before she could think.

"Wait. Where are you going?"

"To get Lizzie."

He didn't bother looking back as he said it, though why he should suddenly despise her so, she couldn't fathom. Brushing aside tears, she propped her hands on her hips and stomped her foot.

"Fine!" she yelled, jutting out her chin. "I'll let you know what I find out."

Whether or not he heard, she didn't know. He kept walking.

Abigail's anger died in the span it took her to reach the Calico Hotel. She'd come to the livery intending to reconcile with Nathan, not damage things further. Were all marriages so filled with angry words and hurt feelings?

A picture of Caroline's happy face popped into her mind. She and John spent most of their time smiling and stealing quick kisses, but when a cross word did pass between them, they resolved it before they attempted anything else.

No, Abigail feared her tense, stressful marriage was a condition unique to her and Nathan. Still, she'd run by the general store when she finished with the aunts and seek Caroline's advice.

Inside the hotel, a chorus of voices drifted from the dining room. It was nigh onto dinnertime, and the restaurant was full. Abigail scanned the faces. Her aunts were not hard to find. The feathers on Aunt Vivian's hat quivered as she spoke, and Aunt Hester Jane's proud head rose high above many of the others, her sharp eyes missing nothing as she scrutinized the occupants of the room.

Unlike the other patrons, the aunts did not have heaping plates set before them—only a simple teapot and three china cups. Abigail couldn't help but realize that one of them was for her, and by the aunts' estimation, she was late, regardless of whether a full hour had passed.

She hastened to the table, curious to discover why they'd ventured a trip without first writing to inquire how she was faring.

"There you are," Hester Jane said. She indicated the teapot with a tilt of her head. "Vivian."

Vivian's fingers trembled as she did her sister's bidding. She slid the cup across the table and patted the chair next to her in a gesture for Abigail to sit.

"Here you are, dear. Won't you join us?"

Curiosity overwhelmed her. Abigail took the seat Vivian indicated, but rather than accept the tea, she folded her hands in her lap.

"The food here is quite good," Abigail began hesitantly, "if either of you are hungry."

"At this hour?" Hester Jane sniffed. She pulled a watch from a pocket of her fitted jacket and peered at the time. "Why, it's barely five o'clock."

But without the entertainment the large cities had to offer, Calico's social life was restricted to barn dances on Saturday nights or the occasional wedding celebration. People worked hard and went to bed early the other six nights of the week. Abigail started to explain, thought better of it, and reached for her teacup.

"I suppose you're wondering why we came all the way out here," Vivian said, her soft voice a clear contrast to her stern sister's.

Abigail swallowed her sip of tea then replaced the cup on the saucer. "I am a bit curious."

"You are Olivia's daughter. That makes you blood, regardless of who your father was," Hester Jane interjected. "We've come to rescue you from this sand pit and give you a proper upbringing—something no amount of talking could convince your father to do."

Confused, Abigail lifted her hand. "Wait, you spoke to my father about caring for my upbringing?"

Vivian's head bobbed like a cork. "Only we couldn't make him listen."

Suddenly, the notion of relatives who cared nothing for her and who had deliberately turned their backs on her and her father flew out the window. Misguided as their reasoning had been, her mother's sisters had attempted to have a part in her life.

She shook her head. "But I thought—"

"That we'd deserted you?" Vivian patted her hand. "That, too, was Anson's doing. He disapproved of our lifestyle, accused us of having been ruined by money, and vowed he'd not let the same happen to his only daughter. We didn't want to stay away. We were just adhering to his wishes."

It was too much to be assailed with all at once. Covering her face with her hands, she attempted to sort through her jumbled thoughts.

"We have distressed you."

Abigail lifted her head. Hester Jane studied her through eyes softened by kindness, her face finally no longer pinched and cold. The moment of compassion was soon dispelled by a stern glower, however.

"We were distressed, too, understand, to find you married and living in a hovel." To the slow shake of her head, she added a *tsk, tsk.* "Still, it's nothing our lawyers back East can't rectify, though it would serve you better to have the situation resolved quickly."

Abigail felt like a leaf tossed about by the force of her aunts' powerful personalities. Still, she didn't like the way they referred to her marriage to Nathan—as though it were a whim to be discarded. "My 'situation.'"

Vivian's patted Abigail's hand. "We're talking about a divorce, dear. It's unfortunate, but given the circumstances, it can't be helped. And don't worry about what the gossips will say. Divorce isn't nearly as frowned upon as it once was. A few dollars sprinkled liberally here and there will go a long way toward expunging people's memory."

Anger gripped her insides. "I'm not sure I understand—"

"A ball, dear. Perhaps even a coming-out party to celebrate your return to Virginia. We'll spare no expense."

The words gave her pause. It had been so long since she *hadn't* considered an item's expense, she couldn't begin to grasp what Vivian offered.

Vivian continued to prattle, but her words were lost on Abigail as she tried to sift through her swirling emotions. Finally, Hester Jane lifted her hand.

"Enough."

Just like that, Vivian fell silent. Like Abigail, she looked to her sister.

Hester Jane took her time refreshing her teacup and stirring in just a hint of sugar. With dainty fingers, she lifted the cup, took a sip, then sat peering at Abigail over the rim.

Well, Abigail could be as patient as she. She waited with her fingers laced in her lap, her gaze locked onto Hester Jane's.

Finally her aunt spoke. "Please accept our apologies. In our excitement, I fear we've overwhelmed you."

That was unexpected. Abigail stiffened.

"Allow me to explain."

Suddenly, Hester Jane's manner became as mild as a kitten's. She took her time recounting the history of Anson's courting Abigail's mother—how the aunts had battled after Olivia's death to convince him that Abigail would be better served growing up in Virginia, and how he had refused. Hester Jane finished with their whirlwind decision to come to Calico to seek out Abigail when they received word of her father's death.

With each word, the lump in Abigail's throat grew larger. According to Hester Jane, the aunts wanted her, had always loved her, and desired to care for her. Looking at their fine clothes and the jewels that adorned their fingers and dripped from their ears, she couldn't help but wonder what it might be like to never want for money again—but only for a moment did she entertain the notion. With a start, she realized she didn't like this side of herself and knew her father wouldn't either. Not to mention Nathan.

Her husband's face and Lizzie's leapt into her memory, bringing with them a hint of a smile to her lips.

"Abigail?"

Jolted from her musings, she looked up to see Gavin weaving through the tables toward them.

He grinned broadly and hooked his thumbs into the pockets of his burgundy vest. "What a surprise. It's not often you grace the Calico Hotel with a visit." His gaze flicked to the aunts. "And who are your guests?"

As Abigail introduced them, Gavin bowed to each of the aunts in turn. "Ladies, it's a pleasure."

Vivian's demeanor changed drastically as her gaze swept over Gavin's handsome figure. She blushed and simpered like a schoolgirl.

"The pleasure is ours," she twittered, her hands fluttering to her chest like twin birds.

Hester Jane cleared her throat, cutting short her sister's flirtatious bout in an instant. Her head tipped at a condescending angle, she motioned to the fourth chair at their table. "Won't you join us, Mr. Nichols?"

Abigail sucked a breath through her teeth. The last thing she wanted to do was to spend time in close proximity to Gavin, but with both aunts urging him to stay, she could hardly protest. To her surprise, he directed a glance her way.

"Do you mind? I would hate to interrupt."

"No interruption," Vivian piped. "We've given our niece so much to think about, I'm sure she's feeling a bit overwhelmed."

"Is that so?" Gavin pulled out the chair, his knee brushing Abigail's as he sat. "I assume it's regarding the purpose of your visit?"

Shocked by the audacity he showed in questioning the aunts about their presence, Abigail stared at them, expecting one of them to verbally chastise him at any moment.

The feathers on Vivian's hat twitched but she remained silent, her head bowed over her cooling tea.

Thinking it odd to see her chatty aunt so silent, Abigail turned to Hester Jane, who sat with lips pursed while she studied Gavin.

"So, Mr. Nichols, what is it you do?"

Abigail hid a satisfied smirk. Good old Hester Jane. Stern as she was, Abigail was surprised to discover that she was beginning to like her.

Gavin handled the change in topic deftly, his fingers smoothing the edges of his mustache. "I work for the mining company. Have for many years. I'm the superintendent, in fact."

"Then you knew my brother-in-law."

"I did indeed." Gavin's lips turned into a sorrowful frown. "Such a tragedy, Anson's passing. I tried to convince Abigail to let me help, but she's a proud woman, much like her father."

The way he said it made it sound like a bad thing, but Hester Jane's chin lifted and she sniffed. "Well, of course she wouldn't accept help from an outsider. She's a Brumsfeld, like Vivian and myself."

Gavin tsked and, to Abigail's horror, reached out to pat her hand. "I'm hardly an outsider, Mrs. Brumsfeld. The Wattses and I have known each other for years, haven't we, Abigail?"

The intimate way he spoke her name, added to the gleaming look in his eyes, made her cringe. As politely as she was able, she slid her hand from beneath Gavin's and laid it in her lap, though she could not bring herself to answer his question.

"Years or not, she is her mother's daughter." Hester Jane spoke the words firmly, leaving no room for argument. Eyes sharp, she tilted her head down and peered at Gavin over her hawklike nose. "And my name is *Miss* Brumsfeld. My sister and I never married."

"Oh—I—forgive me."

"For what?"

"Well, I—just assumed—"

"Do you always assume so much, Mr. Nichols?"

"No. I—"

"Would you care for some refreshment?" Vivian's small squeak came as a surprise, interrupting Hester Jane's assault of Gavin.

Flustered, he turned to Vivian, who was holding the teapot aloft. "Why, I—"

"I don't believe Mr. Nichols is going to have time for tea, are you, Mr. Nichols? We wouldn't want to keep you from your business." Hester Jane's voice was as sharp as her gaze.

Gavin reddened, but he rose from his chair and bowed. "You're quite right, Miss Brumsfeld, though I must thank you for the conversation. It was a pleasure."

Hester Jane inclined her head but, unlike before, did not reciprocate her pleasure. Bumping into chairs from the next table as he backed up, Gavin mumbled his good-byes and left.

Abigail watched in stunned silence. She'd never seen him so flustered, not even when confronted by Nathan. She turned an admiring glance to Hester Jane, who sniffed and turned up her nose.

"I don't like him."

"Hester Jane!" Vivian exclaimed, rounding her eyes.

Calm as could be, Hester Jane took a sip from her cup. "It's true." She cut her gaze to Abigail. "I hope you weren't taken in by that dandy's fancy clothes. He reeks of arrogance and new money."

Abigail's brows lifted. *He* reeked of arrogance?

Hester Jane's lips twitched. "All right, all right. Enough of that. Drink your tea."

Obediently, Abigail lifted her cup.

Vivian made small, distressed noises as her gaze bounced from Abigail to Hester Jane, but neither bothered to explain what had passed between them, a fact which gave Abigail much to consider as she made her way home to Nathan and Lizzie. Something had transpired between Hester Jane and herself—a sort of mutual understanding that was as satisfying as it was surprising.

Her steps slowed as she approached the general store now owned by Caroline and John. Behind her lay the Calico Hotel; ahead, the livery and Nathan. She had family in both places and, for the first time, sensed that the knowledge would tear her apart. As she stepped inside the general store, she could only hope that her friend would offer some direction.

Chapter Twenty-eight

....

Nathan paced the floor of the lean-to, his gaze skipping again and again to the clock above the mantel. Abigail had been gone for over an hour. What could she and the aunts be discussing for so long?

"We've come to take our niece home."

Hester Jane's words stirred a feeling of dread, though why it should be so, Nathan couldn't fathom. He wanted Abigail to be safe and cared for, so why did the thought of her leaving create such a sinking feeling in the pit of his stomach?

Because he wanted to be the one who cared for her and kept her safe.

The thought froze him in his tracks. Behind him, Lizzie collided with his backside.

She giggled and patted his pocket. "Oops. Sorry, Pa."

Nathan looked over his shoulder at her and smiled. "What are you doing back there?"

"I'm walking with you."

Sighing, he picked up his daughter and carried her to the rocker. He'd been so preoccupied with thoughts of Abigail he hadn't even noticed Lizzie. He settled her on his lap and then tilted her chin so she looked him in the eyes.

"Sweetheart, you know how much I love you, right?"

She kissed the tip of her finger and then pressed it to his nose. "Of course, silly bean."

The worry that had been knotting Nathan's gut changed into concern for his daughter. What would Lizzie think, should Abigail decide to go back to Virginia with her aunts? How would she feel?

Certainly Abigail wouldn't up and leave. Not without uncovering the truth about her father. That fact and that alone eased the ache in his chest, but he couldn't lie to himself—it was a temporary reprieve.

He turned his attention back to his daughter and tugged on one of her ponytails. "Lizzie, you like Abigail living with us, don't you?"

Her face split into a smile. "Uh-huh."

"That's good. I'm glad you and Abigail get along. Still, I think I need to warn you, she might not stay with us forever."

The smile faded, replaced by a growing look of terror. "Pa?"

"It's just…" He scratched his head, befuddled. How did one go about explaining divorce to a five-year-old? Or a marriage of convenience, for that matter?

"Is Abigail gonna die?" Her voice broke in a heartrending sob. "What?"

"Momma went away cuz she died. Is Abigail gonna die too?"

Tears sprang to Lizzie's eyes, and Nathan chided himself for having been the cause. "Oh no, sweetheart. That's not what I meant at all."

Lizzie lifted her hands to brush away her tears, but paused midswipe. "It's not?"

Gathering her close, he pressed a kiss to her forehead. "Abigail is fine, sweetheart. It's just that she had some visitors today—family from back East who love her very much and want her to come live with them."

Though the tears stopped, the concern in Lizzie's eyes remained. "But we love her too, don't we, Pa?"

He hesitated, pondering. "Yes, sweetheart," he said at last, his fingers trailing through his daughter's curls. "We do."

"Then why can't she stay with us?"

"Because it's not up to us. Abigail will need to decide for herself if she wants to stay or go with her aunts."

"Abigail has ants?" Lizzie frowned. "Is that like lice, Pa?"

He stifled a chuckle. "Not bugs, sweetheart. Kinfolk."

Lizzie straightened, the set of her chin determined. "Well, I don't care. I'm gonna ask her to stay."

Gently grasping her arms, Nathan turned her so she sat facing him. "Lizzie, as much as we want Abigail to stay, we can't ask her to do something she doesn't want to do."

Her face crumpled with disappointment. "Why not? Why can't we ask her?"

"It wouldn't be fair. Think about how her family would feel. You'd miss her, right?" She nodded. He drew a deep breath, his heart thumping painfully. "Well, so would they."

Lizzie made a *humph* sound and crossed her arms. "I don't care. I want Abigail to stay with us."

He tried to smile but failed and grimaced instead. "So do I, sweetheart."

Steps sounded outside the door. Lizzie sprang from his lap. "Abigail!" Thrusting the door open, she threw herself at Abigail and wrapped both arms around her legs. "You're back."

"Of course I am, silly," Abigail said, laughing as she bent to kiss Lizzie's cheek. "What is all this about?"

"Pa said you—"

"Lizzie." His sharp tone drew both their attention. Nathan lifted himself from the rocker and stood with his hands jammed into the pockets of his trousers. "Run upstairs and change for bed. It's getting late."

"But—"

"Now."

She grabbed a lock of hair and popped the end into her mouth—something she hadn't done in months—and trudged up the ladder.

Lord, please help me, Nathan thought, his hand tearing through his hair. He was a horrible father, but lately Abigail had made him think that things would turn out all right—that she'd make up for what he lacked. God knew how desperately Lizzie needed a mother. Would He see fit to take Abigail from them when their marriage had only just begun?

Left alone, he and Abigail stood facing one another, neither one breaking the silence. Finally he motioned to the table and joined her as she sat.

"How did it go?"

Her hands fluttered back and forth, from the tabletop to her lap. She was nervous. Probably wondering how she would tell him that she was leaving. His jaw clenched while he waited.

"Better than I expected," she said, breaking into a smile.

Nathan's stomach sank.

"There's so much I never knew—so much Papa never told me. Aunt Vivian said they actually tried to convince him to let me stay in Virginia with them, but he refused."

"Really?" He forced a smile.

"Yes."

She chattered on, her voice and face becoming more animated as she spoke, yet with each word, Nathan felt the crevice splitting his heart broaden. His worst fear was realized. Abigail was leaving Calico.

* * * * *

Abigail lay in bed, staring up at the shadows dancing across the ceiling. A thunderhead had moved in as the sun went down, and as a result, bright flashes of lightning filtering from the windows created odd patterns of darkness and light against the timbers. A harsh wind lashed the lean-to, but built by Nathan's skilled hands, the place stood strong. She barely noticed the howling storm outside.

Normally she slept most soundly when rain pattered against the walls, but tonight her mind was too full, too busy with thoughts of the aunts, Virginia, and her father to be able to sleep.

She flipped onto her side, a curious sadness making her eyes brim with tears. She hated to admit it to herself, but deep down, she had hoped the aunts' arrival would somehow prompt a confession of his feelings from Nathan. Instead, he'd seemed happy to learn they'd come in hopes of convincing her to leave. She beat on her pillow with her fist.

Why, God? Why did You let me marry him?

Why couldn't the aunts have come sooner and stopped her from making such a foolish mistake?

No, her marriage wasn't a mistake. Her only fault was in having let herself fall for a man who didn't return her love. She closed her eyes against the pain wracking her heart. He'd warned her, and still...

Clutching the blankets to her chin, she forced her thoughts to turn to Lizzie. She'd seemed so happy to see her this afternoon, even acted as though she wanted to tell her something, before Nathan interrupted and sent her to bed. In fact, Nathan had seemed about to tell her something in the livery, just before the aunts arrived. What could it have been?

Oh, what did it matter? Balling the covers in her fist, she pressed her fingers to her mouth to stifle a growing sob. Nathan was happy the aunts had come, and once she figured out what really happened the night her father died, she'd leave Calico with them.

Forever.

Chapter Twenty-nine

....

Just like the days prior to the aunts' arrival, Nathan rose and left the cabin long before Abigail stirred the next morning. She groaned as the sun peeking through the window beat against her swollen eyelids. Given her ragged emotions last night, she was surprised she'd slept at all.

Tossing back the covers, she slid her stockinged feet from the bed, rubbed the sudden chill from her arms, and padded to the stove to heat a pot of water for coffee—except Nathan already had a pot warming.

His thoughtfulness only served to intensify the sad feelings left over from last night. Pulling out a chair, she plopped next to the table and dropped her throbbing head onto her arms. If only she and Nathan had been given more time to figure out what their marriage could be...

No. She refused to allow herself to dwell on such thoughts. They would only lead to more heartbreak.

Rising from the table, she crossed to the washbasin and splashed frigid water on her face and arms. Afterward, she took her time twisting her hair into a neat knot then climbed the ladder to the loft to rouse Lizzie.

The child slept with her fingers curled around the edges of a blanket, her cheeks flushed and rosy, her hair tousled. She looked like an angel.

Abigail swallowed the sudden lump in her throat and gently patted Lizzie's back. "Up, sleepyhead. The day's a-wastin'."

Lizzie groaned and flopped onto her other side, pulling the blankets up over her head at the same time. "I—li—red."

Muffled by the blankets, her words came out as a jumble of half-formed sounds.

Abigail laughed and tugged the covers from her face. "What did you say?"

"I said I'm still tired…." A yawn cut off her next sentence.

"You'll feel better once you get some breakfast in you. I'll make pancakes," Abigail wheedled. "Sure you don't want to get up?"

A curl flopped over Lizzie's eyes as she shook her head.

"All right, then I guess I'll have to feed your pancakes to Dorsey." Abigail retreated a step and put one foot on the top rung of the ladder.

One of Lizzie's eyes cracked open. "Dorsey's here?"

"I think so. What do you say we go take a look?"

As if drawn by unseen strings, Lizzie slipped from her pallet and knelt by the window. She pointed. "There he is."

"See? I told you."

Scrambling for the clothing she'd discarded on the floor, she started to yank her nightdress over her head until Abigail stopped her.

"No way, young lady. Breakfast first, then a wash. Dorsey will wait."

Her lips formed a pout. "Aww."

Abigail laughed as she climbed down the ladder. She'd miss these morning chats.

The thought left her with a heavy heart as Lizzie scrubbed her face clean and then raced through breakfast. Once they'd washed the dishes and finished straightening the lean-to, Abigail opened the door and let Dorsey sit by Lizzie's side while she twisted the girl's hair into two neat braids.

"Do I have to go to school today, Abigail?" Lizzie rubbed the top of Dorsey's head from the tips of his ears to the end of his nose.

Abigail hesitated, her fingers woven between three bunches of Lizzie's hair. "Actually, I have someone I'd like you to meet. Two someones, to be specific."

"Your aunts?" Lizzie grabbed the end of the braid Abigail had already finished and shoved the tip into her mouth.

Almost absentmindedly, Abigail swept the hair from Lizzie's face. "How did you know about the aunts?"

"Pa told me. He said—" She broke off, her eyes wide.

Letting loose of the braid, Abigail turned Lizzie to look at her. "He said what, sweetheart?"

Her face drooped into a frown. "You might leave and go back to your old home 'cause the aunts love you. But we don't want you to, Abigail. We love you too."

Wrapping her in a hug and giving a squeeze, Abigail wished Lizzie's words were true. Nathan was a kind man and he cared for her, but love? She didn't think so.

"C'mon," she said, drawing away and resuming the braiding of Lizzie's hair. "Let's get you finished up and then you can walk with me to the Calico Hotel to meet my aunts."

"All right," Lizzie said, still pouting. "But I won't like them."

In fact, her pout was still in place when Abigail introduced her a half hour later.

Vivian leaned across the settee where she perched and shook Lizzie's hand. "It's very nice to meet you, dear," she cooed.

"Very nice to meet you too," Lizzie repeated, but by her scowl Abigail knew she didn't mean it.

Turning to Hester Jane, she scooted Lizzie forward. "Lizzie, this is my other aunt, Hester Jane. You may call her Miss Brumsfeld."

The two glowered at one another, and though Hester Jane towered over Lizzie, Abigail had a niggling feeling that her aunt had met her match.

Finally, Hester Jane broke the silence. "Are you hungry, child?"

Lizzie shook her head. "No. Abigail fed me pancakes."

One of Hester Jane's thin eyebrows rose.

Bending to Lizzie's ear, Abigail prompted, "It's 'No, ma'am,' Lizzie."

"No, ma'am," she said, though a trifle reluctantly.

Hester Jane sniffed. "A child who pouts is not polite."

"Neither is a grown-up who stares," Lizzie replied, her chin jutting out.

"Lizzie!" Abigail stiffened. She'd never seen the child so obstinate. She could only imagine what her aunts thought. "Please, don't pay her any mind. She was a little tired this morning—"

Hester Jane stopped her with a wave of her hand. "Nonsense. She's quite right." Her eyes narrowed as she examined Lizzie from head to toe. "How old are you, child?"

Lizzie lifted her fingers. "Five."

"You're not in school?"

"I kept her home so I could bring her to meet you," Abigail said. "Lizzie is a very bright little girl, and she's ahead in her studies."

"I assume by that you mean there is an adequate teacher here?"

"A very good one," Abigail said. "The schoolhouse is on the edge of town, across from the mine."

"Nowhere near as accomplished as the teachers back East, I'm sure."

Abigail felt a strange desire to defend Calico's reputation. "We don't have nearly the books or resources, but we do the best we can."

"Hmm." Hester Jane folded her arms and squinted at Lizzie. "Who made your dress?"

Lizzie fingered the cotton folds. "Abigail. Do you like it?"

Abigail bit her lip. It was far easier to defend Calico than to defend herself.

Hester Jane cast a sidelong glance at Abigail. "You're talented. Your mother taught you?"

"Some. I was young when she died."

Vivian's head bobbed. "Olivia loved to sew. She was very good at it."

Hester Jane's lips pursed. "Olivia was good at many things. It's unfortunate that her skills were wasted."

Ire bubbled in Abigail's belly. "My mother was very happy with my father. Her life wasn't wasted."

Once again, Vivian's gaze bounced between her and Hester Jane.

Slowly, the rigid set of Hester Jane's shoulders relaxed. "Forgive me. I was out of line." She motioned toward the velvet-covered chairs situated next to the fireplace. "Will you stay and visit awhile? I'd like to get to know you both"—her glance included Lizzie—"better."

Though Hester Jane's words still stung, Abigail nodded and took one of the chairs she indicated. For the next hour, Lizzie regaled them with tales of Dorsey and school, and Abigail enjoyed seeing how the aunts interacted with her. She couldn't help but wonder how they would have responded to her, had she remained in Virginia. By the time they rose to leave, Lizzie seemed reluctant to say her good-byes.

"You will come see us again?" Vivian said, patting the top of Lizzie's blond head with affection.

Giving a nod, Lizzie smiled and turned to Hester Jane. She looked up, the end of her braid tucked into her mouth.

"That's a bad habit, you know," Hester Jane said with a sniff, "sucking on your hair."

Her eyes solemn, Lizzie opened her mouth and let her braid fall out. "So is frowning. It makes your face all wrinkly. My papa said so."

"Lizzie," Abigail chided, but Hester Jane's chuckle made her look up in surprise.

"Right you are, my dear." She bent until she looked Lizzie in the eyes. "So then we'll both try to do better. Agreed?"

She stuck out her hand to Lizzie, who took it and gave it a shake. "Agreed."

A moment later Abigail ushered Lizzie into the hall, the aunts' laughter ringing behind them. At the bottom of the stairs, a familiar voice pealed.

"I don't care if they can use the food, Mrs. Baker. It's not my job to provide charity for the Chinese."

Gavin? Abigail clasped Lizzie's shoulder and tugged the little girl closer.

Around the corner, just outside the kitchen door, Abigail glimpsed Mrs. Baker's reddened face and Gavin Nichols's obstinate, angry one.

"I wouldn't call it charity, Mr. Nichols. It's just good sense. The food will only go to waste, and then we'll have to throw it all away. It's hard enough keeping them stray dogs from digging through our trash as it is. Why not give it to Hui Chen's widow? Heaven knows, her and that new baby of hers could use the scraps. I've seen scarecrows with more meat on their bones."

Gavin lifted a finger and jammed it under Mrs. Baker's nose. "Just see to it that any leftovers from the restaurant go to slop my hogs or feed my cattle, understood? That's what I pay you for."

He stormed toward the dining room but caught sight of Abigail and Lizzie standing shocked and silent in the hall. His hand on the banister, he paused mid-stride, cast a glance over his shoulder at Mrs. Baker, and then focused on the two of them.

"Abigail and Lizzie Hawk. A pleasure to see you again, ladies." He tipped his head, amazing Abigail at the speed with which his countenance changed.

Behind him, Mrs. Baker snorted and muttered beneath her breath, her bulk swaying as she moved into the kitchen.

"Hello, Gavin," Abigail said, tightening her hold on Lizzie.

"Here to see your aunts?"

She nodded. "And introduce them to Lizzie."

"Really? I rather thought—" His voice dropped to a whisper. "Well, I suppose I assumed that their presence meant you would be retiring from Calico."

Aware of Lizzie's listening ears, Abigail stiffened.

"You know," Gavin continued, his brows lifting, "leaving?"

"I know what you meant, Gavin. Why would you assume that?"

"Well, we're all aware of the conditions surrounding your marriage to Nathan Hawk. I just thought—"

She shot a glance at Lizzie's upturned face. "You thought wrong. I do not intend to leave Calico anytime soon."

Gavin's smile froze on his lips. "I see."

Abigail motioned toward the kitchen. "Was that Hui Chen's family you and Mrs. Baker were discussing?"

His mustache twitched. "That? Oh, that was just routine business."

"It didn't sound like it," Abigail insisted. "You did see to it that the rest of my father's wages went to Mrs. Chen, didn't you?"

He stiffened and jammed the fingers of both hands into the pockets of his vest. "Of course."

"Then I don't understand. Why are they in such need of food?"

Anger clouded Gavin's face. "It's not my business to oversee what those Orientals do with their money."

Belle's accusations against him came rushing back, and with them a flash of anger. "But it is your business to take what little they own just so they can slave for you when they get to America, right, Gavin?"

He tipped his head and narrowed his eyes. "What? Who told you that?"

Abigail's sudden courage faltered, and she fell silent.

Gavin growled. "Were the Chinese complaining again? Perhaps a cut in their wages will teach them to show a little more gratitude."

Horrified at the sudden turn, she reached out to clasp his arm. "Gavin, no. It wasn't the Chinese I spoke to."

"Who then?" Added to the twitching of his mustache, his eye ticked in time with the tapping of his foot. "Well?"

"Belle McAllister," Abigail admitted reluctantly. "She was the one who told me that you arrange to have the Chinese shipped here and to other mining camps around the country."

Gavin gave a bark of laughter that sent a shiver straight through Abigail's bones. Even Lizzie pressed closer to Abigail at his response.

"Belle McAllister. Of course." Gavin grunted and pinned Abigail with a glower that dripped condescension. "Did she also mention that she hates me?"

Abigail wanted to sink into the floor. Belle hadn't mentioned it, but Abigail had sure enough sensed it in the tone of her voice. She gave a slow shake of her head.

"Well, she does."

"Why?"

"Why?" Gavin crossed his arms. "Because she owes me, that's why. Who do you think loaned her the money to start that ramshackle place she calls a saloon? Me, that's who. And when she refused to pay up, I had her thrown in jail. Someone bailed her out—I never found out who—and made her back payments for her, but ever since then, Belle has hated my guts. If it weren't for the money she still owes me, I'd never set foot inside her place."

For several slow ticks of the grandfather clock situated in the hallway, neither of them said anything. Finally Gavin leaned forward and looked her in the eyes.

"I'm not the villain you make me out to be, Abigail. I'm just a businessman trying to make a living, same as you."

With that, he turned and strode away, leaving Abigail standing openmouthed in the empty hallway, Lizzie staring up at her.

Chapter Thirty

Determined to catch Nathan before he left the lean-to the next morning, Abigail spent a fitful night listening for his footfalls on the ladder. Sometime before dawn slight scuffling sounded in the kitchen, and she slipped from the bedcovers, already wearing a wrap over her nightdress. Nathan huddled before the stove wearing his trousers, a red undershirt, and a look of surprise.

"Abigail. Did I wake you?" After tossing one last piece of kindling on the fire, he dusted off his hands and rose.

"No—I—" He was devastatingly handsome with his undershirt untucked. She gave a shiver that he mistook for cold.

Grabbing a chair, he pulled it close to the fire. "Sit here and get warm."

She sat, but an awkward silence followed. Compelled to break it, she stood and started for the cupboard. "I'll make some coffee."

"Abigail."

His voice was husky and low, his breath warm upon her bare neck. Aware of his proximity, she froze, afraid to move, afraid to breathe. He grasped her arms, gently turning her until she had no choice but to look into his face.

"I'm glad you're awake. We need to talk."

Her heart tripping against her ribs, she let him lead her back to the table. Until this moment, she'd held onto a slim hope that Nathan would ask her to stay. It was obvious by his desire to get this conversation over with—the one where he told her he was happy the aunts had come for her—that her slim hope had been false.

She sat at the table with her palms down on the top. Tears threatened, but she held them back by steeling her jaw and willing resolve into her shaking limbs.

"I'm glad your aunts came to Calico—"

"Belle McAllister hates Gavin Nichols."

"What?"

Despite the fact that she'd tried to prepare herself for what he'd been about to say, she wasn't ready to hear it. She nodded. Fists clenched, she buried them in the folds of her nightdress. "I spoke with him yesterday, when I took Lizzie to meet the aunts. I just didn't have a chance to tell you."

Elbows propped on the tabletop, he leaned forward. His eyes glittered in the dim light of the lantern. "What does that have to do with your father?"

"Remember when Belle told us about the Chinese immigrants and how Gavin cheats them out of their life savings because they'll pay any amount to get here? He claims Belle only said that because he foreclosed on some money she owed him. He even had her tossed in jail. Someone bailed her out, but she's hated him ever since."

She could see the news percolating in his mind. To her surprise, Nathan reached across the table, took hold of her chin, and gently caressed her jaw with his thumb.

"We'll find out what happened, Abigail. I promise you, I won't rest until we know the truth."

With that one simple movement, her heart leaped. She stared into his eyes, hoping for a glimpse of the man behind the strong exterior, some clue as to his feelings—but he pulled away too quickly.

"I'd like to go to the Chinese camp today," she began, hoping to draw him close again.

He ran the back of his fingers against his stubbled chin. "More questions?"

"Actually, it's to see the Chens."

"Hui's family?"

She nodded. "I overheard Mrs. Baker telling Gavin they're in desperate need of food. I thought maybe I'd take them a basket—that is, if you don't mind."

"I think that's a wonderful idea." Pride warmed his voice—at least, she hoped that's what it was. His brow furrowed. "But I thought they had the money from Anson's last paycheck to help them get by."

"They did, according to Gavin."

Nathan shrugged. "Well, I'm still concerned about you going alone, but I guess it's a good idea"—he hesitated, and his steady gaze settled over her—"for both your sakes."

She quirked an eyebrow.

"Lin Chen needs to know that you care about her and her family, and you—you need to know that she doesn't hate you or hold you to any blame."

Sudden insight flashed into her brain. "You spoke to her."

This time he took hold of her hand and held on tight. "I did. She's an amazing woman, Abigail. Strong. Full of faith. She reminds me of you."

With every ounce of her being, she resisted the urge to lean forward and settle into his embrace. This was a temporary reprieve. Hadn't he started to say how glad he was that the aunts had come and she'd soon be leaving? She wouldn't risk damaging any more of her heart.

"Thank you," she whispered softly, sad when he pulled his hand away and smiled.

"Would you like me to go with you? I can leave the livery early."

The temptation was great, but she already owed him so much, and no good could come from spending even more time in his company—not when she already wondered how she would fare once she left Calico for good.

"No, that's all right. It's Saturday. Lizzie will be home. I'll take her with me. I want to visit with my aunts after I finish there, anyway."

He lowered his gaze to the table, probably in an attempt to hide his relief. After a moment, he propped both hands on his knees and pushed to his feet. "All right, then. I suppose I'd best get a move on."

Abigail rose too. "Do you have to? I could make some breakfast."

To her surprise, pain shadowed his eyes before he looked away. "Uh—no, thanks. I'm—not really hungry."

Her heart gave a lurch. Not hungry, or not in any mood to stay here with her? Once again she found herself fighting tears.

Without another word, Nathan turned to go, snagging his hat and a shirt from a hook on his way out the door. It closed with a *bang*, leaving her standing alone in the empty room.

So she was right. He couldn't wait to get away. With that knowledge, Abigail's heart shattered into a thousand tiny pieces.

* * * * *

Nathan strode toward the livery, finding his way by the feeble light of the setting moon and memory.

From the moment Abigail slipped into the kitchen, quiet as a whisper and more beautiful than the sunrise, he'd felt a dull ache

CALICO
1883
CA

start in his chest. It had only intensified when she refused his company in favor of Lizzie's. Obviously she regretted the decision to marry him—even more now that the aunts had come to fetch her home from Calico. Their marriage was a farce, born of necessity, not love. He shouldn't be surprised, and yet...

A part of him had held onto a slim hope that she would come to love him. He'd claimed it was him that would need to learn to love again, to let go of the past and embrace their future together. What a fool he'd been. He'd fallen in love with Abigail the moment she set foot in his life, only he hadn't been willing to admit it.

A donkey's bray greeted him as he entered the darkened livery. No moonlight brightened his way here. He'd need a lantern.

His fingers shook as he fumbled with a match, though he finally managed to get the thing lit and the lantern hung from a nail next to the door. Even with the small circle of light, most of the livery remained in shadow.

Much like what his life would be like when Abigail left town. Lizzie would provide a circle of light, but without Abigail...

A shudder shook his limbs. Too well he remembered the dark days that followed Charlotte's death. He'd been like the walking dead depicted in the Scriptures, a ghost of himself, no use to anyone, especially Lizzie. Well, he wouldn't fail his daughter again. No matter how his heart ached, he wouldn't succumb to the despair he'd felt when he lost Charlotte.

He strode across the livery and snatched a shovel off the wall then gripped it in both hands, his pulse hammering through his veins.

Who was he fooling? He couldn't let Abigail go without a fight. She obviously cared something for them, for Lizzie if nothing else.

At the very least, he could let her know how he felt before she left Calico.

The decision lifted the weight pressing on his chest. Yes, he would speak to her tonight, after she'd finished at the Chens'. That would give him plenty of time to figure out what he wanted to say.

And plenty of time to pray.

Chapter Thirty-one

....

Lizzie's small hand gripped in Abigail's was a big comfort. Her head tilted back, Lizzie peeked up from beneath the pink, frilly bonnet Abigail had sewn for her and waited. Abigail squeezed her fingers one last time and adjusted the basket dangling from her arm before knocking on Lin Chen's door.

The air had turned frosty with the coming of late October. A cloud bank hunkering on the horizon even promised chilly rain later in the day. Abigail pulled her cloak tighter around her shoulders, but beside her, Lizzie seemed oblivious to the cold. She scampered and played, tugging at Abigail's hand so she could reach a leaf that skittered just out of reach.

"Lizzie, be still—"

The door swung open before she could finish and Lin Chen looked out, a crying infant clutched in her arms.

Abigail's throat went dry. "Mrs. Chen. Hello. My name is Abigail Hawk. I'm Anson Watts's daughter." She blinked, horrified by the awkwardness of the situation and her own sudden lack of speech.

Mrs. Chen motioned inside. "You come in?"

She nodded quickly. "Yes, please. Lizzie, come."

Inside the cabin, a pitiful fire sputtered in the stone fireplace. Next to it sat a dwindling stack of wood. No furnishings adorned the surroundings except for a straight-backed chair and a tiny cradle.

Both were pushed close to the hearth. Thankfully, Mrs. Chen was too busy trying to quiet her squalling child to notice their stares.

Tottering to the kitchen, she grasped a scrap of cloth from the counter, dipped it first into a bucket of water, followed by a jar of honey, and pressed it to the baby's mouth. Instantly, the child ceased crying.

Her dark eyes wet, Mrs. Chen finally looked up at Abigail.

"Your baby is beautiful," she said, speaking past the knot in her throat.

Somehow Mrs. Chen managed a smile. "His name Hui, like his fada." She indicated Lizzie with a tip of her head. "This you dada?"

Lizzie's arms circled Abigail's legs and she pressed tight, for once not needing to be reminded to keep quiet.

Abigail's hand dropped to caress Lizzie's braids. "She is my stepdaughter—my husband's child."

Mrs. Chen pondered this a moment and then understanding brightened her eyes. "Ah—stepdada."

Turning to the counter, she moved as though to dip the fabric scrap into the honey again. Abigail shifted the basket off her arm and held it out.

"Mrs. Chen, perhaps your baby would like some milk? I brought you a few things I thought you could use."

Mrs. Chen paused with her hand above the honey jar. On her face was a mixture of shock and joy. "You bring food for my baby?"

Extricating herself from Lizzie's grasp, Abigail eased over to the counter and set the basket down, then began removing the items from the basket, one by one.

She held up a quart jar. "Milk for the baby. There's plenty more where that came from too. I'll bring you whatever you need." Following the milk was a jar of cactus jelly and a loaf of fresh bread. "For you," she said, smiling as Mrs. Chen took the bread in her shaking fingers. The rest of the food—a section of dried beef wrapped in cloth, some eggs, flour, and a small tin of rice—she set on the counter.

Waving her hand over the lot, Abigail said, "It's not much." Especially when she looked about the cabin and saw almost nothing. Where did the woman sleep? Not even a pallet lay on the floor, just a threadbare blanket next to the cradle.

Mrs. Chen hugged the bread to her breast, her eyes brimming with tears. "You angel. Many, many thanks for all this." She bowed as she said it, her dark hair falling loose over her shoulders.

Matching tears sprang to Abigail's eyes as she returned the bow. "You're welcome."

Tearing off a crust, Mrs. Chen soaked it with milk and then pressed it to her baby's mouth. He sucked hungrily, and then his eyes drifted closed.

"You like sit?" Mrs. Chen motioned to the one chair in the empty room. "Little girl, you come sit by fire?" Her gaze questioned Lizzie, who looked to Abigail for the answer.

"It'll be all right," Abigail said, leading Lizzie to the hearth. There, they removed their cloaks and bonnets and folded them neatly on the floor.

Mrs. Chen placed her now-quiet baby in the cradle, covered him with a blanket, and then patted the chair. "Please, you sit here. Please, please," she said, patting and murmuring until Abigail sat and Lizzie scrambled cross-legged on the floor next to her.

Graceful as a young deer, Mrs. Chen lowered herself to the floor next to the cradle and began humming softly to the baby while she rocked him to sleep.

"He must have been tired," Abigail said. At Mrs. Chen's look of confusion, she placed both hands next to her face and feigned sleep.

Mrs. Chen smiled. "Yes, he like you say." She copied Abigail's motion of sleep. A look of worry crossed her face, but another smile chased it away. "He strong, like his fada. He grow good now." She patted the muscles of her thin arm. "Good. Strong. Good food." She pointed to the counter. "Many thanks."

Feeling foolish that she sat in a chair while her hostess occupied the floor, Abigail slid down to sit next to Lizzie. Mrs. Chen watched, her dark eyes curious. Abigail paused in the arranging of her skirt around her legs. "Is this all right?"

Mrs. Chen gave a light laugh that seemed out of place in the dark cabin. "In China, we sit." She spread her hands to indicate the floor.

Oh, yes. She'd seen pictures in the papers back East. Abigail's eyes went to the boots on her and Lizzie's feet. "Oh, our shoes. Forgive me."

Mrs. Chen stopped her before she could tug them off. Mirth and kindness warmed her gaze. "No, please. No need."

Lizzie leaned against Abigail's shoulder and whispered, "Were we supposed to take off our shoes?"

"It's a custom in China," Abigail whispered back, patting her small hand.

"Oh." Lizzie tucked the end of one braid into her mouth.

Mrs. Chen pointed. "You like dip in honey?"

Eyes round, Lizzie shook her head.

"Make taste very good." Rubbing her belly, Mrs. Chen winked.

Finally a smile broke on Lizzie's cheeks. "You're funny."

Mrs. Chen laughed and patted Lizzie's head. "I thought you hungry, like Hui."

She joked with Lizzie as easily as if they sat in a palace warmed by a roaring fire. Suddenly Abigail's trials felt small indeed. For the next hour, she basked in Lin Chen's gentle humor, all the while thanking God for this poignant reminder of how much she had to be grateful for. By the time they gathered their cloaks and bonnets and rose to leave, the sun had crested the mountains, flooding the room with a warmth the struggling fire could not hope to achieve.

At the door, Abigail motioned toward the fireplace. "I will speak to my husband about bringing you some wood."

Mrs. Chen's head bobbed with gratitude. "Nathan Hawk. He you husband?"

Abigail allowed a sad smile. At least for now, she could still claim him as such. She nodded.

"He fine man. Bring some wood already." She motioned to the stack next to the hearth.

Indeed, Nathan was fine, and as generous as her father had been while he lived. She clasped Mrs. Chen's hand. "We'll come again tomorrow with more milk."

Mrs. Chen squeezed Abigail's fingers, her face earnest. "Your fada—he spoke to my Hui about your God. My Hui—he tell me. I prayed Him"—she pointed toward the ceiling—"send me food. He send angel instead." Hands clasped, she laid them against her breast. "Your God, very good."

That was the second time she had referred to Abigail as an angel. Suddenly she knew why Nathan had been so impressed with the woman's simple faith.

"Thank you, Mrs. Chen."

"No, no. You call me Lin." She patted Abigail's arm. "You and stepdada come back for visit. See Hui when he awake." Her arms cradled, she looked at Lizzie. "You like hold baby?"

Lizzie's eyes brightened. "Can I, Abigail?"

"Next time," she said, smiling. With one last bow to Lin, she took Lizzie's hand and led her out the door.

"I like Mrs. Chen," Lizzie said, the skip returning to her step as they made their way past a long row of squatty cabins toward town. She twirled her bonnet on her fingers, round and round. "She's pretty."

"Yes, she is."

"And did you see her hair? It's longer than mine."

Abigail smiled. Lizzie was once again the chatterbox she was at home.

"Yes, I saw it."

"Maybe when I'm bigger—"

A happy bark cut short her next sentence.

"Dorsey!" Pulling free of Abigail's hand, Lizzie ran ahead to hug the black-and-white shepherd that came bounding from the direction of the post office. "Abigail, it's Dorsey."

"I see," Abigail said—but it wasn't the postmaster's dog that held her attention. A distance away, next to one of the cabins, stood Gavin and one of the Oriental workers from Belle's saloon. Gavin's face was dark with rage.

Whether it was eavesdropping or not, she couldn't help herself. She inched closer and moved toward the line of houses to escape Gavin's view.

"I don't care what Belle McAllister told you," Gavin said, his voice quivering with anger. "I don't want you speaking to Abigail Hawk or her husband. Do you hear me? Not one word."

"But Miss Belle say—"

"But Miss Belle say, Miss Belle say," Gavin mocked. "Belle doesn't pay your salary, and she won't get your family here from China." He leaned into the man's face, his tone suddenly threatening. "And let's not forget, Tao, it's thanks to you that those miners thought it was safe to venture so deep into those tunnels. They never would have tried it if you hadn't gone in first and told them it was all right."

Bit by bit, Tao's head drooped lower. Finally, Gavin reached out and clasped his shoulder.

"So, we have a deal, then? You keep your mouth shut about me starting that fire, and I'll do the same about you lying to the miners?"

Tao's head pumped in a dismal nod.

"Good boy. Run along back to the saloon and keep an eye on things for me there. Let me know if anyone else comes around asking questions, eh? And don't worry, Tao, old boy," Gavin said, chuckling as he patted Tao on the back, "our troubles are almost over. Now that those two old biddies have come to fetch Abigail Hawk home, there won't be anyone snooping around in our business."

Though the slump of his shoulders still made Tao look dejected, he did as Gavin said and turned for the saloon.

Fumbling for the shadows, Abigail tried to stay out of the line of sight, but she was too late. A split second later, Gavin's gaze jerked from the man and collided with hers. She froze, terrified by the burning rage blazing from his eyes. Her hands splayed as she grasped for Lizzie.

His face like iron, Gavin took a menacing step toward them. Stumbling backward, Abigail knew she'd never outrun him, not with Lizzie in tow. She did the only thing she could think of: she opened her mouth to scream.

Chapter Thirty-two

....

Nathan eyed the overcast sky. It was getting on toward noontime and Abigail and Lizzie still hadn't returned home. They had apparently decided to stay and have lunch with the aunts.

Jerking the corral gate closed, he looped the rope latch over a fence post and headed toward the livery. The idea shouldn't anger him so, but it did, and so did the knowledge that despite what she'd originally thought about her relatives back East, Abigail had taken a liking to her mother's sisters.

His heart thumped. She'd be leaving soon—and taking a part of him with her.

"Mr. Hawk, hello."

Abigail's two aunts stood framed in the entrance to the livery. Like before, the taller one was draped all in black and the shorter in brown, but a hint of creamy lace peeked from the latter's neck and sleeves. Abigail and Lizzie were nowhere in sight.

He cleared his throat and tried to sound polite. "Morning, ladies."

The taller one, Hester Jane, crossed the yard toward him. A plain black parasol dangled from her arm, but it'd be of little use if the clouds opened up and poured out all the rain they were threatening. He motioned toward the lean-to. "Would you ladies like to come inside?"

"Actually, we were looking for our niece. Is she—home?" The lines around Hester Jane's mouth turned white on the last word, as though it cost her something to say it.

Nathan crossed his arms. What were they playing at? Abigail hadn't been home all day. "Isn't she with you? This morning she said she intended on going by the Chens' house with a few supplies, but after that, she was going by the Calico Hotel. I assumed she was there."

Her head cocked to one side, Vivian spoke and tugged on her sister's sleeve. "Perhaps we missed her, Hester. It could be she's at the hotel now, waiting for us."

Hester Jane jerked a bony finger toward the Asian side of town. "Isn't that where those Orientals live?"

Nathan nodded. "It is."

"Then there's no way we could have missed her, not if she was headed straight over to the hotel afterward."

And so, what did she think? That he was lying? Nathan's patience stretched thinner. "I'm sorry, ladies, I don't know where Abigail could have gotten to, but I'll sure enough send her your way once she gets back. Now, if you'll excuse me, I have chores to finish."

Hester Jane called to him as he turned. "Mr. Hawk."

She said it in a conversational way, not at all like she was irritated or condescending. It stopped Nathan in his tracks. He glanced over his shoulder at her.

"I know you're a busy man, but I wonder if we might have a word with you. Until Abigail returns, that is. Do you mind?"

Mind? You bet he minded, especially since she more than likely wanted to talk to him about letting Abigail go back to Virginia with them. He took his time wiping his hands on an old feed sack before joining the ladies at the entrance and motioning for them to precede him to the lean-to.

Inside, Hester Jane managed to look regal, seated in one of the chairs at the kitchen table. Though she tried to emulate her sister's rigid posture, Vivian only managed to look uncomfortable.

Nathan sat opposite them both, his arms crossed and a glower fixed to his face. Abigail probably would have offered them something to drink. Charlotte, too, when she was alive. Nathan, however, clenched his jaw and waited.

"If you don't mind my asking, how long have you been married to our niece?" Hester Jane asked.

Nathan grunted. He knew what they'd make of his answer. A part of him wished it had been longer. "Just nigh unto two weeks."

"And you were acquainted with one another before Anson died?"

"Yes, since I moved to Calico."

"How long was that?"

"Almost seven months ago."

One corner of Hester Jane's mouth twitched. "Not long."

Long enough considering he'd fallen in love with her during that time. Placing both hands on the table, he leaned forward and stared directly into Hester Jane's eyes. "What is it you want to know?"

To his surprise, Hester Jane copied the motion, her chin squared as she met his gaze. "I want to know that our niece is cared for. I want to know that she's safe, and happy, and most of all, loved. Can you tell me that, Mr. Hawk? Is our niece loved?"

Next to Hester Jane, Vivian fairly quivered as she waited for his answer—but taken aback by the unexpected turn, Nathan fell silent.

Hester Jane's eyes narrowed. "I see."

He shook his head. "If you'll pardon my saying so, you don't see, ma'am. Not at all."

Rising, Nathan made his way to the window and looked out past the dry rocks and sand of the Mojave, to a stand of scrub bushes that dotted the hills. He nodded toward the bushes. "Before I met Abigail, I was like those bushes out there, struggling for something to cling to and soaking up just enough living to keep me alive. If it hadn't been for Lizzie—"

"Your daughter." Hester Jane's eyebrow quirked.

"From my first marriage. My wife died of consumption before we arrived in Calico."

"How long ago was that?"

Sixteen months, twenty-eight days. Nathan returned his gaze to the window. "Over a year."

"But I thought you came to Calico seven months ago," Vivian said.

Nathan clenched his fists and jammed them into his pockets as he thought back to those dark weeks and months he and Lizzie had spent in Oklahoma, where Charlotte was buried. Leaving that place felt like he was abandoning Charlotte, and he'd struggled for days to gather up the courage to leave her remains behind.

He swallowed hard. "Let's just say it took me awhile to get over losing my wife."

It was quiet for a moment, and then Hester Jane spoke. "Then you understand what it was like for us after Olivia died."

Confused, he turned from the window. Hester Jane still sat at the table, her shoulders rigid and her hands clasped, but her eyes no longer looked so hard. In fact, he thought he saw a faint shimmer there.

"My sister was the youngest of the three of us," Hester Jane began, "and we treated her as such, always babying her along, granting her anything she wanted."

Vivian nodded. "You would have thought all that attention spoiled her, but the opposite was true. She was the sweetest, most generous of us all."

"I never could understand how she managed to see the good in everyone," Hester Jane said. "It shouldn't have surprised us when Anson Watts came along and Olivia fell head over heels. He was so much like her—kind, generous. Unfortunately, he was also poor."

Shame written on her face, Vivian dipped her head. "We didn't trust Anson. His nose was always in a book. We thought he was lazy and using Olivia to get at her money."

Lips tight, Hester Jane said, "We were wrong."

"Only—only—we were too proud to admit it."

There was a catch in Vivian's voice, as though she fought tears. In spite of himself, Nathan felt sorry for her. "And so you stayed away."

Their heads bobbed in unison.

"But when we heard that Anson had died and Abigail was alone," Hester Jane said, "well, we boarded the fastest train west."

"Where you found me."

They hesitated, their faces stricken.

Walking slowly back to the table, Nathan sat and stared at his hands. "You asked me if I love Abigail. I reckon that's a fair question seeing as how you've come all this way just to check on her."

Lifting his gaze, he stared first at Hester Jane and then at Vivian.

"The answer is yes, ladies. I do love Abigail. I love her with all my heart."

* * * * *

Abigail woke to sniffling.

Though she tried with all her might, her eyes wouldn't focus, refusing to see past the thick blackness clinging to her like a shroud. A chill crept up her arms and over her shoulders and made the hair on her neck stand on end.

Where was she?

The sniffling grew louder, followed by a hiccup.

"Lizzie, is that you?"

"Lizzie, is that you? you? you?"

Abigail froze as her words echoed—not the ringing cry one cast over a deep valley, but the hollow, muted sound found in…

The mine.

Rolling onto her hands and knees, Abigail felt fine, dusty silt beneath her fingers, mingled with sharp, pointed rocks, and the iron tracks that the ore cars ran on. Fear clutched at her belly.

"Lizzie!"

"Abigail?"

More hiccups followed the first, but at least she sounded close. Abigail tried to calm the terror building in her chest but was still horrified when she stuck out her hands and saw nothing—not even her fingers, when she held them inches from her face.

"Where are you, sweetheart?"

"Here. I'm here. Abigail, I'm scared."

So was she, and her head throbbed. The memory rushed back, bringing sharp pain to her temple where Gavin had hit her. She pressed her hand to her head, trying to ease the ache enough to think. "All right, sweetheart, you just keep talking. I'm going to come to you, all right?"

Her voice small, Lizzie said, "All right."

"We'll make it a game." Sweat dampened her palms. Abigail rubbed them on her skirt before easing to her feet. She had room to stand. In fact, if she stretched her fingers straight up, she barely grazed the stone ceiling. She drew a deep breath. "All right, Lizzie. Let's start with a few questions. What's your favorite color?"

"Red."

Well, that hardly worked. Her answer was too short to get a clear sense of her direction.

"So tell me something about the color red. Why do you like it so much?"

"We–ell," Lizzie said, drawing out the word, "it reminds me of Christmas."

She was somewhere to the left. Her hands outstretched, Abigail turned that way. "Really? Why?"

"Pa says Santa Claus wears a red suit and rides a red sleigh."

"Of course. What else do you like about red?"

"It's pretty. Like roses. You like those, don't you, Abigail? You have rose water."

Though the mountain twisted Lizzie's words, making each sound strange, Abigail could tell she was getting closer. Without sight, however, she cringed, as though she would smash her head on the stone walls. She lowered herself to her knees, crept forward along the iron track, stuck her hand out to feel for Lizzie, and then crept forward some more.

"Yes, sweetheart. I like roses. What other kind of flowers do you like?"

"Hmm—daisies are my favorite."

Thankfully, much of the fear had gone from Lizzie's voice. She talked as normally as if she and Abigail had sat down for tea.

"My momma taught me a game with daisies. You pull off the petals one by one. Do you know it?" Lizzie asked.

"I don't think so. You'll have to teach it to me."

"Maybe after Pa comes." She paused, and when she spoke again, her voice shook. "Abigail, why did that man hit you on the head? Why did he put us in here? Is he mad?"

Just as she finished speaking, Abigail felt something soft and warm beneath her fingers, and then she heard a gasp.

"Lizzie?"

"Abigail!"

Two arms flew around Abigail's neck, nearly choking the breath from her. On her cheeks, Lizzie's tears mingled with her own. She gathered the child close, hugging her tightly until her shoulders ached.

"It's all right, sweetheart. I'm right here. It's going to be all right."

Finally Lizzie's trembling subsided, though she refused to let go of Abigail completely. "I don't like it here. Can we go now?"

Go where? She had no idea where in the mine they were. It had, in fact, taken several minutes just to find her way to Lizzie. Who knew what other dangers awaited them in the dark?

"Soon, sweetheart. First, I need you to tell me how long I was asleep. Was it a long time?"

Lizzie buried her face in Abigail's neck. "Yes. I cried and cried after the man left, but you didn't wake up. I thought you were dead, like Momma."

She couldn't imagine the terror Lizzie had felt, alone in the dark, with what she thought was a body. Abigail shuddered then forced a light laugh to cover her fear.

"Nonsense. I was just taking a nap. See? I'm fine now."

Lizzie's downy hair tickled Abigail's face as she nodded.

More than anything, Abigail wanted to sit quietly and think, but for Lizzie's sake, she kept talking—talking and talking until her voice was hoarse and thirst made her tongue thick. Until all she could find to say were silly nursery rhymes she'd learned as a child. Countless minutes ticked away, and finally Lizzie's body relaxed in slumber.

Her back against the cold wall of the mine, Abigail prepared herself to wait—and pray.

Chapter Thirty-three

....

Abigail had probably lost track of time.

Over and over Nathan repeated the thought, as he finished repairing a section of fence at the back of the corral and put away his tools. Hester Jane and Vivian had left hours ago and still there was no sign of Abigail or Lizzie. But that didn't mean something was wrong. So why did his stomach feel as if he'd swallowed a stone? And why was he as jumpy as a salamander caught between a boy and a stick?

Leaving the livery, Nathan headed toward town. It wasn't as though Calico was all that big. He could stop working, find out what Abigail and Lizzie were up to, and be back before the sun had begun to set over the mountains.

No one at the hotel claimed to have seen the girls all day. The same was true at the milliner. At the general store, a new sign proclaiming the place Gardner's Mercantile had been erected. Nathan went inside and sought out Caroline Martin. *Caroline Gardner,* he reminded himself. She and John were married now.

Caroline rested atop a stool at the rear of the store, her face flushed as though she'd been running.

"Afternoon, Caroline," Nathan said, dashing his hat from his head.

Caroline's eyes sparkled as she looked up. "Nathan, how good to see you." Her gaze flitted over his shoulder. "Abigail's not with you?"

He sidled to the counter, the stone in his stomach growing heavier. "Uh—actually, that's why I stopped by. You haven't seen her, have you?"

Slipping from the stool, she wiped her hands on a frilly apron tied around her waist and came to stand next to him. "Why, no, I haven't. Was she supposed to come by today?"

He worked his fingers around the brim of his hat. He certainly didn't mean to alarm Caroline, but it wasn't like Abigail to disappear for hours, either. "Not exactly. It's just that she went to see Lin Chen this morning, and then she was supposed to visit with her aunts, but she never made it to the hotel. I thought maybe she got sidetracked and stopped by here."

Cocking her head to one side, Caroline propped her elbow on the wrist of her other hand and thought. "I don't think so. 'Course, I could have missed her. John and I have been stocking shelves all day, and I've been in and out, carrying supplies from the wagon." She motioned to tables laden with crates. "I can hardly wait to get all of this unpacked."

Nathan looked around the store. Indeed, she and John had been busy. Most of the old merchandise Mr. Wiley sold had been moved aside to make room for new things—bolts of cloth and ribbons of every color; barrels of rice, oats, and beans; cooking pots and lanterns.

"Where is John?" Nathan asked, cutting short his survey of the store's goods.

Caroline jerked her thumb over her shoulder. "Out back. Do you want to see him? Maybe he knows something."

Nathan nodded and then followed as Caroline led the way past the counter to the rear entrance. Outside, John and the two hands he'd hired sweated as they wrestled fifty-pound bags of flour out of a wagon.

John was a big man, not thin and spry as Mr. Wiley had been. Spying Nathan, John stopped and slapped the flour from his hands in a dusty, white cloud and then moved to join him and his wife on the boardwalk.

"Morning, Nathan."

"John."

He shook Nathan's hand and then braced his hands on his hips. "What can I do for you?"

Nathan cleared his throat. "I'm looking for Abigail. Have you seen her?'

John's dark brows bunched in a puzzled frown. "No. Caroline?"

She shook her head. "I thought maybe you had, since we've both been going back and forth."

Tugging off his hat, John drew his sleeve across his sweaty forehead and then plunked it back atop his damp head. "Sorry, Nathan, can't say as I've seen her." He craned his neck toward the two men still unloading the wagon. "Either of you boys seen Abigail Hawk?" At the negative shake of their heads, he returned his gaze to Nathan. "Something troubling you?"

Nathan shrugged. "Nothing I can put my finger on. Still…" He cast a glance at the sun, which now dipped even closer to the horizon. "She's been gone a long time."

Worry darkened Caroline's eyes. "How long?"

"Since before lunch. I have no idea how long she stayed at the Chens'."

"Well, there you go," John said, nudging his hat back with his thumb. "Maybe something came up and she's still with Lin."

Maybe. Nathan hooked his thumbs in the loops of his trousers. "You're right. I'll head that way. Thanks, John. Caroline."

Caroline touched his arm. "Should I go with you?"

He forced a smile. "Nah, I'm sure she's there. Either way, I'll let you know."

Though she still looked uneasy, she gave a slow nod and stepped back, looping her arm through her husband's.

Grasping a post, Nathan swung off the boardwalk and landed on the hard-packed road with a thump. "I'll talk to you soon."

They nodded, and Nathan turned toward Chinatown.

Lin Chen lived in one of the smallest cabins near the heart of the camp. Strung between the house and a tree, laundry fluttered on the breeze, and Lin was adding more. At her feet sat two baskets, one filled with clean clothes, the other with a kicking baby. The moment she caught sight of him, Lin hurried forward and clasped his hands.

"Mistah Nathan! You come so soon?"

He quirked an eyebrow. "Pardon?"

"The firewood. You come to bring for Lin?" At his look of confusion, she paused and tilted her head. "Miss Abigail say you come tomorrow."

"Abigail was here?"

She smiled and wagged her finger. "Mistah Nathan, you joke with Lin?"

Desperation rose from his midsection. He grasped her shoulder. "Lin, what time was Abigail here?"

Her smile slowly faded. "She come early. Bring milk for Hui."

"And what time did she leave?"

She scratched her head. "She not stay long. Maybe"—she lifted a finger—"one."

"One hour?"

Lin nodded.

One hour. Dismay swept from the bottom of his boots to the top of his head. That meant she'd left just after nine and had been missing for almost eight hours.

Sick at his stomach, he whirled—to go where? No one had seen her. He cupped his head in his hands, feeling as lost and hopeless as he had the night Charlotte died. And then he heard it.

In the distance, a dog barked.

Chapter Thirty-four

....

How much time had passed? Abigail couldn't guess. Except for the ache in her head and the steady rise and fall of Lizzie's chest, she had nothing with which to mark the time.

At the thought of her stepdaughter, Lizzie stirred. "Abigail?"

"I'm here, sweetheart."

Lizzie's body tensed as she stretched and then sat up. "I'm thirsty."

"So am I." Abigail didn't mention that she was also beginning to feel hungry. Surely by now someone had noticed their absence.

"When are we going home?"

Tears stung Abigail's eyes. "I don't know, sweetheart."

"Are we just going to stay here?"

She fought to keep the tremor from her voice. "I think that's best."

"Will Pa know where to find us?"

Would he? She couldn't be sure. All along, she'd been fighting to convince herself that they needed to stay put and let help come to them, but what if help didn't come? What if Nathan had no idea what had happened to them or where to begin to look?

There was no difference in the level of darkness, but she closed her eyes anyway and breathed a prayer. Though her fear remained, she felt a measure of peace when she finished.

It would be all right. Whether help came or not, whether she and Lizzie found their way out or languished here in this mine, things would turn out all right.

God was with them.

* * * * *

Off in the distance a dog barked, but it was the prompting inside Nathan's head that held him transfixed.

"Listen."

The word was a whisper to his spirit, so real he almost felt it. He turned his eyes toward the mine, where the dog's bark had become a mournful howl. Dorsey?

Leaving Lin behind, he first walked and then ran the distance to the mine. Dorsey rose from his haunches as he drew near. The fur on his neck stood on end as he circled the entrance, his bark rising in urgency until his eyes took on a wild frenzy and saliva slathered his jaws.

"Easy there, boy," Nathan said, slowing his steps and putting out his hand. "Come here, Dorsey. That's a good boy."

Slowly the dog's barking ceased, but he continued to whimper as he crept forward and sat next to Nathan.

Nathan dropped to his haunches and ran his hand over the dog's head. "Dorsey, do you know where Lizzie is?" It was a foolish hope, but one he couldn't help but play. "Dorsey, where's Lizzie?"

The shepherd's ears perked, and he cocked his head to one side.

"Where's Lizzie, Dorsey?"

The third time he asked, the dog leapt to his feet and bounded toward the mine entrance. Fear licked through Nathan's veins. What if Lizzie had wandered into the mine and Abigail had gone in looking for her? What if they were both lost in the maze of drifts and tunnels?

Snagging a lantern from one of the ore cars, he lit the candle in the middle and carried it inside. The cage was still at the top of the shaft and locked in place. Lizzie couldn't possibly be down below unless—she'd fallen.

"Lizzie!" Nathan cupped both hands to his mouth and shouted. His voice echoed, but though he strained to listen, no other sounds drifted from the mountain.

Where were the miners?

Struck by their absence, he looked around. Several miners' hats lay scattered about the entrance. The candles driven into the wall for light were unlit, the wicks warm, as though they had been snuffed in a hurry. The entire place felt wrong, vacant.

At his side, Dorsey whined, his dark eyes fixed to Nathan's face.

"What's going on here, boy?" Nathan said, his voice falling to a whisper. His fingers closed around the iron bars of the shaft cage.

And then he saw it. Near the bottom, tangled in the wire mesh, hung a bit of blue-and-white cloth.

Nathan's heart sped. It looked like the fabric from a dress—the same dress Abigail had been wearing that morning when she left the livery. Holding the lantern high, he worked the scrap free and brought it to the light. It was her dress, all right. Worse, it appeared to be dotted with blood.

"What are you doing in here, Hawk?"

The voice from behind nearly scared Nathan out of his skin. Without thinking, he shoved the cloth into his pocket and stood. Gavin Nichols formed a menacing figure in the mine entrance. Light spilled from behind him and cast his features into shadow.

"I asked you what you're doing in here. The mine is off-limits."

Nathan squinted to make out Gavin's expression in the dim light. "Why? What's going on?"

"Just got word that some of the shafts aren't safe. Those fellows from the mining company that were here last week? They wired me this morning saying they didn't want any activity inside the mine until they finished their report."

Nathan's breath caught. Gavin was lying about the men, but was he hiding something more sinister?

Gavin jammed his hand into the pocket of his tweed trousers and fished out a piece of paper. "See? Read for yourself."

It was indeed a warning against the mine's stability, signed with a name Nathan did not recognize. He handed the paper back. "Is that why no one's working the mine?"

"That's it." The lantern cast eerie shadows on Gavin's face, and as he narrowed his eyes, he looked even more menacing. "But you never answered my question. I'll ask you one last time: what are you doing here?"

"Mistah Nathan? You all right?"

It was Gavin's turn to jump. As he whirled, Nathan caught sight of Lin Chen and a couple of other Chinese from her camp. Hiking the lantern high, he shoved past Gavin and stepped outside.

Troubled lines marred Lin's face. She bowed first to Gavin and then turned to Nathan. "When you run off, I go, get friends of Hui. Think, maybe, you need help." Her fingers fluttered through the air as she explained her presence. "You all right, Mistah Nathan? Miss Abigail all right?"

"I don't know, Lin. I think she may be in the mine."

"That's impossible!" Gavin's eyes bulged, and the veins of his neck strained against the starched collar of his shirt. "The mine is closed."

Anger whipping up in Nathan's gut, he spun and advanced on him. "It's not impossible, Nichols." He pointed to Dorsey. "That dog has been following Lizzie around for days. Right now, he refuses to leave the mine. That makes me think she may have wandered in there."

A disbelieving snort blasted from Gavin. Still, one hand worked at the string tie around his throat, and his other hand tore at his hair. "You're listening to a dog?"

He was nervous but trying to hide it. Suspicion flared in Nathan's chest. He narrowed his eyes and formed his words carefully. "I'm going to organize a search party."

Gavin swallowed repeatedly, making his Adam's apple bob like a cork on water. "I'm afraid I can't allow that, Hawk. The mine is company property. If someone were to get hurt in there—"

"You try and stop me and someone *will* get hurt out here." Nathan curled his fists, ready to fight if Gavin insisted on blocking him from entering the mine. If there was even the slightest chance that Abigail and Lizzie were inside, he'd move the entire mountain to get to them.

At the low warning, Gavin stumbled back a step. His gaze darted from Nathan to the Chinese, who watched his every move. "Fine. Organize a search party, but you assume the responsibility for the safety of your men. None of my miners are going in there. Why, they barely escaped injury just today, when a section of tunnel collapsed. You're risking your life, Hawk, but you won't risk my men."

Spinning on his heel, he strode toward town, leaving Nathan alone with Lin and the other Chinese.

Lin stepped forward, her small hands white where she clasped them together. "You think Miss Abigail and little girl in there?" She nodded toward the darkened mine entrance, her eyes clouded with worry.

"I think she might be," Nathan said.

"Maybe they go somewhere else. In town. We look?"

Nathan shook his head. "I don't think so, Lin." He pulled the cloth from his pocket and showed it to her. "I found this caught on the cage."

Lin's fingers flew to cover her mouth. When she looked up, tears misted her eyes. "We help, Mistah Nathan. We find Abigail and your dada."

She turned then and said something in rapid Chinese. A second later the two men took off, one toward the camp, the other toward town. For the first time that day, a tiny bit of the fear pressing on Nathan's chest lessened—but only for a moment. Deep within the mine and rolling up toward the entrance, he heard a faint rumble.

Chapter Thirty-five

....

Lizzie's grip on Abigail's arm tightened. "What was that?"

Though Lizzie couldn't see it, Abigail shook her head. She heard the rumble, too, and it sounded close. "I don't know."

They fell silent and listened. No more rumbles followed the first, but Abigail didn't like it. Something was wrong, and she needed to get Lizzie out of there, fast.

Her mind made up, she took Lizzie's hand and held on tight. "I don't think we should stay here anymore. I think we need to try to find our way out. Do you think you can remember which way we came in?"

Lizzie sniffed, and a tremor shook her voice. "No, I don't think so."

"It's all right, sweetheart," Abigail said, squeezing her hand. "We just need to think of something else."

She stood carefully to her feet, pulling Lizzie along with her. "Tell you what. We're going to walk a few steps one way and then a few steps the other way and see what we find. Sound good?"

In answer, Lizzie's grip on her hand tightened.

"Now you stay close to me so you don't trip on anything. Ready?"

"Yes." Her voice was little more than a squeak.

Abigail's first thought was to travel away from the rumble, but thinking better of it, she wondered if perhaps the sound was from the miners. Maybe they were excavating more tunnels. If she traveled toward the sound, maybe she'd find help.

Drawing a breath to brace herself, she took two hesitant steps forward. The walls of the drift stretched out in front of them—how far, she couldn't guess. Progress was slow, but she put one foot in front of the other, always feeling her way first with her booted toes against the ore car rails and then her hands.

No good. The tunnel could go on for miles. She stopped and drew her sleeve across her brow. The air inside the mountain was clammy and oppressive, but she still sweated buckets. She squeezed Lizzie's hand.

"You all right back there?"

"Yes."

"Good." She took several gulps of stale air, trying hard to calm the racing of her heart. "I guess we should try going back now."

Lizzie clung to her legs.

"What is it, sweetheart?" Abigail said, running a hand over Lizzie's tangled hair.

"I don't want to go back. I'm scared."

"So am I, Lizzie, but we don't know if this is the way out."

Lizzie shook her head and buried her face in the folds of Abigail's dress. "I don't wanna go back."

Abigail hesitated. Either way could be as wrong as the other. Finally she stroked the side of Lizzie's cheek. "All right, then, we'll go forward, so long as we keep moving."

After a moment, Lizzie peeled herself from Abigail's leg and clung to her hand.

"Good girl. Here we go."

Once again Abigail pushed forward, feeling with her feet for the track before them.

"He leadeth me in the paths of righteousness for his name's sake."

The familiar passage of scripture came to Abigail's mind. Well, God would certainly have to guide her here. Deep inside the mountain, she was truly blind.

How long they walked, she couldn't be certain. It seemed like hours. It may have been minutes. All she knew was they walked one moment, and the next they rounded a corner and came face-to-face with a man.

* * * * *

A lantern in hand, Nathan looked out over the crowd. Several of the faces were familiar. Along with Lin, Soo, and the Chinese were John and Caroline Gardner; the aunts, Hester Jane and Vivian; and Pastor Burch with several of the men from his congregation. Even Belle had come, bringing a few of the hands from her saloon. Thinking they might need to dig out Abigail and Lizzie, the men had armed themselves with pickaxes and shovels, and they stood awaiting his orders. He appreciated the numbers willing to help them. Dusk approached, and he knew they wouldn't have much time before night fell in earnest.

"All right, everyone knows the plan. We'll spread out in groups of five. Each group will walk a different section of the mine, but we'll still try to stay close enough to communicate. If anyone finds anything"—he held up the scrap of cloth—"especially anything that looks like it might belong to one of the girls, we all gather up and decide where to go from there. Any questions?"

When no one raised a hand, Nathan stepped back and the groups began making their way onto the cage. He lowered them into the shaft group by group until all that remained outside the mine were the women, John, and two Chinese named Han and Delun.

Nathan stepped toward the three men, but before he reached them, Belle caught his arm.

She gestured toward the mine entrance. "You sure they're in there?"

Impatient to get going, he shrugged. "Not certain, but it's the only lead we've got."

Her head dipped, but not before he caught the worried frown that gathered on her face. "Did I ever tell you about the day Anson Watts came to see me?"

Her voice had gone so low, Nathan had to strain to hear. Surely she didn't intend to tarnish the man's reputation now, when his daughter was missing and possibly hurt? Nathan stiffened and shook his head.

Belle's lips stretched in a tight smile. "It was a few years ago. I was in jail." Her gaze hardened. "Gavin Nichols had me thrown in jail."

"I heard about that."

Speculation sparked in her gaze. "Did you now? I can guess how." She braced her hand on her hip. "Did he also tell you who bailed me out?"

Nathan stilled and shook his head.

"Anson Watts. Never could figure out how or why he came. Just showed up one day with a fistful of money. He paid Gavin what I owed and left. Now, I count that as strange, don't you?"

"I suppose." Where was this leading? Nathan shifted from foot to foot and waited.

"I have an idea," Belle continued. Surprisingly, tears sprang to her eyes. "Deep down, I always figured he wanted me to ask, you know, so he could share something about his God. I almost did— several times—before he died."

She went silent then, her tears drying up faster than water in the

CALICO
1883
CA

desert. When she looked up, her face was once again hard. "I hope you find her, Mr. Hawk. I hope you find Anson's daughter." With that, she turned and slowly headed back toward the saloon.

John appeared at his elbow. "We ready?"

Nathan nodded and turned to Caroline.

"You and the others stay up top."

"We will. Be careful, all of you."

She pressed a kiss to John's hand and then stepped away to operate the cage. Before they could begin their descent, Hester Jane tapped Nathan's shoulder.

"Young man, if my niece is down there..."

Sudden tears filled her eyes, and her voice quivered so that she could not finish. She hadn't taken it well when Nathan told her and Vivian that Abigail and Lizzie were missing, but neither had she cried. It was only now that he realized how deeply the news of Abigail's disappearance troubled her. Vivian, on the other hand, kept a lace handkerchief pressed to her dripping nose.

He squeezed Hester Jane's wrinkled hand. "I'll find her."

"See that you do. And take care of yourself while you're about it." Head held high, she stepped aside and patted her sobbing sister on the back. Though she comforted Vivian, she kept her gaze fixed to Nathan's until they disappeared from sight.

Inside the mine, the muted voices of the searchers calling for Lizzie and Abigail already filled the tunnels in several directions. Small circles of light bobbed down narrow passageways as they made slow but steady progress. Nathan lifted his lantern, though it did little to dispel the deep blackness pressing on every side.

Abigail and Lizzie were in this? And probably without a light to guide their way. He shuddered, thinking of the fear they must feel.

"Which way?" John, too, lifted his lantern, illuminating first one drift and then another that ran opposite.

Nathan pointed toward the second tunnel. "This one. We'll try to keep as far to the right as we can so we don't cross any ground the other groups have already covered."

Han and Delun agreed. Nathan led the way, though several times, John had to caution him to slow down. Nathan could hardly stand it. He wanted to run, screaming, down every tunnel. Instead, they plugged along, making sure they tracked their course with markings on the walls at every turn so they didn't lose their way.

Finally John pulled alongside him, panting. Rivers of sweat coursed down his face, and red grime caked along his nose and eyes. Nathan knew he looked the same, but he wasn't about to give up.

"Nathan, we've gone too far. We need to turn back."

Nathan shook his head and swung his lantern toward the dark tunnel ahead. "No, I think if we go just a little farther—"

John pointed toward Han and Delun, who breathed as heavily as he. "It's no good. We're all tired. We need to meet up with the others and see if anyone has found anything."

Though he wanted to resist, he knew that John was right. What if Abigail and Lizzie had already been found? Or what if evidence of their passing lay in one of the other drifts? Wasn't he just wasting time searching a tunnel they hadn't traveled?

"First…" He drew a shuddering breath. He couldn't meet John's eyes, not with the fear so thick inside him he could almost taste it. He gestured down the tunnel behind them. "Go on ahead. I'll catch up."

John studied him a bit longer and then clapped Han and Delun on the shoulder. "Let's go."

As soon as they were out of earshot, Nathan closed his eyes to pray. He couldn't take one more step—not one—until he asked God for direction. Moisture gathered behind his eyes when he finished, but a new peace filled him as well.

Using a sharp stone, he marked on the wall where they'd turned around and then followed John and the others to the main stope. The searchers who'd made their way back had gathered in a small circle around the pastor, their faces shadowed by concern in the glow from the lanterns. It wasn't the news he'd hoped for.

"What is it?" Nathan pushed his way to the center of the circle. "What did you find?"

His stomach sank as Pastor Burch looked up and met his gaze. The man's face was weary and drawn, and in his eyes, sorrow glimmered.

He stepped toward Nathan, his hand outstretched. "It's not good, son. It's not good at all."

Chapter Thirty-six

....

"Don't scream. Nichols has men posted all around this here cavern."

Abigail's heart pounded. It was hard not to scream with this mountain of a man looming over her. Lizzie whimpered and pressed tightly to her side. Though she wanted to do the same, Abigail simply nodded.

The man held a single candle, which he kept partially covered with his hand. That explained why she hadn't seen the glow of the flame, but what was the man doing in the mine, and why was he cautioning her against Gavin? How did she know whether to trust him?

The man looked to Lizzie and put his finger to his lips. It was then that Abigail caught sight of the scars puckering the skin on his wrist and hand.

Her breath caught. "Tom Kennedy?"

The black pools of his eyes were solemn in the flickering glow of the candle. He nodded.

She hugged Lizzie and her voice dropped to a whisper. "What are you doing here?"

"We heard the blast from the explosion Nichols set to trap you gals in here, and we came to investigate."

Her heart tripped against her chest. Gavin had intended to bury them inside this mountain. She licked her dry lips. "The rumble we heard?"

"That was us setting a charge so as we could clear out some of the rocks to find ya."

"Us? There's someone with you?"

"My brother. He's back a piece, keeping watch." Tom motioned toward the tunnel. "We'd best get moving afore one of them men with Nichols heads this way."

Fear tightened her throat. She nodded.

Tom turned and then peered over his shoulder at them. "Stay close. It's easy to get lost in these here drifts. Just follow the light from the candle."

Even that much was hard. Lizzie's shorter legs struggled to keep up with Tom Kennedy's long strides. Finally he paused, waited while they caught up, and then bent and looked Lizzie in the eyes.

"I reckon you're a mite tired by now, eh, young 'un?"

Her face was scratched and dirty, her eyes wide and frightened. The tears filling Lizzie's eyes nearly broke Abigail's heart.

She clasped Lizzie's hand in both of hers. "Maybe if I carry her…"

Tom's shoulders hitched in a shrug. "Nah. She's a mite overgrown for one as slim as you." He looked at Lizzie and wagged his shaggy head from side to side. "How about it, little one? You let me carry you the rest of the way?"

They had no other choice. Abigail gently pried Lizzie's fingers loose. "It'll be all right, sweetheart. Mr. Kennedy will give you a nice ride, and we'll get out of here that much quicker."

Biting her lip, Lizzie let Tom hoist her to his hip. He handed the candle to Abigail. "You go on ahead now, Miss Abigail. Lizzie and I'll bring up the rear."

The candle clutched in her shaking fingers, Abigail did as he said and moved down the tunnel. After what seemed like ages, the glow from another candle flickered a short span ahead.

Tom tapped her shoulder. He lowered Lizzie to her feet and then passed Abigail in the tunnel. "You two wait here. I'll check to make sure it's clear and come back for ya."

He didn't wait for an answer but shuffled away, his bent shoulders making him look like an old man in the glow from the candle. Ahead, the two men spoke in low whispers, and then Tom rejoined Abigail and Lizzie.

"All clear. George says he heard some commotion back up the mine a piece, but it's all quiet now."

"Gavin's men?" Abigail said.

"Couldn't rightly tell. Mebbe. We'd best keep moving, just in case."

Abigail nodded. Once again, Tom hoisted Lizzie to his hip, only this time she didn't protest. What must she be thinking of all this? Abigail could only wonder—and hope the memory of this experience wouldn't haunt her dreams.

As they drew close, George dipped his head to Abigail. "Glad you's all right, Miss. Tom and I was worried when we heard the blast."

"Thank you for coming," Abigail said. She rubbed her hands up and down her arms as shaking took over.

George gave a curt nod. "We'd best get you safe." He looked at Tom. "You all right?"

Tom grunted. "We'll give those rascals the shake. Ain't nobody knows these tunnels better than the two of us. What about you? You gonna be all right leading those scoundrels the opposite way?"

George closed one eye in a sly wink. "When I'm done with those fellas, they'll be lucky enough to find their own way out."

With that, he turned and headed off down a separate tunnel, his shoulders rocking side to side with his lopsided gait. Moments before the gloom swallowed him up, he scrambled like a monkey up a wooden ladder that led to another level in the mine.

Abigail clutched Tom's arm. "Where's he going?"

Tom's gaze grew serious. "George thought he heard Nichols's men down that way, probably waiting to ambush any searchers that got too close. He's fixin' to lead them away from us, give us a chance to wind our way to the surface."

"Searchers?" Her heart jumped. *Nathan.*

"Yes, ma'am, but it's too dangerous to try and take you out that direction. Nichols's men are planted right smack between us and them. If it weren't for George and his knowing his way 'round this here mountain, we might never have reached you."

He jerked his chin down a different drift altogether. "We're going thataway, opposite the mine entrance. We'll come out on the back side of the hill, out a hole carved by some underground streams. They dried up years ago and the hole ain't much bigger than what a jackrabbit could wriggle through, but it's a mite safer than taking on those hired guns."

Abigail shivered. What if Nathan or one of the other people sent to search for them stumbled on those hired guns? She had no way of warning them. At this point, all she could do was pray for their safety.

She stuck out her hand for the candle, which Tom gave with a smile.

"All right, then," he said. "Let's get you little ladies out of here."

For the first time since meeting up with the Kennedys, Lizzie giggled.

Tom chuckled too. "You like that?"

She nodded.

"All right, then, little lady. From now on, that's what I'll call you." He hitched her higher on his hip and nodded to Abigail. "Let's go."

* * * * *

"What is that? What are you holding?" Nathan's mouth went dry at the sight of the object in Pastor Burch's hand.

"Does this belong to your daughter?" the pastor asked gently.

Nathan took the pink bonnet covered in red dust. It was Lizzie's, all right. Abigail had made it for her. He turned it over and over. At least it wasn't covered in blood. He swallowed hard. "Where—" Words failed him. He cleared his throat and tried again. "Where did you find it?"

Pastor Burch indicated one of the Orientals. "That fella there found it."

Nathan strode to him. "Where?"

The man spoke in Chinese and then pointed toward a dark passage.

Gripping the lantern in one hand and Lizzie's bonnet in the other, Nathan started off. "Let's go."

"Don't reckon it will do you any good to follow that path now."

All heads turned toward the new voice echoing through the cavern. Like a wraith, George Kennedy appeared at the mouth of one of the tunnels, his shoulders hunched and a foolish grin on his face.

Nathan stomped toward him. "What are you doing here, Kennedy?"

"Why, I just figgered I'd take me a little walk." He jerked his thumb behind him. "Now those fellas there? They got different plans in mind."

Shuffling sounded in the tunnel behind him, along with several confused grunts and low voices thick with frustration.

"Which way did he go?"

"I told you, I don't know."

"Nichols will have our hides if we let 'im get away."

"Your hide. I told you we shoulda turned left instead of right."

"I say we never should have left them girls in the first place."

"Hold up, now—is that a light ahead?"

"What are you talking about?"

Suddenly both voices fell silent.

Nathan stuck his head into the passage. "You men come on out." When neither man moved, he continued, "We've already heard you, boys. Best you show yourselves and do your talking out here, especially since there's nothing but rocks and mountain behind you."

After a long moment, the shuffling resumed and two men popped from the tunnel's mouth. Both wore bemused expressions. Only one held a sputtering torch. The other looked far more dangerous with a rifle clutched in his hands.

Nathan eased between them and the searchers behind him. "You boys mind explaining what you're doing in a closed mine?"

The man with the torch glanced at his partner, his eyes large and wild in his scruffy face.

The one with the rifle spoke. "We—uh—we heard you was organizing a search party and come to help."

"That's right," the second man piped. "We got lost is all, before we could catch up with you."

"And you thought you might need a gun?"

Both men looked cornered—not good in a rock cavern where any spark could ignite the anger simmering below the skin of every man. The one with the rifle tightened his grip.

Nathan narrowed his eyes. "You've only got a couple of shots in that rifle, and there's nigh unto twenty of us men. I suggest you lay down that gun and tell us what you're really doing here."

In response, a ripple surged over the searchers as they hoisted their pickaxes and shovels in a show of strength.

The man with the torch swallowed hard and stared at his partner. "Clem?"

Slowly lowering himself to his haunches, Clem laid his rifle in the dust and then lifted his hands. His cohort did the same, dropping the torch.

Nathan turned to George. "You led them here?"

George's head bobbed. "Sure did."

"And you know where my wife and daughter are?"

"Reckon by now, they're just about topside."

The bands squeezing Nathan's heart loosened just a bit, but he knew they wouldn't be fully banished until he laid eyes on the women he loved. He turned to John. "See to those two. I'm sure the marshal will have questions for them later."

Anxious now, he glanced back at George. This man claimed to know where Abigail and Lizzie were, and Nathan wasn't about to waste another second. "Show me."

Chapter Thirty-seven

It seemed they'd walked for hours. Abigail's limbs felt frozen, and the cold made her teeth chatter. It didn't help that the passage they traveled kept narrowing so that they were forced to walk bent almost double. Fighting her heavy skirts, she sweated and huffed merely to set one foot in front of the other. Just when she thought she could go no farther, a breeze stirred the damp hair clinging to her forehead.

Bracing herself against the tunnel wall, she breathed, "Is that—?"

Behind her, Tom grunted. "Lookey there. Stars. We're out." He chuckled and tapped Lizzie on the nose. "Old George was right. But don't tell him I said so."

Lizzie laughed. "I won't."

Tears filled Abigail's eyes and her breaths came faster, rising in white puffs on the frosty night air. She could hardly believe it. "We're out."

"Yes, ma'am."

Still, she stood unmoving, staring out at the patch of night sky, more thankful than she'd ever been to God. He'd heard her prayers and brought them up from the depths.

"Ma'am?" Tom drew even with her. "I think we'd best get you and this little lady in front of a warm fire before the two of you catch a chill."

"Y–yes." Even her lips were numb. She barely managed the simple word.

Tom dropped to his knees and peered through the opening in the mountain. Then he glanced at Abigail. "All clear. I'll go first. You hand Lizzie out and then come out after."

She nodded, watching as he wriggled to get free of the mountain. When his feet disappeared through the hole, he turned round and stretched out his hands for Lizzie.

"All right, little lady. You're next."

Getting out was much easier for Lizzie. She scooted through the hole with no trouble, and Abigail lay on her belly to follow. Tom Kennedy's strong hands grasped her forearms and tugged until she was free. Thankful for his help, she let him steady her until her tired legs were stable enough to carry her.

"Abigail?"

Disbelieving, she turned toward the voice. "N–Nathan."

"Pa!"

Darting around Tom, Lizzie dashed across the stony ground and threw herself into her father's waiting arms.

"Lizzie! Thank God you're all right." He swept her up and held her tightly, then looked over Lizzie's shoulder. "Abigail?"

Switching Lizzie to his hip, he walked—no, ran—the short distance between them. And then she, too, was wrapped in his embrace.

Tears soaked her eyes at the shudder she felt pass through him.

"Thank You, God, for keeping them both safe."

He whispered the words into her hair, and then she could have sworn he followed them with a kiss.

"I was so afraid for you, sweetheart. I thought I'd lost you both. That I'd failed again, and that I wouldn't get to you in time."

Slipping both arms around his waist, she held on with all her

CALICO
1883
CA

might. He was here. She was safe. Best of all, he was whispering the most wonderful things. Closing her eyes, she let all the terror of the past few hours drain from her body and reveled in the feel of her husband's arms.

* * * * *

Anger roiled in Nathan's belly as he watched Marshal Harris slam the cell door and turn the key. Gavin Nichols, unshaven and tired from having been on the run for two days, glared back. It hadn't been easy, but they'd finally tracked him down. Thanks to the Kennedys' testimony, plus that of Abigail, there was no doubt he'd remain behind bars for a very long time—or meet with the end of a rope. Still, it didn't satisfy the urge for vengeance boiling in Nathan's blood.

Immediately, he repented of his ill thoughts. God had watched over the two people he cared most about. If vengeance needed meting out, he'd leave it to Him.

Turning on his heel, he walked to the marshal's desk and waited for him there.

"Well, we've got him," Marshal Harris said as he drew near. He hooked his thumbs on the pockets of his trousers. "Gotta admit, I didn't think we'd catch up to him when he made that southward turn toward Mexico. Reckon it was luck that his horse took lame."

Luck? Nathan didn't think so, but he smiled. "What about Tao?"

The marshal's eyes grew troubled. "No sign of him. If I had to hazard a guess, I'd say his people took care of him. They have a way, you know. Something about dishonoring the family name." He shook his head.

Regardless, it was Gavin that Nathan had been concerned about finding, not Tao. According to Clem and his cohort, Billy, Gavin had been lying about the amount of silver coming from the mine. When Anson had discovered the discrepancy and started logging the silver himself, Gavin set fire to the mine and made it look as though Anson's lantern was the cause, hoping the rumors would be enough to drive him from Calico. He hadn't anticipated Anson and Nathan going back to look for George Kennedy, however. Anson's death was truly an accident. The knowledge brought little comfort to either Nathan or Abigail.

"What about Anson's notebook?" Nathan asked. "Any sign of it in Gavin's things?"

Marshal Harris shook his head. "'Fraid not, though with the witnesses against him claiming they saw him set the dynamite that caused the cave-in that trapped your family, it doesn't look as though we'll need it. We'll have him for attempted murder, if nothing else."

So more than likely, Justice truly had disappeared with the book. Nathan sighed. "And the explosion? I guess that was the excuse Gavin used to convince the miners that the mine wasn't safe."

"That's right."

"But the wire from the mining company said—"

"Just a coincidence. He actually got the wire the day before, when he went into Daggett."

Nathan chewed his lip, thinking. "There's still one thing I don't understand. Why was Gavin so bent on seeing the sale of the mine go through?"

Marshal Harris circled the desk and pulled a packet of paper from the drawer. "Reckon this will clear that up."

His brow furrowed, Nathan scanned the documents. He looked up at the wizened old marshal. "Gavin was part owner?"

Harris nodded. "For years, he'd been using the money he got from the Chinese to buy shares. Problem is, he was more aware than anyone of the mine's dwindling silver, and he was desperate to cover it up."

It all made sense—as much as greed and murder *could* make sense.

Gavin stuck his face through the bars and growled. "I want a lawyer, Marshal. You have no proof I did anything wrong. It's all just hearsay."

Marshal Harris grimaced. "Hearsay or no is not for me to decide. You'll have to convince a judge and jury of your innocence, Nichols, not me." He glanced back at Nathan. "As soon as I hear from the judge, I'll let you know."

Nathan nodded. He couldn't get out of Gavin's presence soon enough. Letting himself out, he stalked the rest of the way to the livery. Abigail was there, and with her, Hester Jane and Vivian. Now that he'd gotten a chance to know them, he had to admit, he rather admired their spunk. How they'd take to Abigail remaining behind in Calico, he couldn't guess, but maybe, with time, they'd come to accept her decision.

A smile twitched the corners of his mouth as his boots echoed against the wooden planks of the boardwalk. Not that he and Abigail had officially made that decision, but he had no doubt she'd stay. After all, hadn't she hugged him when she and Lizzie first escaped the mine? And hadn't they spent the last couple of days learning more than ever about one another?

But has she said she loves you?

The question rooted in Nathan's brain. True, she hadn't said as much outright, but her eyes, when she looked at him, seemed brighter, and she always greeted him with a smile.

Have you told her you love her?

The second question, added to the first, made him pause. He clutched the hitching post outside Doc Goodenough's office. Surely she knew how he felt?

Slapping his hand to his forehead, he groaned. What had Charlotte always told him? A woman needed to hear such things, not just assume them by the way a man acted. Quickening his steps, he made a beeline for the livery. Maybe he hadn't told Abigail that he loved her in so many words, but that was easy enough to rectify. Before one more day went by, he'd tell her exactly how he felt. And then he would ask her to stay.

Chapter Thirty-eight

....

Abigail only slightly heard the words her aunt Vivian was saying. Her thoughts were fixed on Nathan—and what he hadn't said. Her fingers absently working the needle in and out of the fabric of the shirt she was mending, she only pretended to pay attention.

The past two days had been wonderful. Nathan was caring and attentive, barely letting her or Lizzie out of his sight, but every time she thought he might speak the words she most longed to hear, he drew back and stopped before he actually told her he loved her.

Maybe there was a reason behind his reluctance.

At the sudden, unwelcome thought and the rush of despair that followed it, she jabbed her needle through the shirt and pricked her finger. Gasping, she brought her hand to her mouth.

"Are you all right, dear?" Vivian leaned forward in her chair to inspect Abigail's wound.

"I'm fine. Just being careless," Abigail said, giving her finger a shake.

"It's just as well you won't have to do any of that once we get back to Virginia," Hester Jane said, snagging a handkerchief from her reticule and passing it to Abigail. "Working as a seamstress was all well and good while you lived here with your father, but back home, why, there's simply no need."

331

Instantly Abigail wished she'd listened to Vivian's prattle. "Wh– what did you say?"

Hester Jane nodded. "Of course. Now that the truth about your father's death has been exposed, it's only natural that Mr. Hawk will want things to return to normal. The sooner we return to Virginia the better, what with the winter snows threatening back East."

Abigail's gaze carried to the window. The days were growing shorter, the nights cooler. It had begun to look more and more like winter in recent weeks, but leaving Calico?

A sound from the door drew her gaze upward. Nathan stood there, his face unreadable.

"There he is now," Vivian said, rising. The lace overlay on her brown silk dress fluttered as she crossed the room toward him. "How did things go with the marshal?"

Nathan's gaze remained fixed on Abigail. What was wrong? She frowned. "Nathan?"

"Everything's fine. Gavin is in custody, and the marshal doesn't think he'll have any trouble getting a jury to convict."

Then why did he look so angry? Laying her mending aside, she stood. "I'm glad to hear that. The aunts and I were just talking—"

"Yes, I know." He scanned the room. "Where's Lizzie?"

Suddenly unsure of herself, Abigail clasped her hands at her waist. "Not back from school yet."

"When she arrives, send her out to the livery, would you? No need for you to interrupt your planning with your aunts." He tipped his hat to each of them in turn. "Vivian. Hester Jane." A second later he stepped outside, closing the door firmly behind him.

Hester Jane pursed her lips at the silence that followed. "What was that all about?"

Though she didn't respond, Abigail knew the answer. Everything the aunts had said was true. Nathan couldn't wait for her to leave Calico.

Tears stinging the back of her eyes, she turned to Hester Jane. "It was nothing. Now, about Virginia—I think you're right. The sooner I leave all of this behind, the better. For everyone."

Chapter Thirty-nine
·····················

The next few days passed in a blur of sullen silence. Though she and Nathan often crossed paths, he rarely spoke to her, a fact that tore at Abigail's already-tattered emotions. Now that the day of her departure had arrived, she was more filled with despair than ever before.

She stared sadly at the folds of the curtains surrounding her bed. Dawn had begun to pink the sky, and she could hear Nathan stirring upstairs. She knew she should slip from her covers and meet him, perhaps try one last time to work things out, but her bruised heart and battered pride kept her firmly in the bed.

Finally Nathan's heavy tread sounded on the ladder, but instead of heading outside, he paused next to the curtains.

"Abigail?"

Swallowing her tears, she tried to sound normal. "Yes?"

"Are you up? I—thought we could talk."

Irrational as it was, hope flared in her chest. "I'll be right out."

She jerked back the covers, grabbed her shawl, and threw it around her shoulders. Nathan stepped aside as she emerged from the curtains. He hadn't bothered to light a lantern, but in the dim glow of morning, it was easy enough to see that his face was drawn and pale and his eyes red, as though he'd spent as sleepless a night as she. Again, the hope inside her fanned to life.

He motioned toward the table. They sat.

Inclining his head toward the bags next to the door, he said, "You're packed?"

She nodded. "I have a few things left. Not all of it would fit into my trunk."

"I can send the rest of your things later, if you want."

This was not going at all as she'd hoped, no, prayed, it would. She dropped her gaze to her clasped fingers. "Yes. Thank you."

Nathan cleared his throat. "Abigail, there's something I've been meaning to tell you, something I would like to give you—before you go."

Her heart skipped a beat at the look of pain that twisted his features. She leaned forward. "Yes?"

Slipping his hand into the pocket of his shirt, he pulled out a bundle of bills that were rolled and bound with twine. "I don't regret marrying you, Abigail. Deep down, I know that is what Anson would have wanted—for me to take care of you while we figured out what really happened at the mine."

She nodded, understanding slowly dawning.

"But I also promised that I would help you go back to Virginia if that was what you wanted, once all was said and done." He waited, but she wasn't foolish enough to think it was because he hoped she might change her mind. He held out the money. "I'd like you to take this. I know you don't need it, what with the aunts coming to help you claim your inheritance and all. Still, I think it's only fitting that I hold to my promise."

She didn't want it. Her hands shook as she fought to keep them clenched tightly in her lap. Finally Nathan sighed, laid the roll on the table, and stood.

"I hope you don't mind—but the work at the livery doesn't wait.

Not even long enough to grieve. Good-bye, Abigail. I'll—miss your friendship."

With that, he turned and walked slowly out the door, taking Abigail's dreams, her very heart, with him. Feeling as though her core had been splintered in two, she dropped her head onto her arms and cried.

* * * * *

Seated on the tack bench with Lizzie at his feet, Nathan tried hard to pretend that nothing was wrong, but seeing his daughter's tearstained face was almost more than he could bear. Any moment now, Abigail would board the coach that would carry her to Daggett. From there, she and the aunts would depart by train for Virginia.

Clenching his fists, he berated himself for being all kinds of a coward for not seeing them off, but letting Abigail go had been hard enough. In fact, he'd wrestled all night against the desire to fling himself at her feet and beg her to stay. He simply didn't think he could stand watching her actually leave.

Lifting his gaze to the rafters, he breathed a silent prayer for strength. Though he didn't understand God's plan, he knew it had carried him this far. He wouldn't go back to casting doubt now.

"Pa, is Abigail coming back?"

Lizzie's plaintive voice tore at his heart. He reached down and gathered his daughter onto his lap. "I don't think so, sweetheart."

"But why? I thought she loved us."

"Oh, she loves you, Lizzie. You mustn't ever doubt that." It was him she had no feelings for.

"Then why, Pa? Why is she going? Can't you talk her into staying?"

The livery door creaked open and Caroline stalked inside, her hands on her hips and her eyes flashing fire. "That's exactly what I say, Lizzie." She strode over and stood in front of them. "Well? Can't you?"

He drew his brows together in a frown. "Can't I what?"

"Talk her into staying." She rolled her eyes. "Oh, for goodness' sake—Abigail loves you, you know. And you love her, only neither of you is smart enough to admit it." She wagged her finger at him. "Do you know where I've just been?"

Setting Lizzie on her feet, Nathan rose. "No."

"The stage depot, that's where. Abigail is there, and she's crying her eyes out, only she won't let her aunts come and tell you. She made them promise not to say a word."

Nathan still wasn't thinking clearly. His brain felt as scrambled as a pan full of eggs. "But I heard her and the aunts talking. They agreed—the sooner Abigail went back to Virginia with them, the better. "

Caroline gave an exasperated sigh. "Look, Hawk, I don't know what you think you heard. All I know is that my best friend's heart is breaking, and if you don't do something about it right now"—she paused and tears welled in her eyes—"you'll lose her forever. Is that what you want, Nathan? For Abigail to leave Calico forever and you never telling her how you really feel?"

Torn by indecision, Nathan looked from Lizzie to Caroline. It was the hopeful look in his daughter's eyes that finally compelled him to motion. Or maybe it was that he'd wanted to go all along and it just took a nudge from Caroline to get him moving.

He braced his hands against his knees. "Lizzie, do you feel like going for a walk? I think there's someone we need to see."

Clapping her hands, she was up and out the door before he finished speaking. Nathan turned to Caroline.

She clasped his hands and gave him an encouraging smile. "Just tell her how you feel. It's all she's ever needed to know. I promise, you won't be sorry."

But halfway to the depot, he wasn't so sure. What if Caroline was wrong? What if Abigail didn't love him and it was just the thought of leaving Lizzie and her father's grave behind that had her so emotional?

"There she is, Pa!"

Lizzie tugged on his hand, but he refused to let her run ahead. Instead, he walked with her to the platform, under the surprised stares of Vivian and Hester Jane.

Abigail rose slowly as they approached. She was dressed in a blue traveling dress, a hat, and gloves. Looking like that, he had no doubt she belonged in Virginia. She was far too beautiful to waste her life here in Calico. Still, he'd come this far.

He drew to a stop in front of her and tugged the hat from his head. "Abigail…" Everything he'd meant to say stuck in his throat. He loved her so much. Losing her now left him with an ache he couldn't wrestle down.

She stepped closer. "Nathan."

Suddenly Lizzie stamped her foot and jammed her free hand onto her hip. "Tell her, Pa." When he still didn't speak, she turned to Abigail. "He's come to tell you that he loves you, Abigail. And so do I. And so do you." She pointed at Nathan's chest. "Love him, I mean."

For several seconds, neither of them spoke, and then, as if freed from their bonds at the same moment, they both started laughing.

Chapter Forty

....

Abigail's laughter slowly faded. Nathan had come to the depot looking for her, but—

"Is it true?"

Nathan licked his lips and said nothing.

Hester Jane stepped forward. "Lizzie, I think these two need a
moment alone, don't you? Why don't we run across to that general
store and see about getting you a piece of candy?"

She didn't wait for an answer but clasped Lizzie's hand and led
her across the street, Vivian trailing behind. She cast a glance over
her shoulder every so often, right up until they disappeared inside
the store.

Her heart thumping, Abigail turned to Nathan. "I—"

She got no further. Before she could blink, he'd taken hold of
her shoulders and pressed a kiss to her mouth. When at last he let
her go, she almost couldn't stand for the trembling in her legs.

"I've wanted to do that from the moment you said 'I do,'" Nathan
said. Then he shook his head. "No, I take that back. I've wanted to
kiss you much longer than that."

"Wh–what?" she stammered.

He nodded. "It's true, Abigail. What Lizzie said? It's true. I love
you. I think I've always loved you. I just couldn't tell you because—"

"Because you still loved Charlotte."

He hesitated and then shook his head once more. "Because I thought I'd failed Charlotte. I didn't want to fail you too. I didn't think I deserved to love you—or to have you love me."

Of course! Why hadn't she seen the truth before? His words from the mine came rushing back.

"I was so afraid for you, sweetheart. I thought I'd lost you both. That I'd failed again, and that I wouldn't get to you in time."

Tears gathered in Abigail's eyes and spilled down her cheeks. "Oh, Nathan, you didn't fail Charlotte."

Smiling, he traced the path of her tears with his finger. "I know that now. It was only my own grief and pain that made me think so."

Her hand trembled as she pressed it to his cheek. "I love you too."

He stilled beneath her touch, his dear face flushed and his eyes damp with the tears he refused to let fall. Such a man. Just like Papa.

Her fingers slid to the back of his neck. Slowly she pulled his head down, and then, rising on her tiptoes, she copied his action of pressing a kiss to his lips. "I've wanted to do that for a long time too," she whispered, dropping back to her feet.

Eyes closed, he laid his forehead gently against hers. For the span of several heartbeats, they stood that way, drinking in the touch, smell, and feel of the other. Finally, Nathan lifted his head and looked her in the eyes.

"You're not leaving Calico, you know. Not without me."

"Or Lizzie."

"Or Lizzie," he repeated.

"So you'll come to Virginia?"

He didn't even hesitate. "If that's what you want."

She smiled coyly. "But what if I want to stay in Calico? What if I want to be your wife and raise a family with you forever here?"

Nathan's eyes sparkled as he threw back his head and laughed. Wrapping his arms around her waist, he swept her off her feet and swung her in a circle. "Even better, my dear wife. Even better."

About the Author

....

In 2008 Elizabeth Ludwig released her first novel, *Where the Truth Lies,* a mystery that she co-authored with Janelle Mowery. This was followed in 2009 by "I'll Be Home for Christmas," part of a Christmas anthology collection called *Christmas Homecoming.* Books two and three of Elizabeth's mystery series, *Died in the Wool* and *A Black Die Affair,* respectively, are slated for release in 2011. *Love Finds You in Calico, California* is her first full-length historical novel.

In 2008 Elizabeth was named the IWA Writer of the Year for her work on *Where the Truth Lies.* She is the owner and editor of the popular literary blog The Borrowed Book, and is also an accomplished speaker and dramatist, having performed before audiences of 1,500 and more. Elizabeth works fulltime and lives with her husband and two children in Texas.

www.elizabethludwig.com

Author's Note

....

Dear Reader,

Thank you for purchasing *Love Finds You in Calico, California*. I hope you have enjoyed getting to know these characters as much as I enjoyed writing about them!

I first stumbled upon the tiny ghost town of Calico while on vacation with my family. I never expected to set a story there. In fact, Calico wasn't even on my list of stops. My husband and I had simply decided to plan a vacation free from itineraries. So when the giant letters spelling CALICO off Interstate 15 caught my eye, we took a detour and checked out the town. I'm so glad we did.

Besides Dorsey, the mail-carrying dog, and Jim Stacy, his owner, Calico was packed with residents as colorful and varied as the hills the town was named after. Men like Tumbleweed Harris, Calico's last marshal, walked the dusty streets. With a high number of single men and saloons in town, I'm sure he had his hands full keeping the peace.

Alongside Marshal Harris were John and Maurice Mulcahey, two brothers who really did make their home in the Silver King mine, and John and Lucy Bell Lane, longtime residents who lived in Calico long after the silver petered out.

Though I tried to keep the feel of Calico authentic, I knew I couldn't do these real-life pioneers justice. The characters in *Love*

Finds You in Calico, California are an amalgamation of the men and women who lived, worked, and died in the shadow of the Painted Hills. I hope that after reading this story, you'll be inclined to learn more about their past and perhaps even visit Calico yourself.

You'll be very glad you did.

Elizabeth Ludwig

Want a peek into local American life—past and present?
The *Love Finds You*™ series published by Summerside Press
features real towns and combines travel, romance,
and faith in one irresistible package!

The novels in the series—uniquely titled after American towns with unusual but intriguing names—inspire romance and fun. Each fictional story draws on the compelling history or the unique character of a real place. Stories center on romances kindled in small towns, old loves lost and found again on the high plains, and new loves discovered at exciting vacation getaways. Summerside Press plans to publish at least one novel set in each of the 50 states. Be sure to catch them all!

NOW AVAILABLE IN STORES

*Love Finds You in
Miracle, Kentucky*
by Andrea Boeshaar
ISBN: 978-1-934770-37-5

*Love Finds You in
Snowball, Arkansas*
by Sandra D. Bricker
ISBN: 978-1-934770-45-0

Love Finds You in Romeo, Colorado
by Gwen Ford Faulkenberry
ISBN: 978-1-934770-46-7

*Love Finds You in
Valentine, Nebraska*
by Irene Brand
ISBN: 978-1-934770-38-2

Love Finds You in Humble, Texas
by Anita Higman
ISBN: 978-1-934770-61-0

*Love Finds You in
Last Chance, California*
by Miralee Ferrell
ISBN: 978-1-934770-39-9

*Love Finds You in
Maiden, North Carolina*
by Tamela Hancock Murray
ISBN: 978-1-934770-65-8

*Love Finds You in
Paradise, Pennsylvania*
by Loree Lough
ISBN: 978-1-934770-66-5

*Love Finds You in
Treasure Island, Florida*
by Debby Mayne
ISBN: 978-1-934770-80-1

*Love Finds You in
Liberty, Indiana*
by Melanie Dobson
ISBN: 978-1-934770-74-0

Love Finds You in Revenge, Ohio
by Lisa Harris
ISBN: 978-1-934770-81-8

Love Finds You in Poetry, Texas
by Janice Hanna
ISBN: 978-1-935416-16-6

Love Finds You in Sisters, Oregon
by Melody Carlson
ISBN: 978-1-935416-18-0

Love Finds You in Charm, Ohio
by Annalisa Daughety
ISBN: 978-1-935416-17-3

Love Finds You in
Bethlehem, New Hampshire
by Lauralee Bliss
ISBN: 978-1-935416-20-3

Love Finds You in North Pole, Alaska
by Loree Lough
ISBN: 978-1-935416-19-7

Love Finds You in Holiday, Florida
by Sandra D. Bricker
ISBN: 978-1-935416-25-8

Love Finds You in
Lonesome Prairie, Montana
by Tricia Goyer and Ocieanna Fleiss
ISBN: 978-1-935416-29-6

Love Finds You in
Bridal Veil, Oregon
by Miralee Ferrell
ISBN: 978-1-935416-63-0

Love Finds You in
Hershey, Pennsylvania
by Cerella D. Sechrist
ISBN: 978-1-935416-64-7

Love Finds You in Homestead, Iowa
by Melanie Dobson
ISBN: 978-1-935416-66-1

Love Finds You in Pendleton, Oregon
by Melody Carlson
ISBN: 978-1-935416-84-5

Love Finds You in Golden, New
Mexico by Lena Nelson Dooley
ISBN: 978-1-935416-74-6

Love Finds You in Lahaina, Hawaii
by Bodie Thoene
ISBN: 978-1-935416-78-4

Love Finds You in
Victory Heights, Washington
by Tricia Goyer and Ocieanna Fleiss
ISBN: 978-1-60936-000-9

Coming Soon

Love Finds You in Sugarcreek, Ohio
by Serena Miller
ISBN: 978-1-60936-002-3

Love Finds You in
Deadwood, South Dakota
by Tracey Cross
ISBN: 978-1-60936-003-0

Love Finds You in Silver City, Idaho
by Janelle Mowery
ISBN: 978-1-60936-005-4

Love Finds You in
Carmel-by-the-Sea, California
by Sandra D. Bricker
ISBN: 978-1-60936-027-6

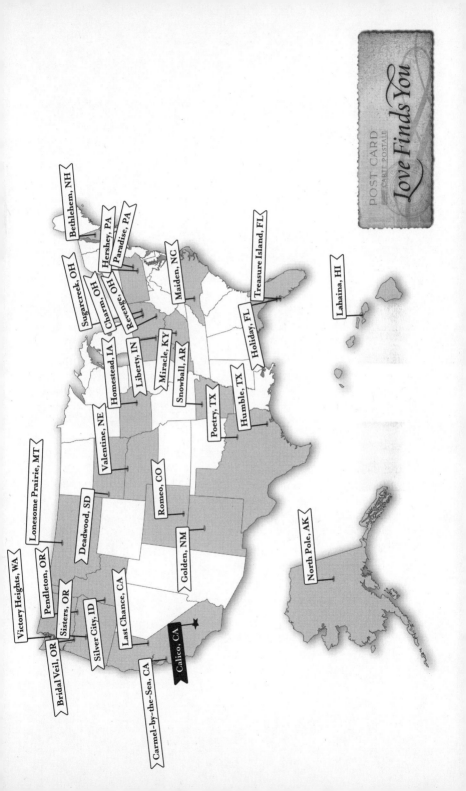